The Ryle of Zentule
Tales from the Netherscape - Book Two

By Michael Green

Cover art by Alexey Rudikov

1st Edition

ISBN: 978-1-950593-03-3

For Jennifer and Bob.

Though the world might crush us all, true
parents hold up the sky and craft a home
so the self might be.

Table of Contents

Chapter 1: Empty-handed

Lysette scrambled to her feet, her face split with agony as the brutox subdued Andy. She was deaf to the calls for retreat from her friends at the portal.

She had dropped her crossbow when she saw the marble roll to her feet. In a flash, she grasped it. For a moment, it rested in her palm. She recalled Andy teaching her to use it.

Almost instinctively, she tightened her grip. She clenched the Argument past the point of pain.

A wrenching feeling ran up her spine as the blade appeared. It weighed nothing. Its sliver light shone out against the glow from the portals.

It's humming, she thought.

Her focus fell to the blade, despite her surroundings. Past the blade, she saw a figure approaching.

A brutox was moving towards her. It bore a spear with a vicious serrated tip that sparkled like glass in the light of the portal. She felt a tug on her hair and heard Taptalles yelling in her ear. He had been for a while.

"What are you doing? Snap out of it! It's coming for us!"

Letty took a breath and swung the blade in a wide arc. As if striking with a heavy bat, she put too much force into the attack and nearly stumbled. Gratefully, instead of being struck down while she was off balance, she saw her enemy staring stupidly at his cleaved spear.

You're not swinging at a baseball! The blade is made of

light!

Her mind tried to adjust to the weightlessness of the weapon. She nearly panicked, not sure how to act. The creature dropped its broken weapon and continued towards her.

"Don't just stand there! Use it like a brush!" Taptalles yelled.

She stepped back and flicked her wrist. In a flash, the brutox toppled into pieces.

"That's it!" Taptalles yelled in her ear.

A pair of brutox, wielding axes, came at her from opposite directions.

Letty slid towards one, and flicked, cleaving its axe haft and splitting the beast apart with a second powerful swipe, before turning to face the second. Its attack came towards her at a ponderous speed.

Letty stepped aside and watched the brutox stumble as it struck nothing. An unimpressed smirk flashed across her face as she looked into the creature's spider eyes.

She flicked her wrist once more and the brutox split in two, its heavy axe making a loud thud as it struck the ground. She spun around to face the mob.

Her brow rose in astonishment as the dozens of brutox stepped back.

Letty approached.

"No! You've made your point! We need to go through the portal!" Taptalles tugged on her hair, screaming, "We have a chance, while they're afraid!"

Letty snatched him off her shoulder with her free hand and tossed him back to Quill, who could

2

only stare.

"You have to go! Letty, just leave!" Andy yelled from somewhere in the mob.

I have to get to him!

Letty rushed forward, swinging wildly. She heard herself crying out as she slashed a way through. The brutox refused to face her, stumbling over each other to escape her flashing blade.

Trained reflexes compelled the brutox to raise their weapons, and an occasional shield, as she attacked, but every offending blade or haft split apart, like paper tearing, leaving its wielder defenseless.

She was wild with the struggle to save Andy, but for every brutox that went down, there were a dozen more still in the way. It had only been moments, but her heart felt ready to burst, and her eyes were brimming with tears. Her throat tightened and refused to allow her more than a gulp of air. She swung one last time, cleaving a blade in two, but instead of falling back, its owner lunged and struck her with a closed fist.

"Letty!" a shocked voice echoed in her mind as her ears rang from the strike.

She stumbled back into Quill and Staza, who pulled her away and held off the charging attacker. The brutox rushed them with his sword, which lacked most of its blade. He fell for a feinting lunge from Quill, and left himself open to a piercing thrust from Staza, who sunk her blade into the creature so deeply that she struggled to free her weapon. Another charged, forcing Staza to abandon her spear and draw her short sword.

Letty looked down at her hand and saw the blade was gone, though the marble remained. With her free hand, she felt that her chin was wet. Rubbing at it, she saw a smear of blood.

Shrill clicks silenced the enemy. The brutox moved all at once. The mob separated, and Andy was held aloft for them to see. Dozens of claws and beastly hands held him tight. Letty saw them wrench his flesh all at once, and he screamed.

"No! I have to help him!" she cried, pulling against Quill and Staza, though she barely had any strength left.

They yelled and pleaded with her, but all she could see was Andy's bloody face.

"Let me go!" She railed against her friends, and even tried to bite them in her frenzy. They were too strong.

"Stop her!" Titus called.

Something struck her head, and she stumbled, holding the marble tightly as her vision doubled.

Don't let go.

She felt herself floating backwards. There was a sudden change in temperature and finally, silence. The breeze coming off the sea was gone.

She was in a warm and dark space. The air was dry and musty.

"Is she going to be okay?" Staza asked.

"She should be fine. Just give her a few minutes," Titus answered, his voice hoarse.

"If you didn't give her a concussion!" Taptalles complained.

4

Letty felt small hands on her face.

"We don't have any minoe!" Taptalles said, reprimanding Quill. "You shouldn't have hit her so hard!"

"She was getting away—I had to do something!"

"Peace! We need peace!" Titus cried. "The lad was doing as he was told."

"I wasn't doing as I was told," Quill complained. "It was the only choice."

"Please, stop it before I loosen your teeth, Quill," Staza said, grabbing him. "We need to show them respect."

There was a long silence.

"You're right. Titus, I was—"

"Don't apologize. I too aired ill-chosen words."

They were silent again.

"I can't see anything," Quill complained, stumbling in the dark.

"I can't believe we left him," Staza said.

"Even if you all bore the Argument, and were properly trained, that still would have been an impossible fight," Titus said.

Letty felt her head throb and she groaned.

"Get that cloth back on her face! She's bleeding again!" Taptalles said.

"How can you see?" Quill asked. "It's pitch black."

"Our kind is blessed with sharp eyes. They even work in darkness," Taptalles said.

Staza felt her way on the ground and tried to put pressure on Letty's nose.

Letty coughed and felt like she was suffocating.

She shot up and took the cloth from Staza's hands. "You're choking me!"

"The blood is still strong!" Titus said, pleased to see her moving.

Quill and the mice stumbled to her side, she pushed them away and held the cloth to her face.

"You might have a broken nose," Staza said. "If only we had some ice."

Letty looked around the dark space and saw only the barest outlines of figures nearby.

"Where are we?" Letty whispered.

"That's what we were hoping to learn from you," Taptalles said.

"I have no idea—" Letty tried to stand but stumbled over an unidentified piece of furniture. Quill and Staza kept her steady.

She stumbled again and felt the marble slip through her fingers.

"No!" She pulled free and fell to her hands and knees. "We need to find it!"

"She dropped the Argument," Titus said.

Quill and Staza bent to help, and so did the mice.

Letty's hands grasped a cold metal bar, she felt around it and realized what it was. *I'm sure this is an office desk.*

Her hand bumped into a metal bin that tipped over with a familiar sound. *That's a trash can!*

For a moment she felt relieved, knowing the desk and can indicated their return to the surface.

A moment later, her mind darted back to the missing marble, and she redoubled her frantic grasping.

There was a flash and Quill yowled. "Found it," he said, shaking his jolted hand.

Letty crawled towards his voice, reached around in the dark, and felt its surface.

She clutched it to her chest. "We need this," she said, incensed. She grasped it and the blade appeared.

Everyone leaped backwards, afraid of being bisected.

The light from the blade was so violent and bright in the complete darkness, that it was still nearly impossible to see.

"You don't understand," Letty said, not bothered by the brightness. "I..."

She wanted to explain how important the marble was, but she couldn't find the right words.

Their concerned looks deepened and they held hands up to shield their eyes.

"Forget it," Letty said, releasing her grasp and putting the marble in a pocket of her torn and mangled dress. "It's not like it saved us."

No one replied.

Finally, Quill spoke, "It was a false feeling of safety. If we never had the marble, maybe Andy wouldn't have tried to foolishly hold them back."

"Right, you know that for sure. Maybe we all would have been captured," Letty snapped.

"This isn't the time for an argument," Titus interjected. "We're here now, and that's what matters."

We're not all here! Letty's face twisted in anger,

though this was lost in the darkness.

There was a rustling sound and Quill struck a flint and started a fire in the trash can.

Letty looked around and realized that they were in an office, but everything seemed outdated, as if the office was many decades old.

"Crazy. It's like out of a black and white movie. There's even a typewriter. And look at that telephone! It has a wheel on it," Letty muttered, though the others didn't understand a word of what she was saying.

Smoke from the trashcan fire filled the room.

Letty coughed and moved towards it. "Put it out!"

Quill grabbed a metal tray from off the desk and put it over the can, suffocating the flames in moments.

"My world is a lot more flammable than yours," Letty said, eyeing a floating ember.

"Yes," Quill replied, "apparently, we're inside something, underground maybe. I didn't expect the smoke to build up like that."

"Well, we still can't see anything, so talking about it is pointless," Staza said.

Letty thought back to her time with Andy in Caspia. She took the marble in hand and tightened her fist. A slight glow shone, and then the blade appeared. She stepped back, startled, as she had accidentally sliced through the door.

"That's too bright," Taptalles said, shielding his eyes.

"And dangerous," Titus added.

Letty released her grip.

There's a point between.

She tried to summon the blade again, only more slowly this time.

Just a little force on the marble.

Her hand glowed and the blade remained hidden.

There was a crackle of light and the blade threatened to appear.

After a moment of practice, she found the right point.

The office was lit in the soft silver glow coming from her hand.

"How?" Quill asked, when everyone else could only look surprised.

"It depends on how gently I hold it. I think my feelings are connected too, but I can't say why. Andy showed me."

"Amazing," Taptalles said.

"The blood is strong!" Titus raised a fist in triumph.

Quill and Staza looked at the mice with pained, uncertain expressions.

"What?" Letty asked, but quickly changed her mind. "Never mind, first we need to figure out where we are."

I may be stuck with crazy mice and snake lady cultists, but we need to do something practical, not stand around.

"Where is the portal?" She asked.

"Back in the hall. It was one way, so don't try to get back to the other side," Quill said, reminded of the trouble they had getting her through earlier.

Letty leaned around the cracked door and saw a hallway. There were other office doors and, looking to the right, she saw the hall ended in a charred wreck. The carpet and walls were stained black, and smeared symbols were visible around the periphery of the far wall.

So, that was the portal. It's probably for the best that it's closed now.

She scolded herself for the thought, but also knew that they could have been killed or captured.

"I expected the portal to leave us in an old cave," Titus said. "It looks like things have changed since I was last through."

Letty nodded.

She looked back into the office. The contrast of the Caspians, in their ornate and wild clothing, standing next to an office desk made her head spin. She saw the mice looking through papers on the desk and muttering between themselves. She felt like she might pass out.

"This will never work. Our clothes are insane," Letty's glance passed over Titus and Taptalles, "and you guys can't be talking or wearing that mouse-sized armor."

"This isn't my first time up here," Titus said.

"It's mine though," Taptalles added, raising a paw timidly.

"Us too," Staza said, looking confusedly at her dress, "what's wrong with our clothes?"

Where do I even start?

"We'll worry about it later," Letty said, wringing her hands, "for now, let's focus on figuring out where we are."

There were no windows for reference, but the papers were promising. As she moved towards the desk, everyone's eyes followed.

She found dusty letters in the trays the mice were looking through and picked up a sheet.

"'From the desk of Lieutenant General Jim Majors, to Dr. J. Koeple: Project IronHawk lead. Please understand that it is with the sincerest regret that funding for your project will cease at the start of the next fiscal year. Use the remaining three months to mothball the project, premises, and equipment. Write letters of recommendation for your staff. Finally, my department will help in fabricating aliases for your subjects. They will receive world-class treatment at facilities across the country. We will take care of them.' This letter is dated 1947," Letty said reaching the end.

"What does it mean? Is it serious?" Quill asked.

"I don't know. It sounds like a government or military project happened here," Letty glanced around the office before continuing, "maybe we're in an abandoned facility."

"That's good, right?" Quill asked. "There'll be no guards."

"Hopefully, but we should still be quiet," Letty said, opening the door and stepping into the hall. She was still light-headed and kept a hand on the wall for support.

She paused for a moment, the others close behind.

1947.

"Titus?"

"Yes," he answered.

"Those portals don't do anything crazy, like taking people back in time, do they?"

Titus shook his head no.

"Why? Is there reason to believe that we're in the wrong time?" Staza asked.

"That letter, it was dated so long ago, and this building and everything here is probably seventy years old."

Titus dragged a claw across the wood paneled floor. "The real question is, what does seventy years of dust look like?" He showed them the thick coating he picked up.

"Probably like that," Letty said.

They went down the hall, away from the closed portal. Most of the office doors were open, and the rooms were in a horrendous state. Toppled chairs and file cabinets leaked out into the hall. Hundreds of loose papers littered every inch of floor space, causing their feet to slip as they walked.

They found a cafeteria at the end of the hall and an open elevator shaft.

"I'd bet anything the elevator doesn't work," Letty said, poking her head in the shaft.

"The what?" Quill asked.

"It's a box on cables that moves people up and down buildings," Letty answered absentmindedly.

She shone her light and looked down. She was surprised when the floor appeared only a few feet below their level. Looking upward, her light faded into blackness, but not before revealing several levels above them.

"It looks like we're on the ground floor—wait no. Maybe we're in the basement."

"Is that a problem?" Staza asked.

"It might be, this looks like a big building. It's strange that all this stuff is still down here."

They stood in silence, unsure what to do, when they heard a small bang in the cafeteria.

"What was that?" Letty asked.

They looked around the corner and saw Titus and Taptalles trying to work a doorknob.

"Well—stop staring and help," Titus said.

Letty saw that they found the stairwell.

"Good job," Quill said, holding the door open. "Stairs I understand."

They climbed to the next floor.

"Wait. We don't know how many basement levels there are," Letty said.

They opened the door on the next floor and found everything looking largely the same, but instead of a cafeteria, there was an archive. The offices still lacked windows.

"This could take a while," Letty said, as they climbed again.

"Does this mean anything?" Quill asked, picking a piece of flat metal off the floor.

"Twenty-eight," Staza said, reading the plate.

"That doesn't make any sense," Letty mumbled, rushing to the next floor.

The others hurried to keep up.

Letty found another sign.

Twenty-seven?

"How?" Letty shook her head. "The numbers are going the wrong way."

It suddenly made sense.

"No—this whole building is underground. We're twenty-seven floors down."

"Do your people often build underground?" Quill asked.

Letty looked at him, annoyed. "We're the same people, Quill. You just don't remember. And no, most buildings don't go down this far."

Resigned to the long climb, they mounted the stairs. After a few minutes, everyone was sweating from the effort, save the mice.

"Are there any laws—or customs—that we should—know about?" Quill asked, through labored breaths.

Letty took this as an excuse to rest and leaned against the rail, signaling a break to the others. "Nothing strange, I shouldn't think. No—violence—stay out of the streets—"

"What? Aren't streets for travel?" Staza asked.

"Yes, but no—" Letty wiped her brow, "we have cars and buses, they use streets—if you're just walking, you have to use—the side-walks. Don't worry—I'll show you when we get up there."

Quill and Staza balked.

"It isn't *that* difficult for humans on the surface. Try being a mouse," Titus said.

Letty stood and continued up the stairs.

After a few more grueling minutes, they reached the top.

"Finally!" Letty said, looking around. She

expected large glass doors that led out onto a street, or perhaps a lobby, instead there was an armored checkpoint.

"Damn," she muttered.

They found a thick glass window protecting a security room and a heavily reinforced door, painted solid red. It featured a large, white number one.

Letty peeked inside the enclosed security room. She spotted control boards and old television screens. They were all blank.

The door to the security room was locked and made of solid metal. Letty kicked it in frustration. "The people who worked in this building had to come in and out somehow."

Her companions were hopeless in this alien surrounding. They all stared, waiting for her to divine the answer. Letty, not wanting to disappoint, paced and tried to work through the problem.

"I bet that door is the way out," she said to the blank faces, pointing to the door with the large number one, "and they monitored it from in there. This was a secret place."

"Why not try the blade?" Quill asked, cautiously.

"It doesn't look like we can escape without it," Staza said, peeking into the security area.

"Good point," Letty said, raising her hand.

"Wait!" Taptalles called out, "What's on the other side of that door? Should we just cut into it?"

"Let's find out," Letty said, summoning the blade.

She struck the red door and felt her wrist sting

15

when the blade bounced back.

Letty shook her head in disbelief.

"It bounced off?" she whispered.

She tried again, softly this time, and again the blade was turned away by the metal.

The mice shared curious glances.

"Almost nothing can turn the Argument," Titus said.

"Nothing, save the Counter," Taptalles agreed.

"Well, they figured something out," Letty said, walking over to the stairwell door. She swung the blade. It sliced through with ease. The bottom half of the severed door creaked, bending the hinge.

She turned and struck the door to the enclosed security area. The blade refused to cut again.

"What's going on here?" she asked, astonished.

"Try the glass," Staza recommended.

Letty did, and the glass split, leaving room for hands to pull the pane apart. She leaned over the window and looked onto the console. There was a large red lever.

"That looks like the one," she whispered, smiling at her friends.

She pulled it and there was a loud click.

The door creaked open.

"That did it!" Titus cheered.

"Right, but we don't know why the blade couldn't slice through these doors," Letty complained.

No one had an answer.

"We need to come back here and look around. I think this place is important," Letty said.

"Certainly, but not today," Titus replied.

"Right, we have to rescue Andy first," Letty added.

She saw uncertain faces.

"What? Obviously we're going to save Andy," she said, challenging them.

"Of course. We will make a plan. But now you need to rest and collect yourselves," Titus replied.

"Letty, you're covered in blood. Look at yourself. You—well, we all look like we've been beaten and dragged through muddy glass," Staza said, plaintively. "We can't do any more."

Letty wanted to yell and head back for the portal, and then remembered it was shut.

She sighed and looked at Quill and Staza. Though they appeared strong, something else played about their eyes. They were afraid.

How couldn't they be? We're so far from their home.

She considered the mice. They were frightened as well. Though fear was a subtle thing on a mouse face, the bend in their ears and coil in their tails was clear enough.

None of them can go home, and now we're in my world, and I'm acting crazy.

The urge to resist Titus's command waned. There was nothing she could do for Andy, not now at least, but inaction felt like betrayal.

"It's just that, he came for me," she said, the urge to cry replacing her desire to fight.

The Caspians each reached out a hand as Letty took a moment to wipe at a tear, catching it before it fell.

17

"We won't forget him. When we're ready, we'll go back to the Netherscape. Right?" Titus asked the others.

"Of course," Quill said.

Staza nodded. "He'll probably refuse to go home until we boot Somni from Caspia. He was so keen to help us," she said with an earnest laugh. "Somni won't make a popular leader if our Mistress stays gone."

"And when we're done putting our part of the scape back together, you and he can be trained as proper Seers. We'll find the Praetor and..." Taptalles sniffled and grabbed his tail.

Titus coughed. "Right. But you, young lady, you must swear to us that you will not pursue unilateral action."

"What?" Letty asked, halfway between laughing and crying.

"You will not try to find Andy on your own." And then to them all, "You must act as a group, and vote on your course, preferably after long discussion, with level heads."

"Why are you talking like that? Why, 'you must act as a group,' and not 'we?'" Letty asked.

Titus and Taptalles both tugged on their whiskers.

"Our people need us; we are both commanders. Once we get you settled, we'll have to return," Taptalles said.

Letty wanted to argue but knew that they had already done too much for her.

"Well, at least we have a plan. Standing around

anymore is just a waste of time." Letty approached the red door and pressed against it.

The sound of clattering bottles and cans met them on the other side. They had to push on the door together to clear the pile of refuse jamming the way. From the look of it, the litter was old as well.

There was moisture in the air, and the smell of decay.

Letty turned and pushed the door back to just shy of being closed. Titus and Taptalles gratefully accepted places on Letty's shoulders.

"Thanks," Titus whispered, "it's filthy down there."

"Yeah, but this is a good sign; I think we're in the sewers," Letty whispered.

She looked back at the heavy metal door and wondered why a whole building was hidden like this. Letty sighed and knew the mystery would have to wait.

They moved slowly down the filthy tunnel and found a single hanging light bulb at the end. It was dead, but it still swayed.

"Where now?" Quill asked.

Letty sighed as she spotted iron rungs on the wall. "Up," she said, raising her glowing hand to illuminate the way.

"I'll have to pocket the marble and climb in the dark," she said, warning the others.

The rungs were slick, and Letty took them carefully. She managed not to slip on the trip up and, at the top, found a wooden hatch blocking their path.

"Damn!" she said, pushing against it.

There was a sudden rumbling.

"What's that?" Staza asked, startled by the noise.

The rumbling slowed, and then ceased. But right as they were taking a breath, the noise started up again, slowly at first, then loud, and then silent.

Strange.

Frustrated, Letty grabbed the marble. "Cover your eyes, I'm going to cut through."

She summoned the blade and stabbed through the hatch. The wood splintered and broke. She moved the blade to the edge of the concrete hole and cut through the perimeter of the hatch. She squinted as debris rained down.

"Watch out," she said, as the panel fell into pieces and tumbled.

"Ow!" Quill said.

She loosened her grip on the Argument and pocketed it before climbing the last few rungs.

They ascended into a grimy space.

"We're in a maintenance room," Letty said, looking at the piles of wires and tools on benches and greasy shelves.

A few old fluorescent bulbs flickered above. Letty pocketed the Argument.

"There's a door," Staza said, pointing past a row of shelves.

"Wait," Letty said, "help me." She was trying to pull a heavy crate over the hole they had just climbed through, "I don't want people going down there."

"Good point," Quill said, stooping to help.

With the crate in place, Letty approached and opened the door.

A crashing noise startled them. The Caspians leaped back and raised their weapons.

"No! It's not a problem," Letty insisted. "It's just the subway." She felt for her pockets, but realized that she didn't have her wallet or her purse.

Damn, no card and no cash.

"What's a subway?" Staza asked, her sword still raised.

"It's like…" Letty paused, not sure how to explain the idea. "It'll be easier just to see it," and looking at Staza, "No need to be alarmed."

Letty stalled before going through the door. *We look insane, and we'll be stopped because of those weapons.* She took a breath before walking through.

Looking left and right, Letty realized that they had stepped out onto a service area, not far from a subway station. Hugging the wall, she led the way towards the platform, and up a few stairs.

"Stay off the rails!" Letty whispered angrily to the Caspians, who didn't understand why she was clinging to the wall.

After hearing her tone, they clung to the wall.

Letty found stairs that led onto the station. She looked out to the platform and saw that no one was looking their way. She stepped up and motioned for the others to follow. Finally, her feet fell onto tiled floor.

Civilization, thank God.

There were people standing and waiting. A few

looked their way, but none for more than a moment.

Titus and Taptalles hid and occasionally peered out from behind her hair.

Staza spotted the exit, but Letty motioned her to wait. "I want to see what station this is." Looking around, she saw the sign, "Marble Hill."

I need to remember that. Marble Hill.

They took the stairs and exited onto the street. It was getting dark, but the streets were still packed. The Caspians gawked.

"What beasts are these?" Staza cried, seeing cars streaming by.

"Look at the way they herd—so orderly," Quill muttered.

"They're just cars, nothing to be afraid of, and they—"

"They aren't beasts! They're contrivances; see their human pilots," Quill said.

"Look at the ceiling!" Staza gasped.

"The sky," Letty corrected. "And that's the setting sun, giver of light and skin cancer," she continued sarcastically.

"Superlative," Quill gasped. "How many people live here?"

"Millions, at least. I'm not sure exactly," Letty answered, slightly annoyed. "Weren't you guys born up here? Pythia doesn't take in young children. So, you should remember what cities look like."

Quill looked aghast. "Be careful, Letty, there are people everywhere. They could be listening," he whispered angrily, as his eyes darted. She saw his grasp tighten on the trident.

"I think I would remember if I'd seen something like this," Staza interjected.

Titus whispered in Letty's ear, "They were likely subject to the same drugs you were, but for years. They were conditioned to obey and forget. Be gentle with them."

Letty sighed. "Quill, nobody is listening to us; they all just think we're silly kids dressed in costumes. The city is full of crazy people. Hopefully, nobody will even notice us."

"Hey! You kids!" An adult voice called out to them.

Really?

Letty turned and saw a pair of police men coming their way.

"Look at these kids," one officer said to the other.

"I think they're going to that comic thing—the convention."

"Yeah—hey, you kids lost?"

"Yes sir," Letty said plainly.

"Listen, the convention is over the bridge at the university. Just cross that bridge and you can't miss 'em," the officer said with a wry expression on his mustached face.

"Thank you, sir," Letty said.

"What about those weapons?" the other asked.

"Plastic, you idiot—listen kids, paint the blades orange if you get a chance—that's policy now. You wouldn't want any trouble, especially from guys like this," he patted his partner on the shoulder. "Usually, I'd have to take them from you, but another policy is community outreach. So just take care of that, alright?"

Letty nodded and the Caspians followed her cue. "Of course, sir, and thanks for the directions." Letty turned and dragged them along and across the bridge, but she still heard the officers, not far behind.

"Did you see that spear thing?"

"Trident Dave, that was a trident."

"Whatever, and the eyes on them, purple eyes."

Letty tried not to stumble as she heard the observation.

"Contacts, Dave, these kids have those colored contacts. They're probably dressed up as characters from some cartoon where everyone has purple eyes."

"How do you know that?"

"Shut up—" the voices drowned out as a traffic light changed and a wave of cars drove by.

"We're going to a convention? What is that exactly?" Quill asked.

Letty was becoming frustrated with the questions. "A convention is a meeting of people interested in a common thing, in this case, comics and movies. There's a convention for fans this way. We should go to that."

"Comics and movies?" Staza asked cautiously, aware of Letty's mounting annoyance.

Letty rolled her eyes. "It's entertainment popular with people our age. We won't stand out so much at a convention, and maybe someone will let me use their phone."

Letty gave the Caspians a sharp look, as she expected them to ask about phones. "A phone is a tool I can use to—communicate, with my parents, or find a map."

They both nodded gratefully.

"A map would be useful," Quill said, looking out over the bridge onto the maze of buildings and streets that ranged on, like a gleaming steel forest, in every direction.

As they walked, a slight breeze rolled in off the water, and the smell of burning diesel put Letty at ease. She had nearly forgotten all of her problems, walking down the sidewalk.

"These people aren't garbed like the others," Quill said, distracted by the growing numbers of convention goers.

They had spotted costumed people sporting giant wigs of various colors.

"It's like a special event; people get dressed up and come out to see one another," Letty said, brushing her bloody dress, "and we look like we fell out of a horror movie. That should help us fit in."

They followed the crowd and spotted the convention hall.

"We don't have tickets, and I can't buy any. We'll ask somebody to—"

"Woah! Look at those costumes!" A chubby man in blue spandex came up to them. He was flanked by a woman wearing golden bracers, a tiara, and bearing a lasso. Finally, there followed a man in a plastic robot suit.

Letty noticed Staza's hand go for her short sword.

"None of that now," Letty whispered, smacking

her hand away from the blade.

"Hey, you guys look great," Letty said with a big smile on her face.

"Not compared to you! What are you from?" The girl asked, eying their outfits.

Quill and Staza looked at each other, dumbfounded.

"Oh—we're doing our own thing," Letty replied hurriedly.

"Really! That's so cool—do you have a script written yet? It looks like a fantasy horror—I love this dress; the ripped part is great!"

Letty smiled like an idiot and waited for the girl to finish. "No—we're sort of designing the costumes first, and then we'll fill in the details."

"Ooh, avant-garde," the man in the robot suit said, while admiring Quill's trident.

"Yeah, say, I lost my purse and phone on the subway—I'm afraid someone snatched it—can I borrow your phone for a minute?"

"Oh my God! I'm so sorry." The man in the blue spandex said, opening a fanny pack. He pulled out his cell. "Here, take as long as you need," he said, handing Letty the phone.

Letty tried calling her parents, only to hear their voicemails. As she was waiting nervously for someone to pick up, more people approached Quill and Staza. The strangers wanted to take pictures together.

"Hey, look at his trident. Very nice!" A man dressed as a pirate, with too much eye-liner, said to Quill.

Letty gave up on the calls and looked up a map. Learning generally where they were, she returned it. "Thanks."

"I made it myself," Quill said, pleased at the interest.

A few girls in bright green and blue wigs were touching the chainmail on Staza's outfit. Staza looked over at Letty, clearly displeased.

"You made this yourself?" The pirate asked, astonished. "Are you a blacksmith?"

Letty rushed forward and grabbed Quill by the shoulder, casting a cautionary glance at him.

"Yes. I've made a few," Quill said, giving Letty a confused look.

"How much for this one? I need it for a new costume I'm working on. Going to be the king of the ocean."

Letty burst into the conversation, "He wants two hundred dollars for this one."

"Only two hundred!" The man was astonished and reached into his satchel for money.

Quill glowered at Letty and whispered, "I'm not selling my trident!"

"We need the money!" Letty whispered back. "And you can always make another one."

Staza tapped her shoulder. The man was holding out two hundred dollars.

"Is there a problem?" he asked, noticing the argument.

"Look man, they just got robbed, maybe give them a little more," the man in the blue spandex suit said.

"Wait, is that actual blood?" The pirate leaned in and looked more closely at Letty. "Did you get beat up?"

"We had some trouble on the way here."

Not really a lie.

"I usually wouldn't do this, but—we have to stick together," the pirate paused, looking closely at the trident. "Is that real blood too?"

Everyone was silent.

"Say no more," the Pirate grinned, "I'll up the price to three hundred."

Quill took the three bills from the man and reluctantly handed over the trident.

A line had formed. A few dozen people wanted to get their pictures taken with Letty, Staza, and Quill. They obliged, accepting money from almost every group who came up to them. Letty shrugged off the annoyed glances from the Caspians.

I can't turn these people down; we might need the money.

Eventually, someone in a security uniform approached. "You can't be conducting business out here – it has to be done inside. Now clear out, before you get banned."

The people scattered, and Letty led the Caspians away from the conference hall and back to the street.

She counted the cash. "Wow, we just made six hundred dollars."

"Is that a lot?" Quill asked, still sour about the trident.

"It should keep us going for a while," Letty said.

"Well," Taptalles poked his head out from

Letty's hair, he was breathing heavily, "is it safe to come out yet?"

"Where are we going next?" Titus asked.

"We'll take the train to my house. Now that we don't have that trident, we shouldn't attract so much attention; though the sword and daggers might still cause us a problem. You know what? Let's take a cab instead. We can afford it," Letty spotted an empty yellow cab and held her hand out.

The driver smirked at their outfits as they piled into his car. Letty sat down for the first time in hours and felt something jabbing her. She reached into her dress and found two things. The first was the contract Andy had signed for Pythia, and the second was the small notebook he had given her.

Chapter 2: Parents

"I must have hidden it after he handed it to me outside Caspia," Letty said, flipping through the notebook. "I've seen this before. It's supposed to be the Infiniteye, but Andy isn't the best artist," she said, showing the notebook to the others.

Quill and Staza weren't impressed.

"It's a sign of the Argument," Staza said plainly.

"It features prominently in Seer history," Quill added.

"What are you kids talking about? Some new book?" the driver asked.

"Oh—it's nothing," Letty said with a laugh.

"My daughter loves that fantasy stuff, and I want to get her something she doesn't already have," he said.

"It's just something we're putting together," Letty said.

"All right," the cabby said, enthused, "good for you, kids. Get in on that market. I wish I was creative at a young age. I bet it goes with those costumes too."

Before Letty could change the subject, the cab had pulled up outside her building.

"Here we are—good luck with the productions, writings, and whatnot. Hopefully this doesn't cut into the budget too much," he said, pointing at the fare readout.

"Thanks," Letty said, paying and tipping the driver.

They stepped out into the street. It had gotten dark and there were fewer people out.

"Okay, be quiet, and I'll try to figure out a story for us."

Letty scrunched her face in thought. Titus and Taptalles also conversed.

"We need to be going now," Titus announced to the group.

"What! No, we're not—" Letty paused, looking at her building and realizing that she couldn't offer up an argument.

They did see us home.

"Thank you for getting us this far," Quill said with a sad smile.

Staza looked around to see that no one was watching and patted their heads.

They bounded off Letty's shoulders and into a nearby shrub.

"We will come and find you when things calm down. Remember, you need to work together," Titus said.

"How do you know where to go?" Letty asked.

"I've traveled these streets before. There's a portal we control not too far from here."

"Where exactly?" Staza asked.

Titus shook his head. "It's dangerous. I apologize, but I can't let you know."

Nobody argued. They shared a long silence before the mice rustled away through the bushes.

"Which direction is that?" Staza asked. "I don't have my bearings here."

Letty took a moment. "East."

"East?" Staza repeated.

Letty sighed, "We don't have time to go over

31

directions."

Staza didn't argue. "At least we know which way they went. It might help when we go hunting for the portal."

Quill nodded, looking up at the structure. "If only Arke could see this. I'm not sure if he'd be sick or inspired. Everything is so perfectly angular and reflective. Am I crushed or elevated?"

Staza looked up at the skyline. Her face betrayed a slight discomfort, where Quill was plainly alarmed.

"Come on—we can stare at buildings later." Letty said, leading them to the door. She typed in the security code, and the door clicked open.

"I think I have a plan, just go along with what I say. Don't mention anything about—down there."

"The Netherscape," Quill corrected.

"Right, nothing about it. Pretend you're from the surface."

The elevator in Letty's building was working, and it fascinated the Caspians.

Letty felt her heart beat faster as they approached the apartment. She hesitated before finally knocking.

They will go insane.

Letty heard shuffling behind the door and some mumbled words before it finally opened.

"Lysette, dear!" Letty's mother cried.

Letty nearly bowled them over. They shared a long hug while the Caspians stood awkwardly at the door. Letty noticed that it smelled a little odd inside.

"Where have you been?" her father asked. "And

what happened to you?"

They stopped hugging to get a look at her.

"You're covered in blood!" he said.

"And who are these people?" her mother
snapped.

"Let's just go inside, please," Letty said, pulling
Quill and Staza in with her.

Letty's parents sat Quill and Staza on the sofa
in the living room before dragging Letty off to the
bathroom. On the way, Letty noticed the sofa had
been moved. She looked around the room, and
realized that almost everything had been disturbed.
Picture frames were in the wrong place, potted
plants had been turned around, and some things
were missing altogether. She could only imagine
how scared they must have been, and expected that
they tore the place apart, looking for clues to help
find her.

Once in the bathroom, her mother put a
washcloth under hot water.

"What is this dress?" She asked angrily, while
scrubbing the blood off her face. "Where did
you even find something like this? Were you at a
Renaissance fair?"

She left Letty in the bathroom for a moment,
to find a change of clothes. While alone, Letty
emptied her pockets. She found the pile of cash, the
Argument, and Andy's notebook and contract. In a
sudden rush she opened a bathroom drawer and hid
everything.

Letty's mother came back with a change of
clothes, right as she was closing the drawer.

"What's that?"

"Nothing." Letty slammed the drawer.

Her mother came over and forced it open.

Letty thought she saw a flash of light, but it was just for a moment.

"What is this?" She asked, pulling out the pile of cash. "What have you been doing?"

Her mother looked down and spotted the Argument.

For a moment they were both silent. Letty's eyes flexed and twinged with pain. She felt lightheaded and realized that something wasn't right.

Letty's mother almost reached out for the Argument, before asking, "What is that, Lysette?"

Letty bent and grasped the Argument. Seeing this, her mother recoiled. There was another flash. Bolts of silver and purple cracked in the air for a split second. Letty's eyes tensed and, for a moment her mother's silhouette was framed by feathers.

Letty grasped the marble and the glow shone out.

There was a creature with a fox face standing where her mother should have been.

Letty screamed and tightened her grasp, summoning the blade. The creature struggled with the knob, and nearly tumbled to the ground as the door opened.

"Quill, Staza! It's a trick! They aren't my parents!" Letty yelled, charging out of the bathroom, after the creature.

Staza and Quill drew their sword and dagger respectively.

"Block the door!" Letty yelled.

She saw a creature standing where her father should have been.

"What are you? Where are my parents?" Letty screamed, tears filling her eyes.

"They're ychorons," Quill said.

"They are pets and spies of the ryle. These ones probably work for Ziesqe." Staza added.

"Do you see those bands?" Quill asked.

Letty saw metal disks on their wrists, ankles, and necks.

"Ryle contrivances," Quill said, speculatively.

The two creatures shared a look.

"Please don't kill us. We will cooperate," the male said.

"Answer my questions then. Where are my parents?"

"They are being treated in a facility nearby."

Letty shook her head and stepped closer. "You don't understand, there is nothing stopping me from killing a few more of Ziesqe's servants; we've been doing it all night. Answer completely!"

Letty felt an arm on her shoulder. Quill was there, giving her a serious look.

"They are behind Ziesqe's office. There is a locked metal door. Behind it you will find your parents and some others. They are undergoing memory alteration," the female ychoron finished desperately, her fox face bent with fear. "Once altered, they would have been returned."

Letty took a heavy breath. They weren't dead. She was torn between crying and laughing. In the end she did both.

"Hold on," Staza interrupted. "We must know more. Tell us what you're doing here."

"We're here to imitate her parents for a time... and to take their daughter in for treatment as well. We were told that you might return, though there was only a small chance," the male said.

"How many guards are posted at this facility?" Quill asked.

"A dozen brutox and one of my kind, who serves as an administrator," the female said.

"Where is Ziesqe? Where would he take a special prisoner?" Letty asked, waving her blade.

They crawled backward. "Ziesqe has many palaces in the Netherscape. I know his favorites are in Pansubprimus and Euboia," the male answered.

Letty looked at Staza and Quill.

"Pansubprimus is our part of the Netherscape," Quill said, "Euboia is another part, but it's very different from ours."

"What? More than one Netherscape?" Letty grimaced, knowing this wasn't the time for more questions and waving her hand in negation. "What will you do if I let you go?" Letty asked, lowering her blade.

"We cannot return to Ziesqe. Our failure will mean re-articulation," the female said.

"He will put a bounty on our heads. We will have no choice but to return to Pansubprimus and flee to Degoskirke," the male added, looking at the female questioningly.

She nodded.

Letty was about to let them leave before asking, "Why do you serve a monster like Ziesqe?"

"We need to eat. The ryle have the food," he said plainly.

"Is any of this true?" Letty asked the Caspians.

"I believe so," Quill replied.

Letty's face softened. "Fair enough. I hope you survive," she said, stepping out of the way.

Letty loosened her grip and the blade disappeared. They looked almost like her parents again. The illusion was strong, and she felt herself sneer in disgust.

They saw this and rushed from the apartment, leaving the door ajar as they left.

"Shouldn't our eyes see through their disguises?" Letty asked.

"As far as I know, the ryle don't wear those etherium powered devices on the surface, they have a latent false self that regular eyes detect, which is constant, even in the scape. Their servants, however, need aid, or they can't work on the surface. Why our eyes see through one and struggle with the other is beyond me."

"One is natural, the other is engineered," Staza added. "The ryle never bother with the devices, because almost no one can see them anyway."

"The illusion vanished when confronted with the blade," Quill muttered, trying to work something out.

"We aren't done for the night," Letty said. "We need new clothes first."

She led them to her room and found a change

37

of clothes for Staza, before rummaging through her father's cabinet for something that Quill could wear.

"We should have killed them," Staza said.

Letty ignored that. Though she already regretted her decision, she wasn't ready to murder defenseless beings, even if they did work for Ziesqe.

After the Caspians received new clothes, Letty returned to the bathroom and peeled herself out of the destroyed dress. She wanted to shower, but knew there wasn't any time. She put on a pair of dark track pants, and an equally dark jogging jacket. She brushed her hair, suffering through more tangles than she expected before tying it back.

Coming out of the bathroom, she burst out laughing at Quill and Staza. He sported shorts that were far too large and a polo shirt, while Staza was wearing a pair of Letty's blue jeans and a green t-shirt. They both looked supremely unhappy.

"You guys look great. Let's go."

Instead of complaining, they followed silently.

Letty nearly rushed out empty-handed, but she ran back in and took the pile of cash and a set of house keys. She locked up and they headed down to the street.

"Cab or the bus? Probably should pay for the cab again. I don't want to be seen, but now we'll blend in," Letty whispered to herself.

They stepped out into the night, and Letty realized that it was almost too late for people her age to be out.

"Look at the sky, it has changed color. It's speckled now," Quill said.

Letty ignored the pondering as she flagged down a cab.

The drive went by wordlessly, though Letty noticed the cabby eyeing Staza's sword.

Should have told her to leave that, but we might need it.

She had the cabby pull over a few blocks from the optometrist's office. They walked the distance, and Letty felt her head hurt as she stared for too long at the sign outside Ropt's office.

"You guys can see that?" Letty pointed at the sign.

"Ryle script," Quill said, wincing, "it hurts just to look at it."

"Seer script still makes me dizzy," Staza said.

"Spend more time in the gallery," Quill replied.

They walked casually around to the side of the building.

"Wait," Staza grabbed Letty, "what's our plan? Are you just going to cut a way in and attack?"

Letty knew that she should stop and listen, but the thought of her parents in there, held captive or being tortured, made her frantic. She became agitated as she tried to slow herself down.

"We need to do this now, or I might not be able to," Letty said. "I'll get us in with the Argument, and you two make sure nothing surrounds me. I can kill them all."

Staza agreed, "The brutox are dangerous, but their weapons can't stand up to the blade."

Quill readied his dagger.

"Alright." Letty took the Argument from her pocket and summoned the blade.

They walked around to the back of the building. An alley ran behind the structure, and across the way was a large metal gate, closed and locked. Letty kept her eyes away from more ryle script on the gate, though, with the light coming from the blade, she also saw a thick coating of dark mist swaying gently towards them.

The mist recoiled upward and away as the blade came closer.

"What is that?" Letty asked.

"It's a snare. That gunk is made the same way the slithers are. If it gets on you, it acts like a beacon, giving you away. The ryle can see it on you. It also makes you sick and miserable. Too much of it will just kill you," Quill finished.

"It's hard to clean off, but it is possible with minoe," Staza added.

Letty had a strange feeling of reminiscence. *I think—wait, I remember mice scrubbing that stuff off me. I thought it was a dream.*

She waved her blade closer to the gate. The mist bubbled and disintegrated.

"Incredible," Staza said.

Letty considered the padlock.

"No time to fool around with this."

She sliced a straight line into the gate and then another, and then a third at the top. They stepped back as the rectangular slab of metal fell towards them and hit the ground with a slam.

Letty and the Caspians shared a pained look.

Letty entered cautiously. Her hand shook with the urge to fend off a sudden attack. Staza and Quill followed with their weapons drawn.

Somehow, the interior wasn't what Letty expected.

"It just looks like a garage," she whispered.

Two luxury cars were parked there, and further back was a closed door. But something else caught Letty's eye. There was a bank of lockers on the right-hand wall. She approached them and saw names written on notes taped to a few of the locker doors. She quickly read them and stopped.

Van Arndt.

She tried the locker handle and was surprised to find it unlocked. Inside was her mother's purse, coat, and her father's wallet, as well as their cell phones. Her own purse was there too.

The sight of it almost made her sick.

"They're here," Letty said, looking away.

She left the lockers and headed for the door.

Staza and Quill raised their weapons in anticipation. She turned the knob and pushed before stepping aside.

A loud whistle shot past her ear. She flinched and pushed herself against the wall.

Another whistle sounded, followed by a loud smack. Letty saw a heavy crossbow bolt stuck in the gate.

A moment later, a brutox charged through the door with his sword readied and his shield raised.

Staza struck from one side of the doorway, leaving his flank exposed to Letty, who stabbed with the blade.

The sword and shield clattered to the floor as

the brutox disintegrated, but more poured in. Letty swung wildly, only careful of her friends, who kept them at bay. Letty's blade tore through the opened door, the bank of lockers, and the front end of one of the luxury cars as she slaughtered the rush of brutox fighters.

One sidestepped her swing and moved in too close. She wasn't fast enough to counter him. Its strong hand grasped her wrist, neutralizing the blade. She struggled and lost her balance as she tried to wrench herself free. The brutox slammed her against the wall and jammed its elbow against her throat, choking her.

A sudden crack knocked the brutox sideways. Letty saw Quill. He had picked up the heavy shield and bashed the brutox with the thin edge.

A second later Quill screamed in pain.

Letty wrenched her hand free from the staggered brutox's grip and stabbed it with her blade before lunging forward and stabbing another. It was too late; Quill was down, with a wound to the back.

Staza roared as she pulled her sword free from the last fighting brutox and rushed to his side.

Quill was trying to stand, but Staza held him down. "Stop! Don't move, you'll make it worse!" She commanded, putting pressure on the wound.

Letty stood there, panicked and feeling useless.

"Look around, they might have minoe here!" Staza yelled at her.

Letty rushed into the next room, her hands shaking. She saw dozens of people lying on tables. Gray orbs floated above each of their heads. Ryle script twisted around the orbs.

She kept her eyes off the script and continued. In the center of the room was a purple orb floating inside a hexagonal glass case. Connected to the case's lid was a clockwork mechanism, featuring gears and probes that pointed at the orb from several directions. One final probe pointed out into the room. The gray orbs above everyone's forehead were like nothing she had seen yet.

A sudden twang caught her off guard. Letty felt like she had been hit by a bus. She stumbled backwards into the wall. A bolt had struck her.

Her vision fuzzed beneath a torrent of pain. She saw the brutox hiding behind a table, it was struggling to load its crossbow.

You need to kill it!

Groaning, she raced across the room, stumbling into something which shattered on the ground. She focused on the brutox and pushed herself forward. The broken glass crunched under her heels as she raised her fist and summoned the blade.

The brutox staggered away and dropped the weapon as she swiped and took its head.

I need to find the minoe.

"Staza! I don't know what I'm looking for!" Letty yelled, slurring her words. She vaguely sensed that the tables held adults, no children, and none stirred at her yelling. The image stuck in her harried mind as noteworthy.

Staza stormed into the room. "Minoe will be in a bottle, maybe vials. Good God!" She put a hand over her mouth at the sight of all the people on the tables. Then she saw Letty. "What happened? I thought we killed them all!"

"One was hiding. It shot me," Letty said, struggling to keep upright. She reached out and slumped onto one of the tables, still scanning the room for something she couldn't recognize.

Gray orbs were scattered here and there, as well as countless mechanical and alchemical components, but they were all alien to her.

"Here!" Letty called out. "There are jugs and vials on this table."

Staza was at her side in moments and set about opening jars. She looked and then took a whiff of their contents.

"I wish I was better with chemistry—I just know it should look like quicksilver, and smell like metal," Staza's hands shook as she inspected everything.

"Is this it?" Letty asked after picking up a jug and smelling something odd.

Staza took the jug from her and looked inside before taking a sniff. "Yes!"

They headed back to the other room, but, halfway there, Letty spotted her parents. The sight staggered her.

"I—just go, Staza! I'll be here," she said.

Staza didn't slow.

"What did they do to you?" Letty reached out and slapped at the gray orb that floated above her father's head.

There was a bright flash and a loud crack.

Her hand was numb from where it touched the orb, though the force of the impact had knocked the gray orb away. She looked around the room and noticed that every gray orb was now rolling on the floor.

The mechanical contrivance featuring the purple orb moved as well.

Letty ignored it and struggled to unstrap her parents. It was agonizing, as moving her shoulder, even a bit, made her twinge with pain.

They're breathing, but they still aren't awake.

Letty worked hurriedly, and frustrated herself with the straps, which, with her wound, were almost too heavy and stiff to wrench free. She cried out as the last strap fell away.

Staza and Quill appeared from the garage. Quill was pale and staggering.

"He's healed. Now stand still," Staza said grasping Letty and getting a look at her.

"What are you doing?" Letty asked, feeling the urge to struggle.

"Quill, help me hold her."

Quill clutched Letty's shoulders, and Staza used a dagger to cut through Letty's jacket.

"Not the jacket, Mom, will kill—"

"Shut up and don't move!" Staza said, her hands shaking.

Staza bumped the bolt in the process and the pain made Letty clench. She squirmed, and Quill struggled to hold her still.

"Just a second," Staza said, poring a few drops of the liquid on the wound. "Here, drink some before I push it through."

Letty winced, but drank. "I don't want—please

45

don't," Letty bit down on her cheeks and braced herself as Staza grabbed hold and forced the bolt the rest of the way through her shoulder.

Letty screamed and tried to claw Staza to get free.

She felt herself blacking out. Her head was swimming as she felt them lower her to the floor. She was overwhelmed by a dull fog, but the bitter pain subsided.

She sensed Staza and Quill rushing back and forth for what felt like hours. Occasionally Staza would pat Letty's head as she passed by.

Finally, she took a deep breath and opened her eyes fully. She slapped herself across the cheek a few times to keep the wave of unconsciousness from coming over her again.

She stumbled to her feet and saw that Quill and Staza had freed every person in the room and were hauling them outside.

Letty looked at her wound and saw it was gone. The jacket was destroyed, but she felt surprisingly good.

"You made it through!" Quill said, struggling with a heavy adult, "The minoe pulled you down to heal that one. Lucky it works fast or we would be carrying you outside too."

"What are we doing?" Letty asked, stepping forward to help.

"We're getting everyone out of here," Staza said.

"Why?" Letty asked, following outside. She saw they had carried everyone out to the side street, including her parents.

drive to her building without causing an accident.

She dropped the Caspians and her parents off in their building's underground lot, told them to wait for a minute, and then drove the car a few blocks away. Recalling several hundred hours of her favorite crime investigation shows, Letty parked in an alley and stopped to wipe the steering wheel, doors, and handles, before returning to the underground lot. Luckily, her parents were now half awake and stumbling.

Careful to keep them from crashing into anything, they got the adults up and into the apartment quickly. Stuffing her parents into their bed was a strange experience, and once she closed their bedroom door, Letty went into the living room and slumped onto the couch.

"We've got them in bed, nobody died, and we have minoe now—"

"Not a lot though," Staza interjected.

"It was a jug full," Letty said, gesturing at their pile of things, but not caring to get up and prove it.

"We used so much on you and Quill."

"Well, it's something at least. That could have gone much worse," Letty said, trying to forget the bolt in her shoulder, Quill's stabbing, her parents on those tables, and the pitiful sight of their possessions in that locker.

"What will happen to all those people we saved?" Quill asked.

Letty had to think for a moment. "They'll probably get taken to the hospital and then let go. The real question is what will the police do? Their jackets and wallets were in the lockers, and that space and those cars are probably owned by Ropt. They'll have to investigate and have a trial. Maybe that'll give us a chance to get Andy."

"Ropt?" Quill asked.

"Yeah, Ropt; it's the fake name Ziesqe uses on the surface," Letty answered.

"Of course," Staza said. "Ziesqe seems so influential. You think he'd be too powerful to bother with the surface."

"How can he be too powerful?" Letty asked.

"Ryle are focused on rank." Quill said. "Ziesqe is strange in personally working on the surface, when he could assign a junior to do it. It is generally believed that a ward on the surface is inferior to a fief in the Netherscape. The reason being that they have to hide up here. They are limited in what they can do on the surface, because, if a ryle threatens to expose its kind in any way, even accidentally, that ryle will be fatally censured. Lower ranking ryle are expected to compete with one another for power, first here, and then, when they accrue enough influence, they can hope to find a foothold below."

Letty bent her brow in confusion and spoke, "Wait, so they build little kingdoms for themselves on the surface and in the Netherscape. They fight each other, but how can this work if they are all independent? Who makes sure they don't accidentally expose themselves?"

"Near Pansubprimus, our part of the Netherscape, there is a place called The City in the Sea. Pythia says this is where the final tier of ryle rule. It is one of their capitols, and they have a leadership there that all the ryle warlords, like Ziesqe, must respect."

Letty still wasn't satisfied, and continued with her questions, "If the ryle are running rampant all over the Netherscape, how is it that places like Caspia and the mouse towns haven't been conquered already?"

This time Staza answered, "It's funny you ask that, because Caspia was constantly threatened until just recently. It's been a Golden Age for us. As evil as Ziesqe is, he provided us with dozens of new pupils, and he offered protection from the other ryle in return for exclusive access to our mistress's talents."

Quill nodded. "Yes, and the mice haven't been doing very well either. They've lost land and towns across their part of the Netherscape. They had something of a civil war less than a hundred years ago. A group called the Vychy split off. They were a secular group that rebelled against Titus's society, the Occidentus Obscurus. The Vychy severed their race's millennia long devotion to the Argument."

"I've heard the word 'Argument' used in weird ways, can you—"

A noise from the other room startled them.

Letty got to her feet in time to see her parents walk into the living room. Both looked groggy and barely cognizant.

"Letty, who are these people?" Her father asked, working up to being angry, though not quite there yet.

"They're her friends, Jim," Letty's mother said,

conciliatorily. "Now, Letty dear—it's rude not to int'oduce—intro—duce," she slurred her words and yawned on her way to the kitchen, before filling the kettle, "—introduce us dear."

"Sure. Mom, Dad, this is Staza," Staza waved and smiled, "and this is Quill," he did the same, though the tension in his eyes wouldn't relent.

"Very unique names, you two. Do I know either of your mothers?"

Staza and Quill fidgeted uncomfortably.

"Good lord, it's two in the morning!" Jim said, noticing the wall clock. "How is it two in the morning? Why are people over this late? What's going on here?"

Letty had been working up excuses and stories, but suddenly felt them all inadequate.

"You don't remember what happened?" Letty asked in an attempt at seriousness that came out more like nervousness.

"Tina, what is she talking about? My head is all foggy—probably because it's two in the morning!"

Letty's mother put the kettle on the stove and glanced up, "I don't remember anything either. Letty, if you wanted to have a party you could have asked; drugging us was not necessary. And you should have invited more friends."

"I didn't know what it was they gave you, but you weren't acting right for a long time," Letty improvised.

"What! Who gave us what? From the top, Letty," Jim said, rounding on her sternly.

"People showed up at the door, you let them in.

52

I wasn't home yet, but I came back with Staza and Quill, they're homeless right now, and we—"

Tina's jaw dropped, "You two are homeless?"

Their eyes widened as Letty's story became more and more fantastic. "Does that explain why he's wearing my shorts?" Jim asked, just noticing.

Quill and Staza slowly nodded.

"Staza's wearing my clothes too," Letty added.

"What happened? Are your parents okay?" Tina rushed over and sat next to them.

"We don't know our parents," Staza said.

"We can't go back home right now," Quill elaborated.

"Of course not. Oh, God, and I asked if I knew your mothers." She rung her hands. "You can stay with us for as long as you need." She looked at her husband and said, "Jim, say you agree."

Jim looked suspicious. "Your home closed? Was that the one a few blocks over—St. Martines?"

Letty spoke before Quill or Staza had a chance, "No, they're from Fulton House, the orphanage past my school."

Jim's brow rose. "Right—they did shut that place down. You poor kids—wait. Lysette, back up a bit. You said there were people here and they drugged us with something?"

"Yeah, I was trying to get to that," she huffed. "We showed up and scared them away. It was a man and a woman. They were dressed like business people, and they were going through everything. They moved all the furniture, look." Letty pointed at the table, chairs, and decorations on the mantle.

"God, they have moved everything," Tina said, mortified.

Her parents made a run through the apartment and continued finding more things out of place.

"I can't find my purse."

"My wallet's missing too," Jim added. "Did you call the police?" he asked Letty.

Letty recalled placing their belongings in her bedroom.

"No, but that's the whole point. We can't call the police," Letty said, looking at Staza and Quill. "They are supposed to be somewhere else, another orphanage on the other side of the city, but the school year is almost over. They can't just leave."

"The police probably won't believe that you scared the thieves away on your own, Lysette," Tina said, looking at Jim hopefully. "The police won't believe her story and the only witnesses are missing children."

Jim still wore a disapproving grimace.

"Whatever drug they gave us wore off. Luckily, no one was hurt, but we need to cancel all the credit cards, and I still think we should still file a police report. I understand why you didn't call the police, Lysette, but your friends should get back to their orphanage." Jim concluded.

"What's an orphanage?" Staza asked, whispering.

"A place for homeless kids," Letty replied.

"We can sort all that out in the morning," Jim said, getting back on track. "About these two, I think it's clear," he paused and soaked up the anxious looks from everyone in the room. "Your mother is right. They should stay with us, for now at least. The condition being, if anything strange happens again, the police are getting involved. If this was a one-time set of coincidences that's fine, otherwise, they leave."

Everyone seemed pleased, everyone barring Tina, who instantly shot up from the couch. "Where are we going to put them?" She stared at Quill seriously. "The girls will sleep in Lysette's room, and you'll sleep on the couch."

Letty and the Caspians stared at each other, unsure how to respond.

"Thank you for your hospitality," Staza said, nudging Quill. "We won't forget it."

"A-absolutely," Quill stammered, "I'll be as silent as a mouse."

Letty and Staza gave him an annoyed look.

"That's what I'm worried about," Tina said, staring at him crossly. "I might just tie a bell to your neck, young man."

"He'll be fine, mom."

"He'd better be, or it's the boot," Jim said, firmly resolute.

The kids shrunk under the silent stares of the adults.

Finally, Tina broke the silence, "I think they get it, dear," she said, before blurting out, "Bedding—I don't think we have enough—Jim, check the hall closet. And make sure the front door is locked! We don't want those people coming back—my God, so much in one day! At least no one's hurt!"

Letty, Quill and Staza all shared a concerned look as the adults left the room.

"Did that go over well or not?" Quill asked.

"You won't freeze tonight or starve tomorrow. So, there's that," Letty said, grinning.

The Caspians both wore expressions that Letty had never seen before.

What are they feeling right now? What am I feeling? It's all too strange. These two are right out of another world, and now they're wearing my clothes, and sleeping here tonight.

For a moment, she felt afraid at how normal they looked, dressed like anyone, and sitting on her couch.

But there's something about them. Something in their eyes. They're wild.

Staza reached out and hugged her. Letty nearly recoiled, startled by the sudden contact.

"It'll be fine," Staza said, releasing Letty. "Just be clearer about the conventions up here. They think that Quill is in danger of breaking some rule."

Letty laughed. "Don't worry about them… I'm more concerned about you two."

Staza and Quill sighed.

"Just don't kill anybody while you're here," Letty said.

"Not unless they try to kill us first," Quill added in a reassuring voice.

Staza nodded her agreement.

Letty rolled her eyes. *There's going to be a problem, but I can't keep an eye on them every second. They aren't stupid; they won't just attack people, but if someone senses how foreign they are and tries to rob them, there will be broken bones at least.*

Less than an hour later, everyone was in bed, barring Jim, who patrolled the hall one last time. Letty heard her parent's door open and close as he finally surrendered his post.

Letty looked over at her clock and saw how late it was.

Sunrise in a few hours.

The sleeping bag on her bedroom floor rose and fell with the rhythmic breathing of deep sleep.

Everything was calm, and her thoughts drifted back to Andy. She shivered.

How can I relax in a warm bed, while he's gone? He's in hell, and I have the Argument.

She bit her cheek to keep from crying.

I don't even know how to get there.

She rolled over and shuddered, the fatigue slowly working her to sleep.

I'm a terrible person. He found me, but there's nothing I can do tonight. I'll start tomorrow. No—they'll take me to school tomorrow. I'll skip class...Andy found a way...he got there. I can too.

Frustration finally gave way to exhaustion, and Letty slept.

Chapter 3: Zentule

Andy was falling. He opened his eyes but there was nothing to see.

A small speck of light appeared. It grew. In moments the speck was blinding. His mind sensed something, yet, before grasping that rogue thought, he came to rest on a soft surface.

Andy shot up. He was in his room.

He stood and felt the floor creak. He bent and looked under the bed. There were no mice.

The Infiniteye was no longer on his ceiling.

Andy rubbed his eyes and shook his head, trying to clear the delirium.

I was somewhere else... wasn't I?

Andy left his room and was surprised to see his parents on the couch. They were crying in each other's arms.

What's happened?

Andy stood still. He felt his head spinning.

He walked up to his parents, but they refused to see or hear him.

There was something not right about their faces.

"Hey, Mom, Dad, are you guys okay?" Andy asked.

His father met his glance, but instead of the calm and reassuring face he expected, there was something cold.

Andy recoiled and crashed into the coffee table.

His father stood, his movement almost mechanical, and approached.

Andy scrambled away. He ran to the front door and burst through onto the sidewalk.

This is wrong.

He looked up.

The sky's wrong too.

It was plain white. The buildings were like sketches. He shook his head, and the details filled out as his eyes scanned the horizon. Everything was flawed, incomplete, and jarring. Andy sensed that he had experienced something like this before.

He felt weight in his hand. Looking, he saw his backpack strap resting in his palm. His mind wrenched, as if overcome by the need to fall asleep and wake up all at once. Moments later, the sensation left, and he felt the sudden urge to rush to the bus stop.

Andy sighed and put the backpack on.

He walked to the bus stop and waited for only a moment before the school bus rolled around the corner. It stopped, and he boarded.

That was close. I was almost late.

He looked from face to gawking face.

What's wrong with everyone? Is it me? Are my eyes that bad?

Dean was there. He looked normal, and Letty as well, but the others were distorted. Their hair seemed flatter, almost painted or made from plastic. Faces were too smooth and lacked their dimples or blemishes. These changes were so fine that Andy doubted himself, doubting that anything was wrong.

He spoke to Letty, "Hey, will you come and sit with me?"

She looked torn between insulting him and getting up.

"Look, I think there's something wrong here, are you feeling it too?" Andy asked.

"The only thing wrong is you talking to us," Emma said, confusion on her face.

Andy looked out the window and saw the bus was moving, though he hadn't felt it accelerate.

One time, the bus drove off while I was still standing. I fell over and skinned my elbow.

"This is wrong," Andy said. "It's like a dream."

The bus disappeared, and all the students fell to the floor. The buildings became translucent. Inside every apartment and behind every wall, Andy spotted ryle. Hundreds of them.

He fumbled for the Argument but couldn't find it.

Each ryle looked his way.

Andy spun about; in every direction there were dozens more. They slowly got to their feet.

He saw turning knobs, and others walking down hollow stairs. They were moving towards him.

He looked for Letty and Dean, but they were gone. All the students were gone.

This isn't real! Andy tried to make himself believe it.

The ryle approached. He heard steps behind him and spun around again. The street was full. They all raised their right hands in perfect unison, their inky claws shining as they moved his way.

He felt something on his shoulder and spun to lash out. But nothing was there.

60

Andy heaved in breath and opened his eyes.

He was in bed. Andy shot up and felt the floor creak.

"This is fake. This is like the Juncture again. I know this is fake!" he yelled.

There was a sudden flash and his room disappeared. Pressure hurt his ears and he felt like he was being pulled backwards, up from the bottom of a pool, until he finally reached the surface.

He heard a female screaming. He opened his eyes, but everything was blurry. He saw a shape contorted in agony. Its hands were clawing at its face, and it was screaming.

Andy felt his ears pop worse than they ever had. His face was sweaty, and his head hurt like he had just been cracked with a bat.

There was a purple and silver orb floating above his face. He tried to move, but restraints pressed against his arms and legs.

The screaming continued and then gave way to a wretched voice. "I can't do the surface; I've never seen it!"

Andy's vision cleared, and he realized the creature reminded him of Martin.

An ychoron?

Ziesqe had a single finger laid against the ychoron's forehead. It wore something that looked like a full-body piece of metallic clothing. It reminded him of what an artistic jeweler might create if one commissioned a swim suit made from necklaces.

Andy stopped staring at the odd clothing long

enough to see that the creature was tearing its feathers out. It shook with pain, but continued to mutilate itself, as if the alternative was worse.

"Off!" Ziesqe's voice thundered through the room.

It shook its head and begged. "The Seer has resistance; it even knows about the junctures. I'll try again!" She screamed.

The door opened and other ychorons appeared. They were also wearing jewelry harnesses, though each was unique.

Ziesqe reached out and tore the jeweled harness off the offending ychoron and threw it to the ground.

The ychoron crumbled to the floor in a torrent of weeping.

The others rushed into the room and took her away. One stayed to clean up the small pile of multi-colored, bloody feathers scattered across the floor. The faces of the other ychorons were neutral, but there was tension there, as if they had practice at remaining blank.

Ziesqe walked to a window and looked out. Flashing light from beyond played across his fleshy, tentacled face. The last ychoron left the room and closed the heavy stone door, leaving Andy alone with Ziesqe.

Ziesqe's fingers tapped, as if in time with some thought. He nodded his head, tilting it this way and that, before finally turning towards the bed. Andy reflexively closed his eyes.

Ziesqe's footsteps came closer and closer, until

Andy sensed the ryle was standing only inches away.

"Look at you," Ziesqe murmured. "An ancient artifact, renewed, alive and breathing. You're putting my best dowsers through their paces. This isn't the first failure, but this is the first time you overcame the suppression. If I were human, I would likely apologize for what you witnessed moments ago."

Andy opened his eyes. Ziesqe stared at him placidly, his claws grasping a bedpost.

"But you can see what I am. I will not speak untruth. That unpleasantness is a sign by which you might divine your future."

Ziesqe paused, as if expecting a question or plea. When none came, he continued, "I was hoping for a few lucrative years of experimentation with you, a committed seer. It seems that you know more than you should. Explain."

Andy looked away.

Ziesqe chuckled and placed a clawed finger on Andy's forehead. The sound of it echoed in his mind and a sudden pain shot up behind his eyes. Andy clenched his teeth and pulled away as hard as he could, but the pain only ceased when Ziesqe removed his finger.

"Our arrangement is a simple one. You must not annoy me. Use whatever faculties you possess to achieve this end, and, from the start, realize that the inverse of this pointless resistance is even more tiresome."

Andy gulped.

"If you succeed in not annoying me, I will

reward you with the continued existence of your kin. I shall repeat myself for emphasis: Do as I wish, and those you love will survive. These are simple terms. Do your best to never need reminding."

Andy stared at the ceiling. *I need to focus. If I keep this monster occupied until he gets bored with me, I'll be protecting my family. If I do this, it might keep Letty safe.*

"I—"

Ziesqe tapped him with a claw for silence. "We'll take the air first—have a leisurely stroll, and determine if you can be acclimated. I have seen a number of your kind lose their simple minds only moments after awakening. There is more than just physical danger here." Ziesqe tapped him again with a claw. "Think like you never have before, Seer. Cleave to that which survives, and nothing else. Smother the weak and squeamish, false certainties that infest surface existence. Take account of your morality, of your ignorance, and of your lauded humanity. You must purge yourself of such caprice. If you win this war with yourself, you might endure to enjoy the comfort of hiding beneath sheets once more."

Ziesqe left the room, and, moments later, more ychorons appeared. They bore clothes. Andy was unchained and then groomed by several feathered arms. The tickling feathers made him sneeze, but they held him still as he did so. They brushed and trimmed his hair, and sponged the grime away. They measured him and altered his silken undergarments. Andy stepped behind a screen to change, and was surprised when they laid out a chainmail suit. The rings of mail were quite fine. They seemed too small to be of any good.

These won't protect anyone.

Andy tore at a piece of the mail to prove the point to himself and was surprised at its resilience.

An ychoron grinned at the sight, but said nothing.

Andy dared a look at the creatures. Their jewelry jangled as they worked. One took the shirt and motioned at him to put it on.

Andy's first instinct was to resist, but he thought better of it.

"What's the point of this?" He asked.

The sudden question startled the ychorons. They were nervous, and none answered.

They probably remembered what happened earlier, all those feathers. People everywhere are having their lives ruined because of me.

Andy felt his stomach clench.

That changes today. Even if it means I'm a slave for the rest of my life.

Andy put the mail on. The ychorons provided belts and cinches that, when strapped on, made the weight of the armor almost disappear.

Andy hopped in place and stretched his arms; he bent over and lifted his knee to his chest. The ychorons stopped their work to watch.

"It's not that bad," Andy said.

When he was finished trying out his armor, they approached him with fine silver and blue robes. He stood still as they carefully applied the robes in layers.

Andy thought they were finished, but a final box was opened. In it were four heavy obsidian bracelets. The interior of each bracelet was ringed in ryle script that flickered and pulsed.

Andy recoiled when he saw the bracelets. He clenched his fists and sized up the ychorons.

I can probably fight my way past them. His eyes traveled to the door. But out there...

They sensed his intentions and looked ready to run from the room.

He remembered his family.

"Go on then," he said, holding out his arms.

They shared a long look before placing the bracelets on his wrists and ankles. It took two of them to slip the necklace over his brow.

No burning. No pain at all?

Andy felt his forehead and found his bronze laurel was missing. He almost asked about it but realized they would have no idea.

"What are these?" Andy asked, inspecting what he supposed were his new shackles.

They did not answer.

They mustn't be allowed to talk to me. If Ziesqe comes in and I'm asking them questions, he'll probably think the worst and have them tortured.

Andy cringed.

And that would be my fault too.

He sighed and let his questions go unaired.

They led him to the door and held it open. Andy stepped out into a wide, plain hall. Every surface was cold slate gray. The way the hall was carved made Andy claustrophobic. The width of the hall and horizontal fissures running in the stone made it feel like the whole building was crushing down on him, even though the ceiling was well out of reach.

He heard a wave of gibbering coming from nearby. The ychorons pulled him gently from the center of the hallway and pushed him against the wall.

One end of the hall writhed with motion. Countless shapes stormed closer. As they approached, Andy recognized that they were slithers, thousands of slithers. He braced for the attack, but they simply charged past.

In the center of the swirling mob, Andy spotted a severed ryle head. Bulbous and bearing more tentacles than a regular ryle, the thing was being carried by the horde. Instead of ears, it had large, bat-like wings it flapped to keep upright. It squealed and gestured with a tentacle.

In a flash, the crush of slithers turned down another hall.

Andy stared with wide eyes at the ychorons, who only seemed slightly annoyed at the delay.

Resigned to never getting an answer, and satisfied that Ziesqe wasn't within earshot, Andy still had to ask, "What the hell was that?"

An ychoron gave him a sympathetic look.

They led him down the hall and through a pair of wide, slatted wooden doors.

Wow.

A long pool of dark water ran down the center of this central hall. In some places there were benches and tables, and over the pool ran the occasional flat bridge, though these all lacked rails. There were stairs leading off the space, and other wide, slatted doors. Columns ran the length of the hall and occasional flashes of light shone from rectangular holes in the ceiling. Countless ryle heads milled about, each with an attendant group of slithers. A few convened in the pool, their heads leaned together in confidence. Ychorons rushed this way and that, each wore their unique piece of body-enveloping jewelry. He spotted a group of brutox, too. Tall, pale mantises guarded doors, while a troop of heavy beetles stepped silently over the polished floor, their greatswords resting on their shoulders. Several creatures stopped and stared as Andy came in.

Andy was led down low stairs into the hall and realized, as he went, that the pool was wider than he thought.

The proportions are off for everything in this place.

He saw a large gorilla-like brutox harnessed to a cart, which was filled with massive slabs of ribs. Andy realized he was in something more akin to an indoor avenue than just a hallway.

Running his hand over the hewn-stone, Andy peered into the rooms adjoining and saw eating halls, libraries, and rooms full of strange instruments and alchemical equipment.

This place is huge. I could never make a run for it.

As they approached the end of the hall, Andy realized that it didn't end with a door or wall, but opened to the Netherscape. The rough slate floor continued outside unchanged. Light from the sky above flashed and reflected off the walls, floors, and weapons of the brutox. As they left the roof behind, Andy gazed up and saw the smooth walls of the structure reaching into the air.

Multiple floors above.

And higher still was a sky running wild with glittering bolts of lightning. He shielded his eyes.

Andy heard the water jostle and looked over at the pool. A large mass of dark purple and green mottled flesh had parted the surface. A single red eye stared his way.

Andy flinched and backed away, stumbling into the ychorons. They laid their hands on him, and he realized that they were trying to calm him.

"What the hell is that thing? It isn't a ryle—is it?"

No answer came as the eye sunk into the black water.

Andy shivered as his hand searched fruitlessly for the Argument that once rested in his pocket.

The ychorons gently forced him to move again. They walked out onto a carved promontory. Andy looked out past the walls of the palace and saw thick jungle bristling in the wind and shining with moisture. The lightning storm in the sky was almost constant, and the perpetual shifting of light and shadow across the palace and the expanse of forest beyond made Andy's stomach clench. The countless undulating boughs, thick with purple fronds and swaying vines moved like some nightmare ocean, concealing unknown terror.

I feel like I've seen this before.

A piercing screech nearly made him stumble. He looked over the promontory and saw centipedes the size of cruise ships wrestling inside stables larger than airport runways. Their clawed legs were as tall as trees and tore chunks out of the floor and walls as they clashed.

"I have to be seeing things—it's probably a trick of the light." Andy's jaw dropped.

The fury of their struggle kicked up dust that swirled and obscured their spiky limbs. They filled the air with ear-piercing screeches and snapped their mandibles with such speed that Andy felt their cracking ring out. The sensation reminded him of overly loud music that rattles the bones. When he felt his body shake with the sound, he knew his eyes weren't deceiving him; they were huge.

Andy recalled Ziesqe's speech to him from earlier. He stared at the ychorons, desperation in his eyes, begging for an explanation.

Here I am, begging the fox faces for an explanation. Ychorons are the only thing my mind considers rational now.

The thought was so absurd, he didn't know if he should laugh or cry.

"Those are the ravagers. Now, please hurry, or we'll upset the Master," said one, whose feathers were currently checkered blue and yellow.

They pulled Andy away from the promontory and directed him to a long, gradual stair that led down into an expansive rectangular stadium. The walls of the pit, like every other surface he had seen, were immaculately angular, despite their hewn surface and the natural striations in the stone. A stadium, also carved like the pit, rose on all four sides. Wooden planks lined the seats, presumably for the comfort of these monsters. On the far side, beneath a red awning, sat Ziesqe.

The seats were filled with ychorons and brutox, as well as dozens of other, full-bodied ryle. The sight of these other ryle was a surprise.

They reminded him of Ziesqe, but he didn't trust his eyes to tell the ryle apart; he had seen only two.

All at once they noticed him. A hush came over the hundreds of creatures. Ziesqe stood and neared the edge of his balcony. He held out a hand to Andy and gestured towards the pit.

Andy's attending ychorons led him to a side stair well, and they went down into a hidden armory.

He was presented with tables full of arms, and then the ychorons turned and left.

He wants me to fight.

Andy felt his stomach sink.

I must pick a weapon.

Andy approached the first table and handled weapon after weapon. He found them all too heavy or cumbersome.

I'm used to the Argument. It's so lightweight that everything else feels ridiculous.

Finally, he picked up the lightest blade, a rapier. The swept steel guard covered his hand as he gripped the weapon. It was delicate and pleasing to the eye.

I'll probably be killed.

Andy turned to leave before pausing and grabbing a dagger.

Just in case.

He stopped again and chose a second dagger.

He tucked one into the belt at his waist, and put the second inside the sandal wrappings that ran up to his calf.

I'm going to die.

Andy walked through the doorway and stepped out into the pit. A score of slithers were waiting for him. He felt relief at that.

The slithers here look fleshy, not like the ones I saw at the ossuary fortress.

Andy recalled his first battle at Cair Fromage. The slithers there had been like these. Andy knew the brutox also consisted of several forms.

Ziesqe put a claw up to his mouth and then held it out to the crowd. They were silent.

Ziesqe's voice filled the arena, "Can you see it? Look past the boy and behold our primordial foe in his terminal brilliance. Recognize, if you can, the great privilege before us: that of bloodied history and her song unfolding, for a moment, in these halls." He held out his clawed fist and pointed at Andy. "There it stands, reaching through a thousand pages and a thousand years alike to gift us these seconds. I will hear his feet on the sand, nothing else."

Andy sensed every creature in the stands clench.

I'm a piece of history for them. Or maybe I'm more

*like an aged bottle of wine, something they will enjoy for a
moment, and then forget.*

"Weigh the Seer!" Ziesqe's voice snapped like
thunder and the slithers attacked.

Andy swung at the charging creatures, keeping
them at bay. The group split apart and tried to
encircle him. Andy swiped and struck one. It rolled
across the ground and lay still.

It isn't inky.

He rushed through the gap and spun to cut
down another.

The slithers changed course, but their plan was
the same.

Andy backed towards the wall to keep them
from surrounding him. He swung and struck
another, but felt a poke in his legs. He reached down
with his free hand and grabbed the offending slither
before sending it flying, like a discus, out of the
arena. He realized the rapier wasn't the best weapon
for this foe. It was light, but as he swung, he realized
that it was intended for stabbing thrusts, and these
enemies were far too small to stab. He could only
hope to catch one with a lucky slash.

Maybe I can set them up.

Andy leaped over a pair with a grunt and rushed
to the other side of the arena before slowing.

Let them catch up... and now!

He turned and swiped in one fluid motion.

A pair fell to the attack, but a third caught and
held onto his blade before climbing towards him.

"Get off!" Andy growled swiping with his free
hand at the slither, while backing away from the

others.

He managed to slap it off his hilt, but not before another pair were up his legs, stabbing with their tiny blades as they went.

Now I understand the tiny chainmail.

Andy ignored the stabbing and stomped a foot down onto one, before slashing another in two. He reached and grabbed for one slither, but it stabbed him in the hand, and crawled to the small of his back.

"So that's how it is?" Andy yelled, slamming his back against the wall, and crushing the elusive creature.

The last slither had stopped stabbing him. Andy felt all over for it and turned around. He spotted it climbing up the pit to escape.

Andy took a deep breath. *That wasn't as easy as I'd hoped.*

He wanted to check and see if he was bleeding, but he felt that the wounds would be tiny, like dozens of pinpricks. Andy hoped their weapons hadn't been poisoned.

There was a murmur in the stands. Andy saw Ziesqe with his right elbow on his left knee, and his tentacled chin resting on his palm.

What am I thinking? Poisoned needles? They put armor on me, and Ziesqe could have me killed at any time. They have no need for poison.

Andy stood and took in all the faces. Those faces, however, were concerned with Ziesqe.

What now?

After a long moment, Ziesqe got to his feet and

swept a glance across the audience.

Andy saw the creatures shifting uncomfortably.

"Striped, pale mantis. Subdue him without a weapon," Ziesqe commanded.

A mantis brutox shot to its feet and in two bounds was flying through the air. Its wings, startlingly pink, flashed for a moment as it landed soundlessly in the pit.

The creature was twice his height.

Andy raised the rapier. For a moment he felt pity for the monster standing before him.

Does it have no choice? It has to subdue me, while I have to kill it.

Andy scowled up at Ziesqe.

The mantis saw this and lunged; its vicious serrated arms suddenly spread wide.

In the moment before it collided with him, Andy realized, *It doesn't need a weapon!*

The mantis slammed into him. He felt massive pressure clamping down on his ankles.

The mantis pulled, and he felt the floor slip out from beneath him. He was being held upside down. Andy stabbed with the rapier, but the mantis's other claw slapped the weapon away. The mantis turned and presented Andy to the audience with the barest trace of a flourish.

The crowd erupted with guttural cheers. Andy reached for his waist and found the dagger there. He pulled himself up and stabbed the mantis between two plates on his underarm. The beast cried; a clicking moan echoed across the arena. Its limbs slackened, releasing Andy, who rolled to his feet and plunged the dagger into the mantis's midsection.

He felt the immense pressure again. This time it had caught him around the chest, making it hard to breathe. He was lifted again. The mantis clamped down harder, and he heard his robes shred. A moment later he felt a pop as the mail links beneath tore apart.

The mantis stared him straight in the eye before using its mandibles to clamp down on his hand.

Andy screamed as it bit into his wrist.

The crowd was wild with excitement. Ziesqe held out a claw and there was silence, but the mantis ignored it all.

Andy felt his vision tunneling as he gasped for air.

The mantis twisted its mandibles, forcing Andy's hand back in an unnatural direction. Finally, Andy heaved in a breath and dropped the blade. The mantis released his hand and instead snapped at Andy's face. He felt a slash across his cheek.

Andy grasped the mantis by its plated throat with one hand and held its snapping face away. With his injured hand he reached down to his ankle and fumbled for the dagger there.

The mantis realized, but it could only strike with its wounded arm. With some chainmail still resisting, Andy shrugged off the blow.

Andy stared into the creature's eyes as he lifted the blade.

It knows what's coming.

He tightened his grip on the dagger, raising it high, and plunged it into the mantis's throat. The pressure on his chest released, and he tumbled to the floor.

The mantis clutched at its throat for an awful moment before finally surrendering, its pink wings flexing open in the final moment.

He stared at the creature's broken and bleeding body, while his own shook with pain. His robes were shredded and even the mail beneath was torn apart in places.

Andy felt unexpected sadness for the now lifeless creature. Its broken body, somehow beautiful in death, where it was terrifying in life.

The crowd was silent. Andy slowly turned from his foe, afraid to face the crowd, but equally afraid to stare for any longer. He looked up and watched Ziesqe, who sat in silence.

The creatures, unsure of how to respond, whispered cautiously and kept their eyes on Ziesqe, who finally stood and spoke, "I fought this Seer on the coast outside the Python's den. He wielded a piece of the Argument."

There was a murmur, but Andy saw this was common knowledge.

A few of them were probably there.

"I assumed it was a fluke. Of course, every now and then a Seer slips through the cracks. Even less commonly, one stumbles upon the Argument."

This seemed reasonable to the audience.

"But this boy fought before us, armed with metal blades, not artifacts of the conflict."

That brought them all to silence.

So what? Of course it would have been easier with the

Argument.

Ziesqe held out a hand and stared into the distance.

"Can you hear it?" His voice finally came, soft and with a hint of pain. "Can you see it around us? The extinct hand of humankind. The boy speaks with the Voice of the Dead God. Yet, there is no sign of the Usurper."

This caused a commotion. Ziesqe lowered his hand and cocked his head in disapproval as the crowd grew bolder with its disagreement.

A loud ychoron flared bright red and yelled, "The child is a skilled fighter, yes, but it must have been luck!"

Whoa. That guy's headed for an execution.

Many others complained openly, and this shocked Andy, considering how servile they had been until now.

Something about what he said was too much for them.

Ziesqe raised a claw. "You forget yourselves," he said.

The crowd came to its senses and quieted.

After a long stare at the loud ychoron, now colored black, he spoke, "That mantis would have felled a dozen humans. But here, something else spoke to us. It reached out and stabbed your brother through the throat."

The crowd grumbled.

"Let's be clear, friends! Look at him, go look," Ziesqe snapped a claw, and growled a command Andy couldn't hear.

A team of ychorons rushed out into the pit,

grabbed Andy, and tore off the ruined robes. The bloody chain beneath gleamed in the flashing light from above.

"Look! How could any of you say that a human child, of the debased surface, would even be able to stand, and only stand, before my mantis. Look at his corpse, now ruined, and by what? Any child, any one of billions, would have cried and pleaded in the moments before death."

There was no reply.

He's saying that I'm not myself. Andy paused, and considered that for a moment. *Haven't I been saying that the whole time?*

Ziesqe waved at the ychorons, and they directed him out of the pit. Andy stumbled as he went, and when they reached the armory, he fell to the ground, his hands clutching at bloody wounds.

The ychorons carried him to a medical room. They removed his destroyed armor and applied minoe to his wounds. Finally, one offered him a drink of the quicksilver fluid, and Andy felt better, though this time it was many minutes before he could stand.

"Probably a few broken ribs," one ychoron said to another.

"How could he endure? The pale mantis is our deadliest."

"The master may have a point," the other responded.

"Our master is most erudite, but this is heresy," the first ychoron looked at Andy as he spoke.

"His wounds, how severe were they? Should he

have been able to fight and win, let alone survive?"

"I can't say. How often do we treat Seers?"

There was a silence as they worked.

"Llanyly will probably be executed."

The other laughed. "Why did he call out like that?"

"Perhaps the shock of such a claim moved him to insubordination," the ychoron said, shrugging.

Finally, Andy had to speak, "What exactly was that claim? What did your Master mean when he spoke about me?"

They were both silent.

"Oh come on, I'm just a kid, remember?"

That earned him suspicious glances.

"What's going to happen to me?" he asked, nursing the now healed wounds on his torso, and looking as helpless as he could.

One of the ychorons rolled its eyes, though the other looked sympathetic.

"You've been assigned chambers and a guard. You should also keep armor on, whenever in the halls. The spawn may try and kill you if they get the chance." The sympathetic ychoron spoke curtly.

"Spawn?"

The ychorons both huffed a quick laugh.

"Certainly, you've seen them. The damnable flapping heads that are waging petty wars all over Zentule."

The other laughed. "I'd like to see them campaign off the palace grounds for once."

"Indeed, a nice excursion in the Nightmare would set them right."

"And Zentule?" Andy asked, digging further.

The ychorons shared a condescending look.

"The Voice of the Dead God?" One scoffed.

The other broke out in laughter.

"Guys, please. I have no idea what's going on here."

"Zentule is the name of this palace and its grounds," the sympathetic one said.

"Raised by our master out of the murky Nightmare itself, and now a living testament to ryle ingenuity."

"So, you do respect Ziesqe. Because a moment ago you didn't sound like it," Andy said.

They were taken aback.

"Our master allows his ychorons and brutox more freedom of thought than any ryle I've seen, and I've worked for a few in my time."

"That's right, you were with Juukvel not long ago."

The sympathetic one nodded. "We might take it for granted, Llanyly certainly did. We'll wait and learn where we stand, but I hope Llanyly is executed. I would hate for the palace to fall to the rot of such a base insurrection."

Andy had never heard such a sentiment in his life.

Executed for speaking out. And they think it's a good idea. Just when they were starting to make sense...

The door opened. A brutox of beetle type stepped in and stared at Andy.

"They are going to take you to your chambers. Remember to stay armored, and do not try to lose your escort. They are there to protect you."

The medical ychorons gave Andy one last condescending look before turning back to their organizing.

The brutox bore a battle axe. He let it rest against his shoulder. Andy followed him to a hall that was narrower and darker than the one he had been through before.

A dozen other brutox were standing nearby. All were the stout and hardy beetle type, save one. The odd one out was another pale mantis. The mantis towered over the other brutox, and the plates of its body were outlined in sharp pink. It was bulkier, compared to the one he had fought, and showed signs of old damage on its plates. Heavy cuts had left their mark.

Andy stared at the mantis and saw something akin to emotion on its alien face. There was a trace of pain and anger in its eyes, but only for a moment.

"I didn't want to do it," Andy said plainly. "Ziesqe will kill my family if I don't cooperate."

At hearing this, the beetles glanced at the mantis, who was still. The mantis turned and led the way.

The brutox led him through the hall to a set of circular stairs. They came out to a wider hall, though this one was busier than the last. After a few minutes of walking they turned back onto the main hall with the pool.

Andy scowled at the motionless water, knowing something hid beneath.

There was commotion up ahead, and the beetles

readied their axes.

Is that another human?

Andy thought he was seeing a giant man in shackles screaming his lungs out.

It is, and he looks familiar.

The man was tugging on the chains and tripping his captors.

The man leaped over a wall of stumbling brutox and rushed away, pulling about two dozen chains, each connected between his limbs and a brutox captor. The scene nearly had Andy falling over with laughter, especially when the captors slid across the floor, their carapaces throwing up sparks.

The beetles looked to the mantis, who watched in silence.

The man lunged at one of the flapping heads. He grabbed it and swung the beast by its tentacles.

Alarmed, a brutox jumped onto his back and tried to weigh him down. More brutox clambered onto the first, and after a long moment the warrior finally fell to his knees.

What a monster, that guy! Andy grinned.

The beetles tapped the blades of their weapons against their plated chests in something akin to applause.

Finally, the mantis began moving again. Andy and the brutox followed, though, as they passed Andy slowed to get a closer look at the warrior.

I remember, in Caspia they called him Thrag.

"Thrag?" Andy asked the writhing mass of bodies.

A mere, half-second later the pile of brutox

erupted outwards. They all flew the distance their chains allowed before smacking into the ground.

Andy ducked as one arced past his head and landed in the pool.

Eyes wide, Andy got a closer look at Thrag. The man was craggy beyond belief. He looked like he'd been carved from a chunk of marble. His threadbare clothes and furs were torn to pieces and barely hung together over his rippling bundles of muscle.

He stared at Andy, his manic eyes swimming and his mouth slowly moving, as if he were speaking phantom words.

He's insane.

Andy felt his face twist with pity.

The brutox readied their weapons, but they didn't pull Andy away.

"Thrag?" Andy asked again.

Something came loose in Thrag's mind and he seemed to focus.

"Caspian! We need—" Thrag lunged towards Andy and grabbed him.

A beetle plunged his axe into Thrag's shoulder, but the man didn't blink.

"What! What did they do to you?" Thrag grabbed Andy by the jaw and pulled him forward, his own brazen face contorted in frenzied sympathy.

"I'm fine, Thrag!" Andy complained, trying to free himself from the crushing grip.

"Can you speak! Where is your sight?" Thrag looked around. "They have us, Caspian!"

A score of brutox weapons tore into him. He released Andy and began to rip his chains asunder, oblivious to the wounds.

The beetles surrounded Andy and pulled him away. The sounds of violence echoed down the hall. Andy struggled fruitlessly against his guards to see.

Finally, he slipped free and looked back. Thrag was motionless on the floor. Andy stood and stared for a long moment, almost unbelieving.

Andy felt his body wrack in agony. But he knew something was wrong.

How has he not been killed up till now? I saw him fight a mantis barehanded. He was a wild man, and he knew Caspian, who's been dead for—well, longer than I've been alive at least. How has he stayed alive this whole time?

Andy considered an alternative.

Maybe he wasn't always so suicidally crazy. Either way, he kept calling me Caspian. Pythia did too. I saw a likeness of Caspian once—the mosaic Musi and Arke were working on. I look nothing like him.

Andy scowled and watched as ychorons rushed to clean up the mess and take the wounded to the medics. Strangely, the brutox holding the chains continued their watch over Thrag's body, as if no one had given them permission to stop.

Finally, the mantis stepped up beside Andy and gave him a blank look.

I'm being rude to my captors.

Andy sighed, and followed his guards.

Chapter 4: Following Footsteps

Letty walked into her first class of the day: history. A few glances held on her longer than she liked. She refused to meet their eyes, wondering how much they knew.

She had only missed two days of class while she was in the Netherscape. Emma waved, while Becky, Brook, and Quinn gave her six raised eyebrows.

Hurray.

Letty took her seat, and she tried to keep from sneering.

"Where have you been?" Becky and Brook asked in the same instant.

"That boy people saw you with, the Lice boy— some people think—well, people are talking, Letty," Quinn said, displeased. "This looks bad, and we couldn't even reach you."

"I told you, she was grounded after the museum field trip. She has strict parents; obviously they took her phone," Emma retorted, before Letty had a chance.

"Right—" Letty said, ready to let it go, but she continued dryly, "I donated my collection of last winter's clothes and they found out."

"What's wrong with that? I do—"

"I do that too! Oh, we're so alike, you know," Becky preened, interrupting Brook.

Quinn wasn't convinced.

"I'm basically off limits for the rest of the week," Letty said.

"Yeah, okay, so you're grounded for the week,

but where were you for two days?" Quinn asked.

"My parents know how much I love you guys. Going to school wasn't enough of a punishment," Letty said, hiding her face in her backpack. She found her cell and saw a dozen missed calls and ten times as many text messages. Letty rolled her eyes and dropped the phone back into her pack before retrieving her binder.

"That's not fair!" Brook complained.

"We need to talk; everything went crazy when you were gone," Becky rambled.

Finally, Ms. Aldridge walked in.

"Ah, Lysette is back. I'd like your report on— what was it? Valley Forge, I believe. Now please, you already had extra time."

Oh God. I didn't do it.

"I'm sorry, Ms. Aldridge. Due to private circumstances, I didn't actually have a chance to—"

"See me after class," she interrupted calmly, before writing the day's lesson on the white board.

Letty's face flushed red, and she clenched her fists.

Damn! I was on a roll in this class! This will sink my grade. Hell, everyone is staring again.

Dean walked into class quietly and tried to dodge the teacher's line of sight. He made it to the desks before nudging one, attracting Ms. Aldridge's attention.

"Lunch detention," she said.

Wow, she must have a hearing aid or something—that was ridiculous.

Dean stopped as he saw Letty. He looked to

Andy's empty desk and then back to her.

"Take your seat, Mr. Loggia!" Ms. Aldridge was beginning to fray.

Dean rushed to his seat, but Letty felt him staring her way for the rest of the hour.

The bell rang, and she rushed to leave, but Ms. Aldridge stopped her cold with a glance. She stood by her teacher's desk as everyone left. Dean, Emma, and Quinn all tarried on their way out, clearly trying to listen in. A glare from Ms. Aldridge sent them running.

"So, where were you, and why didn't you do that report?" Ms. Aldridge asked.

"Call my parents, please. I don't want to talk about it," Letty said, looking at the ground.

Ms. Aldridge leaned back in her chair. "Well, I will call your parents. I hope nothing happened. I can always refer you to the school psychiatrist if you want to talk to someone more privately."

She isn't mad at me.

The woman was concerned.

I wish she was mad at me. I feel even worse for lying.

Letty turned down the offer and thanked her before trying to leave.

"We just found out that Lysander—Andy, is missing. His parents have been calling. He's been gone since Sunday. You don't know anything about that, do you?"

"No, ma'am," Letty said, biting her cheeks.

"Okay. I wish you could tell me what happened, because, as it stands, you'll have lunch detention today for not handing in your report. I'll give you more time, but don't let this—whatever it is—sink your grades, young lady. It isn't as important as your future."

Letty nodded and walked out.

She felt herself start to tear up.

In homeroom, Mr. Holt made an announcement about Andy's disappearance. He asked if anyone knew anything. He gave Letty a plaintive look which drew more attention her way. When he asked to talk to her after homeroom, she ran out, sick of the scrutiny.

Her next few classes went by with no issue, and she even felt herself calming down.

Finally, lunch came, and she went to the cafeteria to grab a tray. Her friends followed.

"Can't you skip detention? Like, do it tomorrow—we need to talk," Brook said. Letty thought Brook might explode with questions and pointless insinuation.

"I don't think it works that way," Becky said.

Letty gave them a sad look before heading back to the hallway.

At least I get to eat lunch in peace—provided Mr. Holt leaves me alone.

Dean bumped into her, and she scrambled to keep from dropping her tray. "Watch out!" she snapped at him.

"I'm so sorry, Lysette—I wasn't paying attention," he stammered, picking up his milk carton and brown-bagged lunch.

Damn, he has lunch detention too. I was hoping for peace.

Letty rolled her eyes and rushed down the hall with Dean a few steps behind.

In Mr. Holt's classroom, she suffered a stern glare for walking out earlier.

Mr. Holt closed the door, but as he did so Emma appeared out of nowhere with a tray of food and slammed into him. He was doused in milk and rectangular strips of pizza.

"Emma, why?" Mr. Holt exclaimed.

"Sorry! Oh my god! I'm so sorry," She said. Letty spied the slightest smirk at the corner of her mouth.

Mr. Holt looked at Letty as if she was responsible.

"You want lunch detention that badly, fine, you can have it for the rest of the week. And I'm sending a note home to your parents," Mr. Holt said as he headed towards the washroom, dripping with milk.

"Fine—thanks, Mr. Holt," Emma said, walking into the classroom.

She gave Dean a cruel look before sitting down next to Letty.

"Where were you?" Emma's tone was almost desperate. "I went to your place and your parents—they were crazy—it was like they didn't even know me or remember you! What's going on? I thought you were dead, and they were in denial!" Emma rambled, her face going flush.

"You don't want to know, and you wouldn't believe me if I told you."

Emma wasn't satisfied and stared with entreaty.

"Look, I'm grateful that you cared enough to check on me, but you don't want to get involved."

"The weird thing is, Andy's parents still remember me. And now you show up, and he's still gone," Dean said, butting into their conversation.

"Don't talk to us!" Emma retorted.

"Wait, you said Andy's parents still remember him?" Letty asked.

"Yes, they do, and I'm sure your parents remembered you too. Not to call you a liar, Emma," Dean said rationally.

"No," Letty said, shaking her head, "the people Emma saw at my apartment weren't my parents."

Dean grimaced.

"There's no point in even talking about it; you won't believe me," she said softly.

Silence.

"Dean, look, I need you to tell me what Andy was up to before he went missing," she said firmly.

I need to find out how he got into the Netherscape.

"Why? Are you looking for him?" Dean asked.

"Yes. I'm going to find him."

Dean shook his head. "I barely know the guy. I almost wish I didn't. The last thing we did together was go to the Masters Gallery with his dad."

The Masters? I should check it out.

"We talked about him getting glasses at the museum. He was shaken up about it. You don't think he ran off because he didn't want to get glasses, do you?"

Letty shook her head. "I saw him at the optometrist's. That's all I remember, until…"

The images of Caspia and Andy being captured flashed before her.

"I managed to escape, but he didn't make it," Letty said, looking down at her uneaten food.

Emma and Dean shared a concerned look. That made Letty angry.

I don't need them; I've got Quill and Staza. They're fearless and they know the truth, unlike these two.

Letty sighed and tried to eat.

At least I know what Andy was doing before that day at the optometrist, but I don't know what happened to him after.

Eventually, Mr. Holt returned. He still looked too damp to have only suffered a polite mishap. He sat down and glowered at them for what felt like ages. Letty could barely stomach half of her pizza before the bell rang.

She rushed her tray to the cafeteria before getting to her next class. The rest of the day went by slowly, but she finally had a plan.

When school was out, she went to the park and found Staza and Quill being spoken to by a police officer. Startled, she rushed over.

"Look, you can't be fighting in the park. I don't care if it was only with sticks, you could hurt someone or yourselves. If you have to busk, maybe try juggling or playing an instrument. I don't want to see this again, all right?" the officer finished. Gratefully, it was well-intentioned chastisement.

They agreed, and the officer continued down the path.

Letty tried not to grin.

He was on them about play fighting with sticks and not truancy.

92

However, after another look at her friends, she could see why he made that mistake. Something about their bearing made them seem older than just their looks implied.

"Letty!" Staza said, pleased to see her.

"The surface is a strange place. Apparently, sparring in an open space is in breach of your code of conduct," Quill said judgmentally.

"I thought those people were watching us though. They even dropped their money on our jackets."

"You made money again?" Letty asked, surprised.

Staza held out a handful of small bills and coins for Letty, who laughed in astonishment.

"Making money isn't usually this easy, but, come on—we should get something to eat. I'm starving. Also, I've learned a few new details, and we need a plan."

Letty took them to a diner famous for its hamburgers. Of secondary appeal was its large, open patio.

Only a few people sitting outside. This is good, we'll have some privacy.

After confusion at the counter, Letty ordered for all of them. They stepped outside with a tray of hamburgers and a second of French fries.

"It smells—interesting," Staza remarked as they sat at a shaded table.

Letty ran back in to grab the drinks.

Better just get tea; they probably won't like anything too sugary.

93

Returning, she noticed nervous expressions on the Caspians. She hoped they wouldn't hate the food.

"Extraordinary," Quill said, daintily eating a fistful of fries.

"One at a time," Letty said, trying not to grin.

Quill leaned back from the table as he considered a fry. He watched as a business man walked away from the restaurant, unwrapped a burger, and took a bite.

He grimaced. "Walking while eating? Can't you see the ingrained haste of your civilization? Look at this hamburger for instance," he lifted his burger, "The elements of food bundled into a self-contained package. What is this?" He picked up a bun and flopped it back and forth.

"That's the bun," Letty said, a wry look on her face.

"You see! That's exactly my point." He nibbled on the bun before continuing, "This tasteless hunk of baked dough was designed only to make the mobility of the hamburger possible; it detracts from its flavor."

"Eat the damn thing, Quill," Staza said, after a bite of her own.

Quill did so, and his face lit up.

"Well—contrivance of haste or not, it has appeal."

Staza took a sip of her drink. "What is this?" she asked.

"Iced tea," Letty said.

"Mhh, we have tea as well. Though I've never

had it served over ice before. It's refreshing," she said, pleasantly surprised.

It's like they prepared for disappointment. Letty smiled, trying not to rush through her food.

They enjoyed a few quiet minutes. Quill spoiled it by claiming the noise of the street was an adulteration of the sound of flowing water. A car horn blared, only triggering a wave of honking from aggravated drivers. The Caspians both shot from their seats, but, after Letty explained, they enjoyed the rest of their meal in relative calm.

"The way I see it, we have two problems," Letty said, pushing her tray away. "First, we need to figure out how Andy got into the Netherscape, or failing that we need to find a different entrance. Afterwards, we need to learn where he is in the Netherscape."

Quill and Staza both agreed.

"I've learned from Andy's friend that they visited a certain art gallery, before I saw him at the optometrist."

"Andy has allies here?" Quill asked. "We should work together."

"No, that's not a good idea," Letty said, thinking about how Dean responded to her. "He would slow us down."

"This is good news! We have a lead now," Staza said.

Letty nodded and continued, "I will do everything I can to find out how we can get back. Just remember, that once we're there, I'll go back to being useless. You two will have to figure out where they have Andy, assuming he's still…"

There was silence.

"Look, Andy is valuable to them. He's still alive; I'm sure of it. And you aren't useless," Quill laughed. "With the Argument, you're a better fighter than the pair of us."

That made Letty feel better.

"We talked about it," Staza said, looking at Quill, "and we should try to find the exact portal Andy used. A different portal will likely lead to other parts of the Netherscape."

"What do you mean, other parts?" Letty asked. "You mentioned it last night, but I didn't have time to ask."

"Well, the Netherscape doesn't work like the surface. There are dozens of Netherscape domains, but you can't just walk from one to the next. There are a few paths that allow travel by sailing or airship, but the fastest way to travel is to take a portal, and preferably a safe one," Quill explained.

"Last night we took a potentially unsafe portal," Staza added.

Quill nodded before continuing, "We come from Pansubprimus, but there are many other domains, some of which we know next to nothing about."

Letty wasn't happy to hear this.

"Well, why do you call it the Netherscape then, if all these pieces aren't even connected?" Letty asked, a little annoyed.

"At one time they were connected. The Axiomatic wars took their toll on the Netherscape, far more than the surface. Despite where it stands today, the Argument was the stronger side for centuries," Quill said.

"Andy could be in any of the other Netherscape domains," Letty said, coming to grips with the new facts. "Do the ryle control all of them?"

Quill scowled. "No. Some of the domains are inhospitable to all living things, even the ryle."

"Well, even if we find the right portal, that doesn't mean Andy will be in Pan—what? Pan-prime?"

"Right, he's with Ziesqe, who I imagine can go anywhere he likes." Quill said.

"How the hell are we going to figure out where he is? We can't just walk up to a ryle and ask, 'Hey do you know Ziesqe?'"

"We might learn something if we go back. Maybe we can ask our Mistress," Staza said.

"We can't risk going back to Caspia right away. Maybe in a week or so," Quill said.

"But we need to do something now! We're wasting time, and who knows what they're doing to him!" Letty said.

Staza and Quill shared a sad look.

They think it's impossible.

Letty sighed and let her head fall into her hands. Her hair tumbled over her face.

"Letty," Staza stood and put a hand on her shoulder, "anything could have happened. But no matter what, we're going to search with you. Right?" she asked Quill.

"Of course. We owe him that much at least."

Letty stood and went to throw the trash away.

She put the trays on top of the bin, before turning to her friends with a small smile. "I appreciate it. Let's go to the gallery."

Letty texted her parents and let them know that she would be home late, before finding the route to the museum on her phone.

"We'll take the subway, and remember, it's nothing to be afraid of."

At the station, Letty bought tickets for the Caspians, and had her own subway pass ready. Quill and Staza followed close behind, and she navigated the crowds and serpentine tunnels with the skill of a native. They arrived at their platform with a minute to spare.

Letty noticed that Staza and Quill were on edge, clearly nervous, and likely claustrophobic. The crush of people was oppressive. Their eyes shifted from person to person, and she noticed their hands resting above what she expected were hidden daggers.

It's not even that busy, but they're freaking out. I should do something.

"It's okay, just hold my hand," Letty said, reaching out and taking both of their hands.

Quill and Staza seemed offended, but patronizing them had the desired effect. The shame of it calmed them.

The train arrived, and they jostled onto a car. Quill and Staza both took the opportunity to free their hands. They stood near the door.

"Grab hold," Letty said hurriedly, as the train accelerated.

Quill and Staza were both quick on their feet. They stood firm, though their nervous expressions returned.

"We are in an underworld, but it's the surface's underworld. And you can just come and go? No, there was a machine gatekeeper," Quill wondered loudly enough to attract attention.

"The subway is for transportation. Think of it as a huge car on tracks. But because there are so many people in the city, it's always crowded," Letty whispered.

"A crowded underground road," Quill muttered to himself, his eyes still darting from face to face. "Fantastic."

After a few stops, a busker came on board with a saxophone. Staza and Quill couldn't help but stare.

Great. Don't make eye contact, or he'll come over here.

Letty nudged them, but it was too late; the fellow was on his way over.

He played to Quill and Staza's fascination. Staza opened her bag, and to Letty's surprise pulled out a sketch pad. She started a quick drawing of the man in pencil. He was wearing a heavily patched sports coat over a green button up shirt, as well as jeans also covered in patches and various logos.

He played the theme songs from a few television shows she knew.

He's not bad.

Letty held out a few dollars, and the man accepted them.

"God bless you," he said, pleased that they were entertained.

"Hold on," Staza said, ripping the page out and handing it to him.

The man was taken aback when he saw the drawing. He rustled around in a pocket and found a safety pin. He pinned the page to the front of his coat.

"I'm wearing this today, but tonight it goes up on the fridge. Thank you, young lady." He walked off and readied his instrument for another song.

A moment later, they heard him playing in the next car.

"So, this is how your society works. People trade performances," Quill said, fascinated.

"Well," Letty wanted to disagree, but, after some pondering, she couldn't disagree. "Maybe it is. Sometimes the performance, or service, is making food, or teaching a class, or playing music for just three people on the subway."

The train stopped, and Letty realized this was their station just before the doors closed.

"Come on!" she said, grabbing the Caspians and rushing.

They made it off, though a conductor on the platform blew his whistle and pointed disapprovingly their way.

"Sorry, I haven't been to this stop before," Letty said.

They took the stairs outside and walked the few blocks to the museum.

"Andy came here with Dean, not too long ago. I think he had his sight at the time, and we need to keep an eye out for anything that he might have seen. Titus told me that a few paintings contain messages only people like us can see."

"We're Sensates, Letty, or Seers, depending on who you ask," Staza said.

"Seers, right," Letty said, with a strange feeling. "Titus told me that places like this are trapped and patrolled by ryle, or their servants. This time around we can't depend on Titus to keep us out of trouble."

"Keep us out of trouble?" Quill repeated.

"Yes. The mice also patrolled museums to keep an eye out for young Seers, like us, and to help us avoid the traps. Sadly, it's hard to do that as a talking mouse. Titus did his best, but I still got snagged. That's how all this started."

"Of course," Quill said, annoyed at his forgetfulness, "that was their purpose in the first place."

"Wait," Staza interjected, rooting through her bag. "We spent some of that money today."

"I noticed. That bag is new, and your sketch pad too. I didn't know that you drew," Letty said.

"I don't really, ah—here they are," Staza produced three pairs of dark sunglasses. "These should hide our eyes."

Letty was impressed.

Such an obvious solution.

They put their sunglasses on and walked into the Masters.

"I hope it works, because we look ridiculous," Letty muttered, as they were waved past the line by a guard, after he had seen Letty's student ID.

A kindly old lady gave them a map as they

passed her stool.

In the first hall they visited, Letty spotted distracting and bright colors on a painting.

"There's one," she whispered.

They slowed and looked.

The canvas featured people dancing. One dancer, a man in a pinstripe suit and trilby hat, stood out. The stripes on his suit shone in the bright colors that Letty associated with the Infiniteye.

"Are you seeing that? His clothes are like nothing else," Letty said, nudging Staza.

"Yes, but look at the frame," Staza replied.

Letty felt her skin crawl at the sight of grasping tendrils, which she hadn't noticed until Staza's warning.

The frame undulated with dark purple trim. Tendrils lined up with the carved motifs of the actual frame underneath. She realized the tendrils were moving, and they were moving slowly towards her, stopping about a few feet from where they were rooted.

Letty felt her stomach sink. She was suddenly paranoid. Staza nudged her away, and they moved on. Though Letty couldn't shake the feeling that someone had seen them stare for too long at the painting of the dancers.

As they walked through the hall, she looked back and noticed that the tendrils moved to stay pointing at them.

That's how the first painting got me; I was too close.

Letty sighed and then said, "That painting was trapped, but I didn't see a message for us."

"Not every artist set out to put secret words in their work," Quill whispered as they moved through a crowded room.

A picture of water lilies also shone with a brilliance that made it feel like the pond was trembling beneath a wind.

"Like that," Quill continued. "The painter has used pigment that only we can see, but he may never have realized that other people couldn't experience it the way he intended."

The idea astonished Letty. *How could a painter not know that he was a Seer?* She looked at the painting in wonder. *Well, I didn't know until recently. What if nobody told me? Maybe I would just think that I was a little different.*

They walked into the next hall and found it full of statuary. None of it stood out to Letty, but she began to doubt herself. *What if I see something and I don't realize it's different?*

"You aren't seeing anything?" she asked.

"There are some marvelous pieces, but nothing for us," Staza said.

Quill considered a statue of a man chained to a rock. A large bird of prey stooped over him, and a fallen torch burned nearby.

"Prometheus, punished for that most egregious sin," he said, looking up for an answer.

Letty drew a blank.

"He defied the gods and gave mankind forbidden knowledge," Staza finished, her expression chagrined.

"You have mythology too?" Letty asked,

remembering the story of Prometheus.

Quill gave her a speculative look. "Of course. We share most of the same history, though a fair portion of it is suppressed up here."

"It's suppressed down there too, Quill," Staza rebutted.

As they left the statuary, Staza grabbed Quill and Letty.

"Careful, turn around," she said quietly.

Letty did so, but looked over her shoulder, and saw purple tendrils lining the doorway. A thin screen of mist also filled the doorway. She hadn't seen it when they were approaching, and even now she could barely distinguish it.

"Good catch," Quill said, trying to slow his breath.

"Nobody saw us turning around," Staza said, motioning them down another hall.

Letty's paranoia and nervousness returned. She looked around and noticed the little black domes that hid security cameras.

Maybe someone saw us. I shouldn't alarm them, or should I?

"Do you see those little black domes?"

They both looked and nodded.

"Guards can see us through those, on television screens, but there is no guarantee that someone is watching on the other end."

Quill and Staza stiffened, realizing the domes were everywhere.

"I'm starting to think that we should get out of—" Letty paused as she saw something familiar.

"I see it too," Staza said, looking at a painting.

Letty sat on a nearby bench.

"There's something there," Quill said.

"The sign of the Argument," Staza whispered. "There on the drum."

Letty opened her backpack and found Andy's notepad. The Caspian's joined her on the bench as she flipped through the pages and found a rough sketch of this painting, followed by several abortive attempts to draw the Infiniteye. There were also a few words he had written, but they were from another language.

"Andy was here! He saw this." Letty showed them the sketches. "What did you call this?" she asked, pointing at the symbol.

"It's the sign of the Argument—essentially a religious symbol. Its creation is punishable by execution in some places. The ryle spent extra effort hunting down those who could make it," Quill said.

"I don't think there's a person alive now who knows how to paint it anymore," Staza added.

"Is there a trick to it?" Letty asked, inspecting Andy's awkward attempts on the notepad.

Quill nodded.

"Why don't they destroy it?" Letty asked, staring carefully at the militiamen.

"Our Mistress says the ryle have a fascination with Seer artistry, even though they can't see what makes it special: those pigments that give off the brilliant shine," Quill whispered, looking over his shoulder.

"In Caspia, Titus told me that Andy discovered

the truth about optometrists from another painting. This one here is by the same artist," she read the placard next to the painting. "Rembrandt. We know that Andy saw the Infiniteye here. So, moving forward, Andy would associate the eye with Rembrandt's good information. Do you think that changes anything?" she asked.

"I don't know, but it's a start," Staza said.

Letty stared at the painting and saw the Seer script. She had the urge to lean in, but, even though she saw no tendrils on this painting, she was afraid.

"Can either of you read these letters?" Letty tapped a copy of the painting in Andy's notebook. "I don't know the language."

They both shook their heads.

Wait. Hold on.

She found her phone and pulled up a translation application. She typed in the text.

"Dutch," she said. She read the translation, "The symbol guides our steps."

"If Andy translated the message, he would have been keeping an eye out for the symbol," Quill said.

"I'm sure he did," Letty responded, feeling hopeful, and then nervous as if the hope was premature.

"She's right," Quill responded. "All we need to do is recreate the day everything started. We need to discover where he was. I'm certain that somewhere on his path he came across the symbol, and after reading that," he pointed to the translation, "he would have followed it and found a portal or the mice."

"Titus said he just walked into their city," Letty said.

Quill's face lit up.

"This is good news," Letty added, "but I don't know where he was. I can hardly remember where I was that day. Who knows what he did after the optometrist? He could have gone anywhere."

"Well, it wasn't going to be easy. Do we continue tomorrow?" Staza asked.

Letty checked the time on her cell and the angry messages from her parents. "Yes. We need to get back," she said, standing and stretching.

They were careful on their way out of the museum and had to avoid two inky screens of tendrils before finally exiting.

As they returned to the subway, Staza stiffened beside Letty and bent to whisper in her ear, "Someone's following us. They have been since the museum—I'm sure of it."

Letty grasped the Argument.

"Stay with me," Staza said, stepping ahead of the group and leading the way.

When they rounded a corner, Staza broke out into a run. Letty and Quill followed. They turned down the nearest alley, and Staza drew a dagger from beneath her borrowed jacket.

"What are we doing?" Letty asked, a glow coming from her hand.

"Put that out!" Staza whispered.

Letty loosened her grip. She hadn't realized that she was clenching her fist.

Footsteps came closer.

In a flash, Staza reached out and pulled their pursuer into the alley with them. Their bodies tumbled to the floor, but Staza came out on top, and had her dagger at the man's throat.

Letty felt her eyes focusing, and after a few seconds she realized the man was a ryle. The ryle wore a tailored suit, and Letty suppressed the urge to laugh at the curious sight.

"Do you see it?" Letty asked.

Quill and Staza nodded.

The ryle made a sudden move, but Quill struck with his right leg and knocked a pistol from the ryle's grip.

"Do it again! I'd love to learn the color of ryle blood!" Staza leaned forward as she whispered.

The ryle's fleshy face contorted in surprise.

"What do you want from me?" he asked.

"Why were you following us?" Letty replied.

The ryle's face twisted into an expression akin to annoyance. "Look at you," he hissed, "why do you think I was following you? No wonder your side lost."

Staza gave the ryle a few gentle slaps with the flat end of her dagger. "Careful now, don't forget that you're an inch from bleeding to death."

"Just kill me," the ryle said, pushing himself closer to the dagger.

"No—you don't get away that easily." Letty said, pulling Staza back.

"They'll do worse when they find out three mature Seer children just avoided all of my snares, and then...overpowered me in the street."

Letty huffed. "Where are your brutox?"

The ryle huffed right back. "Brutox? At my age? I'm alone in this garbage ward, pulling museum duty. I've spent years looking for you little rats. Here are the first ones I find and look what happens. I'm useless spawn at this point."

The Seers shared a surprised look. Letty almost felt bad, but Staza had a grin on her face, and Quill could only shake his head in astonishment.

"Tell us, do you know a ryle named Ziesqe?" Letty finally asked.

"I know five!" The ryle hissed.

"Zyzqe Ziesqe," Quill said.

"Ah, that tart. He calls himself Ropt up here. Yes, he's come into some serious trouble recently," the ryle paused, his beady eyes going as wide as they could. "Of course. It makes complete sense. You are the thorns in his side, eh? And now you're on a rampage through the city? Tell me, is this a full-scale rebellion, or just an isolated incident?"

They gawked at how quickly the ryle figured them out.

"I just would like to know if I'll be remembered as a casualty of a treacherous coup, or a fool who couldn't do his job," the ryle rambled, resigned to whatever came.

"Hey," Staza gave him another slap, "pay attention. No editorializing. Where does Ziesqe reside in the Netherscape?"

"I'm not his mother!" the ryle complained gratingly.

Quill laughed, and gave the ryle a soft kick in

the ribs. "I'm starting to like him."

"And why would I tell you anything?" The ryle countered.

"Fair enough," Letty said, considering. "How about, you tell us everything we ask, and we let you go."

"Yeah," Staza interjected, "and if we find out that you lied to us, we'll come back. Don't forget, we know where you work," she concluded, a conciliatory expression on her face.

The ryle coughed up a nervous laugh, as if it were a joke. His eyes shot back and forth between them. "Fine," he finally agreed.

"So, back to Ziesqe," Staza said.

"He's one of the richest and most powerful in the city. I don't know what to tell you. He has interests all over the surface, Pansubprimus, and Euboia. His famous palace is in the Nightmare. It's called Zentule. They made a big performance about him building the first settlement in the Nightmare for centuries."

Letty took the pistol and pocketed it. "That wasn't so difficult," she said.

Staza and Quill released the ryle, and stepped back, their daggers at the ready.

The ryle stood and brushed itself off. It turned to leave, but then spun towards them, a weak purple blade shot from its hand.

It swung at Staza, and she parried with her dagger. The two blades locked. Staza's blade quickly gave way as the purple sword burned through. Letty felt a sudden pain behind her eyes flare at the sight of the ryle's blade.

She grasped the Argument and drew her own blade. The pain in her head evaporated in an instant.

The ryle stumbled backwards in shock. Its face contorted in agony.

She swung her blade, and the ryle pulled away, as if he wanted to keep the blades from meeting. He was too slow, and a loud crack echoed in the alley. The pea sized purple orb shot from the ryle's hand. Letty's blade also fizzled and the orb flew from her hand as well. Recovering from her stumble, she turned and recovered the Argument while Staza and Quill held the ryle at bay with their weapons, though Staza's dagger was cut almost to the hilt.

"It's a piece of Counter-Argument," Quill said, unimpressed.

Letty, her orb in hand, walked towards her foe's weapon and felt the urge to strike out at it. She summoned her blade.

The ryle yelled, "Don't!"

She struck, and the Counter-Argument burst apart in a small explosion. A stain of what looked like smoky, black and purple glass stretched for many feet, even climbing walls and a metal trash can.

"No! You can't imagine how expensive that was!" The ryle whined, before promptly receiving an elbow to the face.

Staza waved her destroyed dagger inches from his face. "I made this myself, it was one of a kind!"

Quill restrained her.

"We should kill it," Staza complained. "It's

traitorous!"

Letty blinked, realizing that Staza was serious.

"Hey!" A voice yelled. They saw a burly man in an undershirt standing at one end of the alley. "What's going on here?"

Letty gritted her teeth at being found. "Listen!" she said to the ryle. "We know where to find you."

A few more people appeared next to the burly man.

"Run!" Letty whispered, leading the way.

They ran out of the alley and slowed to a fast walk when they turned the next corner, but they didn't relax until they descended into the subway station and hopped on a full train.

"We should be fine now," Letty said. "Hopefully no one called the police; there are cameras everywhere."

Those people will think we were mugging that ryle, and he'll probably tell them the same, but will they call the police?

Letty felt anxious and scanned the length of the car for any activity. She gave Staza a questioning glance.

"I don't think anyone followed us," Staza said.

A station later, some seats opened up. Letty sat and felt the shape of the gun in her pocket. She remembered it was a revolver.

What am I going to do with it? I don't want to throw it away; we might need it.

She remembered Andy being disarmed by Ziesqe, and something similar just happened to her.

If Andy had a second weapon, he might have escaped. I

shouldn't toss the gun.

Letty looked at the others.

Quill behaved like I expected, but Staza... I need to remember that they come from a violent place. If I'm not careful, she'll kill someone before I can stop her.

Staza sighed and Quill noticed.

"You still have your sword," he said.

"I can't carry it openly," she complained. Letty sensed that Staza wanted to insult the sad state of surface civilization.

"Well, we did learn where Ziesqe lives," Quill said.

"He said Ziesqe could be in many places," Staza retorted.

"What was that name he mentioned? The Nightmare. Do you know it?" Letty asked.

Quill shook his head, and Staza slumped in her seat.

Letty leaned back and looked out the window as a station rolled by. Bright lights flashed between pillars as they slowed to a halt. The doors opened and closed with barely a handful of people moving on and off.

The rest of the ride was quiet, and as they left the station Letty received a call from her father.

"I told you, we went to the gallery. It was fun. No—we're on our way back now. We'll be home in a few minutes."

Letty listened for a long time.

"No, we'll be back in a minute. I swear. We're just down the street," Letty's voice was suddenly nervous, and the Caspians could tell. "Yes, that's fine."

Letty put her phone away, but her face had gone pale.

"What's wrong?" Staza asked.

"The police came by while we were gone. They have questions for me," Letty said.

Chapter 5: Deliberation

Andy lay on the bed, gazing up at the slate ceiling. The light coming through the frosted glass window flared and kept him awake. He put a pillow over his eyes, but found the flashing lights were the least of his problems.

He rolled over and saw the plain, wooden table. A pitcher of water sat next to a slab of something too sweet and gray for his taste, though he had eaten half of the mystery pastry, despite that.

He felt guilty about Thrag, and far worse about his parents. He tried to accept it: This was his life now. He was the newest piece of Ziesqe's collection. Thrag was once part of his collection as well, though that hadn't worked out.

Andy sat up and saw his new suit of mail resting on a chair near the door. It sparkled against the light from the window.

Thrag couldn't have been here for more than a day or two, though they didn't give him a fancy suit of armor.

Andy started to resent himself.

Maybe, if I just slam my head against the wall for a few hours, I'll lose the ability to feel guilt, or time, or boredom. He chuckled, thinking he might have just figured out Thrag.

He flopped back onto the bed, but a moment later the door burst open and a handful of ychorons poured in. They bore clothes, buckets of steaming water, brushes, and best of all, a tray of what passed for food in Zentule.

"Up, up—you've work to do," an ychoron

commanded.

They didn't wait for Andy to sit up before manhandling him.

He ignored the brushing and cleaning, focusing his attention on the platter of supposed food. There were strips of purplish meat, which smelled appealing. Yet the orange loaf of bread and its attendant bloody speckled butter, looked more like a Halloween novelty than potential breakfast.

Curious, Andy reached for the loaf. A swift ychoron swatted him away. "Not until you're presentable, human!"

The ychorons were largely uniform in color this morning, with most feathers appearing in solid and dark earthy hues. Most were brown, ocher, or slate, as if to match the walls. The defining differences between them lay in scarring or, most often, in their full body jewelry harnesses. Each piece was markedly different in design, material, and construction. Some featured twisting copper cable, while others were mostly chain links made from precious metals. One, cut like a toga and lined with rubies, stood in contrast to the majority, which were reminiscent of bathing wear.

With his silk underclothing tied on straight, Andy prepared for his chainmail. His hair snagged on the mail links as they lowered the chainmail shirt over his outstretched arms.

Andy yelped.

"That's what you get for rushing."

Finally, they garbed him in fresh robes, much like the ones he had worn yesterday.

"I can dress myself, you know. Next time just leave me the clothes."

They laughed.

"Dress himself!" One moaned, "Maybe if we wanted to watch paint dry, we'd let you try!"

"You rhymed!"

"Did I—ah, try and dry!"

Andy smirked at the ychorons. They reminded him of the kids in drama club at school.

Once free, Andy dashed to the chair and started devouring his breakfast. "What's this?" he asked, suspicious of a chunk of meat, "Forget it—I don't want to know," he said tearing a piece off with his teeth.

"Ravager spawn," an ychoron said, put off by Andy's voraciousness.

"Mmmh," Andy replied, taking a serrated knife to the loaf.

The bread was still steaming, and the butter had the slightest hint of cinnamon to it. He grabbed at something randomly and took a bite. It was fruit, striped purple and lavender. It had delicate ocher flesh and a pit at the center. Finally, he paused at what looked like a tall glass of teal milk.

"Seriously? Teal milk?"

"Aphid nectar. It's a delicacy."

Why not? Andy took a sip. His eyes widened. It was cool and had the faintest taste of vanilla. He finished the glass.

"Fine then; what is today? Do I fight the giant centipedes bare handed?"

"Call them ravagers, and no. We are going to the

golden library."

Andy felt a weight lift off his shoulders. *They aren't likely to kill me in the library.*

Feeling oddly refreshed, Andy approached the door and swung it open. He saw that his guards were surrounded by slithers. Among the horde of slithers were the flapping heads.

When they saw Andy, the horde went wild. The beetles braced to keep them back, but the slithers climbed the walls and ceiling and a moment later were pouring into Andy's chambers from above.

The ychorons slammed the door closed. Andy looked around for a weapon and could only spot the chair. He leveled it, but saw the ychorons had the assault under control. Their hands darted like lightning, snatching the slithers off the walls and jolting them with their strikes.

A few moments later, there was a pile of fried slithers, and the ychorons leered at Andy like he was being foolish. "Put that chair down before you break it."

He obeyed.

"I think we know what's going in the stew tonight," one said with a chuckle, dropping the last slither onto the pile.

Shuddering, Andy neared the door and peeked through. He saw the beetles throwing flapping heads across the hall and occasionally into the pool.

"How are you supposed to work around here?" he asked.

The ychorons laughed, ushering him out of the room.

Andy fell in with his guards, who, melee settled, were at ease.

I've been down here too long if the insects are starting to look relaxed.

They marched down the main hall, and, only a moment later, turned down a side passage before taking a set of stairs upward. At the top of the stairs was a round chamber with doors that led into different colored libraries.

They approached one featuring a dark, golden carpet. Once inside, Andy noticed dozens of ryle sitting around tables, going over large tomes and charts. A few ryle were writing at lecterns, while ychorons were organizing the books and rushing back and forth with writing materials.

Scores of ryle lifted their heads to watch Andy and his escort cross the room.

Approaching a platform topped with a fine chair, the brutox directed Andy to sit.

His escort fanned out, surrounding the platform. The mantis, who seemed in charge of his guards yesterday, was nowhere in sight.

Ychorons laid a few books on a table across from where Andy was seated. They opened the books to specific pages. Andy strained to look and saw drawings on those pages.

The ychorons then set up glass jars on the table. On one side sat two glass jars, one full of purple stones, while the other was full of jade stones. On the other side of the table were three jars, each empty, though there were placards in front of the empty jars, facing away from Andy.

An ychoron took a chair and sat to watch the empty jars, a plain piece of paper in one hand, and a quill in the other.

Andy stared, and a memory from Sentinel's Watch rose in his mind. He realized there would be a vote. There were three choices and, somehow, two pools of voters. Andy tried to imagine what the placards read.

Death by ravager. Death by slither horde. Death by whatever lives in the pool in the hall.

He stifled a grunt; his instincts about libraries were still in effect.

All would be terrible ways to go, though they would probably be quick.

Ryle and ychorons lined up to inspect the books, take a stone, and then cast it in one of the empty jars. The two pools of voters were now clear: ychorons and ryle.

Andy sat still, rolling his eyes for what felt like hours as the procession moved through the library to cast votes. There were quite a few ryle, but there were far more ychorons. Andy noticed there were no flapping heads, brutox, or slithers taking part.

Slithers can't be capable of much thought, but the brutox are more than they seem.

Finally, the pale mantis arrived, trailed by another dozen brutox. These were more like spiders to Andy's eyes, and they bore crossbows, quivers full of javelins, and maces.

The brutox set about clearing the library. A scuffle nearly broke out as an incensed ryle pushed a table over in protest. Andy was shocked to see a spider club the ryle over the head.

It was surprising, but, clearly, the hierarchy wasn't as rigid as he expected. Of course, the brutox were obeying orders. Since ryle war with one another, brutox warriors and enemy ryle must come into conflict.

That made sense to Andy, but the sight still unnerved him, and he couldn't say why.

A few minutes after the room had cleared, Ziesqe arrived with a pair of ychorons in tow. One's feathers shone verdant green. It was sheathed in shining brass strands, sewn in a way that evoked spider webs. The second was orange with a blue face, garbed in braided cables of matte black metal.

Ziesqe wore a simple, honey colored coat over a black button up shirt. His pants matched the coat. Andy found this strange, as the other ryle wore various types of robes—much like the ones he was draped in—but here was Ziesqe in fashions that looked like they were from the surface, if several decades behind.

Ziesqe accepted a piece of paper from the attending ychoron, who shuffled away as quickly as possible. Andy assumed the paper was an account of the votes.

Ziesqe considered the paper before showing it to his attendants. Some conversation passed between them before he approached Andy.

"Have you figured it out yet?" he asked.

Andy took a moment before answering. "They show up, look at the books, at me, and then cast a vote."

"That's a summary of mechanical occurrence, and possibly the weakest answer you could have given. The ideational occurrence—what happened in the realm of motive—was my focus, though a guess as to what was concluded would not have gone amiss, either." Ziesqe snapped a claw and gestured to the table. His attendants picked up the books and brought them forward. "This might make it clearer for you."

They held the books open for Andy to see. There were images of paintings, statues, and even sketches of humans wielding the Argument. They wore disparate outfits, some featuring armor, while others bore flintlock muskets, and still others were garbed as royalty. Andy looked to the other book and saw a rendering of a mosaic featuring a familiar man in classical armor. It bore a strong resemblance to the mosaic he posed for in Caspia.

"They were voting on if I am Caspian," Andy guessed.

"Ha!" Ziesqe chortled, and an awful shriek came from his throat. "What a thing to say. Quite close, but no. I merely asked them if you resembled this slain hero." He pointed to the mosaic and continued, "One jar for yes, one for no, and one for undecided. Can you guess which won?"

"Undecided?"

Ziesqe inclined his head and held out the paper. Undecided won by a large margin, with yes and no nearly tied. "Curiously, my spawn were more likely to see a resemblance, though I expect the undecideds were hedging their bets on the safest—

read, least likely to upset me—option." Ziesqe paused to let Andy absorb the information. "Now, before I tell you why I've done this, I'll need you to think back to yesterday. I asked how you knew what a Juncture was. I need you to tell me now," Ziesqe said politely, but Andy could tell that underneath lay an expectation of obedience.

"I made a deal with Pythia," Andy said.

The ychorons looked wary at this.

"Hmm. The details please," Ziesqe said, folding his arms.

"I would serve Pythia with my abilities as a Seer, and with a piece of Argument, one night a year. In exchange, she would free Letty, and we would enjoy safety from you in her lands."

"I see. I think we know where this goes next," he gestured at the verdant ychoron, "Inxa, would you relate the notice in question?"

"Certainly," Inxa said, unrolling a piece of paper and then reading it, "Inexperienced warlord Q'telwe is slain in his holding: Nicomedia fortress, Disputabat. His forces defeated via infiltration, executed by unaffiliated goblins, supposedly led by a rogue ychoron and a youthful Seer. These reports are unconfirmed."

"Those goblins weren't unaffiliated; the snake knows when not to wave a banner," the blue and orange ychoron quipped.

"What did you find in Nicomedia?" Ziesqe asked.

"She wanted a way into the Juncture..." Andy silenced, as the ychorons were tittering at his claim.

Ziesqe held up a hand.

"I got us inside," Andy said, annoyed.

Even Ziesqe looked torn at hearing that. "That Juncture in particular has been sealed for quite some time." Ziesqe paused, and held a claw to his chin. "History tells us that a meeting took place there, before it was sealed. Those who attended never returned. Did you see any evidence of them?"

"Yes."

That surprised Ziesqe. "Were they trapped? How many were left?"

Andy shook his head. "All that remained were blood stains. Pythia claimed that it was ryle blood."

Ziesqe blinked.

"There was something inside the Juncture. Something monstrous that chased us. I bet that it killed those ryle."

"Describe it."

"That's not so simple. The monster was invisible. It was man shaped, about the height of your pale mantis, but bulkier. Its body, mostly blades. I saw it tear a massive table in two, and then lift both halves, one in each hand."

"Axiomechina," Ziesqe mumbled.

The blue and orange ychoron hadn't heard her master. She asked Andy, "How can you describe its dimensions if it was invisible?"

Ziesqe nodded. "Fair point, Zava."

"It was Pythia's idea. She managed to—what was the word she used—fold? She folded the blood on the table and moved it with her will. She threw a glob of it at the monster, and then we could see it."

Ziesqe unfolded his arms. "Obnoxious, traitorous, and yet, occasionally ingenious."

"We evaded the monster for a time. I had some trouble with Pythia at this point—"

Ziesqe snapped his claws. "Details, Lysander."

"She tried to get me to stay. She spoke a prophecy. It claimed that I would be your prisoner." Andy paused.

The ychorons looked to their master, curious about his response, but he was placid.

"She thought that I could avoid capture if I stayed in the Juncture. I tried to leave, but something happened in there. I don't remember most of it. I only escaped because the monster kept chasing us, and eventually it jarred my memory."

"He's lying," Zava spat.

Ziesqe held raised his hand. "He's omitting. He hasn't lied yet."

Inxa rushed towards him. "I'll cut off his nose. It'll improve his aesthetic, and teach him respect for the truth."

Andy leaned back and nearly knocked his chair over. She reached out and pulled him forward.

Ziesqe clicked, and she stepped back.

After a tense moment, Ziesqe asked, "This prophecy, what were the words?"

Andy shook his head. "I can't remember all the words. Most of it had to do with me and you in particular. She said you would torture me with that dream device."

Silence.

"She said that you would like me and hate me all

at once."

"So far this is true," Ziesqe said.

Andy sighed, seeing they expected more. "Finally, she said that I would spend my life being tortured. She claimed the torture would benefit you, but none of that made any sense."

Inxa grinned sarcastically, while Zava was perturbed by the conversation.

"Inxa," Ziesqe spoke, as he gestured her way, "will you explain the fyr to our young friend?"

"Certainly," Inxa said, considering where to start. "Ryle civilization runs on etherium, negative etherium in particular, but there is so little of the positive stuff that it isn't worth mentioning."

"Why did you then?" Zava sneered.

Inxa ignored that. "Ychorons as a species are born from ascended slithers, who are born from raw etherium. The same is true for the brutox queens, and the brutons, and the ravager spawn. I'm sure you follow by now. The problem is that the supply of etherium derived from the Counter-Argument could not meet our needs."

"Wait—Counter-Argument fuels etherium?" Andy asked. *The mice had etherium tipped weapons, and the minoe was made from it too.*

"Again, either false-Argument or Counter can be synthesized into positive or negative etherium respectively. There is no demand or supply for the positive element, so we omit it from our discussions altogether. The important detail is that a piece of Counter-Argument, even one the size of a marble, can be made to bear a hundred brutox, thousands of slithers, or, eventually, something special, like me."

Ziesqe held out a heavy orb the size of his fist.

Andy saw something glitter in the ychoron's eyes as they stared at the orb. *Yearning and revulsion, simultaneously.*

"Yes, this piece, while it may look small to you, could become another ravager," Inxa said, her eyes still locked onto it.

Ziesqe curled a lip at them and flexed his fingers around the orb. It vanished, but Andy felt his skin crawl as the air shimmered around Ziesqe.

"Wait, you said the supply was running dry centuries ago," Andy interjected.

"Yes it was, until the revelation. A ryle, Archmaster Mazij, pioneered the fyr. He discovered that your cursed bloodline paradoxically contained the true salvation of our civilization."

"The point, Inxa," Zava complained.

Inxa batted her eyelashes at Zava. "History deserves an occasional flourish," she responded, before continuing, "Our salvation, when broken down into mere mechanics, involves the capture and imprisonment of your kind in devices like the one you awoke from a day ago. The process of monitoring Seer consciousness in the dream-state and accelerating that consciousness into a flux of piqued terror is fyr-threshing. When fyr is attained, the product is essentially Counter-Argument."

"We call it precursor, but it becomes the fuel of our civilization," Zava added.

Andy tried to wrap his mind around what he was being told. *They torture people like me, the Seers, because the torture itself produces their Counter-Argument.*

"What, so an orb just rolls out of my ear when you torture me?"

"It is expelled as condensate from the lungs, though success has also been had in extracting it from the blood. Generally, the condensate pools into a connected container. We believe the precursor is simply the Seer's natural response to the fyr."

"Why aren't I in the machine then? Or am I?" Andy asked, suddenly alarmed at the thought.

Ziesqe snorted. "You will never be productive, Lysander. Not even in a thousand dream years would you yield a mote of etherium. We have tried. That is why you woke up yesterday."

"So, the prophecy was false. I won't be of value to you."

"Regarding net loss and gain, you've already cost me two skillful fyr-threshers, and that's just since you arrived. The mantis died at my command in the pit, so I won't fault you. The brutox lost in capturing you are another story, but all this is incidental. Now the prophecy: Pythia nullified it herself when she took you inside the Juncture. The fyr draws motivation through the Junctures, particularly the Junctures under ryle control. Can you see the issue here?"

Andy considered for a moment. *The fyr nightmares were just like the Juncture. Nothing made sense, and the shifting places and people eventually tipped me off.*

Finally, Andy spoke, "Pythia was so desperate to get me into the Juncture because she hoped to cancel her own prophecy."

"Precisely!" Ziesqe's voice echoed loudly. He moved towards Andy and locked eyes. "And the question is why? Why you? Why would she care to simply give you what I pay so dearly for? Why did I arrange this charade of voting today? Why did you survive the pit yesterday? And the vexation that changed my plan: Why did Thrag call you Caspian?" Ziesqe's stare was intense, but Andy tried not to look away.

An ychoron flanked by a pair of brutox appeared with a scroll. "I beg your forgiveness, Master."

"Not now!" Zava snapped at the messenger. "He is busy."

"It is critical," the messenger retorted snidely.

Ziesqe took a deep breath and finally broke eye contact with Andy.

The messenger held out the scroll.

"Just the pertinent points," Ziesqe said.

The messenger was uncomfortable, but he didn't need to be told twice. He unfolded the scroll and read. "Zyzqe Ziesqe: Hierophant Prime of the 187th Ward. You have allowed your surface holding to fall into primitive hands. The fyr devices have been made secure, at great cost to your peers. It is in the best interests of our species that you report to the Maelstrom for ascension this year. Do not let your heretofore untarnished record become damaged any further. You are meant for greater..." the messenger looked up from the scroll, "it goes on—"

Ziesqe snatched the scroll from him, looked at it

129

for less than ten seconds and then nearly ripped it in two. To Andy's surprise, he relented and handed the scroll to Zava.

The messenger slowly backed away as Ziesqe resumed staring at Andy.

"Such failure," he said.

"You knew it was coming," Zava said.

"Is it time to flee?" Inxa asked.

Ignoring them, Ziesqe's eyes flamed, his brow tightened and finally, he leaned close and whispered to Andy, "In the ruins of my ambition lie such fragments, and you, Lysander, are the mortar. With you, these fragments might shape a victory beyond yesterday's hope, but have I the genius to shape you?" Ziesqe grimaced and turned away. "Zava, with me. Inxa, mind the boy."

Ziesqe stormed from the room, with Zava right behind.

"What's happening?" Andy asked.

Inxa wore a look of deep concern.

Andy stood, stretched, and finally nudged Inxa.

"Hands off, human! You're unclean," she snapped.

"Fine," Andy said walking away.

She huffed and followed. The beetles formed up around Andy, but they did not bar his way.

"So, what was the big deal about that scroll? Something about ascension?" Andy asked coyly.

"The big deal is that we might all end up with different masters," Inxa sounded genuinely upset as she spoke. "And I'm sure this catastrophe can be traced to you as well," she said, disgusted by his closeness.

I wonder what happened. Andy grinned. *I hope it was Letty, and I hope that Ziesqe can't worm his way out of the punishment. He won't make very good martyr out of me.*

Full of energy, pleased his captor was suffering, and surrounded by his personal bodyguard, Andy went for a stroll. He took corners and stairs at random, and eventually found a barracks. The lazing or sleeping brutox sat up on their wooden slabs to stare. A few were eating in a nearby canteen. One dropped a fork in surprise as Andy and his guard passed.

Andy reached the far end of the barracks and only found a training area.

"How about you lead us outside? Somewhere with a view, please," Andy said to Inxa, who was fidgeting, deep in thought.

Inxa looked around and realized where they were. "How the hell? Come on, you idiot. Voice of the Dead God indeed..." she continued cursing him until they mounted the stairs.

A minute later, they were in the main hall again. A horde of slithers rushed by and nearly tripped Inxa, who was still distracted. A beetle kept her from falling, but in that moment, Andy saw her feathers flicker. It looked like electricity flashing. Andy recalled Martin.

"Why is it that ychorons here don't change their colors very often?" Andy asked.

She gawked. "Very often?" she repeated. "It takes several minutes of focus, or fear."

"I knew one of you—I'm sure his feathers

changed color, and it didn't take minutes. He could do it in seconds."

Inxa was aghast. "He did this at will? Not like Llanyly yesterday; he was scared out of his mind and his feathers went black. Who was it and when did it happen?"

"Martin. He changed often, when I was with the Broken Teeth."

She shook her head in confusion, "What? No wait, are you thinking of someone changing clothes?"

"I'm not stupid," Andy complained, "Martin was a friend of mine. He saved my life, and he could go invisible."

Her eyes widened.

"So, that's not something all ychorons can do," Andy said, regretting his loose tongue.

Inxa looked to see if anyone was watching, and besides a few ryle spawn flapping away, no one was paying attention.

"Come on," she pulled him forward.

They stepped out onto the promontory. Andy looked down into the ravager pit and noticed that they were missing. He grinned at the thought of something so large going missing.

"Where did they—"

"Be quiet and answer my questions," Inxa said, an eye on her surroundings. "Did your friend wear a coil?" She fretted as Andy looked unsure of what a coil was. "A piece of jewelry like this," she took hold of the brass spider webs that draped her body.

Andy opened his mouth, but paused. *Maybe I can*

work a deal here.

"I have a few questions too," He said.

Inxa's eyes went wide with fury, and she grabbed him by the robes. The beetles saw this and laid gentle hands on her. She slowly released him.

"I'm not used to impertinence," she said in a tone almost apologetic.

Andy wasn't sure what to ask first. "What is Ziesqe's plan for me?"

Inxa shifted on her feet. "I—I don't know as of now. It has changed, in the last hour even; I know that much."

Andy was not satisfied, and she could tell.

"Why do you think he told you so much today? Why have us explain economics to you?"

Andy agreed with her assessment. Why would Ziesqe bother explaining anything to him?

"I don't know," Andy mumbled. "Maybe he doesn't hate me as much as Pythia predicted."

"Ha!" Inxa scoffed. "He isn't an irrational creature; do not expect your own failings in the ryle. When he acts, it is with purpose, and not out of emotional uncertainty."

"Well then, why did he tell me about the fyr? It doesn't make sense. What does he get out of it?"

"He told you because he suspects that you might be the next target of the Usurper. He believes that the Voice of the Dead God is stirring in you, and that through experimentation he can prove it."

"Who is the Usurper, or the Dead God? Does that mean there is a Living God? Why would he think that I have anything to do with them?"

"The Dead God was the creator of the Seers, if not humanity and all existence. The Usurper is a more recent phenomenon, if still centuries old. The Usurper was the downfall of the Seers and still exists as an occasional thorn in our side. Be careful, some think you are already taken by the Usurper, a long dead hero named Caspian. This is clearly not true; Caspian was quite different. Perhaps he is hunting for you."

Andy stood in silent confusion.

"Moments like this make me think that you are nothing but an accident," she sighed, "he watched you, and had us watch too, as he slowly fed you information. He suspected we would spot knowledge that you, a child, shouldn't have. We were waiting for the same thing when you showed fighting talent that a child cannot possess."

Andy was silent.

"Why the vote?"

"Mostly distraction. Though the data was curious, the sample was already poisoned by Ziesqe himself, when he spoke his momentous words about you yesterday. Now you will answer my question."

Andy took a long moment and looked out over the jungle they called the Nightmare. Countless treetops bent in the wind. *I can do impossible things because a Dead God acts through me? And somehow, this Usurper is involved. She said I might be his target.* Andy let his head sink in disbelief.

Inxa clicked her tongue to get his attention.
Right, her question.

"Martin wore no clothes; he wore no jewelry. He

went only in his feathers."

Inxa narrowed her brow. "He isn't an ychoron; the term is ychorite. Did he have the power to go unseen? Completely unseen? There was no outline or blur?"

She's really interested in this.

To counter her, Andy asked the first question that came to mind. "Where are the ravagers?"

She reached out to slap him, but relented.

"They're being harnessed and rigged; I don't know for what purpose. The orders were likely just given. They will be in the docks at the gateway as we speak," she looked around, "it also explains where everyone's gotten to. Now answer!"

"The first time I met Martin, his face appeared to me, and his body remained invisible. There was no blur, or anything I could see that gave him away." Andy thought back to his time with Martin. "He mentioned that he worked with a master. Now, I know that he meant a ryle master. It was Bock? Bock-something." Andy narrowed his brows, trying to remember.

"Boqreq?"

"That might have been it."

She looked contemplative.

Andy raised a wrist. "What are these?" He pointed to his ankles, and tapped his heavy necklace.

"They're well made, these torques," she said, admiring the obsidian.

"That's not what I asked."

"They are usually used to track stock, but since

I can't see what's written on the inside—the part that's touching your skin—I don't know what's etched on them."

"I see." Andy paused. "So, if I'm part god, why do I never know what's going on?"

To Andy's surprise, she laughed.

"You aren't a god, no matter what you think. Though there is clearly something special around you. Of your ignorance, well..." she shrugged condescendingly.

Andy felt like he could get away with being snarky, and he asked, "Where can a guy get a piece of Argument around here? I'm starving."

She chuckled again and jabbed him in the arm. "We'll get you fed. You know, you aren't so bad, for a human."

Andy wanted to chuckle, but he had to ask, "Do you see many, outside their nightmares?"

She didn't answer.

Chapter 6: The Right Path

Letty opened her eyes.

She heard Staza mumble in her sleep, "That's good, but do better or I'll—"

Letty grinned and rolled over. Her clock read: 5:57 AM.

She had the habit of waking up minutes before her alarm went off. She despised the noise it made and considered it a good morning if she turned it off before it blared. Staring at her ceiling, she got a feel for what she had to do that day.

I need to dodge the police again. I certainly don't want to talk to them. We figured out where Ziesqe might have Andy; Zentule, whatever that is. But I still don't know how he got into the Netherscape.

Letty flipped the alarm off a moment before the clock ticked over to 6 AM.

Wait. Why don't I just ask Andy's parents?

She remembered Dean saying he had spoken to them and that they seemed normal, unlike the replacements waiting for her the other day.

They obviously don't know where he went, but maybe they can give me a clue.

Letty threw off her covers, stood, and felt the cold floor on her bare feet.

Nothing like sleep to sort out problems. It's so obvious. Why didn't we think to ask them before?

She walked over to Staza's sleeping bag and gave her a nudge.

Staza lashed out and grabbed Letty's wrist, pulling her to the floor. Letty felt another hand at her throat.

"Wha—oh, Letty, is that you?"

"Rrrss," Letty grumbled through Staza's grip.

"Sorry." Staza released her.

"It's fine. I should have been more careful."

They stood and heard the adults shuffling in other rooms.

"Letty, breakfast in a few minutes," her mother said, knocking on the door.

They ate at the table, and her father turned on the morning news.

"Thank you," Quill said awkwardly, holding up his food. "The toast is nice and crispy."

Tina and Jim both gave him a suspicious look.

"Look at that," Tina said, pointing at the television.

A news anchor was reporting on a human trafficking ring, discovered at a local optometrist's office. The screen cut to a reporter talking to a detective, "have you ever found anything like this before?"

"Nothing—it's the most outlandish case we've seen in decades. Luckily, none of the victims were hurt, though several are suffering severe drug induced amnesia."

"What kind of leads do you have? Do you know who is responsible?"

"We do have a few leads, and we are still reaching out to several persons of interest."

The detective held up a picture of Ropt.

"If anyone has seen this man please call the local—"

"Don't forget, Letty, you need to be here tonight at six. The detective is coming by to interview you," her father said seriously, ignoring the television.

"What about—" Letty paused, staring at the Caspians.

The police can't know about Staza and Quill.

"We didn't mention them. And I'm not happy about lying to the police. I won't do it again. Make sure you are here after school. Do you need me to pick you up?" he asked, an edge in his voice.

"No, I'll make it," Letty said, knowing she wouldn't.

She pushed her plate away and stood. "Let's go."

The morning sun was low in the sky, and there was a chill in the air. Frost stuck to almost everything still shaded by the towers. Blades of grass, weighed down with ice, crunched underfoot as Letty led the Caspians over a thin strip of lawn and across the street.

"Remember, we meet at the burger place, but stay in the park nearby if I need to find you earlier," Letty said firmly.

"Yes, of course. We aren't idiots," Quill said, getting further away.

"This city is bigger than you can imagine." Letty replied, before rushing back over to them.

"What?" Staza complained at Letty's reluctance to leave them.

She pulled a felt-tip pen from her backpack and wrote her cell phone number on Staza's wrist. "If you get lost, borrow a phone from somebody and call me. This is my number," Letty said, her face as stern as she could make it.

"I will, but don't worry about us, you've got the difficult task," Staza said, giving Letty a hug goodbye.

They went their separate ways, though Letty still fretted.

She saw the school-bus coming and ducked into an empty entryway before it passed.

She used her phone's map to find the correct street, but then went on memory.

I've seen this place dozens of times driving by, but I never paid attention.

She sighed, realizing how many row houses were on this block.

She texted Emma: "Hey, I'm not going to make it today. I'm visiting Andy's parents; would you ask Dean what their address is?"

"WHAT?" Emma replied.

"Just do it please, for me."

"I cannot believe you."

Letty stood, staring at her screen.

"4153 Hurst Lane. Never ask me to do something like that again. Everyone's staring at me now."

"Thanks. Don't tell anyone what I'm doing."

That wasn't so bad.

Letty walked down the street and found the house.

She approached the door and felt a sudden apprehension.

They aren't going to be happy to see me.

She took a deep breath and knocked.

No answer.

She tried the knob, but the door was locked.

She knocked again, louder this time.

The door opened. "Yes?"

Letty saw Andy's mother. Her eyes were dark and bloodshot; she seemed stooped and her hair was a mess.

"I'm sorry, I—" Letty stammered, unnerved by the woman's appearance.

"I know you. Don't you go to school with Andy?"

"Yeah; everyone's worried about him."

"Will you come in, for a minute please?" She asked, choking back a sob.

Letty felt conflicted, but agreed, and went inside.

"Honey, we have company," she said, loud enough to be heard further back in the house.

"Who is it?"

"What's your name, dear?"

"Lysette," Letty said, sitting down at their kitchen table.

"Ah, I remember meeting your mother, the other day..." she trailed off, and wiped her eyes, "please forgive us, Adam hasn't been..."

"It's fine, I just wanted to talk," Letty said, feeling responsible for their pain.

She tried to stay calm, but watching Andy's mother fret confusedly in the kitchen was too much to bear.

These poor people.

She bit down on her cheeks to keep from crying.

"You must be hungry, please eat." Andy's mother came back from the kitchen with a plate full of scones and some fruit and butter. She put the plate down, and a door opened.

"Who is it, Joss?" A man came out. He was unshaven, wearing a white shirt and wrinkled slacks.

"It's Lysette, a friend of Andy's. They're worried about him over at the school."

He offered his hand to shake. Letty shook it. "Adam Vanavarre. I remember your mother, she seemed rude, but actually wasn't. I suppose you're the same."

"Uh—" Letty shied away.

"Be polite, Adam," Andy's mother insisted.

"You were there the day he went missing," he said plainly.

"I—"

"And now that place is on the news. People are waking up with amnesia, and some of them are claiming to have children that no one can find; they can't even find records of these missing children."

"Stop scaring the poor girl! What can she know that we don't already?"

"Did Andy say anything to you at school? Was there anything strange?" He asked, ignoring his wife.

"We…" Letty didn't know what to say. The man's bent face almost broke her heart. She wanted to confess to everything. She opened her mouth, but Adam continued before she had a chance.

"It's just that he didn't want to go. He was insistent about not going—and we made him. I forced him to go get his eyes checked. It's routine—"

he coughed and shot up from the table, the chair toppling behind him.

He left the room and slammed the door.

Andy's mother came back from the kitchen a minute later with another plate. This one was full of reheated bacon and eggs. Letty almost felt hungry, but she knew it would stick in her throat.

"What happened? Can you please tell me?" Letty asked after choking down a piece of bacon.

"We were in the car, leaving the... place. Andy just opened the door and bolted. Adam lost sight of him a few streets over," she paused, taking a small bite of bacon. "I'd swear he yelled something at us, something like, 'I'll be fine.'"

"What streets were you on when Andy got away?"

She shook her head. "We've been all over. Someone said they saw him in the park. The—I can't even remember what it's called, it's a few blocks east of the optometrist's. But someone saw him. It was just some pedestrian, but they said he was bloody and drinking from a water fountain." She shivered.

Now we know where he went.

"We're going to look for him," Letty said plainly.

She smiled a small, hopeless smile. "You're a good girl to come here and comfort us. Thank your parents for me."

Letty ate a few more bites, out of politeness, before getting up and heading for the door.

"Will you come back and see us again?"

"I'll try."

Letty opened the door, but Andy's mother

143

followed her out onto the porch.

"How did we avoid what happened to those other people?"

Letty took a deep breath and tasted burning diesel in the air. "I think Andy and I might have screwed it up for the doctor," Letty answered plainly.

Andy's mother smiled. "That sounds like my boy. I only saw that doctor for a moment, when we had to carry Andy out—he passed out from vertigo during the test—but when I saw him, I knew something was wrong."

Letty nodded and walked away.

She heard Andy's mother sobbing.

Letty didn't look back.

Poor people.

She turned and headed towards the park. It would take some time to get there, giving her a chance to think. However, a few blocks down the road she was startled by a siren. Looking over her shoulder, she saw a police car pulling over.

Letty continued walking.

"Young woman—hello!"

She looked and saw the officer pointing her way. "Stay right there," the woman commanded.

Damn. What did I do?

The officer parked and got out.

"Let me see your ID, please."

Letty got her wallet out of her backpack and found her school ID. She handed it to the officer.

"Why aren't you at school, Mrs. Van Arndt?"

Letty knew she looked guilty and doubted whether she could talk her way out of this.

After a prolonged silence, the officer opened the passenger door of her cruiser. "Come on. We're going to school."

Letty hung her head in shame and got in.

The officer radioed in the situation, and Letty felt her face redden.

This is ridiculous. I hope nobody sees.

"Is there anything you want to tell me, Lysette? Anything going on at home?"

"No, ma'am."

"What are you doing out here instead of in class?"

"You wouldn't believe me if I told you," Letty said, sighing and looking out the window.

"Try me."

"You've heard about the people they found at the optometrist's?"

"Yes. I was there for that. We think a thief broke in, saw what was happening, and called us."

"So the thief ran away? Because they were probably wanted for other crimes?"

"That's the current theory, but I don't see what that has to do with you?"

"I—well, I know someone who's missing. He was at that optometrist a few days ago."

"Oh?"

"Yeah. I skipped school to visit his parents."

The officer regarded her doubtfully but said nothing.

The drive to school only took a few minutes. Letty noticed how well behaved all the other cars were when they saw the police cruiser in their rear-view mirrors. The only problem was that they obeyed the speed limit a little too strictly.

The cruiser pulled into the school's parking lot, and they stepped out.

"I should write you up for truancy, but since you aren't in the computer for anything else—" she paused, as if thinking carefully about what she would say to Letty. "Decent people have to look out for one another. I respect that you were comforting a suffering family, but you need to do it after school hours. Don't let me catch you again, or I won't be so friendly."

"Yes ma'am," Letty said, relieved that she wouldn't walk onto campus wearing handcuffs.

Letty sped up as she approached the doors. She gave an unfamiliar man standing on the school steps a wide berth as she went.

"Lysette Van Arndt?" The man asked.

"Yes," Letty said, as she felt her eyes straining. The man's glasses reflected the sun, and the glare made her look away.

"My name's detective Fairbanks. I came by your home last night to talk to you, but you weren't there. I'd like to talk with you now."

Letty kept herself from recoiling. "What do you want to know?" she asked in the calmest voice she could manage.

"First, why are you here so late? And second, why did you arrive in a squad car?"

"She's fine detective, she was just visiting friends."

Letty turned and saw the officer standing by her

146

car.

The detective glanced at the officer. Letty thought that his skin looked bruised.

"That's fine, I just have a few questions for her," he said to the officer, before focusing back on Letty. "I can place you at a scene where multiple kidnappings occurred. What do you have to say about that? Do you admit to being at Dr. Ropt's establishment the night that dozens of people were found?"

A tentacle moved across his tie. Letty stepped back, and nearly stumbled on the steps.

He's a ryle!

The detective stepped forward and held up a piece of paper. Letty felt her eyes tense.

The Infiniteye.

"I know what you are," the detective whispered.

"Is there a problem, detective?" The officer stepped towards them.

"No, no problem. I'm on the optometrist case, just following some leads."

The officer approached, not satisfied.

He straightened his tie and folded his piece of paper. "Leads are hard to come by when everyone has amnesia. And that's the strangest part—nobody remembers anything," he said, looking at Letty.

"Of course," the officer said, and then, patting Letty on the shoulder, "go on now, get to class."

Letty struggled to keep from running to the door. She stepped inside and had to lean against a wall to calm herself. A student with a hall-pass walked by and gave her a weird look, but Letty hardly noticed.

They know who I am. They know where I live.
She felt shattered.
What can I do?

"Miss, may I see your hall-pass?" a woman with a clipboard asked. Letty recognized her as an administrator.

Letty focused. "I don't have one. I'm going to class now—I just got here."

"Okay then. You'd better hurry," she said.

Letty nodded and rushed off. She had to check her phone for the time, learning second period was in session, but right as she approached the classroom door, the bell rang.

Students burst from every doorway and swarmed in all directions. The complete silence of the halls instantly collapsed under the weight of a thousand voices.

Letty stood as they passed, moving up or down the hall in a shambling mass. She felt herself wanting to laugh, but there was also something unbelievably sad.

I can never go back to this.

"Letty! Oh my God, where have you been? I was so scared," Emma nearly bull-rushed her into a row of lockers.

Letty returned the hug. "I was a little late."

"A little—it's third period now!"

"Oh yeah, I wasn't sure," Letty said, looking at the numbers on the doors, and trying to remember which way she needed to go.

"I'll see you at lunch," Emma said, concern

on her face. "You have science now; it's that way." Emma pointed down the hall.

Letty laughed. "Thanks," she said through the laughter.

I'm losing my mind. Of course science is this way.

She got to class and wasn't sure which seat was hers. She waited for the others to fill up the desks before an empty seat became clear. She couldn't hear the teacher and barely kept her book opened to the right page. It felt pointless.

After what felt like a second, the bell rang. Looking down at her notebook, Letty realized she had written nothing. The student who sat in her desk during the next class was standing there, giving her a mean look.

Pay attention, Letty!

She rushed to pack her things and get out of the way. Once in the hall, she followed someone that shared her fourth period class.

"—Lysette?"

Letty stared at her instructor. "Excuse me?"

"Non, non, en français s'il vous plaît!" Her instructor said, plainly annoyed.

A few people giggled.

"Uhm—Excusez-moi?"

"Faites attention," he said, looking away and asking the next question to another student.

Letty felt her face redden.

She tried to pay attention to the rest of French, but the memory of the detective stayed with her.

What should I do? I need to find Andy, but what about after? What if they take my family again? Should I stay away? Would that keep my parents safe?

The bell rang.

Letty sped to the door and elbowed a few people on the way. She ignored the affronted grumbles and headed towards the cafeteria.

Once there, she saw her friends, and spotted Dean, off by himself.

"Letty!" Emma called out to her. "Over here!"

Letty ignored her and walked to the door that led to the P.E. area. Once outside, she kept an eye out for instructors.

There's a good spot behind the row of pines.

Letty hunched low and avoided a pair of gossiping instructors on their way to lunch.

She ducked behind the pines and climbed the fence. She grimaced as dozens of prickly branches slapped her face and rearranged her hair.

She kicked a leg out over the other side and nearly snagged her blouse, but she carefully unhooked it, and climbed down the other side, eager to be free and find the Caspians.

She rarely left school this way and needed a moment to get her bearings.

I better watch out for another squad car, or I'll be truant again. Letty sighed at the thought.

She walked as quickly as she dared down the sidewalk, afraid of the attention running would bring, but equally afraid that she was being chased. Glancing over her shoulder, she saw no one.

She arrived at the burger place, but Staza and Quill weren't there. Feeling hungry, Letty decided to have lunch. She ordered and took a table outside.

She looked around at all the corporate people, who, like her friends at school, were let loose for an hour and expected back in their seats promptly. She grinned at the sudden long line that now stretched onto the sidewalk.

I can't laugh though. It's a tragedy; we go from wanting to avoid responsibility to plunging in, till they don't even have to use the bell.

Letty leaned forward and looked closer at a girl across the street.

Is that Emma?

She stood and stared at a crowd of people crossing the street, but lost track of the familiar face.

Probably just another skinny blonde.

Letty sat back down.

I've got a guilty conscience. I've been lying to everybody, and this can't end well.

"Hey! You're early," Staza's voice came to her from nearby.

Letty saw Staza and Quill, both shouldering heavy packs.

"We bought provisions," Quill said proudly.

"Wait—you did what? Don't tell me you wasted all that money," Letty got up and took the heavy backpack from Quill before opening it.

Hmm. Survival rations, sleeping bag, canteen, flint striker.

"Did you guys go to a camping store?"

Staza nodded. "We're not going back to Caspia; we'll need supplies."

"And that paper money wasn't going to do us

any good down there," Quill added.

Letty found herself agreeing.

"Did you learn anything?" Staza asked, sitting down.

"Yes. I spoke to Andy's parents. Now we know where Andy went on the day he disappeared," she said.

"Where?" Quill asked, surprised and impressed.

"There's a park not far from the optometrist's office. Someone saw him there. We'll go after you eat, and then we'll start our search. It might take days, but we'll ask around. Maybe other people saw him," Letty said, feeling guilty again.

"All right," Staza said, hopefully. "This could be going a lot worse; I think we should be grateful for how lucky we've been."

"You're right. We are still free, and no one has died, so far," Letty said.

"It's a shame we aren't here under better circumstances. I've never had so much to wonder at," Quill said, taking in the traffic.

He and Staza were about to go inside to place their orders, but Letty gave them a quick explanation of how to do so.

"We aren't children, Letty. We saw you order yesterday," Staza complained as she turned to go, holding her money in a tight fist.

Letty grinned as they went, but then remembered the ryle from earlier.

Even if I told them about the ryle detective this morning what good would it do? We have a plan. Andy is more important right now. They know I'm a Seer—we'll worry about it later.

She thought about their plan and felt doubt. She imagined approaching a thousand strangers and realized that she should go back to Andy's house, for a picture to show people.

She dropped her face into her hands and tried to keep calm.

He came after me, and we will find him because it's the right thing to do.

"Hey, how are you feeling?" Staza asked, sitting down with a tray.

Letty popped back up. "Just a little tired."

"Me too. It's hard sleeping on the couch with your father leaning in to check on me every hour. That floor creaks," Quill complained, and the girls laughed.

Letty felt herself calming as Staza and Quill ate lunch and sniped at each other in their playful manner.

These are the only people I can be honest with anymore, but I barely met them a few days ago.

"Don't you feel anonymous here?" Staza asked, finishing her burger.

"What?"

"I would feel crushed beneath all these people. In Caspia, each one of us has a talent, unlike any other. We are all valued, to a greater or lesser extent, based on what we provide for our society," Staza said.

Quill looked like he wanted to disagree, but didn't speak.

"I do feel that way sometimes. But it can be nice

to be anonymous; it takes the pressure off," Letty answered.

Staza didn't like the sound of that. "Pressure is one parent of excellence. Discipline is the other, and the two together improve one's character. Without pressure of some kind, I don't see how anyone can live up to their potential."

Letty was startled by Staza's reasoned stance. "I probably have to agree, but there are problems with mandated pressure and excellence," Letty said, careful to leave out Pythia.

She expected that Staza and Quill had followed her implication, but neither responded.

After a moment of awkward silence, Letty realized everyone had finished eating. "Let's get going," she said, standing and busing the table.

The park was over a mile away, but Letty chose to walk the distance.

Quill pointed across the street, and they saw the yellow police tape. A few squad cars still surrounded Ropt's office.

They crossed the street, traveled the last few blocks, and made it into the park.

"This is the place," Letty said.

"A little pocket of life nestled between the sheer mountains," Quill said arching his neck to look up at the buildings.

They walked up and down the paths, asking the cart vendors if they had seen anyone matching Andy's description, but no one remembered. Letty dreaded mentioning his bloody shirt.

After an hour's worth of bothering strangers,

they took a break on a bench near a fountain.

Letty watched a leaf fall into the water. A gust of wind picked up and shook many more from their branches. Falling, they sparkled in the sunlight, twisting and diving in their descent.

Both Quill and Staza had unshouldered their packs and were looking worn from the failure. None of them wanted to air their thoughts, so they sat in silence.

Letty noticed a man sitting on a nearby bench. He was looking her way. The man was heavy set, bald, and wearing a suit.

He's staring.

Letty felt nervous.

I hope he's not a ryle. I can't always tell right away.

He gave her a nod, folded his newspaper and walked off.

Letty was about to suggest that they leave, but Staza sat up and spoke, "Hey, look over there." She pointed through the trees at what looked like a rail-bridge made of brick.

Letty sat up and saw a bright patch through the branches. "There's something on the wall. It's shining like Seer script," she said, almost not believing.

They headed towards it. Letty looked over her shoulder as they went, but saw no sign of the man, though she did see a couple at another bench in the distance that reminded her of Emma and Dean.

Letty laughed. *That'll be the day.*

"What's funny?" Quill asked.

Letty was about to speak when she caught sight

of the Infiniteye, scrawled plainly on the bridge. It looked, for a moment, like any other piece of graffiti in the park.

Letty laughed again.

"It's just there, in plain daylight. If Andy came through here, he would have seen it for sure," she said, feeling her spine crawl with fearful anticipation.

"Certainly," Quill said, grinning at their luck.

In the tunnel under the bridge they spotted another symbol drawn beside an old rusted metal door. They pulled at the handle, but it wouldn't budge.

"I'll cut a way through," Letty said, palming the Argument.

They looked both ways down the path and waited until there was no one in sight. Letty summoned the blade and plunged it through the locking mechanism. She loosened her grip and the blade vanished. The door creaked open. A brick hall lined with beer bottles and other garbage awaited them on the other side.

They passed through and closed the door. Letty made the Argument glow, but Staza had a flashlight out and lit the way.

"We're definitely coming back to the surface to pick up more supplies. We can make a dozen spears and tridents and sell them again," Staza said, sounding entrepreneurial.

"Our Mistress won't like the sound of that, but the rate of exchange is well in our favor," Quill said, shifting the heavy pack. "Look at all we bought for so little."

*They probably could be millionaires with their
attitudes.*

They tried to advance down the hall, but the
hundreds of bottles and cans were too much. They
lined up, one behind the other, with Staza and her
flashlight up front. She made her way, careful of the
debris.

"That door was locked. Where did all these
bottles come from?" Letty asked.

"They're probably a cheap early-warning
system," Staza said, as they continued down the hall.
They moved slowly as Staza cleared the way with
her feet, but every few steps, someone grazed a can,
despite their efforts.

"I hope no one's on guard wherever we're
going," Quill whispered, watching his feet.

They turned a corner and saw a quicksilver wall
at the end of the hall.

"A portal," Staza said.

They approached and stared at its surface.

"Andy came through here. I'm sure," Letty said,
about to step through.

Staza grasped her. "Wait," she whispered.

Staza took off her large pack and retrieved her
short sword and scabbard. She put the baldric on
over her clothes and drew the sword. Quill had his
dagger ready.

Staza almost stepped through. "One more
thing," she said rooting through her bag.

She pulled out the revolver they had captured
from the ryle.

"Oh my God!" Letty said, carefully taking the gun from Staza.

"What?" Staza asked, her eyes wide as if she had made a deadly mistake.

"This is a gun," Letty said, a little shocked. "It's very dangerous."

Staza looked at her strangely and raised her sword. "So is this," she said, not following.

"No—you don't get it; this can kill you from far away. And it could go off accidentally, like if it bounced around in your bag, you could have died."

"I didn't realize," Staza murmured.

She had learned from her father how to handle and be safe around guns, but the thought of the Caspians carrying a loaded pistol, without a care, nearly sent her into spasms of outrage.

"You took this from my room without saying anything." Letty wanted to chastise them, but knew it was her fault.

I should have told them what it was. I just didn't think – everything was so crazy; this was almost nothing. I was just going to leave it hidden in my room.

"What? It's a weapon from your world. You need a way to fight, if you lose the Argument. Remember what happened to Andy? Ziesqe disarmed him, and he had nothing to turn to," Quill reasoned, and Staza nodded.

Letty stared blankly.

He's right.

"This pistol is like a tiny crossbow, but loud and it can shoot six times before reloading. It can kill with a single shot," Letty said gravely.

"Efficient," Staza said, eying the revolver.

Letty unloaded it and put the cartridges and pistol in her pocket. She felt her heart pumping—the sensation of culture shock had never been stronger.

I thought that deep down they must remember something from living on the surface, but this proves that they don't.

"Do you want to lead the way?" Staza asked Letty.

Letty readied the Argument and summoned the blade. "Sure."

She stepped through. Staza and Quill followed.

Once on the other side, they all stood in silence.

"Are we huge, or is that tiny?" Letty asked.

"The mice," Quill said, approaching and examining what appeared to be the work of a miniature civilization.

Tiny beings had carved a huge and complex fortress into the walls of the cavern. A cobblestone path led forward. They moved slowly, each fascinated by the skilled work on everything in sight, from the ballistae, to the arches and battlements.

"The Infiniteye," Letty said, spotting the symbol amid decorative carving.

"I see it over here too," Staza added.

Eventually they ran into a chain that blocked the path, and further ahead there were more blocking the way.

"Do you smell that?" Quill asked, carefully stepping over the first chain.

"Something's burning," Letty answered.

They negotiated the chains and left the cavern, stopping before a smoldering wreck.

"What happened here?" Staza asked.

Stone buildings had crumbled and were smoke stained.

"This is the mouse city," Letty said. "The siege Titus was returning to. This was it."

"It looks like the mice lost," Staza said.

Quill searched one of the discrete piles of rubble. "Letty's right. This is one of their floating blocks. Hundreds or thousands of mice lived in each of these."

They looked around and counted a dozen such wrecked structures.

"That can't have been all of them though, this space is too big for only these few," Staza said, gesturing across the expanse behind the strange city walls.

"Yes, and where are the bodies? There aren't any corpses in the wreckage," Quill remarked.

"Did you say that these floated?" Letty asked.

Quill nodded.

"Maybe they escaped," Staza added.

Letty sighed, hoping that they all got away.

"I don't know why, but I feel like this was my fault," she said, trying to link the chain of events in her mind.

Staza grasped her hand. "Don't start thinking like that. This is a place of war. The mice have had enemies for centuries."

Quill nodded.

Letty knew they were right, but standing in the ruins, it was hard to stop moping.

They walked through the wreckage and closer to the city gates.

"Is that a wall?" Staza asked.

"A city wall made of statuary." Quill laughed. "This is Sentinel's Watch. The last bastion of the Occidentus Obscurus."

"Not anymore," Staza said.

Quill arched his neck. "Look up; the cavern lights should have been our first clue. We're back in Pansubprimus."

Letty looked up and remembered the colorful sky. *He called it a cavern. That means there's a roof up there.* There were several colors pulsing back and forth chaotically.

"But it's not right; the cavern is in flux," Quill noted.

"Have you ever seen that before?" Staza asked.

"It's a sign of change. It's reacting to the defeat of this city," Quill said.

Letty spotted a thin strand of amber color among the others; it stretched into the distance.

"How far are we from Caspia?" Staza asked, also spotting the amber.

"A day, I think. I don't know the roads. We could follow the Amber," Quill said.

"We aren't going to Caspia," Letty snapped.

Neither answered.

Staza looked to the ground. "Maybe we could pass by and look. Just to see how they're doing. Maybe if our Mistress is back, she'll make a portal for Letty…" Staza trailed off, realizing how unlikely that was.

"Ziesqe's forces will still be all over the surrounding scape," Quill said, shaking his head, "and Pythia, helping Letty—" he scoffed.

"Yeah, she hates me now," Letty said.

Letty saw they wanted to hear more, but she didn't want to offend them with her opinion of Pythia.

I'm pretty sure I called her a cow and told Andy to kill her.

"So, where?" Staza asked.

"There are portals for hire in Degoskirke; maybe we could find Ziesqe's estates that way. We have to pass through Vychy land to get to the city, and they aren't friendly to Seers," Quill said.

Staza laughed. "I'm not afraid of the mice."

Quill looked at her sternly. "I've read that they move in warbands of many thousands. They'll be wearing tiny armor, and wielding small pole-arms and crossbows, but imagine a thousand needles shot at you," Quill said.

Letty cringed at the thought. "Can we go around their land?"

Quill shrugged, and said, "We haven't sent people out here since I became a pupil, so we don't know what the borders are today. With this city coming down, there will be a land grab for the defeated territories."

"Well, at least we know which way to go," Letty said, moving towards the destroyed gates.

"Oh, my, God!" A familiar voice echoed from

behind.

Oh no.

Quill and Staza spun in a flash, weapons raised, but Letty turned far more slowly.

No, please no.

She saw Emma and Dean standing there, with their mouths ajar and eyes wide.

Chapter 7: Hyadoth

Andy heard the door open. "I'm getting up. Just give me a minute," he mumbled.

"There is no time for this!"

He opened his eyes, and, instead of his mother, he saw a green fox face.

Andy screamed and rolled sharply out of bed.

The ychorons laughed up a storm.

Andy peeked out from under his blankets. One of them was jolting with laughter. Her feathers shifted color slightly.

He felt hands around his arms, pulling him up.

"You've got a big day ahead," Inxa said, before turning to the others and overseeing his preparations.

"I can dress myself, damn it!" He pulled away to another chorus of laughter.

"Just surrender," Inxa insisted.

Andy did, and endured another thorough scrubbing.

"So, am I fighting the ravager today?" He asked as they finished layering his robes.

Inxa rolled her eyes. "Today we mount the ravager. This way." She opened the door as a fight outside was dying down.

Andy stepped out and saw armies of slithers engaging each other on the walls and ceiling. The flapping heads were leading charges and squealing up a storm. Andy spotted one getting mobbed by a dozen slithers. They piled onto it and held on anywhere they could. The extra weight meant the flapping head couldn't stay aloft, and it spiraled pathetically down into the black pool.

It's always a bad day for someone.

A giant beak emerged from the water. It silently swallowed the head before sinking back into the depths.

Andy tapped Inxa. "What the hell was that?"

"A wife, I expect, though who can say?"

"A wife?" Andy thought he hadn't heard that correctly.

She nodded.

Andy stopped walking and looked back at the water.

"Ziesqe's wife?" He asked incredulously.

Inxa looked at him like he was acting strangely. "Yes. One of many."

Andy sputtered, and then burst out laughing.

That poor bastard! It explains everything!

Other ychorons and brutox stopped what they were doing to stare, but there was no end to his laughter.

Inxa gestured to the beetles, and they hoisted Andy, carrying him along.

"Do they—hahahaha, do they swim upstream to spawn? Hahahahah!" Andy was crying, his ribs ached and his cheeks burned, but finally the laughter sputtered out.

"Insane, these humans," Inxa said as they came into an expansive foyer.

Creatures were rushing through the halls with cargo, food, weapons, bundles of pegs, and sheets. He saw through the fortress gates. Several large tents swayed awkwardly.

"That's odd," Andy said, wiping tears from his cheeks.

They navigated the bustling foyer. Andy gawked at a giant pile of casks, and then at a rack of dozens of lanterns. "Field trip?" he speculated.

They stepped through the gates, and Andy got a closer look at the tents. They were moving, if slightly.

"Wait a second."

The slate path that exited the gate terminated, and stairwells to the left and right led down. Straight ahead, past the point where the slate ended, there was something else. Curved, ribbed, and reddish brown. Andy looked to the left, and then to the right.

"That's the ravager?"

"Of course."

No way I'm getting on a giant bug.

Andy slowed, but his guards picked him up again. He considered resisting.

They'd just drag me on, anyway.

Andy settled with complaining. "Really?" he moaned at Inxa. "Is this really the best way to travel?"

Inxa ignored him, and waited for a load of casks to be brought aboard before stepping on. She waved the beetles forward, and they carried Andy up the gangway. Andy looked down the gap between the ravager's plated back and the ground so far below.

This is the dock. It almost makes sense now.

The beetles put Andy down once they were

166

aboard.

"Okay, great, giant centipede. But why not just use portals? I know they exist," Andy whined.

"For such a force, portals are prohibitively expensive. At least the manual ones are. There are a few permanent ones, but they have fixed destinations," Inxa said plainly. "And besides, there is something you have failed to grasp about the ryle: They love attention and status. And almost nothing is more expensive and impressive than an armed retinue mounted on a fleet of personal ravagers."

Andy felt that his eyes might roll right out of their sockets. *I understand buying a sports car, but this is a whole new dimension of overboard.*

"What are you doing, Inxa?" an irritated voice called out from the dock.

Andy saw Zava coming up the gangway.

"What is it now?" Inxa complained.

"We need to get him in his cage—now! Before the guests arrive!" Zava grabbed Andy by the arm and pulled him towards one end of the ravager.

"Who's coming?" Inxa asked, following along.

"Did I hear that right? I'm going to be put in a cage?" Andy interjected.

They ignored him, and Andy felt his stomach sink.

But I can't be that surprised.

"I know The Farsighted and the Bloody-Eyed will be here for certain."

"I spotted a blue ravager out past the walls," Inxa said.

"That'll be the Marshall as well," Zava said

absentmindedly.

They approached a platform. A large metal cage was being assembled atop. A chair sat inside, as well as several chains and shackles.

Andy felt sick.

"Go on then, and be quick about it." Zava smacked him on the back of the head.

"Leave him be, Zava. He's just a child," Inxa said haughtily.

"Oh, and you've taken a liking to our enemy? Is that in fashion now?"

Inxa laughed. "As much as bullying the defenseless has always been popular—with the mediocre."

Zava's expression soured.

Andy sighed and mounted the platform. A beetle held the cage door open for him, and he sat in the chair.

The beetle was about to attach the shackles, but Andy raised a hand and did it himself. He needed assistance with the last one, which went around the neck. The beetle helped and the ychorons watched, the looks on their faces indiscernible.

"Straighten out his robes; he has to look presentable," Zava complained to the beetle before growling and jumping onto the platform to do it herself.

Inxa followed, and the two arranged Andy's chains and robes for a regal effect.

"Don't move if you can help it. Behave, and I'll get you anything you want for lunch," Inxa said.

Andy felt a tear roll down his cheek. He saw it

fall on his hand, not far from the obsidian bracelet, and the silver shackle. He was surprised to see the tear.

I guess that makes sense. This is the worst thing that has ever happened to me.

With the cage door finally closed and locked, the ychorons shared satisfied glances.

"He will be pleased. Now, let's get back; the guests could arrive at any moment," Zava said, turning to leave.

Inxa gave Andy one last look before following.

Andy took a long breath and tried to keep himself from crying.

Hey, if I'm a good boy they might feed me my favorite snack!

Andy sniffled and let his head rest on the bars.

Maybe we can go for a walk too.

The sarcasm only made him feel worse. Andy tipped his head back and felt the tears come.

He looked up through the bars at the streaks of light across the sky. They burned afterimages over his vision.

He tried to focus on them, but the welling tears blurred the flashes together. He blinked and pushed the tears away, but nothing would focus.

"AAARGH!" A throaty voice bellowed.

Andy saw Thrag slamming his fists against the bars of another cage and pulling against his chains. A team of lumbering, ape-like brutons, surrounded by dozens of armed brutox, were carrying him up the gangway.

He's not dead! They did stand ready by his corpse.

They must have known... Is he immortal? He took so many wounds, and he looks fine, well, minus the cage and chains.

Thrag burst into a tirade as he reached fruitlessly through the bars of his cage. "You there, insect, bring me your tender skull! YOU'RE DELICIOUS! And I'll have that one with the claws for seconds! I bet you taste like lobster! You there! Monkey bird abomination in the whore's chains, wouldn't you like me to take care of this insect problem of yours? I'll kill them all for free, just open my cage, and I'll let you and your slave race live. What! Can't you hear me? I don't eat your kind; your bones give me splinters in unmentionable places!"

A dead silence filled the air as every eye turned to the madman. Andy saw Ziesqe in golden and white finery watching the debacle from nearby. Thrag spotted him too, and his bellowing took a different tone.

"I sailed the darkest sea on a raft sewn of severed tentacles, ripped from the faces of your lords. I traveled to your homeland and tore down your towers, like they were paper. I plucked your monkey birds and made feather gowns for women long dead. I ground your bug shells into pulp to dye my rags," Thrag spoke between heavy breaths, his fists and legs working against the chains and the cage.

Finally, Thrag unbalanced the team carrying him and tipped the cage. His hand reached out and snapped the neck of the closest brutox. He went for another, but then screamed as his body wracked with spasms.

"Settle down or I'll do it again!" an ychoron with an electrified pole yelled at Thrag.

Thrag flung imaginative obscenities at the ychoron.

He endured another shock before they finally got his cage up and moving again.

Andy couldn't help but smile. *He will never give in.*

Andy looked down at his own chains and felt pathetic. There was only a single guard keeping an eye on him. Thrag had more than he could count. *Well, he probably doesn't have family to worry about.*

They carried Thrag to the other side of the ravager. *Of course they're keeping him away from me. They don't want a repeat of the other day. I wish I could talk to him. He's crazy, but what does he know? More than me at least.*

Thrag's bellowing died away in the distance. *That was the high point of my day.*

But Andy pushed himself to pay attention. *If Thrag can cause trouble while in a cage, maybe I can too. I need to keep myself from breaking down.*

Andy watched as pieces of ballistae were carried aboard and teams of brutox assembled platform mounts for the weapons. Ordered ranks of brutox appeared. They carried long barbed poles which sputtered flames from their tips.

Tents and pavilions were erected here and there, and a low fortified wall encircled the perimeter of the flat space on the ravager's wide back. The larger pavilions featured empty flagpoles, while one bore Ziesqe's banner. Andy recalled the banner from his first meeting with Quill.

They work so quickly.

A trumpet blasted, and Andy strained to see the gangway.

Giant ants, colored neon orange and dark brown, formed up on the dock. They carried halberds and bore banners featuring a clawed hand outstretched over a chessboard.

I've never seen ant brutox before. They look nimble.

Another ryle appeared in the crowd. As tall as Ziesqe, but maybe four times the width. His bulky frame was encased in orange and gold-plated armor. Andy realized that his face differed greatly from Ziesqe's as they clasped forearms in greeting.

This new one's face is covered in white stripes. Is that scarring? It looks too regular.

The guests came aboard, but Ziesqe waited at the gangway.

A new squad of armed Ychorons appeared. They formed two columns on the path to the gangway, one side colored white, the other black.

I haven't seen ychorons go armed yet, but these ones are huge.

They all carried massive two-handed swords with wavy blades. Andy also noticed that none of these ychorons had tails.

The ychorons shouldered their blades as an older ryle walked through the two columns, up to the gangway. Ziesqe rushed to help him.

This ryle leaned on his walking stick, and a large apparatus was harnessed over his coat. It featured lenses and optic devices. A slender, auburn ychoron followed with a quill and scroll at the ready.

Andy watched Ziesqe and the older ryle talk. Occasionally, the older one would pause and look over to his attentive auburn ychoron, who would scribble feverishly, presumably transcribing the conversation.

They were escorted to a pavilion, and a new banner went up.

The next group was rather plain. A simple squad of beetles followed a female ryle. She wore an unadorned white dress, though the dress betrayed armor underneath.

She and Ziesqe shared an embrace.

Now hold on, I thought the beaked octopus monsters in the long pools were ryle females. She's shaped like him.

A few words passed between the two before she walked off with her group.

He talked with the others for far longer. For them to be so casual, while everything else is so formal—

The next arrival was also a female, though she was quite different from the others. Her skin was blood red. She was taller than the rest, and her muscled flesh was tattooed all over with jagged symbols. She went nearly naked, and Andy realized the ryle body wasn't that different from the human.

Her brutox were likewise blood red, armed with barbed tridents. They were also equipped with blades they had lashed to their wrists and joints. They reminded Andy of man-sized locusts, if locusts frequented gymnasiums.

The brutox and ychorons backed away to make way for the red company.

Ziesqe held a hand out for her, but she pushed

past. "Where is the Dead God?" she bellowed. Andy heard her from half-way across the ravager.

Ziesqe tried to calm her, but she wasn't having it. Andy spotted other ryle coming out of their pavilions to see what the noise was about.

Another guest was tapping her feet on the dock, angrily waiting to be announced, but the ruckus meant that she went unnoticed by everyone save Andy.

She was wearing an ivory gown covered in raised gold foliate patterns. Her slender tentacles were swept up over her head in an odd display, and held in place with stiletto daggers. She wore long, black velvet gloves and boots. Her escort consisted of stately manti, all dressed in livery to match her. They bore no weapons, but Andy remembered how dangerous they were, even unarmed. An ychoron attended her. His feathers were alternately golden and ivory, and he held a leash. At the other end of the leash were a score of mice, all also golden and ivory.

They look like intelligent mice.

Andy remembered Titus and Taptalles. His eyebrow nearly shot off his forehead, his lip curled, and he felt his heart beat faster at the sight of the restrained mice.

Ziesqe was pleading with the red ryle as she headed towards Andy's cage.

"He's right here," Ziesqe said, annoyed at the breach in protocol.

She walked up to the platform and stared.

Andy stared back.

Her face contorted, and then she laughed. A little at first, but then more and more, until she bent over.

The other ryle approached. The old, the stout, the plain, and finally the golden and ivory all watched the red with annoyed faces.

Finally, the golden and ivory ryle snapped. "Step aside, you effuse viscera, and let your betters see!"

The red ryle snapped straight up and tore a trident from one of her guards. She crouched, and a set of dragonfly wings tensed open on her back.

The elegant ryle didn't move, but her entourage surrounded her, their bladed arms suddenly opened and ready.

Ziesqe raised a claw as brutox and ryle everywhere were ready to fight. "Peace! Or I'll throw you both overboard myself."

The fighters lowered their weapons and came out of their stances, all save the red ryle.

"You have wasted my time, Ziesqe! This pathetic human can barely keep itself from wetting the floor!" She pushed through the crowd, her locusts close behind.

"Wait! Just wait! He will prove himself."

"This is an insult. And the price of insulting me is double!"

Ziesqe was seething.

"You will receive ten percent more."

"FIFTY!"

"Twenty or leave," Ziesqe pointed to the gangway.

A little reverse psychology there.

She huffed and was suddenly calm.

The other ryle all tried to speak at once, but Ziesqe cut them short, "Yes, the increase applies to you all!"

They were satisfied.

"And now, I would like to welcome her ladyship, Z'tiela Veloiz of the velvet touch. She joins us from a successful campaign against the last enclave of heretic mice in Pansubprimus."

Z'tiela Veloiz bowed slightly and gestured with a flat palm at the mice her ychoron was leading. "I'm certain it was luck, Ziesqe. Though the fine manti you've bred for me are luckier than most."

"Mistress Veloiz!" Andy called out.

Everyone turned a glance his way.

"May I speak with your prisoners for a moment?"

She looked shocked at the breach of propriety. Despite her scornful glance, she was lost for words.

"Please, your ladyship, encouraging him might help us tomorrow," Ziesqe said.

Veloiz rolled her eyes and waved for her ychoron to satisfy Andy's request.

The golden and silver ychoron approached the platform carefully, the mice following. Andy counted seven.

Ziesqe watched curiously as Andy got to a knee inside his cage and looked the mice over.

"I've heard the worst has happened. Your city fell. I feel that part of the responsibility is mine."

A few of the mice refused to meet his gaze.

He couldn't tell whether they were ashamed of themselves or furious with him. He could see the true color of their fur under the gold and ivory paint.

One mouse, a cold gray beneath his gold paint, looked up at him. "It isn't your fault, Lysander. I spoke with Titus before the end, we know that you had an obligation, and that it pained you not to join us."

"It would have been different if you were there!" said another mouse, shaking a fist at Andy. This one was dun colored underneath. "You had the Argument; you could have cut the brutes down! But look where you are now!"

Andy balked. He looked down and shook his head. "What happened to Titus and Taptalles?"

The mice conferred. One thought he might have seen Titus, but none could confirm that either still lived.

"Quite a few cyclostones escaped. Maybe they made it," the gray said.

"And damn them for cowards if they did," spat the dun mouse.

"That's enough from the vermin," Z'tiela complained, which prompted her ychoron to tug on the leash and pull the mice from the platform.

Andy had to bite his cheek. *They didn't deserve that.*

There was a sudden rumbling. Andy looked up and saw the sheer surfaces of Zentule moving away.

"We're underway," Ziesqe said, breaking the silence. "This human's day is coming. Follow this way and see my other capture."

"Anyone can take the barbarian!" The red ryle complained, "But why would you? You'll only waste good brutox keeping it caged."

The ryle left and their assorted, colorful guards went with them. When the crowd cleared, Andy realized that, besides his own guard, another ryle had remained. It was the female with whom Ziesqe had shared only a few words. Up close, he found his attention focusing on the plainness of her dress, in comparison with the others. Plated indentations in the fabric revealed the armor underneath. She simply stood there, staring.

Andy tried to ignore her. He watched the compound sink into the distance. The acreage outside Zentule's walls was cultivated, and a few scattered towns dotted the landscape. He saw efforts to remove trees.

He also saw villagers, but the ravager was so tall it was hard to get a good look at anything near.

How high are we—fifty feet? Maybe more.

Andy stood on his toes, and then climbed his chair and almost crushed his head against the bars to see over the pavilions. He saw two other ravagers, also mounted for war. A minute later, he spotted a third.

It's almost camouflaged.

The blue ravager nearly blended into the sky. Its deep-green underbelly was reminiscent of the surrounding trees.

A minute later, the ravagers converged in a line, and then the jungle closed in on both sides in a frightening rush.

The guards at the fortifications went on alert. A loud crashing noise echoed back to him from far ahead.

Andy looked behind him, down onto the wake of the ravagers. Felled trees filled the path behind them.

Andy listened to the noise. It sounded more like thunder than anything else.

Maybe if I'm a good boy they'll let me out to see. Andy sighed, stepping off his chair and sitting back down.

The plainly dressed ryle was still staring at him.

Andy almost snapped at her, but paused and wondered if he might make use of this. "I thought ryle females were giant octopus monsters that lived in the water," Andy called out with a chuckle.

"We can be, or we can be like this. You cursed us with this choice."

Andy twisted his face. *What did she say?*

She stepped forward and slowly put a clawed hand through the bars. "I'm called Kal, Kal Burriasqe."

Andy blinked, surprised at her behavior. He instinctively raised his hand to shake hers. "Andy," he said blankly.

"Thrag," she spoke the name and just stared at him, particularly his eyes.

"What?"

She ignored him and continued, "The viper."

"Do you mean Pythia?" Andy asked.

She tilted her head slightly. "Caspian."

Andy rolled his eyes. "What did you mean when

you said I cursed you?"

"Hmmm," she nearly purred with consideration. "Centuries ago, when the Struggle was rife, the Argument struck a heavy blow by giving the females of our species a choice at birth. We might retain our traditional, water-bound form, or eschew fertility for a life in bodies like these. At first it was considered a misstep for the Argument, as our forces nearly doubled in a generation. As you can imagine, only a faint few cared to live trapped in the water. Your Argument was farsighted and nearly won the struggle, as our population declined rapidly thereafter. Life for a ryle in the field, at that point, was quite short. The Counter then replaced that choice with chance, regaining the balance, but retaining females, like me."

It sounds like the Argument had the upper hand, but how could it change a whole species?

"What I don't understand is, how can I be the Voice of the Dead God, if I'm also supposed to be Caspian?"

She grinned. "No, no. One might say, you speak with the Voice of the Dead God. That being, if it still exists, has no body. As to the distinction between Caspian and the Voice, we ryle are blind to that which is yours. Are there two flagging deities on the side of the Argument? I have heard this equated with being committed to the Argument. Either way, it is foolish of them to call you Caspian. His presence has always been clear, when he takes a body. He is still considered the greatest human hero, yet, true historians know him for what he is: a failure."

"Fine, but why did Thrag call me Caspian?"

"Thrag is an insane murderous curse, worse than the Nightmare jungle. You said his name, then he snapped, because you look vaguely like the first Caspian."

"First Caspian?"

"Yes, his original body, before his supposed ascendance, before he became the Usurper. This is the point most stick on: After he ascended, did he replace the Dead God? Is it Caspian speaking through you? None of us know, but locked inside you is the answer."

Andy was astonished. *Caspian is the Usurper.*

"Ziesqe is convinced that you harbor the potential to attract the Usurper. He believes that your amazing skill and luck are not chance. He believes that the Dead God is speaking through you, and to that voice, follows the Usurper."

"This whole thing is ridiculous. I don't see what Ziesqe is getting out of it."

"You will—" She paused, frowning. "What's so ridiculous about stabbing a mantis through the throat?" she asked, her eyes so intense that Andy avoided meeting them.

"It was all I could do," Andy complained. "Why is it so impossible for me to have fought and lived? I had weapons and armor."

"A mantis is living weapons and armor. It was designed by your host, Ziesqe the Just."

"The Just?" Andy blurted out, surprising them both.

"Indeed," she said looking around. Even the nearby beetle had jumped a few inches at the outburst.

Andy shook his head, "I'm sorry, I just…" he rattled his chains to make his point. "Your species imprisons children in nightmare machines to create food your enslaved servants need to live."

"Etherium can do far more than that. Though I can understand why you see us as a parasite race, but remember that all predators prey on those beneath them. Your species is predacious as well."

Andy knew what she was saying was false, but he struggled to stay calm. "No. It's not the same. Torturing intelligent victims for decades and hunting to survive are not the same."

She put her clawed hand through the cage and stroked his cheek. "There it is. That key difference between us. The noble part of your savagery—the intoxicating will to suicide of your race—the sixth sense of morality."

Andy reeled at her touch, and she looked almost hurt.

"Excuse me," she said, pulling her hand out of the cage, before turning away.

"Thrag," Andy called to her. She stopped. "Thrag isn't the only person to call me Caspian."

She stood for a long moment, before finally leaving.

If I speak with the Voice of the Dead God, whatever that is, how the hell am I still stuck in this cage?

He tried to reflect on everything he knew.

Both Thrag and Pythia called me Caspian. But Pythia,

182

well, she's a little lonely, and maybe I look a bit like him. But Thrag is crazy, he might have called me anything.

Andy felt doubt.

But he didn't just say anything, he said something very specific, and so did she. I wish I knew who he was. What did he do to become their devil? Why is he the Usurper? I shouldn't have scared the ryle away, she might have told me more.

He racked his brain, but nothing else would fit.

Andy leaned back in his chair, watching the tops of the tallest trees rush by. He rested his eyes, but opened them again when he heard a crack.

The brutox, armed with flaming lances, were leaned over the side, spouting gouts of flame into the jungle. Andy realized the ravagers had stopped moving.

He stood on his chair and saw a scuffle breaking out on the deck. A furry blur was racing across the ravager, knocking over crates and tearing through tents as it went. The brutox were stumbling over each other to get it. It leaped over the side, the lances spitting flames after it.

What was that fuzzy thing? Andy laughed. *Maybe the reason they call this jungle the Nightmare.*

His beetle looked at him, a trace of scorn about his chitinous face.

"What? I'm stuck in a cage; any distraction is better than nothing," Andy complained.

The beetle had little to say.

I've heard one talk before. Was he an exception, or do they prefer not to speak? Either way, the ryle don't care about discussing sensitive topics around the brutox.

183

The ravagers continued moving and the flame lancers stood down, though the ryle and their escorts weren't bothered by the attack.

Andy returned to his seat, and tried to get comfortable, but a minute later an ychoron approached his cage with a tray.

I've seen him before. He arrived with the older ryle.

The auburn ychoron motioned to the beetle to open the cage. The beetle did so, and the ychoron handed Andy the tray.

He could smell the food, and tried to remove the lid, but found it stuck.

The beetle closed and locked the cage, but the ychoron did not leave.

Andy struggled with the lid, before he finally noticed a recessed lock built into the tray.

"Are you serious?" Andy nearly slammed the tray into the wall of his cage.

The slender ychoron gave him an apologetic look. "I know it's tedious, but politics being what they are—one must create a need, and then satisfy it for a price."

"What can I possibly know?" Andy whined, suddenly aware of his hunger.

"I heard from a certain local that you have already met one of my kind."

"Yes," Andy said, calming.

"You called him, Martin?"

"Yes. He was remarkable, and nothing like any of you."

Andy recalled that Martin had put him in a box once.

"You said that he had certain talents?"

Andy's spine crawled. He felt regret for his being so loose with what he had seen. *I hope this doesn't get Martin in trouble somehow.*

The ychoron sensed Andy's hesitation. "I was his companion for some time. We worked together, with Master Boqreq."

I see. Martin did mention his old master.

"But back then he was called Amalcaav. I see that you are allies, and I must tell you that at one time, Amal—uh, Martin and I were also allies."

Andy saw sincerity in his eyes.

"Martin and I were successful products of our master's breeding, though there are always unexpected results."

Disarmed by the ychoron's frankness, Andy spoke up, "I'm Andy. What's your name?" Andy held his hand out in greeting, but, realizing that it would look like he was begging, quickly lowered it.

The ychoron eyed his hand but didn't seem bothered. "My name is Alek. It's been a while since I've spoken to a human."

All the ones you know are hooked up to machines, right? Andy felt himself sneer, though he kept his face calm.

Alek noticed Andy's expression and stepped back.

"Tell me something about Martin," Andy said, trying to change the tone of their meeting.

Alek paused, but then stepped forward again. "He had a hard time controlling the link between emotion and feather-dilation."

"What's that?"

"Oh—what's that indeed. It's a half-baked term to describe the opening and closing of junctures in the feather filaments. There are three channels in every one of our feathers. Each channel corresponding to one of three colors. From those three, all others are made. Our bodies control this process involuntarily, when we are young, but as we advance some of us can develop more control."

Andy recalled Martin changing color with his mood. He nodded at the memory.

"So, Martin is unique in having this trouble?"

"More or less. Though there are a few breeds who cannot change color at all, and most of us will drift in color if we don't pay attention. In fact, you might have spotted those speckled ychorons."

Andy nodded.

"Their master was showing them off. While Martin wouldn't have been good on parade, he was excellent in other ways."

"About your question, Martin is well; at least he was the last time I saw him. He is leading a goblin mercenary team. And yes, he does have the ability to become completely invisible. I've seen it in action."

Alek's eyes widened. "I see, he developed. It's probably how he escaped. And now he's in a position of military leadership..."

Andy gave him a questioning look.

"Our master dances on the line when he creates such high-functioning specimens. Amal—Martin and I were created at similar times. I've never been able to cloak for more than a second at a time; I'll pass out if I try for longer. On the other hand, I've never experienced the impulse to run away," Alek had an almost stupefied look on his face. "Goblins? Of all things. And he leads them?"

"He's skilled, and he shares command with a goblin leader. They are impressive."

Alek gawked in wonder. "Should I tell any of our peers? They probably won't believe it."

Andy wanted to tear the lid off the tray and dig in, but he suffered in silence, and waited for Alek, who finally shook himself out of his pondering. "Thank you for your earnestness, Lysander. I hope you live up to your guardian's high expectations. Such is best in life."

He handed the key to Andy, who unlocked the lid and saw an oddly colored dinner. He scoffed one more time at the locking tray and ate with his bare hands.

A slice of onyx-tinted steak and orange mash sat steaming. The first bite of mash revealed exotic tones. The spices underscored the sauce, which was tart and smoky in a way he never tasted before. But the core of the meal, the steak, despite its color tasted familiar, even delicious. He closed his eyes and tried to drown out the noise as he took another bite.

It's almost like a home-cooked dinner.

Andy tore through his meal and, after a few peaceful minutes of watching the treetops float past, he felt himself falling asleep. He nearly fell from the chair as he drifted.

Better stick to the floor.

Andy got off the chair and lay on the floor of the cage. He rolled over and over. It was massively uncomfortable, but eventually his fatigue won out and he slept.

He flashed in and out of wakefulness, his eyes registering figures and faces looking in on him through bars. They were talking to him, and he was talking back.

"Morning killing—I'm an animal. Feed me, before I feed myself."

His eyes popped open.

"Do you know that your ex-lover has named her city after you?" Veloiz asked conversationally.

"I'm not Caspian," Andy said, pulling an unfamiliar blanket from between his arms and legs.

He shot up and looked around. He was still chained, but the cage was gone. He had been sleeping on a mattress on the floor.

When did they move me?

"Ah, the boy is back," Veloiz said to the ychorons nearby.

Andy looked around and spotted many of the ryle, all sitting in chairs, surrounded by harried ychorons. They were tired. There were piles of pages stacked here and there, several broken quills, and ink stains on the floor.

"What's going on?" Andy yelled. Creatures leaped at the sudden noise.

I don't remember them moving me.

Andy lunged, aiming to grab a pile of pages from a nearby ychoron. The ychoron stumbled backwards, knocking over an ink jar and slamming into Ziesqe's chair.

Ziesqe glared, which sent the ychoron off in a hurry. "We've been having a most trying conversation for the past few hours," Ziesqe said.

"On the contrary; I'm now convinced that Caspian is nearly upon this boy. Voice of the Dead God or not, another intelligence shares his body. Xyth can do nothing but confirm him—he won't dare a test with the Argument." Kal said, with a tired yet excited look on her face.

"We can only hope," Ziesqe muttered.

The ryle nodded, as if Ziesqe had implied something dire.

"What did I say?" Andy demanded.

Ziesqe held a claw to his head in annoyance. "Softly, Lysander, or I'll have you gagged."

"Nothing of import, really. Just historical trivia, and threatening rambling," Master Boqreq said, going over his notes. "We mentioned events and places, and the voice inside you occasionally made reply with information that you could not know, young human."

Kal nodded. "It will take research, but I think some of those answers predated even Caspian's original life."

"Well, you have good timing either way, Lysander. We're almost to Hyadoth, and this day is about you, not us," Ziesqe said, getting to his feet.

The ryle and their ychorons sorted their notes and cleared up. The brutox were back on high alert. Andy felt tension in the air.

Inxa came rushing his way with silver robes.

"We need to get you dressed. They let you sleep in."

Andy cooperated, and asked, "What's happening to me today?"

Inxa fretted over the layering of the robes. "I don't know exactly, but I expect Xyth, ruler of Hyadoth and custodian of the Maelstrom, will want proof of Ziesqe's claims. The other ryle here will back him up, but proof will still be needed."

"Proof of what? That I'm Caspian?"

"In a way," she said, working on his sleeves.

"How do I prove that?" Andy asked, already guessing the answer.

"Through answers, or possibly, another combat."

Andy sighed.

"Armor?" he asked hopefully.

"No armor," she answered. "But you will be better off this time."

Andy stared questioningly.

"In one of his chests I saw a sealed reliquary."

"What does that mean?"

"It means that he's brought a piece of the Argument, possibly to arm you."

Andy's eyes widened, and then sharply narrowed.

"What does he get out of all of this? If I am Caspian, or however it works, shouldn't you just execute me and get on with enslaving humanity? Apparently, I can't make etherium like the other Seers, so what's the point?"

Inxa finished with his robes and gave him a conflicted look. Her feathers bled into a darker green. "My master has his reasons, and the scale of them is past my understanding. I know that this current plan is recent, likely formed when his ward was compromised," she said, more for her own understanding than Andy's.

She had the brutox unlock his chains and then led him to the fore of the ravager.

A litter had been made up with flowing silver drapes and a cage built over the seat. Andy stepped inside and sat down. Inxa was about to close and lock the cage, but Zava came up and interrupted her.

"Leave it open, the master has one final touch to add."

I wonder what it could be. Maybe they'll shave my head, or glue on some facial hair.

Andy looked over the sides of the ravager and saw the jungle had given way to dark, marshy wastelands. Ragged and disorganized buildings dotted the landscape and, approaching quickly, was a distinct city. The sky surrounding this city was dark and swirling with clouds that blocked out the flashing light further above. Something jagged interrupted his view of the clouds. Andy realized that a massive angular tower, the color of the dark clouds, reached up from the center of the city and rose higher than those clouds.

Andy felt a slight burning on his arm. A speck of dark purple liquid had fallen there. It stung and bubbled before he wiped it away.

Ziesqe approached the cage door, with something bundled in a red cloth. He bent down and opened the bundle.

Andy was surprised to see a helmet, like those worn by knights. The full helm was made from a metal that shined like silver. The faceplate was delicately modeled into a roaring lion. Its mane was short, cropped into ringlets that fell on the brow beneath an embossed wreath.

"What is it?" Andy asked.

"An artifact. Your scribes referred to it as the first debater's helm, or sometimes as the Casque of Destruction."

"Why are you giving this to me?"

Ziesqe laughed as he put it over Andy's head. "I'm lending it to you. The piece is priceless and mentioned in a number of your legends. I'm surprised you don't recognize it."

Andy flashed an annoyed glance at Ziesqe before the Casque closed over his head. He felt a click, and it shut tight.

Andy took a breath, afraid that it would be hard to breathe, and found the air to be surprisingly fresh. He had the sudden urge to rise and stretch.

Ziesqe pushed him back down to his seat, but Andy pushed back and slammed Ziesqe's hand into the top of the cage. Andy rose to leave the cage, but Ziesqe slammed the door, and it locked tight.

"Not now. Save it for Hyadoth."

Andy put his hands on the bars and pulled, but they would not bend. He expected they might.

"Don't make me regret this," Ziesqe said as a guttural roar pierced the sky.

More of the dark purple rain gushed down onto them.

Andy screamed out in pain as it hit his skin. He brushed it away, but more came.

"Sheets, damn it! Cover him!" Ziesqe commanded, quickly draping a silver cloth over the cage to keep Andy dry.

As abruptly as it had begun, the rain stopped.

Andy watched the little purple drops converge again and again, droplet after droplet, until they were large blobs of purple filth. A huge mass of the stuff crushed an interfering brutox.

Everything on the deck backed away, and even Ziesqe was shocked.

Finally, the globs formed into a massive grotesque face, reminiscent of a bloated and aged ryle. A huge beak emerged from behind its tentacles.

"What do you bring into my lands? Cowards are not welcome here." Its eyes pulsed as it focused on each ryle present. "Is this another scheme to avoid ascension?"

"Within this human is the Voice of the Dead God. The Usurper is moving swiftly towards him, I swear it and my peers attest it," Ziesqe spoke firmly.

"Where did it find the Casque?" The head shook violently, seeing Andy in the cage.

"The boy invaded my palace and infiltrated my strong room. He is drawn to it, and now the Casque is locked in place. It will not allow itself to be removed."

"I will remove it, along with his head!"

"No, my master, there is more!" Ziesqe called out.

The head shook, and a red light shone through

from inside the mass. It exploded. Acidic gunk rained down. Brutox writhed in agony, and ychorons screamed as they were struck.

Moments later, other ychorons rushed forward with vials of what Andy assumed was minoe. Andy avoided the worst of the gunk, with Ziesqe's aid, but Zava carefully handed him a silver vial. "Put it on your skin where you are burned. You need to be whole for the test. Assuming there is going to be a test," she mumbled, glancing around at the masters for some indication.

Arguments flared between the ryle, but the ravagers continued on their path.

"Make ready to dock! Keep an eye sharp for vaulters," a voice commanded.

"He will press the test," Ziesqe muttered to Kal. "But will he demand the Argument?"

"Not likely," Kal said.

"We should turn around," Boqreq insisted.

"It's too late, Xyth has seen us all and the Maelstrom will have our names. We are now committed to this course," Ziesqe said.

The next few minutes were a flurry of activity as the ravagers entered through the city walls and slipped into the docking channels.

Andy lifted his eyes to the many towers and tall tenements that overhung the docks. Though smaller than the mountain fortress, the local towers still loomed far above the ravagers. Misshapen creatures looked down from balconies.

Are they ryle, or ychorons, or brutox?

Ziesqe's brutox flew into action as the locals

tried to rush the ravagers at the dock. Fights broke out and were quickly ended as the locals fell to the deadly efficiency of Ziesqe's brutox. A few were even thrown overboard, to be trampled fifty feet below.

A local green-skinned ryle leaped down onto the deck from the buildings above. "A million mouths yawn to meet you, traitors!"

The red ryle thrust with her trident and caught the green before it could dodge. "Let them hear my reply!" She hissed, hurling its body into the crowd on the dock.

The stout ryle led his brutox in a broad sweep off the ravager and onto the dock. A few sporadic fights broke out, but, after the red ryle had shown her disregard for life, the locals relented.

With military precision, Ziesqe's company took the docks, and Andy was carried on his litter over the gangway. Andy found himself missing the quiet dignity of Zentule.

He saw the mountain fortress. It reached into the sky and stood taller than any building her had ever seen. A swirling mist emanated from the highest tower, which reached out like a factory smokestack, pumping inky vapor into the air.

"Disgusting place," Ziesqe commented as he walked. His brutox were hunched and bared their weapons as they moved in teams to clear the path and inspect every alley and building entrance for potential ambushes. Other brutox kept their eyes and crossbows aimed at the windows.

Thick rain fell sporadically. Bursts of red flame in the sky, emanating from around the fortress, heralded the momentary downpours. Andy spotted chunks of the fallen rain forming arms and legs or jaws. But more often than not the piles were pounced on by a horde of inky slithers. The fortress walls tapered gently and glistened like the surface of a lake. As he looked closer, he thought there was movement there, movement akin to winds playing across water.

"What's on that tower? It looks like it's moving," Andy asked Ziesqe.

"The city of Hyadoth is overlooked by the Hyacap; its surface runs with the overflow of low grade etherium and precursor that is processed inside. What you're seeing is thousands of potentials killing one another in their struggle to spawn from the runoff."

Andy looked back up. *That's thousands of creatures?*

Veloiz, who wasn't pleased by the distraction, stepped up to Andy's cage. "Directed evolution, my dear human. Ychorons first formed that way from the slithers, oh, a couple thousand years ago. You won't find mention of them before a certain point."

Andy gawked, disgusted and terrified by what he was hearing.

"Oh, but you do look brilliant in the Casque. And, if it comes to an Axiomatic fight—ah," she paused and looked at Ziesqe, "you did remember the…"

Ziesqe put a hand under his robe. Andy saw red armor underneath. Ziesqe produced a spiked metallic container hanging from a heavy chain.

"Oh good," she said, satisfied.

"What's that?" Andy asked.

"Hopefully you won't have to find out," she answered, dodging a falling slither and then impaling it with her heel.

The city had been built without order. Buildings had crumbled into sink holes now full of stagnant dark water. The streets winded in some places, and intersected regularly in others. Canals and changes in elevation between levels of the city meant an occasional waterfall as dams had given away here and there, creating rapids in unlucky locales, and dangerously wet stairs in others. Andy spotted red and purple flesh in the water. He also saw hordes of flapping heads, though the ones here were of many colors and varied shapes.

As they moved closer to the center, Andy saw that the fortress, the Hyacap, as Ziesqe called it, was indeed covered with thousands of writhing forms. The same scene up there repeated itself down in the streets when the occasional blobs of rain grew large enough. Andy saw creatures that looked like enormous hunched ychorons with wild, monstrous faces chained in front of the less dilapidated manors and warehouses.

They approached a wide set of stairs and descended. They were entering a round pit surrounded by a massive, yet ramshackle stadium. A promontory, jutting from the bulk of the fortress, overlooked the pit. Andy saw figures looking down from balconies on the promontory.

Ziesqe's company took control of the stairs that

led down into the pit. Ziesqe himself entered first. He walked across damp sludge to a wooden podium left in the center of the pit. Half-formed arms and mouths rose from the floor to grasp at his feet, but they barely slowed him.

He stood by the podium and raised a hand.

A great raucous booing poured from the monstrous audience. Andy saw hundreds of banners and many thousands of creatures filling the seats.

There was a rumble, like thunder, and the creatures in the stands became silent. Andy saw crimson stains appearing on the Hyacap. The crimson became more and more prominent, and then it moved, and snaked its way to the promontory, where it amassed in a huge droplet.

"What the hell is it?" Andy called out.

No one answered. They were all fixated. The ychorons were trembling, and even the ryle looked to be second guessing their plan.

Wind whipped up from a dead calm to a sudden gale. Banners were torn from poles, and even the large brutox bent to keep balanced.

The crimson droplet strained and tensed under the violent wind. Andy made out shapes, like arms and wings, underneath the surface.

"This will never work!" Boqreq complained as his knees gave way, and he had to be held up by his ychorons.

"Be quiet, you old fool," the red ryle grumbled loudly.

"Give it a chance," Kal yelled through the wind,

"either way, the onus is on Ziesqe; we're merely his witnesses. We cannot be punished."

The droplet burst, and a red-skinned monster strapped with fleshy muscle and purple veins clung underneath the promontory.

It released the stone, and its leathery wings snapped open and caught the air. It glided over the arena, banked upward, stalled, and fell with practiced precision.

It's colossal.

The monster crashed onto a high perch overlooking the arena. The ground shook and chunks of masonry exploded outward under its bulk. It took a heavy breath, and Andy saw a great pallid beak flash from underneath its thick growth of tentacles.

Its black eyes glistened and focused on Ziesqe, who had grasped the podium.

It makes Ziesqe look like a toy. It must be thirty feet tall.

"Lord Xyth, high Custodian, we, your servants, have come to confirm that this prisoner speaks with the Voice of the Dead God. He will soon be taken by the Usurper. We ask leave of ascension to maintain a prison that will keep him contained for many decades to come!"

Xyth's wings fluttered and tensed as he listened. The wind died down, and he stared in silence at Ziesqe.

"You grasp too long at this penultimate life," Xyth's voice rumbled through the air.

Ziesqe was silent. He glanced down in shame.

"This child Seer wears the Casque." Xyth raised its bulbous head and claws to the audience. "Is he foolish enough to allow a child into his hold to steal an artifact? Am I to believe this?"

The audience exploded with angry yelling.

"Believe what you will, but the law of ownership means that this artifact cannot be separated from me," Ziesqe said, rising to his full height.

Xyth rumbled with guttural laughter. "We shall remove the child's head before testing him then."

"No!" Ziesqe called out defiantly. "This is the Voice of the Dead God! This is Caspian's next host! If I keep him enchained it will guarantee peace for our people for the extent of his natural life! If, like proud idiots, we kill him, the Usurper will find another host! What would the Maelstrom say when they discover this?"

"How would they learn, after I grind your corpse into slush?"

"Ah—I thought we might hit upon this impasse," Ziesqe said. "And for that reason, I have supplied five of the most powerful ryle in Pansubprimus and Euboia to serve as my witnesses. I should have mentioned them sooner and saved you the posturing."

Xyth flexed his corded muscles. Andy heard them stretching from all the way across the arena.

Ziesqe introduced the famous ryle in his company. The audience grumbled.

"He's done it," Kal whispered. "Ziesqe has snared him."

"Test the child," Xyth finally said.

"Steel?" Ziesqe said, questioningly.

"Argument," Xyth answered.

A cheer erupted from Ziesqe's company, and even the audience had to applaud the anticipated combat.

"The test will bring Caspian!" Ziesqe cried. "Empowered and unchained, you would unleash him?"

"You had better hope he kills me. Let us hear our old enemy; I will find proof of the Usurper and chain him for you!"

Ziesqe rushed back up the stairs, grumbling furiously. The cage was unlocked, and Andy was pulled out by a dozen grasping hands. Ziesqe was there, staring at him.

"Listen to me now, Lysander. If you try to kill me, or any of my compatriots here, I will tear your body into pieces." Ziesqe grabbed Andy's wrist and tapped on the obsidian bracelet. "These will make you a stain on the walls, don't forget that."

Andy was confused. "How could I even try? And why did you put this stupid helmet on me?"

"You'll see in a moment. But do not forget, we are off limits. Do you understand?" Ziesqe asked seriously.

"I'm not stupid," Andy complained. "What do I have to fight this time?"

Ziesqe took Andy by the arm and led him down into the arena. "Don't worry about that either."

Andy looked up and saw the crowd cheering and booing in a frenzy. Xyth held out a massive clawed hand. Crackling black light swirled around his body and, with a flash, there appeared a huge piece of the Counter-Argument.

Xyth sighed and grasped it; his body lost its outline as a deep purple blur filled the surrounding air.

"He's not as stupid as I thought," Ziesqe muttered as they moved to the center of the arena. "Avoid attacking him as well."

"Attack him? Why would I ever do that?" Andy screamed.

He felt his knees shaking. Red and yellow plated brutox were entering the arena. They were shaped like wasps. Andy shuddered at the sight.

His breath quickened as his eyes darted. *Dozens of wasps. They're making me fight so many.*

"A weapon!" Andy cried as Ziesqe walked away.

He reached into his robes and pulled out the spiked container. He held it out by its chain for Andy to see.

The wasps were circling and leveling their spears, while others held shields, providing coverage for their fellows wielding crossbows.

Ziesqe stopped, turned, and took hold of the canister. He twisted the top apart and out came a large piece of the Argument.

Andy felt his eyes flex. His muscles seemed to tense on their own and a strange sensation of excited anticipation made him feel almost giddy.

What the hell is wrong with me?

The audience gasped, and a number rushed back from the front rows, as if afraid. The brutox saw the Argument and were unsure of what to do.

Andy wasted no time in charging straight for the glowing orb. One of the smarter wasps pushed past its shield bearer and rushed at Andy, trying to cut him off from the Argument. It fired a bolt from its crossbow.

The bolt whistled past Andy's head. Andy leaned back and slid, hoping to pass under the wasp, but it dropped its weapon and grabbed him.

Andy reached into the wasp's quiver, grabbed a bolt, and stabbed the creature in its eye.

Its grip released, Andy rolled to his feet, just in time to see a second wasp leaping through the air, its clawed hand outstretched for the Argument.

No!

The wasp didn't even touch the Argument before there was a loud crack. The wasp was vaporized into a thin cloud.

Andy rolled and grasped the Argument, more bolts flying by; one bounced off the Casque.

The piece of Argument was so large that Andy couldn't get his hand around it.

How do I grasp it then? If I can't grasp it, I can't form the blade!

Andy stood in shock for a moment, but the wasps were still fazed by the incineration of one of their own.

I've got it!

Andy held the Argument up to his eye.

Chapter 8: Mouse Country

"What are you doing here?" Letty yelled at Dean and Emma.

"We saw you leaving—and those strange kids—" Emma stammered.

Letty stomped up to them, and plowed right over their explanations, "No—I don't care; go back! Just turn around and walk out, right now!" Letty insisted, pushing them.

"Letty—please," Emma begged.

Letty felt hands around her shoulders. Quill and Staza held her back.

"Letty, you need to calm down," Staza said. "I've never seen you act like this."

"No! It's too dangerous for them."

"Look," Dean interrupted, he was forceful at first, but successively quieter as Letty glowered him down. "I'm Andy's friend too, and I bet this has something to do with him. We just want…"

"How the hell could you two ever work together, anyway? I feel like I'm going insane here!" Letty moaned.

"It wasn't easy," Emma answered. "But I'm your friend too. Whatever this is," she cast her glance up at the chaotic ceiling, "we need to stay together—is this like a theme park?"

Letty sighed, and pulled free from Quill and Staza. She turned around and shook her head. "So stupid."

"Greetings, and welcome to Pansubprimus," Quill said diplomatically. "This is Staza, and my name is Quill."

"I'm Emma."

"And I'm Dean."

"I take it you two know Andy?" Quill asked.

Dean nodded, but Emma spoke, "I know Andy, but I'm here for Letty."

"I'm not going back, Em!" Letty snapped. "I'm going to find Andy."

"Why? This place is weird—" she glanced at Quill and Staza, "no offense."

"You don't know the half of it, but he saved my life. I can't live with myself if I don't find him."

Letty's earnestness silenced the others.

"If that's how you feel, I'm going to come along," Emma said.

"So am I," Dean concurred.

"Look, you two are less than useless, you are literally dead weight." Letty sighed and put her face in her palms before continuing, "What are you going to do, Em? What are you going to do when something tries to kill us? Are you going to curl up into a ball and cry? Of course you are! And you, Dean! I'd rather have a dozen Emmas over one of you! You'll lose your glasses and cry about how bad the food is! You'll try to argue with the first giant bug we meet."

Emma and Dean wilted under her tirade.

"Do you see them?" Letty pointed at Quill and Staza. "They are from here; they were trained to fight from a young age. They are fearless killers; what are you—"

Staza interrupted her, "Enough, you're being

cruel."

Emma looked like she was about to cry, while Dean's face turned a new shade of red.

"She's right, you know. The Netherscape is dangerous all over, and Pansubprimus, or the part we're currently standing in, is no different. If you come with us, you will see bloodshed," Quill spoke stoically.

Dean swallowed, and Emma's face twisted with anxiety.

"You said giant bugs?" Emma asked, "Like how giant?"

"Wait till we see a ravager," Staza said, sounding morbid.

"A ravager?" Dean asked with a stammer.

"Turn around, and go back," Letty said softly.

They both looked like they wanted to, but, somehow, neither did.

Letty felt Staza's hand on her shoulder. She relented and said, "Fine, do this to yourselves, but don't slow us down."

Quill approached the newcomers. "Good news," he said with a smile as he handed Dean one of his packs, "share the load, friends."

Staza handed a pack to Emma. "We'll need to forage for extra provisions now, but more hands will be helpful. What weapons do you two carry?"

Emma and Dean shared another fretful look.

"Weapons?" Emma asked.

"Are you a hand to hand fighter? There might be a use for that, especially since you look so helpless," Staza mused.

"Not really," Emma said looking at her hands.

Staza grabbed Emma's hand and stared at it in disgust. "Soft and painted," she said, before tossing it aside. She looked Dean up and down and shook her head.

"Well, Andy didn't look like much either," Quill replied.

"Let's move," Letty insisted, tired of wasting time. She headed toward the gates leading out of Sentinel's Watch. Their disagreement ended, everyone followed along, though nothing had been settled.

"Yes, Andy did surprise us," Staza agreed with Quill, "but he was a Seer, and these two don't have a touch of the violet."

"What does that mean?" Dean asked. "Does it have to do with Andy? I noticed that he had violet eyes the other day."

"So does Letty," Quill said.

"Really?" Emma said, pushing ahead and trying to get a look at Letty's eyes.

Annoyed, Letty pushed her away. "Yeah, they changed color. It's what started everything," she said.

"We have them too," Staza said. "Everyone in Caspia is a rescued Seer."

"What's Caspia?"

Letty groaned and picked up the pace.

Hopefully I'll tire them out so they stop with the questions.

Quill and Staza answered as well as they could. Quill continually responded by saying, "We haven't sent out an expedition in a while," and Letty realized that their knowledge of the Netherscape was almost as limited as her own.

Quill stopped them on a path surrounded by soft, rolling hills covered with blueish grass. He looked over his shoulder back at the mountains of Sentinel's Watch.

"So, we've been going Pacward. Now that we've cleared the mountains, we need to veer sur..." Quill scratched his chin and looked off towards the horizon. "Shame the ceiling is disordered. We won't be able to navigate by it for weeks or more."

"What is he talking about?" Dean asked.

Staza gave Dean a slight shove. "Quiet, he's thinking."

"That way!" Quill said, pointing towards a stone tower. "I believe that guards what was the border between the Vychy and the O.O."

"Who?" Dean asked.

"They are mice."

Emma made a scornful face. "Not the mice again, Letty."

"They're real, dammit! Quill and Staza have seen them too."

The Caspians both nodded.

"Either way, all you need to know is that the good mice were friendly with us, but now their city is destroyed—"

"Most of them probably escaped," Quill cut in.

"Thank God," Letty continued. "And the Vychy are bad mice, who will not be happy to see us."

"Why won't they be happy to see us?" Dean

asked.

"It's religious," Letty said, not wanting to get into it.

"And who cares? They're just mice. What can they even do?" Emma joked.

"They're pretty resourceful," Letty said.

"As much as they are despised in Caspia, it must be said that they are warlike," Quill muttered, his eyes still scanning the horizon.

"Why do you despise them? And what is Caspia anyway?" Dean asked, nervously aware of how annoying his questions were becoming.

"Our Mistress—she isn't exactly fond of the mice," Staza said.

Dean's questioning expression deepened, and he stared at Letty for an explanation.

"Ugh. Caspia is like a school, only it has one of those annoying teachers who pretends to be like one of the students, but she's really just a prissy dictator. I guess she dislikes the mice too," Letty rushed through her explanation, and kept an eye on the tower they were approaching.

Quill and Staza both stared wide-eyed at Letty.

"What? It's true."

"Shouldn't we hide from the tower?" Emma asked.

"The mice are capable of bursts of speed, but we're much faster, given time. We should be able to cross their lands before they can get an army together to stop us. We'll have to hide when it's time to sleep, though. They could catch up with us as we rest," Quill said.

"It doesn't sound like you've thought this through," Letty said.

"I'm sorry. I'm doing my best. We've never been out here before," Quill said.

"What do we do if they catch up with us?" Letty asked.

"You have the Argument," Staza replied.

"I don't want to kill any mice, even if they aren't the friendly kind."

"Ow!" Dean cried out.

Letty looked and saw a tiny needle stuck in his arm.

"Cover your faces!" Quill yelled, taking off his pack and holding it up as a shield. "They're shooting at us from the tower."

Letty did so, but felt a few pinpricks before she finally raised her pack to shield her face.

They rushed past the tower.

"It'll only be a moment," Quill said, stifling another cry.

"Humans are not welcome on these lands!" A shrill rallying call went up from the tower.

A loud crack sounded out and Quill stumbled to the ground.

Letty and Staza turned to help him back to his feet. A bolt stuck out of his thigh. It was about the size of pencil.

"Damn ballista! It got me!"

Quill stumbled along, wincing as he went. Emma and Dean were shocked and yammering, "What are we going to do?" and, "He's wounded! We need to go back!"

"We have minoe in one of these packs, it will heal this up in a flash," Quill said, between jolts of pain. "The wound isn't all that bad."

A loud pop, like a firecracker going off made Letty look back over her shoulder at the tower.

"They fired a flare," Staza said.

"What does that mean?" Letty asked.

"They might have reinforcements able to intercept us up ahead. We should get off the path, and hunker down to heal my leg. I'll only slow us down until we do."

Quill was in too much pain to travel far. "Good idea," Letty said. "Wait until the tower is so far behind that they can't spot us leave the road."

Emma and Dean looked like they were regretting their decision.

But they know it's too late to go back now. Idiots.

Letty and Staza held Quill upright so they could move faster.

They kept up the pace until everyone was sweating.

"The tower is out of sight," Dean said, looking over his shoulder.

"Over there, in the trees," Quill sputtered, pointing to a growth far off one side of the road. On the other side, the landscape gave way to long, stretching fields and farms, though the tall orange wheat, or tuber filled vines, were often taller than the mouse-sized farmhouses that kept them.

"We can't see them, but the mice who run these farms can see us," Staza said.

"Or at least hear us. They've got sharp ears,"

Letty said, thinking back to when she was with Titus and Taptalles.

"That's why—hiding in the trees—ugh," Quill muttered between groans of pain.

They left the road and crossed into the trees.

"Well, it'll be easy for them to track us into the woods," Dean complained.

"It's not like we're going to stop, right?" Emma asked.

"Just shut it, until we heal Quill," Letty snapped.

Letty felt safer as they entered the coverage of the forest. They pushed on until the plains disappeared behind branches and leaves.

"Here," Letty said, stopping.

They took off their packs, and a moment later Staza had found the flask of minoe.

"We stole a good amount from the ryle, but we can't waste it," Staza said, breathing heavily and taking a long moment to inspect the wound. She cut Quill's pants off at the knee, and he muttered something about evening out the other side.

Staza ignored him and gave the bolt a slight tug. Quill cried out. Staza winced in realization. "We need to push the bolt through the other side before we heal the wound," Staza said.

Letty remembered this happening to her in that garage. Quill's eyes had rolled back inside his head.

"Wait—what did you say, Staza?" Emma asked. "Push it through?"

Staza grasped the bolt. "It will cause far more damage to try and pull it out. Watch," she tugged on the bolt, and Quill screamed, his hands flailing wildly. Letty saw the flesh of his leg rise with the bolt.

"Hold his hands down, you two!" Staza ordered.

Emma and Dean rushed to obey.

"The bolt is barbed; it will tear his leg to pieces if we pull it out. Even with the minoe, he won't be walking for hours at least."

"Do it," Quill said, biting down on his cheeks.

Staza took a breath and pushed the bolt through. Quill heaved and knocked both Emma and Dean over.

"He's strong!" Emma said, getting to her knees and grabbing Quill's arm again.

"The flask, Letty! Now!" Staza said, as she pressed down on the wound.

Letty struggled with the flask and finally poured some of the liquid onto the wound.

"And the other side, get it on a cloth and hold it there," Staza said, lifting Quill so Letty could reach the bottom of his thigh.

Letty held the cloth in place for a few minutes before the wound closed.

"That's impossible," Dean muttered. "This would save lives..."

"On the surface," Letty finished for him.

"Right, the surface," Dean stared, fascinated and grimacing like he might throw up at the same time.

Emma, on the other hand, looked like she'd already thrown up.

Letty found the bloody bolt on the ground and held it up. It was barbed.

Emma fainted.

"Damn it!" Letty yelled. "Someone, wake her up, please."

Dean leaned over to help, but then stumbled as well.

"I'm fine," Dean groaned pushing himself up onto his elbows. "All the blood. It just gets to me."

Emma mumbled before coming to.

"We can't go on like this. We'll need to camp here," Staza said, rubbing Quill's cheek.

"Fine, but we carry him further into the woods," Letty answered.

"You don't need to carry me," Dean stammered.

"Be quiet," Emma snapped. "They're talking about Quill."

They shouldered their bags. The surfacers were unsteady, but Quill was still worse. Letty and Staza had to carry him and several packs.

"He was shot. What happened to you?" Staza asked the surfacers, "Afraid of a little blood?"

Dean was silent and looked at the ground as he trudged on.

After a few minutes of huffing and puffing, Staza's eyes shot up.

"What?" Letty asked.

"Water. We're near a stream." Staza pointed through the trees. "That way."

Moments later, Letty heard it too. They passed a few more trees and saw a swiftly moving stream. It was about ten feet across, and two feet deep.

"Will it keep the mice away, if we cross?" Letty asked.

"It might," Staza answered. "We should cross

and find a place to camp for the night."

Letty and Staza held Quill between them as they moved into the water.

"Wait!" Letty called out, as her foot slipped. They fell into the water.

"Get up!" Staza yelled.

Dean and Emma also fell prey to slick rocks. Drenched, the group lifted Quill and emerged from the water on the other side.

Letty felt snide. "Sorry. I tried my best; I'm not used to carrying bodies across rivers!"

Staza ignored her as they continued.

Less than a dozen trees further, both Letty and Staza gave out under the weight.

I shouldn't have been rude. She was carrying most of the weight.

Letty looked over at Staza, who leaned against a tree, canteen in hand.

"I'm sorry for snapping like that," Letty said.

"What?" Staza answered, confused. "Oh, that. Don't worry yourself. The real trouble happens when weapons are drawn. Don't think I can't kill you before you can get at that Argument in your pocket," Staza said, grinning.

Letty didn't doubt it.

"What was that about, Letty?" Dean asked. "Something about arguing?"

Letty rolled her eyes and pulled the marble from her pocket. "This is an Argument. For some reason I can 'wield' it."

She grasped it tightly and the blade shot from her hand.

"What the—" Dean scrambled away from the flashing light. "You're doing that?"

"Yes."

"Does that help us in any way?" Emma asked.

"I could slice through that tree if we had to, but I'd rather not," Letty loosened her grip and the blade fluttered out.

"Wow..." Dean stared open mouthed. "Magic is real."

"I don't really know if it is. Everyone keeps saying that it's religious," Letty said, annoyed at the recollection.

Staza saw them looking her way for an answer. "We don't learn a great deal about it either. I can tell you there was a war, for thousands of years, between the human race of Seers and the ryle— purple tentacled fiends—with their many races of warriors and servants. The war swung back and forth, with the Voices of either side making major changes to the world. One such early change was the creation of the Netherscape. Another change split the Netherscape into many parcels. All of that ended when the ryle crafted their scheme to separate the Seers from the rest of humanity. This happened about five hundred years ago. Once the dust settled, religion fell out of favor, and is now looked down on. Almost no one wields the Argument anymore, well, barring Letty here, and Andy."

Dean looked confused. "So, that thing she just did is part of your religion?"

"Not mine," Staza said. "No, but it would have been if I was born centuries ago. Humanity has to come to accept that we've lost to the ryle. The best we can do is live free in Caspia. Pythia takes care of us if we do our duty to the city, and we do."

"After all this is done, you're just going to go back to Caspia?" Letty asked.

Staza shrugged. "I don't know about Quill. He has always been a romantic. I can see him getting inspired by Andy and dying a Seer's death."

"Wait, so you're telling me that this race of purple tentacle monsters—the ryle—has control of all of mankind?" Dean asked.

"Well, I don't know much about the surface. From what we're told, there aren't that many of them. The ones that control your society likely do it from places of power," Quill said.

"Yeah, like their use of optometrists." Letty explained how Ropt and Ziesqe were the same person. "You see, he just pretended to be human, and almost nobody can see his true form. We have these violet eyes, and it's people like us they hunt, because only we can see them for what they really are," Letty finished.

"My optometrist, who prescribed me these glasses—my optometrist? He was a ryle?" Dean worked himself up into a frenzy.

"Calm down," Staza said laughing. "It's been like this for centuries. Life goes on."

But Dean wasn't satisfied. "It's an affront! Don't you see, human progress is all a lie if it was directed by these ryle. They've been keeping us stupid and distracted. Is any of this true? Did Andy and you really see them?"

Letty gave Dean a sympathetic look. *He might crack; this is too much for him.*

"And one of these ryle has Andy now?" Dean asked, dazed.

"Yes, but we have an idea of how to find him," Staza said.

Letty found herself staring at Emma, who almost seemed excited. "Hey Em, why aren't you freaking out like Dean?"

"What, me? Oh, it's just that this sounds like—" she paused and looked up. "I can't explain it, but I always knew there was more to life. Now it feels like we're doing something important, even if I am useless."

"You're insane," Dean said, still on the verge of pulling his hair out.

"I didn't expect octopus monsters, or giant insects, but it's better than going to class," Emma said.

"I forgot about the giant insects, thank God we haven't seen any—wait, you think this is better than class? We could die! Didn't you see what happened to Quill? This whole thing is nuts, and you're nuts for not wanting to leave," Dean insisted.

"No, she isn't," Quill interrupted, groggily.

"Quill!" Staza hugged him.

"Too tight, careful," he complained, and she let him loose.

"Thank God you're okay," Letty said.

"Thank the minoe too. And you," he pointed at Dean angrily, "your insufferable cowardice woke me from my sleep. The girl has the heart of a warrior."

Emma looked startled.

Quill continued. "She wants to live and die for something more important than that sedentary mush of slave distractions they have you addicted to on the surface. Of course it scares you, because even if neither you nor she realizes it, she is living proof that humans can aspire to more than self-satisfaction."

Everyone was silent for a moment.

"Yeah, that's what I was trying to say," Emma added with a smile.

"Well, I hadn't really considered the whole crusading aspect of it. I mean, if our lives are basically worthless anyway, I can see coming along," Dean looked at his feet as he spoke.

Quill reached out a hand and grasped Dean's arm. "Forgive me, I was full of fire."

Staza laughed. "When weren't you full of fire, or a number of other things?"

They laughed, and Dean stopped looking so abashed.

After divvying out the rations and filling their canteens with water from the cool stream, everyone but Quill set about organizing a camp. They spread out their sleeping bags and discussed setting up an order of watch for the night.

Letty took the first watch, and timed two hours out on her cell phone.

No reception, but at least the alarm will work.

She listened to the stream nearby and tried to stay awake.

Should I wake Staza and Quill early? Maybe we can

leave these two behind.

She thought about it for a moment.

They would never make it back to the portal. It's too late now, and we don't have the time to take them back. Even if we did, they'd just refuse to leave, especially now that Quill shamed Dean... and complimented Emma.

She shook her head.

I still hate it.

Letty looked through the leaves and watched the colors pulse on the cavern ceiling above. She leaned back against a tree trunk and considered each sleeping bag. *It doesn't look like Emma or Dean are sleeping. I can't blame them.* She checked her cell phone and saw the alarm was about to sound. She turned it off.

Time's up. But I don't want Emma or Dean on watch, that's probably how they'd fall asleep.

She nudged Staza awake and offered her the phone to use as a timer, but Staza shook her head and tapped her brow, implying she didn't need it.

Letty crawled into her sleeping bag, rolled over, and was asleep in an instant.

What felt like moments later, a hand grabbed her shoulder.

"Letty." It was Quill's voice. "Letty, wake up," he said softly.

Letty pushed her hair out of her face and yawned. She rolled over and saw Quill. His eyes were locked onto something. She sat up and looked around.

Mice, everywhere.

"How the hell?" Letty whispered.

"They weren't there one second, and then there were thousands," Quill whispered.

"I'm glad you're up," an annoyed mouse spoke from the crowd. "Now, answer plainly, what are all you humans doing on our land? Who did you run away from? Some fool ryle not keeping track of you?"

Letty couldn't spot the speaker, but stood up, and her sleeping bag fell around her legs. "We don't belong to anyone. We're just traveling."

"Oh—right, traveling." He laughed. As if prompted, hundreds of other mice joined in. The effect was gratingly shrill.

Dean and Emma sat up in their bags.

"Mice..." Emma mumbled, still half asleep.

Dean leaped to his feet and stumbled over his bag to get away, but as he turned, he saw more in every direction. "We're surrounded, wake up!"

"Be quiet, Dean," Letty said.

"Look at their kit; they might be telling the truth. Those clothes look like surface work to me," another mouse said to the leader.

"Posh! How would you know surface work?" a third exclaimed.

Letty spotted the leader. He was a blotched yellow and blue. He wore armor brighter than the others, and was followed by a banner-mouse.

"I was with the O.O. a while back; we went up a few times. Those clothes aren't far off what we saw. They're not ryle slaves—I promise you that."

The leader considered this. "Well, I suppose we will have to confiscate your possessions and then imprison you for trespassing. Nothing else for it."

Letty had heard enough. She found the Argument in her pocket and held it out to them.

She was surprised when they shied away at the sight.

"I know you aren't fond of religion. So stay out of our way," Letty said, grasping the marble and producing a silver light.

There was a long silence as the light filled the forest. The mice were unsure.

"At them!" their commander yelled.

But none of the soldiers moved.

Letty tightened her grasp and produced the blade. The soft light gave way to the blade's bright flickering.

"The blood is strong!" A mouse exclaimed. Another uttered the same words. Letty heard their small voices echo with the mantra.

"Silence that squalling! I'll have none of that!" The commander yelled.

I thought these were Vychy mice.

"Attack!" The commander bellowed, slapping and shoving at the mice nearby, his other officers took note and harassed their mice as well.

Letty saw Dean waving to her. He pointed at the mouse commander and put his wrists together, pretending they were bound.

He thinks I should have the leader captured. It's worth a shot.

Letty raised her blade threateningly and called out, "Seize your officers!"

A few mice obeyed instantly, while others froze

in confusion. Only seconds later, swarms of regulars were disarming their officers and tying them up

"I say! Treason! This is mutiny—" the leader called out, before being gagged.

"Please forgive him, young Seer! The secularism runs deep in the noble houses of Vychy. Please, show us mercy!" a gray mouse called out.

"What do we do with them?" Quill asked.

"I don't know," Letty said, still taken aback by their sheer numbers.

"These mice will be punished when their masters learn of this incident," Staza said sadly.

"They'll have us executed, my Lady," the gray said.

"We can't just leave them!" Emma insisted.

Letty sighed. "Those of you who would join us are welcome. Now plug your officer's ears, and cover their eyes," Letty ordered.

"Do you really plan to bring these mice with us?" Quill asked critically.

Letty ignored him.

Once the officers were sufficiently deafened, Letty continued. "Who wants to join us? We are traveling far from here. Raise your hands if you do; have no fear if you don't."

A large majority raised their hands.

"I've family back in Vychy, ma'am, I can't just go on an adventure," a brown mouse lamented. Several others echoed the sentiment.

"That's fine. Whoever can't go will be tied up and left with the officers. When one of them eventually gets loose, they'll find you and assume that you are still loyal," Letty said.

"Good plan," Quill added, though he scowled at the mice.

The mice also agreed, and they tied up those who didn't want to join.

Emma was satisfied that nothing bad would happen to the mice, and Dean was full of silent consideration.

The gray called out to Letty. "But which of us is to be in command now? We can't work without officers."

"Have a vote," Letty said.

"A vote!" A mouse yelled, pleased at the idea.

"Yes, a vote! Haha!" Another replied.

"Is there a problem?" Letty asked.

"No problem, my Lady; it's just that we've lived so long with democracy outlawed. This is a streak of very serious rule breaking," the gray said.

They rushed enthusiastically to have a vote, but first the applicants had to give speeches.

Letty looked at her friends with a sarcastic grin. "Let's have some breakfast, this might take a while."

Emma tore into her bag and found a box of toaster pastries. Staza produced granola, and even a few energy drinks from hers.

"I'm not allowed to have these," Dean said with a devious grin, as he cracked open a can filled with the noxious smelling drink.

"Don't go crazy," Letty said.

A few minutes later they were packing their trash and rolling up their bags.

Letty found the mice arrayed and ready to go.

224

The prisoners and family-bound mice were tied up in a long line. About ten percent were staying behind.

"So, who is it?" Letty asked. "Who has been elected to lead?"

"My Lady," the gray mouse said, making a bow. He looked dashing in his newly acquired breast plate.

"What do we call you?"

"Fidelio," he said.

The mice seemed confused at this.

"I'm taking a new name! I never want to hear the old one again. And you should all do the same: we live a new life now!" Fidelio called out.

Letty pondered at the name. "Fidelio—I like it."

Chapter 9: Cataclysm

Ziesqe felt his innards clench as Lysander held the Argument to his eye. This wasn't the plan.

A blinding flash tore through the arena, but all Ziesqe heard was the sound of the boy screaming.

"It's too much for him—he's too young!" Boqreq yelled, surging forward, only to be held back by the General.

"Stay back!" Kal yelled, "None of us can touch him!"

"I'm going back to the ravagers," Veloiz said fearfully. The ychorons, and even a few brutox were also eager to retreat.

"Xyth brought down history by arming the boy with the Argument—he'd better be up to the task of crushing him or a thousand scholars will name us the bearers of cataclysm!" Ziesqe yelled scornfully at the fearful.

"Will your thousand scholars divine our names from what mangled flesh the Usurper will leave behind?" Boqreq cried.

Veloiz fretted, and pulled a piece of the Counter-Argument from her purse.

"Don't!" Kal nearly slapped the overwhelmingly expensive orb from her hand. "It will attract his attention; we must not use the Counter unless absolutely necessary!"

"Do as she says!" Ziesqe snapped at his fearful peers.

At least Kal is as steadfast as I had hoped, Ziesqe thought.

Lysander's voice deepened in pitch, though the scream wouldn't relent. A burst of silver light shot from his body. A moment later, the dozen brutox who had surrounded him were gone, as if they had never stood.

Perhaps we should back away. Ziesqe motioned his party to retreat a few dozen paces from the edge of the arena.

A circle of green appeared beneath Lysander's feet and spread.

"What is that? There on the floor, the green," the General stammered.

Boqreq flipped a lens over his eye. "It's grass."

Grass?

"The boy is giving way to the Usurper!" Kal yelled over Lysander's constant scream, which finally subsided.

"This was a fool's plan—drawn in haste!" Boqreq cried, though none of the others even met his eye.

Lysander was different. Nothing had changed, but Ziesqe was certain that it was no longer the boy. He stood straight and proud, his arms at his side and his chest puffed out. The boy looked up at the lord of Hyadoth and laughed.

"Xyth, old boy! Is that you? My word, you have packed it on, haven't you?"

"That voice! The boy is gone!" Kal insisted. "It's him!"

Forget the voice and listen. He knows Xyth! Ziesqe ran a claw through his tentacles in astonishment.

Xyth leaped from his ledge and slammed onto

the earth of the arena. His red muscles flexing in anticipation.

"Caspian." Xyth said with certainty. "I watched you die once. I will have that pleasure again."

Why did you have to know him, Xyth? My plan would have worked, but if you crush the boy's body, I'm back to failure.

The circle of green relented as it approached Xyth.

"So much ingested poison—look at you. Like a titan of the Maelstrom. Why aren't you on to your change of life then?" Caspian looked around. "Where are we? Low-ryle sprawl in every direction, maturation tower so massive it must be making up for something. We aren't in the City in the Sea. It's usually built in better taste; at least it was the last time I destroyed it."

Xyth tensed.

"Does that upset you? You, a clear failure? My occasional cataclysm stimulates your economy, not to mention all those ryle architects. I give them a chance to apply a unified vision onto the ruins."

Xyth's muscled frame twitched as Caspian spoke.

Why isn't Xyth attacking? Ziesqe felt an uncomfortable realization branch through his analysis. He's afraid. *He's actually afraid of the boy— well, it's not him anymore. It wasn't him in the first place.*

Caspian raised a hand to the sky and a crackling bolt of light pierced the clouds that spewed from Xyth's tower, the Hyacap. A flash of blinding light bled down through the clouds and shot into

228

Caspian's outstretched hand.

"Ah!" Caspian ran and leaped free of the arena in a single bound. "We are in Euboia!" He started laughing.

"He took Argument from the storm!" Boqreq yelled.

Xyth's haggard face twisted in confusion and then fear. He raised a claw and commanded everything in earshot. "If you wish to live through the night, kill that human!"

The local inhabitants weren't keen on the order.

Caspian ignored the threat. "You built your city here, of all places! You live under my sky to spite me! Don't you have a name for my jungle, just there beyond your border?" He paused for a moment and Xyth leaped up to his level. "Yes! You call it the Nightmare! For this insult alone, I will level your works!"

Xyth slashed out with a claw.

The creatures around Ziesqe gasped at the speed of the strike.

But Caspian had flipped out of the way. He stood up straight, flourished dramatically and bowed.

"Tut-tut! You shall not touch me."

Xyth made a fist and twisted his forearm. Purple light crackled around his hand before a golden blade shot into the air. Black flames climbed its length.

"It's too late, old friend. I'm out now," Caspian said.

"You've barely any Argument in you." Xyth sneered, lumbering forward. "One blow will make you helpless. A second will leave a stain."

Caspian leaped again onto the stands. He raised his hand to the sky, and spoke as if lecturing a child, "What do you think swirls in the sky above these blessed lands? How much Argument roils in the air above us? I will take it Xyth, but tell me, do you think it will be enough to kill everything here?"

Xyth's eyes bulged, and Caspian scoffed, before turning and racing with unnatural speed towards the Hyacap.

"After him!" Xyth's voice blared so loudly that Ziesqe and the others felt their ears ring.

Only a few creatures turned to give chase. "Whoever brings me his head will bathe in pure etherium!"

That got them moving.

But Ziesqe was unsure of how to react. *What's Caspian planning? Can he destroy the whole city with so little Argument, or even with what stirs in the sky? Can I salvage these shambles?*

Ziesqe looked up at the storms through the clouds.

Caspian is a known boaster, but his face was certain.

"What do we do?" Veloiz screamed.

"Silence!" Viqx, the red warrior raised a hand to slap Veloiz, but the General stepped between them.

Xyth roared and leaped into the sky, his red form streaking and melting away into a mist.

"He's gone back into the clouds. I'm not sure he can stop Caspian," Ziesqe muttered.

"There is a theory that the lightning in the skies above Euboia is a storm of diffuse Argument," Kal

230

said, trying to put everything together in her mind.

"That's a legend, a stupid story meant to scare the spawn!" Viqx argued, slamming her trident on the ground.

"Like the Nightmare?" Veloiz countered. "It's a curse of the Argument."

"Yes, Caspian thinks so, and Xyth is behaving as if it is true. Caspian said he wants to level Xyth's works! Does he mean to destroy all of Hyadoth?" Ziesqe asked, visibly frustrated.

"Caspian was supposed to be chained and questioned! Not armed and released!" Boqreq cried.

"Xyth knew him in a past life; his pride was piqued. None could have foreseen this!" Veloiz insisted.

"If this falls apart, it's on you, Ziesqe!" Boqreq interrupted.

Ziesqe grabbed him by the collars. "It has fallen apart! But blood is in the air, old man. Stand by your commitment or ascending will be your last concern."

Kal, who had ignored the disagreement, spoke. "He has utmost mastery of the forms; he can do almost anything the Dead God could. All that limits him is a source of Argument."

"And?" Viqx yelled, annoyed at the lack of action.

"The Counter-Argument is powerful, perhaps a hundred times more so than the Argument. But our side is diffused. I cannot imagine how much Argument hides in the storms above. Caspian assumes much, and if he's right, he could do things we cannot imagine," Kal concluded.

Viqx growled and raced after Caspian.

"Wait!" Ziesqe called out. "We must return to the ravagers!"

Viqx paused, the lithe tendons on her long red arms and legs twitched as she raised a furious brow to Ziesqe.

"We take the ravagers through the city! There is no other way to keep up with him," Ziesqe said, turning and motioning their large party to move at the double.

A moment later, he saw Viqx and her locust brutox had followed.

"Piloting ravagers through streets is a capital offense in any city!" Kal yelled as they ran.

"There might not be any city left if we don't reign him in!" Ziesqe argued. "It's the only way our plan can still work!"

"But how can we? We have no leverage. Worse yet, we may not even be able to find him!" the hefty general, Puktifa, huffed and puffed as he complained.

"Don't forget," Ziesqe held up an obsidian rod. "I can lead us to him—"

"To his necklace!" Kal corrected.

"To his necklace," Ziesqe repeated, "and if we're in sight of him, and the worst should come, we can kill him all the same. Caspian or no, the bracelets can rip his body to pieces, and we'll still be heroes."

"What if Caspian knows how to take the torques off?" Veloiz asked.

Then we are done for. Someone in the arena will let the Maelstrom know what we did. If we don't stop Caspian, it will mean the worst for us, and me most of all.

They found their path to the ravager docks largely abandoned.

The garrison left behind to guard the ravagers was bloodied from local raids, and grateful to see their masters return.

"Mount up and cast off!" Ziesqe ordered. "General, would you care to lead your blue and cover us?"

General Puktifa agreed with a slight incline of his head and Ziesqe grinned at the gesture. *He's still breathing too heavily to give an answer, so he bows. At least his vanity has provided us with options.*

The General rushed to the other ravager berths with his escort.

"Tie everything down, including yourselves! We're going over the city!" Ziesqe called out.

There was barely enough time for Ziesqe to rush to the head and strap in next to the helmstox, a massive mantis, who steered the ravager by pulling on its antennae.

The ravager mounted its berth and set foot onto the dock itself. Ziesqe looked over his shoulder and saw the slower ychorons and brutox flying overboard; he cringed at the loss. Veloiz was screaming as a chest of her fine, color-coordinated outfits shot open and tumbled over the side. The stream of clothing caught onto the armored hide of the ravager and flapped wildly as they rushed headlong into Hyadoth. The change in perspective made the city look even more tightly packed and poorly planned than it had on foot.

The helmstox worked the antennae keenly, with delicate twitches and motions. The ravager responded with a precision that Ziesqe didn't realize was possible from the leviathan. They maneuvered between tall rickety buildings, and winded through zig-zagging streets, clipping structures and bouncing wildly as the varied city elevation made the ravager struggle to keep its body level.

Ziesqe grasped the rail and pulled himself up to look out over the rear. He saw his other two ravagers, and the General riding on his blue. The other ravagers were following closely behind, but they weren't as expertly piloted, and had ripped through several structures, leaving a trail of destruction in their wake. Ziesqe shuddered at the thought of having to pay for so much destruction.

He rolled his eyes at himself and started laughing.

Veloiz struggled up to the helm, a cable lashed around her wrist, which she nearly climbed to get there. She looked disgustedly at him. "Laughing, are you? It is certainly not the time!" she yelled.

"It's never been more the time, my lady!" Ziesqe cried, astonished at what he was doing.

She slapped him so hard that his tentacles whipped around. "You need to make some use of this debacle! Now, what are we going to do?"

Ziesqe took a heavy breath and found the ebony rod. He pointed it out across the city and felt for vibrations, but the shaking of the ravager made it difficult. He pointed it towards the Hyacap and barely felt the rod buzz.

"He's on or near the tower!" Ziesqe called out.

A searing column of light flashed in the sky, causing the ravagers to grind to a halt and everyone on board to wince and shield their eyes. The light glared blindingly for several painful moments, before finally flickering out.

"What happened?" Veloiz shrieked.

"There!" Kal yelled, pointing to a silver blast halfway up the tower.

The ravagers lumbered into motion again as their pilot's eyes readjusted.

Ziesqe grabbed the binoculars from the helmstox and focused on the blast. He saw Caspian slicing his way through the tower. The silver blade shot clean through from one side to the other.

He's destroying the Hyacap.

The tower creaked and shifted.

"Hold!" Ziesqe yelled. "It will come down!"

The ravager halted, and the others fell in on the sides.

"But we don't know which way it will fall!"

Ziesqe's claws dug into his harness as the tower creaked and groaned, shifting first this way, and then the other. Even the ravager swayed back and forth, as if anticipating which way to run. The creaking itself rung with a concussion that forced dust and debris to fall from buildings miles away.

A second silver flash lit up the sky, and the tower crumbled onto itself.

Ziesqe almost heaved a sigh of relief, but a moment later, the crumbling masonry and exploding steel supports unleashed a torrent of wreckage in every direction. A thick mix of fluid was bursting from the lower portion of the Hyacap. What remained of the tower buckled and creaked so loudly that the ravagers twitched at the noise.

"The precursor stored inside will burst loose. Millions of gallons," Boqreq muttered.

Kal came forward. Her usually stoic appearance was long gone. "The precursor, Ziesqe! It'll pour out into the city! It will come in a wave and mutilate everything!"

The helmstox looked at Ziesqe, afraid and unsure.

"Higher! We need to get above the wave," he commanded.

Ziesqe looked around and saw several tall towers belonging to petty ryle, not far behind, on the path they had cut through town.

"Back! Back to those towers!" Ziesqe ordered, and the ravager swung wildly about.

He saw the other ravagers following his lead. Lighter debris was crashing down all around. Panes of glass thirty feet tall spun through the air like massive translucent blades, slicing through weak structures.

The ravager hit the first tower and Ziesqe was pushed back against his harness as they pulled straight up. The creature climbed faster than he expected. He looked down and saw the other ravagers trying to mount the same tower.

Idiots!

"No! It's too much weight!" He screamed, but the blast from the crumbling tower was far too loud.

He grabbed the helmstox and pointed to the next tower over. "Get us over there!"

The mantis looked at him with a surprising amount of incredulity.

"Now!"

The mantis was unsure how to convey that command to the ravager, but it directed the beast to the far side of the now shaking tower. Then, much to Ziesqe's shock, his helmstox leaped over the side.

Ziesqe pulled against his harness to see. The mantis was holding onto the ravager by its facial plates and pointing at the next tower.

The ravager seemed to understand as it unhooked its front legs from the tower before making the leap.

The mantis held on by an antenna as the ravager spanned the distance. Ziesqe felt weightless for a moment before the ravager grasped onto the next tower. Many of the ryle and ychorons behind him were screaming and weeping. Viqx, however, was laughing uproariously.

"Bring me death!" She yelled, between fits of insane laughter.

Ziesqe saw his other compatriots and noted that Boqreq looked like he was going to be—or just had been—sick all over the deck.

Ziesqe looked out at the other tower and saw the wave of debris crash into it. A torrent of dark purple filth rushed underneath the dust cloud.

"How much Argument will Caspian still have left? That act must have drained him!" Boqreq yelled.

Ziesqe tried to count the ravagers. He realized that one was missing.

"What will all that precursor do?" Veloiz asked, "Is there any way we can catch some of it?"

"It's raw," Kal countered. "It's the mutagen he poured over his tower to breed new strains. You don't want to touch it."

"I'm not an idiot, girl! But it's still valuable!" Veloiz insisted.

"Not more than our lives!" Boqreq argued.

Ziesqe raised a claw for silence.

They waited for a few minutes as the debris settled, and the crashing roar finally deadened to a dull rumble.

Calls from the other ravagers got Ziesqe's attention. He directed their ravager to climb down and off the tower. The other ravagers did likewise, though one tower crumbled and collapsed in the process, leaving the ravager that was clinging on, tumbling to the ground.

It pulled itself out from under the debris. Much of the crew was lost, though the pilot was still in control.

Around the far side of the first tower they found the missing ravager, half submerged under debris.

"Have them bend down, and we'll pick up any survivors," Ziesqe commanded.

A moment later he realized that a gushing torrent of etherium was bubbling up around the collapsed ravager. The creature was tensing and shifting under the debris.

"The mutation factor will be too great!" Kal

insisted.

"She's right," Boqreq added, shocked at the sight. "This is happening all over the city."

For a moment Ziesqe wasn't sure what to do.

"Stake it! Kill the beast before it becomes exponential!" Viqx screamed, unharnessing herself.

"Yes, we must," Ziesqe said, focusing.

She was leaping through the air, her wings flashing like fire for a moment before she tucked them in and dove onto the mutating ravager.

Ziesqe looked over and saw her and the ravager's pilot drive a huge steel stake through the creature's thick skull.

"That might not do it," Kal said. "I've never seen that much precursor spilled before."

Viqx flew back aboard, carrying the pilot of the lost ravager.

"Up!" Ziesqe called out.

The helmstox pulled back on both antennae, and the creature rose.

The blue ravager pulled alongside, and the General called out, "What's the plan?"

"We chase the boy!" Ziesqe yelled, holding the ebony rod, and pointing.

The fleet moved out over the destroyed city.

"We're making better time now that everything has collapsed," Veloiz commented.

Caspian is moving. But what's he planning?

Ziesqe saw the thick clouds that spewed from the now fallen Hyacap slowly thinning.

The ravagers slowed.

"What's holding us up?" Boqreq asked.

Ziesqe looked overboard but recoiled as a barbed tentacle rose from the street below. The ravager veered away. Ziesqe had glanced long enough to see fleshy appendages and writhing forms lifting from the rubble of the ruined city.

"The land crawls!" Kal yelled.

The other ryle grasped their pieces of the Counter-Argument. Blades, shields, and purple, glowing armor appeared.

I didn't want it to come to this, but there's no choice.

Ziesqe did likewise, peeling off his robes to reveal the crimson armor beneath, and grasping his priceless piece of the Counter-Argument. Curiously, Viqx only summoned a blade. He looked down at his solid steel armor, tensing and flexing the nerves and muscles across his body before a glowing suit of Counter armor rested above the steel. Two suits had always felt more secure than one. He recalled ryle grown complacent from so much dominance. Calling the etherium armor took effort and mastery, and those failed ryle had mistaken a hefty orb of Counter for protection enough. When the moment came, a crossbow or dagger in the hand of the lowest creature could fell the mightiest ryle. Though the steel chafed, and others might sneer, he wouldn't make their mistake.

A tentacle came crashing onto the ravager, but Viqx struck with her blade. It sliced half-way through. The tentacle cracked and fell.

"Well done!" Kal said, using her axe to chop through another bladed arm swiping their way.

"The ground is coming to life. Giants are trying

to rise!" Veloiz screamed.

"Of course they are!" Viqx yelled at the wavering ryle.

"Our eyes are the first to witness such horrors!" Boqreq muttered.

Ziesqe felt the rod and motioned for the helmstox to steer slightly to the left.

Ahead of them was a living forest of misshapen limbs tearing and ripping at each other.

Ziesqe heard a shrill clicking. They looked back and saw the General's blue ravager being pulled down by a colossal tentacle, tipped with a lobster claw.

The brutox on board swung and chopped with their weapons, but it was useless. The General fought at the head and dislodged the claw, but their ravager was giving way. Its legs stabbed out in a hundred places at the living floor, but it couldn't kick free. A second and then a third arm rose and clamped on. A massive, toothed jaw snapped up from the earth and subdued the ravager.

"We need to go back!" Veloiz yelled, manic frenzy in her voice as she approached the helmstox. "Pilot us out of the city!"

Viqx restrained her.

Ziesqe grasped the rail as he saw the General's blade flutter out.

"We can't! We have to keep moving," Ziesqe spoke, though he refused to look her in the eye.

"Why? That is our fate, if we stay!" Veloiz yelled desperately.

They shifted and felt a drop. A scaled leg had

kicked their ravager sideways.

Ziesqe was about to call off the pursuit before he saw a flash of silver light.

"There!" he called out.

The base of the tower jutted from the wreckage of the city. It looked like a huge stump, covered in a thick layer of rubble.

There was another flash, and then a red flame burst into the sky.

Caspian is fighting Xyth.

The ravager hit the sloping side of the tower, and its legs failed to get traction on the slick layer of precursor still coating the walls.

"Don't slide into that stuff; if enough gets on our hull we'll start to mutate," Boqreq called out to the helmstox.

The helmstox nodded, though his fine precision had given way to more desperate articulation on the antennae. The ravager seemed to ignore the instructions, until it finally jumped forward, onto a large piece of fallen wall that lay on the side of the slick tower.

The ravager climbed higher and higher, sticking to the debris, before finally skirting the crest, where Caspian had sliced the mountain-sized tower in two. Ziesqe looked over his shoulder and saw no sign of his other ravagers.

He sighed at the massive cost.

The ravager pulled itself up the edge and finally came to rest on level ground. They could feel its massive body heaving from the exertion.

Ziesqe unharnessed himself and rushed to

the rail, the others right behind. A pool of boiling precursor bubbled in the tower's stump. Chunks of curved wall floated on the surface of the pool.

Ziesqe grabbed the binoculars. He spotted Xyth, held aloft by silver veined tentacles. Caspian leaned at the edge of a chunk of fallen wall and had his hand in the pool. A nexus of branching silver cords grew out into the pool from where he touched. The branches pulsed with light.

"He's killing Xyth," Ziesqe said. "Do we stop him?"

"We have to," Veloiz cried. "He will reward us!"

"I'm not sure," Kal replied, "He may feel that we are at fault for all of this. It might be best to let him die, and then defeat Caspian."

"Yes," Boqreq said, "that way, we control the story. We defeat the enemy and save the ruined city, no Xyth to contradict us."

"Interesting plan," a lilting voice replied.

Ziesqe nearly flew out of his skin.

They turned and saw Caspian sitting at the head of the ravager. The helmstox slowly backed away.

"He still wears the bracelets!" Veloiz shrieked. "Blow him to pieces!"

If I do, Xyth will fall into the etherium, and that alone should be the end of him, and we will be responsible. But, if I don't kill Caspian now, he might escape beyond the range of the rod.

Ziesqe felt his stomach sink.

It wasn't supposed to happen this way.

"Now, if you don't mind, I'm busy with an old friend," Caspian said in a friendly tone.

"You aren't going anywhere!" Ziesqe yelled, holding up the rod, as the others fell silent. He grasped the bottom half and twisted the top.

A small crack echoed off the debris. Caspian was nowhere in sight.

"Did it work?" Kal whispered.

They stood in silence, everyone looking for Caspian's body.

"There!" Kal called out, pointing.

Ziesqe looked through the binoculars. Caspian was still alive and laughing.

"It failed. He's still wearing his head," Boqreq moaned. "Can you get nothing right?"

"He kept the bracelets from exploding... he is centuries old, perhaps he's experienced them before," Ziesqe said.

Cursing his stupidity, Ziesqe looked through the binoculars again. He saw that Caspian had lifted the visor on the Casque, and was talking with Xyth, who was still held in the air by a score of thick tentacles.

"What in hell's name?" Ziesqe waved for the pilot to lower the ravager. The ravager bent its many legs and Ziesqe hopped over the side. He heard a few grunts and footfalls behind him. He kept low and moved around the debris that rested on the rim of the trunk.

Are they simply talking? Certainly not after all that!

Ziesqe peeked around a corner and spotted them.

Xyth was speaking between bouts of laughter, "Do you remember the Kaiser? Hahaha, the oaf was Victoria's grandson; can you imagine if she knew what happened?"

"Now, now, big lad, that's just the supposition—
that he was a fool and all—but it was von
Hötzendorf who really made that whole war
happen. Weren't you in with the Austrians at the
time? I mean, before you began impersonating
a zeppelin?" Caspian asked, leaning back on the
broken wall.

Xyth laughed. It rolled out, a raucous and
resonant warble, shaking the rubble loose.

They're discussing history!

"Conrad was a poor commander, yes, but
the Empire was foolishly conciliatory with its
possessions from the outset. Imagine trying to do
business at the time; the railroad tracks weren't
standardized! Every part of the Empire had their
own type. A train would end up in a station, and
the track would suddenly be wrong. A centralized
nation simply organizes and has another train
waiting on time, but—"

"On time!" Caspian spat, laughing.

Xyth failed to rebut and joined in the mirth.
"Good years though," Xyth finally replied.

"What the hell are you remembering? The worst
thing possible kept happening until we finally ran
out of worst things. I was glad when you all finally
killed me." Caspian paused for a heavy breath. "And
on that topic, I'm afraid the bumblers who let me
loose have declined to retreat."

"Oh," Xyth grunted and snapped his beak. "Are
you going to kill them too, the ungrateful spawn?"

"If I see them, but they have someone I need."

245

"Caspian?" Xyth started. "When I knew you during the war, your body was quite different; how is it I recognize you so, after so many years and with you in a child's form?"

"Sharp eyes don't see the body," Caspian said, standing.

Maybe I can get Lysander to the fore in the boy's mind, and push Caspian away.

Ziesqe paused for a long moment, hesitation cloying his limbs, he clenched and finally called out. "Lysander!"

"Ah, the boy, what will happen to him?" Xyth asked, not surprised at Ziesqe's sudden arrival. "I've never understood how you took their bodies."

"Not now, Xyth," Caspian answered, getting to his feet. "And that's quite a rude question."

"Lysander! Do you ever wish to see your parents again? We are almost ready to go home!" Ziesqe called out from behind the broken piece of wall.

The wall split apart as a silver blade cut through. Ziesqe stumbled away and nearly slipped into the lake of etherium. He looked back and saw Caspian, only a few feet away.

"There, there, young man, don't think to—" Caspian's voice cracked, as his body twitched.

The boy is trying to regain control.

Caspian's head tilted down, as if confused.

Now!

Ziesqe raised his claw and a purple blade shot out. He swung, but a silver shield appeared around Caspian's hand, and he deflected the strike with such force that Ziesqe flew off his feet and slammed against the split chunk of wall. His hefty piece of Counter rolled away.

"Ziesqe!" Kal screamed and rushed at Caspian, who slapped the air and sent her flying.

"Careful, or you'll end up in the soup," Caspian said, as he ambled slowly over to the ravager.

Viqx raised her blade. Caspian only sighed and lowered the visor on his Casque.

Her wings flexed and she leaped into the air, but not towards Caspian. She flew towards Xyth and sliced through the tentacles holding him aloft.

Caspian stopped. "You idiot!" He raised a hand towards Xyth, but it was too late. The lumbering ryle slipped from the few remaining tentacles and crashed into the pool of precursor.

Caspian broke out into a run. "Thrag! Wake up!"

He's going for Thrag? Ziesqe pulled himself to his feet and grabbed his piece of the Counter-Argument.

"We need to leave, now!" Kal screamed.

The pool of etherium gurgled, and a bolt of piercing, violet light shot out from its churning surface.

The ryle rushed towards the ravager, but Caspian was already aboard.

I must get the boy to the forefront. He will reason with me.

Ziesqe and the others climbed aboard. Caspian was about to slice through Thrag's cage.

"Lysander! Think of your parents!" Ziesqe yelled. He snapped a claw at the helmstox and pointed to the horizon.

The ravager was on its feet in moments as the erratic flaring of light cast shifting shadows across every surface. A deep groaning rumble echoed through the air.

"I can't!" Lysander's voice called out from inside the Casque.

"No! I'm not going back!" Caspian yelled.

Ziesqe ran up to them, but stopped short as a flickering silver blade swiped inches from his face. The blade was unhoned.

"He's weak!" Viqx cried.

"Stay back!" Ziesqe ordered.

Ziesqe loosened his hone and struck Caspian's blade. A small crack pushed him back a few feet, but his foe had slumped over.

Caspian isn't careful with the Argument and uses it so extravagantly in every motion. Destroying the tower and battling Xyth must have drained him, but it barely showed when we were fighting.

Thrag flew into a slurring fit as he watched. Viqx leveled her blade as he bent the bars of his cage.

A small, marble-sized piece of Argument rolled from Caspian's hand.

"I'm alive—" he said with a weak voice.

"Lysander! Take off the helmet! You can save Lysette if you only take off the helmet!" Ziesqe commanded.

"Letty—I," Andy's voice was barely audible. He fumbled with the helmet, and finally it cracked open.

The boy lay there, silently, as if asleep. Zava and Inxa, who had remained hidden for the ordeal, came to return him to his chains.

Once he was out of sight, it didn't take the few remaining brutox long to calm Thrag with jabs of their electrified lances.

Ziesqe looked back to the ruined city of Hyadoth. "Caspian was free for less than an hour, and he managed to destroy the city."

"Destroy it?" Veloiz snapped, "Nothing will live here for centuries!"

"It was a failure for the historians," Boqreq agreed, venom in his voice.

"The advantage is ours," Kal insisted. "We decide what they hear at the Maelstrom."

"We aren't even out of danger yet!" Veloiz complained, pointing across the city.

Ziesqe was silent as they moved through the wreckage. He saw the lumbering forms of ravagers, covered in extra heads, bearing legs that pointed in every direction. Beneath those were fields of building-sized beasts of indiscernible species ripping one another to pieces.

The helmstox avoided the obvious fighting, making a course straight for the city walls. The ryle and the few remaining brutox bodyguards took up watch. They fought off a rogue tentacle that tried to pull them down.

Ziesqe looked back to the ruin of the Hyacap and saw the mutated body of Xyth wrack and spasm. His bloated body was even larger. Ziesqe felt his heart break at the sight of the once proud ryle.

A shuddering groan rolled out over the ruined city. *Its old master will rule still, his armies and subjects replaced with mindless abominations, though not a one as fearful as he.*

When the border of the city finally fell away behind them, Ziesqe called the helmstox to a stop. "We need to convene," he said to the ryle. "We have lost one of our own," he took a deep breath, "and our plan is failed."

Kal looked like she wanted to rebut, but Ziesqe held out a hand.

He looked around at the others. Viqx was not that bothered. She even seemed pleased at being a part of so much slaughter. Boqreq, on the other hand, was barely standing. Veloiz was frazzled and had a manic look about her eyes. She was fond of the General, and he will be as etherium-cursed as anything else in that city. Finally, Kal herself was not discouraged. He saw her racing mind, written clearly in the tense lines that played about her face.

"I will accept the responsibility for our failure, alone. If any of you should decide to go to the Maelstrom, I will not try to stop you," Ziesqe said.

Boqreq rounded on him in a fury. "You are absolutely responsible! They won't even force you to ascend—" Viqx reached out and snapped his neck with a single hand. She flung his body overboard and ordered her locusts to slaughter Boqreq's remaining brutox and ychorons.

"You said you wouldn't try to stop anyone..." Veloiz complained. Her voice, softer and softer, until it finally petered out.

"I did," Ziesqe said, "but I can't speak for Viqx, who does as she pleases. It seems that traitors do not please her."

Veloiz had no comment.

"Very well," Ziesqe rushed ahead brusquely. "I've concluded that there is no explaining this away. Even if we tell the most slanted version of events, the facts are: The Casque was known to have been in my collection, the Argument he wielded was also supplied by my estate, and there are certainly other survivors. These survivors are already racing to be the first to report what has happened. We cannot lie about the previous facts. Our actions have destroyed the capitol city of Euboia and consigned its master to an end worse than death."

Even Kal didn't care to argue with that.

"We must now be proactive. To regain the Maelstrom's approval, we must do no less than capture the city of Degoskirke."

Unbelieving faces met his words. Veloiz was the only one to rebut, "That is a stupid jest, and a waste of our dwindling time. Capturing the free city is a fool's punishment."

"Yes, and fools we are. But we have an advantage none of our foolish forbearers have ever enjoyed." Ziesqe paused, inclining his brow towards Andy.

The ryle were confused.

"Degoskirke is the greatest city in Pansubprimus, and it is free."

"Of course!" Veloiz interrupted, "but that's why being assigned to Degoskirke is a death sentence. It has been free for centuries, and you, oh great bumbler, propose to capture a city with the boy who destroyed a city?"

"That was Caspian; don't forget that." Ziesqe raised his hand to silence the protests. "I can see the boy, and only the boy, being the critical difference between our attempt and all those who have failed before."

They were silent.

"We must play off this failure."

Kal nodded, "I see where this is going."

"What is the key characteristic of Degoskirke? What has made it difficult for us thus far?"

"Their militant secularism and a founding document that explicitly outlaws our kind," Veloiz replied.

"Yes," Kal said, "but their defense cleaves both ways; Seers are just as taboo and equally outlawed."

"Get to the point," Viqx snapped. "What good is the Seer?"

Ziesqe smiled. "Young Lysander here could simply walk through the streets and flash his blade for a moment. The sight would strike terror in the city's inhabitants, who, bearing neither Argument nor Counter, must rely on their cumbersome weapons to even threaten him."

A few grins spread here and there.

Veloiz, however, disagreed. "And what is to keep Caspian from stealing his body again?"

Ziesqe smirked and looked to Kal.

"It was a combination of the Casque and the Argument that empowered Caspian. The Viper meddling with the boy has accidentally taught him some resistance, buying us some time with little fear of the Usurper's presence—unless we invoke him purposefully," Kal said.

"I have made an arrangement with the boy, and I'll make another," Ziesqe said. "If he serves us in taking Degoskirke, we will release him onto the surface, and leave him to his family. He is a moral creature, and I know how you will complain, but we can compel his cooperation. It will only take a little creativity."

"You mention Seer morality; they historically balk at killing innocents," Kal said.

"And he won't have to. If simply waving the Argument in public doesn't stir an uproar, we'll have him do something moral. Perhaps he could hunt down and massacre the corrupt philosophers of the city." Ziesqe's head rolled back and he laughed uproariously. "We'll be doing good, but the thinkers will certainly whip the people into a frenzy against him. We won't have to do a thing, until—Anyone have a guess?"

"We capture him publicly, taking credit for saving the city," Kal said.

"Exactly. And in this way, we can see the laws changed, and move into positions of power on the heels of rescuing the city."

They were pleased with this; even Veloiz had calmed.

"It's genius. The Maelstrom will struggle to hunt us while we're there. We will have cover for as long as it takes," Kal said, standing tall again. "And when we do finally conquer the free city, the Maelstrom will have no choice but to allow us to remain, to preserve the coup. We should be free for decades, allowing us time to contrive another crisis that only we can solve."

The lightning above was sparse and the scape had sunk into a darkness that didn't hinder his eyes. Ziesqe took a long moment to look out over the jungles. *It's not a bad plan; it certainly isn't genius. Though it all depends on him.*

Ziesqe looked over at Andy in his cage. He was sleeping soundly. Ziesqe picked up the Casque and turned it over in his hand. It was still ringing with the echo of the Argument, and it burned to the touch. He considered throwing it overboard.

That catastrophe should never be allowed to happen again.

Ziesqe lifted his arm, paused, and then lowered it.

You never know.

Chapter 10: Sidetracked

"May we know your name and those of your companions?" Fidelio asked.

"Of course. I'm sorry for being rude. I'm Letty. This is Emma and Dean; they are friends from the surface. Neither are Seers, as far as I can tell anyway."

"Thank God," Dean muttered.

"And these two are Quill and Staza, they are my friends from Caspia."

That caused the mice some trepidation.

"Caspia?" Several repeated the name.

"Are you in league with the Viper, my Lady?" Fidelio asked.

Letty looked over at Quill and Staza, who at first only seemed bemused by the whole production, but became increasingly irritated by the stares.

"No," Letty answered cautiously. "I was a guest there for a while. It's dangerous for my friends back at Caspia, so they are with us, for now at least."

"We're seeing this through to the end," Staza said firmly, with a sharp eye for the mice.

"Well—" Fidelio awkwardly changed the subject, "—now that's settled, may we know our destination?"

Letty paused. *What harm could come from telling them? I don't think that they've tricked us.*

She looked over to Quill and Staza. Both folded their arms. *They probably think this is a waste of time.*

"We are headed to Degoskirke. There is another like us. He's with the ryle, but we intend to save him," Letty said.

Fidelio had a glassy-eyed look, as did many of the mice.

"Which way?" Letty asked.

"Oh—" Fidelio sputtered. "I believe that you were headed the right way, but I can't say for certain. None of us have ever left the nor-most part of Pansubprimus, but traders occasionally come through the goblin town of Steustace. We should travel there and see about arranging travel. Perhaps one of the traders would like our services as escorts."

"Steustace?" Dean muttered the name incredulously. "Pansubprimus? Did drunk bankers name your country?"

Fidelio raised a sharp brow Dean's way. "We're ready to travel whenever you are, my Lady."

Letty grabbed her pack, and the others did likewise, before pushing off through the woods and across the stream. The mice slowed them considerably. They had to pause as the thousands used chunks of bark as rafts to ford the river in teams.

"How many mice are in your company?" Quill asked.

"Near six thousand," Fidelio said, "we are the Rex Legion, or were... I'm not certain what we are now."

Quill and Dean had more questions, but Letty found Staza whispering in her ear as they crossed the stream.

"They're slowing us down, Letty."

"You're right, but we can't just tell them to go

back," Letty argued.

"They aren't our responsibility," Staza countered.

Letty wanted to argue but couldn't think of what to say.

"Let's just get on with it then," Staza moaned, seeing Letty's obstinance would not give.

The mice crossed the stream and led them back to the road.

"This way!" Fidelio called out, pointing surward.

After a few hours of silent travel through open and cultivated countryside, they came upon another tower.

"Let us take the lead, my Lady," Fidelio said as he led his mice ahead of the party. "Walk in a straight line if you would," he said, gesturing for the humans to get behind each other.

The mice marched in columns and surrounded the humans. The mouse-sized tower, which was no taller than she was, came closer and closer.

"What if they shoot at us again?" Dean asked nervously.

"Shh!" Fidelio hissed.

"Halloo there! Mice of the Rex, what do you have?" A red mouse with a tall feather in his helm stood on the road outside the tower.

"Warden of the Sur! Fair morning! We have new stock, and the Goldmanes want these ones sold right away. We're headed to Steustace."

"Aye, the Goldmanes don't know decent mounts when they see them."

"No point in that," Fidelio replied. "The war is over. Sentinel's Watch is fallen. Ryle got them in the end, not us. I can't believe you haven't heard."

The warden didn't look pleased to hear the news. "No news out here." He rubbed at his eye. "Well, there will always be another war." He laughed awkwardly, "Maybe we'll get some damned relief here on the border."

"Indeed."

"Ryle got em, you say?" The Warden asked.

"Yes, though we don't know how. I suspect they came from further lantic, through the woods on the coast."

"Well, they must have, otherwise we would've seen them cut around the mountains onto our plains." The warden scoffed. "No ryle army crossed this border. That's for certain."

Fidelio nodded and gave a salute as they passed the tower. "Good day, sir. We'll see you on the return."

The Warden returned the salute and watched as they passed.

They marched in silence for a long time before Fidelio finally spoke, "We should be safe now. Though we won't be able to bluff our way past whatever comes next."

Everyone took a breath and their ranks loosened.

Letty walked back to Staza. "See, they were useful after all."

"You could have sliced that tower in two. Or we could have taken the extra time and stayed off the road to avoid the border guards," Staza said.

There's no pleasing her. Does she hate the mice, or am I being foolish?

Letty sensed that the mice were hearing every whisper. She rolled her eyes and hoped there wouldn't be any trouble.

They marched in silence. Staza and Quill were calm enough, but when Letty heard them whisper to each other, there was something different. Emma and Dean looked like they were in a daze, though Dean twitched at the slightest cough or scrape.

Letty gazed ahead and saw trees thick in the distance. The soft plains gradually gave way to rolling hills.

They crested a hill, and, surmounting the pines, a church spire rose into the sky.

"Steustace!" A mouse called and pointed.

"That's not what I expected," Letty said.

"It looks like a church," Dean commented. "What is a regular old church doing down here?"

"Maybe Seers built it," Letty guessed.

As they went downhill, they lost sight of the spire, but they came upon a sign carved into a standing stone a few minutes later. There had been Latin characters scrawled onto the stone, but they had been covered by claw marks, making the sign illegible.

"Left here," Fidelio said.

Letty turned the Argument around in her palm, wondering about what had made those marks.

The group turned, and after a few bends the road became a steeper path.

"I didn't know there'd be so much hiking," Dean said.

"Feel free to turn around," Letty mumbled.

"Do you hear that?" Fidelio asked, cutting off Dean's reply.

"What?" Letty tried to listen, but could hear nothing.

"Goblins," Fidelio said, his face betraying confusion.

"So, we're on the right path," Letty replied.

"They're wailing, sir," a mouse said to Fidelio, while pulling on his ears.

Minutes later, Letty heard the noise too.

They climbed the last rise and saw hundreds of shabby tents and the local goblins, moping and wailing.

A pair of goblins on guard duty saw them and came running.

Letty grasped the Argument, and even the mice leveled their halberds.

"Humansies and mices! Thank the Gib you've come!"

"Steady on!" Fidelio said.

"What's wrong?" Letty asked.

"Do we really want to know?" Dean grumbled.

"The monster! She's eaten our chiefses! All we has is judge now, and no one likes him! We can't go home! We're stowed in tents, and no traders will come through! It's the end of Steustace!" The guard wailed, and his moaning set off a chain reaction in the hundred goblins who had rushed to see the humans.

"Monster?" Letty asked the others.

Quill and Staza both shrugged.

"You say it ate your chief?" Letty asked.

"Ate's him all up! And not only him!"

"It keeps us up all night, stomping around town, asking tricky questions and eating whoever speaks wrong!"

The goblins set off wailing again.

"Perhaps we should return to the road, my Lady," Fidelio said, alarmed by the manic goblins. "There must be another way."

Letty looked at her friends. None were pleased, barring Emma, who still seemed amazed by everything.

"Fine!" Letty said. "You guys go back to the road—I'm going to try and help them. If I can kill whatever is eating them, I'll catch up."

The goblins heard this and cheered. "Right this way, Misses! I'll open the gate for yous!"

Letty stomped off, surrounded by the suddenly raucous goblins.

"We're here to get Andy! Aren't we?" Dean asked.

"He helped the mice on his way to save me. I can't just walk past; I need to see if we can do anything!" Letty yelled back to them.

She couldn't make out what the goblins were saying in their ceaseless rambling.

As they approached the wall, many goblins broke off from the group. Finally, it was only Letty and the guard with the key. His hand was jittery, and he kept looking over his shoulder.

"What kind of monster is it? Is it a brutox or a ryle?"

"No—no Missus, it's not brutoxy, not squiddy. It's cat lady, gray shiny fur."

What could that be? Gray fur?

The goblin was quaking in its mismatched boots.

"It's fine. Give me the key and I'll go," Letty said.

The goblin handed over the key before turning and running back to the tents.

Goblins...

Letty reached the rickety palisade that surrounded the town. She searched for a place to use the key but saw it was only a wooden gate.

Why the hell did he give me a key?

Letty pushed the gate open and looked inside. Like its wall, Steustace was poorly built.

She stepped inside and saw a clump of silver fur stuck to the gate.

What creature has silver fur, and can talk? Letty's mind flashed with images of talking mice, giant insects, and squid monsters. *Well, anything is possible at this point.*

She walked into town. The contrast between the wood and stone buildings made her sneer.

Look at these rickety goblin buildings sitting around that church. It's so strange.

The slanted roofs and ramshackle walls of the goblin shanties creaked in the soft breeze. The harsh angles of the old stone church drew her eyes upward. A stained-glass window above the doors featured a multicolored Infiniteye.

Seers built this.

She walked to the church and saw a metal plate next to the door.

St. Eustace Abbey.

Letty felt her brow raise. Steustace? She sighed. *Goblins... But you think the mice would know better.*

She went up to the door and turned the latch. The door stuck.

It's locked. Ah—

She tried the key and the latch clicked.

Letty felt suddenly nervous and looked back at the gate.

She took a breath and palmed the Argument. Grasping it brought the glow. She pushed the door open, and looked down the length of the church. Lying at the base of the altar was something large with the frame of a four-legged animal. Its body rose and fell, and she could hear its strong breath from all the way across the church.

The goblin eater.

Letty bent low and inched forward. She kept lower than the well-worn pews.

The beast grumbled a few, half-formed syllables.

It sounds like a woman.

Letty's elbow grazed a pew, causing it to creak slightly.

The creature raised its head and sniffed at the air.

Letty cringed, and slipped down an aisle.

It took long heavy breaths, and almost sounded like it was purring.

Letty peeked around the pew and got a better look. It had the head of a woman and the body of a lion. Heavy wings curled on its flanks. The creature had dead, blank eyes.

Is it looking at me?

The creature yawned and lazily got to its feet. It saw her.

Letty stood sharply and summoned the blade. "Stay back!" she yelled.

"Who is lost?" The creature asked in a slurred accent.

"What?" Letty replied, afraid and confused.

"A truth blooms into tomorrow. A fallacy sleeps behind my teeth. Which will you be?"

What is she saying? Are these riddles? She sounds like the Greek lady from next door.

"Who is lost?" the creature asked.

Me? No, I'm not lost. Is it metaphorical? Are we all lost? No, that's stupid. Maybe she's lost. The goblins want her gone, but she stays.

"You. Are you lost?"

The creature stepped forward, her eyes hungry for more.

It's a sphinx!

"A sphinx is lost!" Letty burst out.

The creature stopped and sat. She looked almost sad.

"How are you lost? This isn't your home?"

The creature looked up through the damaged ceiling. "The paths have broken. Eyes are dim to signs."

Maybe she means the ceiling. It's been going crazy since

Sentinel's Watch fell.

"A Seer's oath to timeless keepers stands to this day?"

What does she want me to say?

Letty paused, and the sphinx stood, loping slowly her way.

"The oath to Voice and God lives in your blood?"

Her paw tensed and revealed claws.

Oh no! I don't know what she wants me to say!

The sphinx came closer and bared her teeth.

Letty raised her blade and swung. "I'm sorry!" She cried.

The blade passed right over the creature's frame, as if it was nothing but light. Letty gasped and stumbled backwards, keeping distance between her and the sphinx, who was moving faster and faster.

"The Voice, it moves scornfully," the sphinx stopped and looked to the ground.

"I'll help you. Just stop eating people," Letty said.

The sphinx raised her head. "A deal," she said, coming still closer.

Oh God. She braced for the worst, but saw that the sphinx's claws had retracted.

Letty stood still as she moved to within an inch of her face. She could hear the sphinx purring. She rubbed her cheek against Letty's.

She's huge.

The sphinx pushed past her, like an annoyed cat, and opened the church door with a paw.

Letty followed, and they stepped outside.

Wait, did the goblins have her locked in here? Maybe

they expected me to kill her.

Dean yelled, as he stumbled back into the gate. Emma looked just as scared, but kept her footing as she backed away.

"What is that thing?" Staza yelled, drawing her sword.

"It's a sphinx!" Letty called out to them.

Dean stared at them from behind the gate. "Did you answer its riddle?"

"I think so," Letty said. "We need to help her on her way."

"Where is it going?" Quill asked.

"I'm still working on that," Letty replied. "Stay back. I'm going to ask her a question. Be careful, because my blade won't hurt her."

"What?" Quill asked, surprised.

"The blade went right through her, as if she wasn't there," Letty replied.

The sphinx stared for a long time at each face. "The Voice gave many shapes to its servants," she finally spoke. "How could they harm each other?"

"What does that mean?" Dean asked.

"I think she's saying that she's made of the same stuff as your Argument, Letty. That's why you can't hurt her," Staza reasoned.

"That makes sense," Quill agreed. "But why haven't we ever heard of a crea—"

"Ah! A sphinx," Fidelio announced excitedly.

Letty saw the sphinx's eyes raise as the mice came through the gate.

"Don't eat them either, please!" Letty begged, stepping between them.

"Eat us?" Fidelio said, surprised, "We're natural allies! At least according to the stories."

The sphinx approached the mice and pawed at Fidelio, who backed away, while keeping a smile plastered to his face.

"Shamed converts, these," the sphinx said plainly.

"Fidelio, do you know where the sphinx needs to go?" Letty asked.

Fidelio looked up at the creature nervously, despite his earlier excitement. "A pair of sphinxes guard an ancient temple on the sur side of the Cyclo Mountains, not far from here."

Letty smiled and said, "That's lucky, if she just wants to go home—"

Quill interrupted. "Fidelio, how do you know that? The part about there being sphinxes in the mountains, I mean."

Letty didn't appreciate the interruption, though she felt it was justified.

"Well," Fidelio cleared his throat, "my grandfather patrolled the foothills around the mountains. He told us they followed uncertain animals and twice came upon a hidden temple carved in the rock. They went inside, and found creatures with the heads of women and the bodies of lions—he didn't mention the wings though. The sphinxes asked them questions, but they ran both times. They knew that if you failed to answer the question, the consequence was becoming dinner."

"Detailed story," Dean said, looking at the others. "Sounds like he's telling the truth, as far as he knows. But how did this happen in the first place? What is she doing down here?"

"As far as I know!" Fidelio blustered.

Letty ignored the mouse and said, "She must have left for some reason." She stared questioningly at the sphinx.

The sphinx looked up at them with a grin on her face. She pawed at Fidelio, who put a friendly expression on, though he was plainly quivering.

"I don't know why she left, but I think the ceiling going crazy," Letty pointed upwards, "confused her. She was lost and came here by accident."

"What do we do with her?" Staza asked.

"Well, that's clear; we take her home." Letty said. "It can't be far."

"That's not what I mean. The problem is that the goblins aren't going to be happy if we just walk out of here with that creature. They'll want revenge," Staza said.

Letty shook her head. "I don't know, they might just be grateful if we get rid of her."

They stood there for a few minutes, everyone silently thinking of a plan. Letty was continually distracted as the sphinx played with the mice. Dozens of them had overcome their fear and climbed onto her. She was gentle with them.

"Wait. Let's get all the mice on her, and just pretend like she's been subdued," Letty said.

There were a few incredulous looks.

"Well, I can't think of anything besides covering her in a sheet," Dean said, "I say we go with Letty's idea."

After piling the sphinx high with hundreds of armed mice, they approached the gate.

"Maybe the goblins will help us get to Degoskirke, after we get her out of here," Staza said.

"That's the best plan we have right now. They might know a safe way across the ryle lands," Quill agreed.

"It might not work if they know we befriended the sphinx, so everyone: weapons up, and act like she might kill us," Letty commanded as they opened the gate.

"What if she doesn't go along with the plan?" Staza asked.

They all stared at the sphinx for a sign of her intentions.

The sphinx gave them an inscrutable, almost sarcastically blank expression.

"We'll just have to find out," Quill said.

They walked the sphinx out of the town, but the goblins were still some distance from the gate.

"Which way, Fidelio?" Letty asked.

Fidelio, who was sitting happily on the sphinx's shoulder, pointed back through the goblin camp. "We need to go back the way we came and turn lanticward. The way isn't marked, and it might take us some time to find."

Everyone, save Emma, scowled at the news, but before anyone could voice a grievance, the goblins spotted them.

"They gots it!" A shrill voice called out.

The goblin guards tried to keep the civilians away, but they rushed headlong towards the sphinx, who growled and bared her teeth, causing the crowd to bolt again.

"It looks like she's going along with the plan, unless she's just being herself," Letty whispered.

"Stay back!" Quill and Staza both pushed curious goblins away.

"Do you want to get eaten?" Emma asked a few curious green faces.

A bold goblin yanked on the sphinx's tail, which elicited an overwhelming roar. The sphinx bucked the mice off and turned around to swipe at the goblin, who tumbled away, lost its footing, and rolled a dozen times before landing on its face.

The mice all scrambled to climb back on, but the roar was enough to send even the goblin guards running for their tents.

After they passed through the camp, Letty looked back at the few pointy faces peeking out of tent flaps at them. "We'll be back! But you can go inside your town now! It's safe!"

After they had gone some ways down the road, they saw the goblins packing up their tents.

"Why did you go there anyway?" Staza asked the sphinx, who looked at her with a calm face.

"Priests once. They could see, and would share the Voice," she said.

"What do you mean? Share the Voice—how is that possible?" Dean asked.

The creature ignored him.

"I think she means that whoever lived at that church once helped her with a piece of the Argument," Letty said, holding out her own piece to show everyone.

The Sphinx eyed the marble hungrily, and even leaned towards it.

"Careful, Letty," Quill said.

Letty hid the Argument and asked, "What is your name, sphinx?"

The creature looked from Letty's pocket up to her eyes. "Aleta."

They loped along the road and turned right at Fidelio's direction. "I think this is the way," he pronounced hopefully.

"Aleta, how long have you been out here?" Letty asked.

Aleta gave her a curious look but remained silent.

"Don't upset her," Dean whispered.

Emma came up to Letty, who was considering another question, and nudged her. "I'm hungry, Letty. Can we stop for lunch?"

"It is about time," Quill said.

Letty nodded. *Everyone's treating me like I'm in charge.*

"Fine, let's stop to eat."

The march came to a halt, and they sat beside the road. The mice set up watches in the trees and Aleta lay against a mossy trunk. She spoke in verse and told stories to the mice.

With her paw upturned and full of attentive mice, she spoke, "Thrice ten and century plied— have these eyes lidless been—watchful against the sunless sky—of my sunken climb. In that time, I have supped on flesh and the tender breast of

271

nightmare beasts and once on a sigh-filled yes.
There there, glassy, mousy eyes, tremble less, for
filled of you, am I."

Letty was listening but felt a tug at her shoulder.

"What if we can't find her a way home?" It was
Staza. "The others aren't happy about this."

"I know," Letty whined. She followed Staza and
approached the group. They all looked up from their
packaged food.

"So?" Quill asked Staza.

"Look," Letty said sternly. "I don't know why I
feel the way I do, but I'm certain that helping Aleta
is important. But I understand why you don't agree,
so I'll make you all a deal: If we don't find anything
in a few hours, we'll send her on her way with the
best advice Fidelio has, and then get back on the
road."

Her friends shared a look, and a moment later
they nodded in agreement.

"It wasn't a waste of time either," Quill said.
"Now the goblins are indebted to us, and maybe
Aleta will help, if we find the way to her temple."

Emma held out a protein bar and asked, "Will
you come and sit with us?"

Letty felt her guard lowering. She sat between
Emma and Dean.

"So, Andy's caught up in all this," Dean said.
"Every time I blink, I feel like I should wake up, but
each time I open my eyes it's all still there."

"It's funny," Staza quipped, "I felt the same way
on the surface."

Quill huffed a sound of agreement. "How

can you stand it up there? The noise, and endless people everywhere you look." He rolled his eyes at the recollection, and Staza nodded. "The food was superb though; I'll give you that."

"And the supplies," Staza added. "The stitching on everything is inhumanly precise." She held up a pack and pointed at the sewing.

Letty laughed. "I knew you guys felt that way; you did a good job of keeping calm though. And Staza, the stitching was done with a sewing machine. Maybe we can get one for Caspia."

"Sewing machine?" Staza mumbled, half in disbelief.

They were silent. Emma and Dean looked at Letty for an explanation.

This probably isn't the best time to tell them about Pythia. I have nothing nice to say.

"I'll never get over cars," Quill said, distracted. "You don't have to feed them."

"Well, that's not exactly true," Dean said. "They eat, in their own way."

"I still can't imagine how you live with it," Staza said.

"Cars?" Dean asked.

"No," Staza replied quietly. "I saw so many people on the surface." She paused, searching for the right words, "It was crushing. You probably won't understand, but—I know that I'm someone down here. I can't explain it. Down here, there is no one else like me. I have value and purpose in Caspia, and so does everyone else. I might be one of the best fighters, and that means people look at me with appreciation, like I do for them. But on the surface," she shivered at the memory, "I was nobody to thousands, and I can't remember a single one of their faces. How can you live like that? You have no—" she struggled for words.

"Community," Quill added, and Staza nodded.

The surfacers were silent. Letty wasn't sure if Staza was wrong.

"Well, let's get back to it," Fidelio said loudly, breaking in on their flagging conversation.

The humans took the chance to leave the awkwardness behind. Everyone stood; the bags were packed and shouldered in minutes.

"I say we just keep on this way. Eyes sharp, everyone; we don't want to miss a clue," Fidelio said, after accepting a place on Aleta's well-muscled shoulder.

The woods thickened as they continued, and eventually the road gave way to several trails. Letty allowed Fidelio to lead the way, while she kept an eye out.

In a flash Aleta roared and bolted towards a tree, Fidelio flying off her shoulder and the other mice ducking for cover. She climbed up the tree in a few bounds and swiped at a large blue and green bird.

The bird released a shrill cry and took off, barely dodging Aleta's claws.

"Shame," Aleta said, landing softly on her paws and following the bird as it went. "They were made for me."

Letty saw Aleta licking her lips as the bird

twirled and raced through the branches. A chorus of other birds picked up the call. Letty spotted four or five circling their group for a moment, and then they all flew off in the same direction.

"I think we should follow those birds," Letty said.

Dean rolled his eyes. "Why should we follow the economy-sized peacocks?"

Letty wanted to answer, but instead watched Aleta's eyes as she tracked the birds. A moment later, her feline limbs pressed up and down, she arched her back, and her claws made indents in the earth.

She wants to chase them.

"Guys—" Letty stumbled back as Aleta bounded away from the group and after the birds. "Follow her!" Letty yelled, regaining her balance.

Letty ran a few steps after her. *The mice! They can't keep up, can they?*

Letty looked back at Fidelio.

"Just go! We'll follow your tracks," he said, shooing her onward.

Letty turned and ran. Quill and Staza were strong runners, and could have left her behind, but they stayed by her side. Emma and Dean flagged from the outset.

A few minutes later they had lost sight of both Aleta and the mice. Letty slowed to a stop. She was breathing heavily and hunched over. Emma and Dean caught up.

"We lost her!" Dean complained. "Nothing to do now but go back and try to find the mice."

275

"He's right, Letty," Emma said, also gasping for breath.

"No, the sphinx left a trail," Staza said, pointing out a broken branch. "We could follow her for miles."

"Will you lead the way, please?" Letty asked.

Staza did, pointing out crushed leaves and damaged shrubs as they went.

"Well, at least we don't have to worry about missing P.E.; we should be in top shape when we get back," Dean said.

"Yeah," Emma agreed, still out of breath, "I never expected to be running through the woods with a backpack on. I mean, forget the mice, goblins, and sphinx, this alone is weird enough."

Letty wanted to join in, but she was focused on Staza, who followed Aleta's serpentine trail so expertly that they never slowed.

"What's P.E.?" Quill asked, leaving the tracking to Staza.

"It's the easiest class," Emma said.

"Speak for yourself. The locker room—and showering—what a nightmare," Dean insisted.

"Letty, are we going in circles?" Emma asked.

"No, and if you guys paid attention, you might realize that," Letty snapped, annoyed at her friends.

"Sorry," Emma whispered, half apologetic, and half hurt.

A moment later Staza spoke to Letty as if continuing a conversation, though her eyes stayed on the ground. "You don't belong up there after all. They're too soft for you—that whole earth full of grown toddlers. I'm afraid your friends will infect Quill. He's already a soft heart."

"What was that?" Quill asked, breaking off a conversation about classes with Emma and Dean.

"You're soft, like the surfacers," Staza replied.

"I certainly am not!"

"Wait! Be quiet," Letty said, hearing something. They all listened.

There's noise. What is it?

"Water," Emma said.

Letty looked at her, surprised.

It is water.

"This way—the tracks are headed towards it," Staza said, picking up her pace.

The sound of rushing water intensified. They broke out through the trees and onto a rocky shore surrounding a stone filled-pool beneath a waterfall. The moss on the rocks was slick, and Letty nearly slipped as those behind pushed through the branches.

"Slowly!" Staza yelled over the water, "Don't push!"

Letty looked up and saw hundreds of blue and green birds swirling around the rocky waterfall. They nested in the trees all over, and their cries only added to the noise.

Atop a pile of slick rocks lay Aleta, the fringes of her mouth stained red. Her tail lolled lazily, and she looked up at them.

Dean and Emma balked and descended back behind the wall of foliage.

Even Staza and Quill found the bloodied sphinx

unnerving. They raised their weapons as if by instinct.

"I hate to sound like the surfacers, Letty, but is this the best plan?" Quill asked.

I'm not sure.

Letty felt herself relenting.

There's no point wasting more time. I don't even know what I expected.

As Letty was about to turn away, she spotted a blur of bright colors on the periphery. She examined it, but felt her eyes tensing as she stared.

It's a bird, but it's so bright, it's like looking at a flood light.

"Do you see that?" Letty asked, pointing at the bright bird, which now sat upon a rock.

"Birds, Letty," Staza said, "though that glare." She raised a hand to cover her eyes.

"No, there's something else." Quill said, also spotting the colors. "What is it?"

"I think it's one of the birds," Letty replied, watching its outline move and preen unlike any of others.

"But how does it shine like that?" Staza asked.

Letty saw Aleta rise and cast a glance at the pack of birds nearby.

"No!" Letty yelled, "Don't eat that one!"

Heedless, Aleta pounced and the flock burst into the air.

"Damn! I lost it!" Staza said, holding a hand over her eyes as hundreds and then thousands of them took wing and circled through the air.

Letty was buffeted by dozens of flapping wings

as the birds in nearby nests joined the others.

Letty's eyes went wild trying to spot the one special bird, but each glistened as it coursed through the air.

"There!" Quill cried out, spotting it.

In a flash, the cyclone of birds stopped spinning. The mass broke apart into thousands of single birds traveling in their own directions.

No two are going the same way.

Letty rushed out onto the slick rocks, keeping her eyes up and on the blur.

"Letty!" Staza called after her.

Letty heard someone slip and crash onto the rocks, but she refused to look back.

She passed into the cover of the trees again. Her face stung from the branches snapping as she rushed.

There!

The blur sat for a moment high among the branches, before taking off as she came into sight.

"Do you see?" A voice asked, startling her.

"Oh God!" Letty sprung away from the sudden presence.

It's just Aleta.

"You scared the hell out of me," Letty said, her eyes back on the canopy.

"Do you see what I cannot?" Aleta asked again.

"Maybe, I spotted a bird unlike the others," she said.

"My beacon," Aleta mused, not winded in the least by all the bounding.

"Hopefully the others are okay; I think one

might have fallen into the water. They'll catch up," Letty said, chasing after the blur.

"This path is here and now," Aleta said cautiously, though Letty didn't understand.

"Staza followed your trail to the waterfall, she can do it again."

They continued after the bird. Letty realized that rushing towards the creature only scared it into immediate flight again, so she paced herself, and tried to catch her breath. Aleta strained under their slow pace. They gave chase this way for some time, until Letty finally lost the bird behind another screen of branches.

She and Aleta pushed through a wall of shrubs and found themselves just past the edge of the forest. The land ahead was steep and rocky. Letty scanned the horizon.

"Does that one shine?" Aleta asked, pointing with a paw at a pile of boulders.

Yes, it does.

The bird had alighted on a rock and looked their way. It flexed its wings before taking off again.

Letty scowled at the rugged hillside. There was no easy way up. She took a breath and climbed a rock. Even from a higher vantage she couldn't spot a route forward that didn't involve leaping from one boulder to the next.

"Well, here goes," she muttered.

She bent her knees and leaped, landing firmly on the neighboring boulder before looking for the next leap.

"This isn't a good idea," Letty murmured as she

jumped again. "They won't be able to track us over the rocks."

She looked back for Aleta but couldn't see her.

"Aleta! Don't go far, please!" she called out.

Letty jumped again and continued looking for the bird. She couldn't spot it either.

She moved to the next rock, and heard a clatter, as of stones tumbling. Her immediate urge was to crouch, but her footing was stable. She looked around but couldn't see what made the noise.

Lost the bird, and the sphinx, and my friends, and the mice. Now I'm leaping over pits like an idiot with no idea where to go.

Letty landed on a tall, jutting boulder. Every way forward, and even the ways back now all seemed too far to span in one jump.

But I made it when I came from that way.

Letty tried to convince herself to leap back, but her mind told her it was too far.

"This was a terrible idea," she said.

The thick forest was farther back than she expected. Desperate, she looked down into the pit.

Maybe I can get down and climb back up somewhere else.

The pit looked to be about ten feet deep.

Too deep.

Her heart beat faster. She rushed to the other side of her boulder.

"That's a fool's way," Aleta said, looking up at her with a vexed expression.

Aleta! She's here!

Letty stared wide-eyed at the sphinx. She was

speechless for a moment, before finally asking, "There's a better way?"

"These are my grounds," Aleta said, trotting between the boulders.

Letty climbed down the side and slipped the last few feet to the ground.

There are paths down here! I couldn't see them from above.

She bent low and followed Aleta, who had the advantage in this terrain. Letty had to crawl underneath a low passage. Aleta paused impatiently, her tail patting the ground.

"I'm sorry; I wasn't made to crawl under boulders," Letty complained as she caught up. Aleta huffed before moving on.

Letty skinned her knees as she rushed, but she refused to slow down for fear of losing Aleta again. She passed under another boulder and stood to stretch her back. She groaned in pain, and Aleta gave her an angry scowl before looking up at a boulder.

The bird!

The shimmering bird that had led them was sitting on the rock and idly fussing with its feathers. Aleta had spotted it and was bent low, as if ready to pounce.

She made a powerful leap, and with her clawed paws bounded up the side of the boulder and swiped at the bird, who was off in a blur, cawing angrily.

Aleta landed heavily back in the pit, her eyes craned skyward after the complaining bird. "I return with nothing," she said under her breath, before moving on.

I saw her eat not too long ago. She remembered Aleta tearing a swathe through the flock of birds.

Letty followed and took a turn under the next boulder. She gasped when the raw stone gave way to hewn walls and stairs.

Letty wanted to stop and look at the carved images on the walls, but Aleta was getting further ahead. Despite the haste, Letty noticed that several carved figures had their hands raised to their eyes, as if they were inspecting something.

Letty took the stairs, which looked especially worn, as if Aleta had gone up and down that exact way so often that it had worn the stairs smooth.

How long has she been here? How often has she gone in and out of this place?

Letty climbed and climbed until the stairwell opened onto a high promontory that overlooked the rugged hills and forest beneath. A carved bench overlooked the view; she gratefully sat to catch her breath.

Looking over her shoulder, Letty saw a wide ravine separate her promontory from another cliff face. The far side looked to be right out of a history textbook. It struck her as an ancient temple, carved into the rock. Stairs led to a smooth wall preceded by plain columns. An obelisk, made from black stone, stood before the temple, offset from the path and ringed by flagstone circles. There were markings all over the obelisk, but they were too far away to see in any detail.

"That's it! We're here!" Letty said.

Aleta walked by, her tail wagging in impatience.

"Almost," she said, bent low with her wings flexing.

The wings were a good size, yet they seemed too small for Aleta's heavy frame.

"What are you—" Letty nearly fell off her bench in surprise as Aleta bounded forward, her wings spread wide.

Aleta leaped across the ravine to the other side, her wings flapping madly.

"What am I supposed to do?" Letty yelled across the distance.

Aleta raced up the stairs and into the temple. A moment later Letty heard strange rumbling growls echo from inside.

"Aleta! I don't know how to get across!"

Letty stood and approached the edge. The distance was much farther than she could leap.

Maybe she'll come back out. But what was that sound? Is it safe here?

She waited, ready to run at the first sign of danger, but nothing happened. Aleta did not return.

Letty felt tricked. *I got her here, and now she won't even help me across. I wasted everyone's time, and now I don't even know where they are.*

She looked back to the promontory and down to the forest. *They're lost in there, trying to find me, and I chased the lion woman.*

Letty sighed, and turned to go, but stopped in her tracks.

The bird was standing squarely in her path. It stared at her quizzically.

"Yes, you led me here too, thanks for that," Letty said, irritated.

The bird chirped and hopped. It walked back towards the stairs that Letty had taken up to the promontory. It looked over its shoulder at her and hopped again.

Letty sighed and followed the bird, who led her back to the hallway full of carved images. The bird hopped down the stairs sideways.

Poor bird wasn't made for stairs. I think it's trying to help me... that or it's one more waste of time, when I should be finding Andy.

The bird hopped up to a carving on a wall and waved a wing.

Letty approached and saw the carving was much like the others, featuring a woman in plain robes holding a stylized eye with long eyelashes up above her face. She was inspecting the eye.

What does this have to do with anything? It looks like an older version of the Infiniteye.

The bird hopped and chirped.

Letty reached out and touched the carving, looking for hidden switches or panels.

The bird flapped.

"No, that's not it." Letty said.

The bird used its talons and beak to climb up Letty's pants.

"What—hello, yes, why don't you get back down—off please!" Letty stammered, increasingly skittish at its disregard for personal space.

It cawed and snapped at her fingers when she tried to brush it away. Using its beak, it tapped at her pocket. It was tapping against the Argument.

"What, this?" Letty produced the Argument.

The bird hopped down, flapped its wings, and chirped wildly.

"What do you want with the Argument?" Letty asked.

The bird flew up to the carving, and then back to the ground. The motion was exasperated and wholly unnatural. Letty suddenly felt like she was standing at the whiteboard, lost for an answer, while the classroom chuckled.

It must be so obvious.

Letty stared at the carving.

Maybe.

She held the Argument up to her eye.

There was a rush of sound. She closed her palm and found that the Argument wasn't there.

"What's happening to me?" she called out, not hearing her own voice.

She looked at the bird and saw a bird-shaped wireframe instead. A glowing silver core blossomed with light from its center.

Letty stumbled backwards. The movement filled her with a sense of vertigo. She was screaming, but she could only hear a dull roar of overwhelming white-noise, like a million voices speaking at once. She struggled to breathe.

"Calm," a voice sounded in her mind.

She looked over and saw the wireframe bird standing closer.

"What's happening? I don't understand!"

The bird shrank away from what Letty knew

was her loudest volume, though she still couldn't hear herself.

"Focus, calm," the voice repeated.

Letty lay there for a long time before she felt the noise subside. The bird stayed by her side, silently watching.

What's happening to me?

Letty looked at the bird and felt a calmness.

She remembered the Argument disappearing from her grasp. *That's what the carving was showing. It does something to you. This was supposed to happen.*

With that conclusion firmly in mind, Letty stood and immediately felt her head spin. She took a breath and leaned against the wall.

The bird hopped ahead and mounted the stairs.

"We're going back up?" Letty asked, barely hearing her own voice.

The bird, looking almost like a skeleton surrounding a star, looked her way and then continued.

Letty followed along, keeping a hand against the wireframe wall for balance. It took ages, but finally they came out onto the promontory again.

With terror she took in the world all around. It was too much.

The sky seemed to scream at her with a thousand flashing voices, each yelling over the other. Every strange surface, and even blank space, was infused with text. Bands of millions of letters and numbers were insistently present in the forefront of her mind, but each only for a moment as her eyes arced across the ceiling. One color and band of writing violently gave way to the next. Letty clasped her hands over her ears, but that did nothing.

"It won't stop!" She yelled in horror as her eyes retreated across the horizon, looking for something less loud to rest on.

She shut her eyes but could still see through her eyelids. She covered them with her hands, but saw through those as well. The wireframes of her arms and hands were interlaced with a glowing silver cord that pulsed with what she thought was her heartbeat.

Terrified, she shrunk down and grasped her knees, sinking her eyes as close to the ground as she could. She felt herself slide down the stairs, but was too afraid to reach out and slow her fall. She slipped down a few more stairs, her eyes locked to the comparatively normal floor.

She was gasping and crying but couldn't hear herself.

"Calm," the voice sounded in her mind. She just now heard it, but somehow felt like it had been speaking for a while.

Letty lay there shaking.

"Calm."

This is awful.

"Calm."

Finally, sore from being still for too long, she dared to roll over. She didn't know how much time had passed, but the noises had quieted, and she no longer felt overwhelmed.

She found herself relaxing when she regarded

the bird, who was still nearby, waiting. Letty pulled herself into a sitting position and dared to look up, an inch at a time.

For a moment, she felt embarrassed at the thought of herself lying on the floor and crying at the sky.

I'm glad no one was around for this. But how do I go back to normal, or am I going to be like this for the rest of my life? Why did the bird do this to me?

"What now?" Letty asked the bird, confident that she could stand and walk again, though looking up was still too much.

The bird hopped towards the ravine. Letty followed, careful not to look at the terrible ceiling. A moment later, she dared to raise her glance a hair. She saw a glowing bridge spanning the gulf.

I couldn't see it before.

The bridge was made of stone blocks as far as she could tell. Its glow made it difficult to see much detail, though it plainly had no guard rail.

Maybe it wasn't there before.

The bird stood by the phantom bridge and looked her way.

Letty stepped closer. She got to her knees and carefully reached out, touching the glowing stone.

It's solid.

She got back to her feet.

Why didn't Aleta take the bridge then? She's been here forever.

The bird rustled its feathers and cocked its head toward the temple entrance.

Aleta didn't know which bird to follow either. She isn't

a Seer.

As much as she wanted to head back to her friends, Letty kept going.

She took another breath and stepped onto the bridge. It supported her. She took another step and was standing over empty space.

It wouldn't be so bad if everything weren't trying to scream at me.

Letty felt her nerves get the better of her. The voices grew louder. Her eyes focused randomly on strings of words in the bridge or cliff side below. Those strings of words inflated to massive size in her vision.

No, not again!

She felt her legs shaking as she took another step. She got down to her knees, afraid to go further as the voices grew louder.

"Calm, focus," the voice returned to her.

Yes, calm. I need to be calm and focus.

"Breathe."

Letty focused on her breathing.

Calm. Breathe. Focus.

After a minute, she realized that the voices had quieted, and her vision had stopped snapping onto things of its own will.

Calm.

She stood and took another step. A moment later, she was across, though her legs were shaking. She breathed a heavy sigh of relief, and immediately regretted it.

"Flesh!" Came an echoing voice.

Letty felt the earth rumble and saw a glowing

red blur flash out of the temple and lunge for the bird. The wireframe sphinx was red at its core and glowing like a dull flame.

"No! Aleta, stop it!"

The bird flapped away. A hair slower and it would have been taken by the sphinx's claw. Aleta growled and turned on Letty, snarling and bending low to pounce.

"Stay back!" Letty felt an unexpected fury erupt from within, her palm tensed and she saw a vision of the blade in her grasp. A rushing burst of sound accompanied as her sight returned to normal. The Argument had rushed from her eyes down her arm.

The glowing silver blade flickered from her right hand. She held it just shy of the sphinx's face.

"That's enough! I'm sick of you!" Letty yelled.

Aleta, who looked far thinner than she had a moment ago, also had a new sickly pallor to her skin. She shied away from the blade.

Wait, this won't work. I swung the blade at her before and it just passed through.

Letty felt suddenly nervous, but kept the blade up, as it deterred the sphinx regardless.

What happened to her? She looks different.

The sphinx still displayed the urge to attack, though there was something else. She growled but bowed low and backed away.

"Aleta?" Letty asked.

As if prompted by something unseen, the sphinx turned and raced to the ravine before leaping and flapping across. She bounded to the stairs and disappeared.

"What the hell was that about?" Letty asked, loosening her grip on the Argument.

She heard a caw and looked up at the obelisk. Her bird had alighted at the pinnacle and was looking at the temple entrance.

Letty shrieked in fright as Aleta reappeared from the temple door.

"How?" Letty stammered, looking back to where the sphinx had been a moment ago.

Aleta looked like herself again.

There are two. Letty realized. *I was attacked by the second, who I hadn't met before.*

"My sister was starving," Aleta said, looking longingly off towards the forest.

Letty cringed, realizing how close she had come to a violent end at the claws of a hungry sphinx.

There was a slight gust of wind, and Letty heard a faint flapping sound. It wasn't the bird, who still sat placid. Letty saw the edge of a piece of parchment flapping against the back of one of the columns.

Letty approached, but stopped as Aleta made an aggressive move towards the temple door. Letty stepped back and looked at the sphinx, who was now eying her dangerously.

Now she's acting more like a sphinx. Am I going to hear the riddle? I need to get a look at the paper, it might be important.

Letty moved carefully towards the column, keeping her focus on the sphinx.

She reached for the parchment and gave it a slight tug. It stuck.

She edged forward, but this time Aleta growled and lunged.

Letty dashed to the far side of the column and saw the parchment was held in place by a dagger. In a rush, she ripped it away and bolted back towards the ravine.

Aleta followed for a few paces, growled, and then returned to mount one of a pair of plinths that flanked the entrance.

Letty stood tense and ready to run, but when Aleta let her head rest on a lazy paw, she knew the danger had passed. She looked at the parchment, which now had a large tear running through it.

"Acolyte—heed this warning. Typha is a man-eater. Brother Aelinga has just learned this lesson, and most brutally. Wait in the hall for me to return before attempting to enter the Serapeum. If you must enter, don't forget to clear any Axiom nearby, not only your own. I should be back from the Abbey shortly," Letty raised a brow as she finished reading aloud.

I know Aleta isn't afraid of eating goblins, if she's anything like her sister. And what's this about clearing Axioms?

Confused, Letty put the parchment in her pocket.

Letty stepped forward. As if sensing her presence, Aleta's head shot up and her posture tensed.

"Do you have a question for me, Aleta?" Letty asked.

Aleta grinned. "How can one enter so armed?"

"That doesn't sound like a riddle. Aren't you supposed to ask me a trick question about aging or holes in buckets?"

Aleta was silent.

Maybe it is a riddle.

Letty stared at the old message again, but nothing jumped out at her.

How can one enter so armed?

Letty felt for her backpack, but realized that she had either lost it or taken it off long ago.

I don't have that pistol on me. Maybe she means the Argument. Is that what the message is referring to? An Axiom?

Letty approached the obelisk and set her Argument down on the ground. She didn't like leaving it and now felt unarmed.

Scowling, she carefully returned to Aleta, watchful for any aggression. Aleta sat up and bared her teeth.

No? I was sure that was it.

"I'm unarmed, Aleta. That's what you meant, right? How can one enter..." frustrated, Letty trailed off and read the message again.

'Clear any Axiom nearby, not only your own.'

Letty looked around.

I don't see anything else. Wait...

Letty walked behind the columns and looked on the ground.

Sitting behind a column, not far from where she had grabbed the parchment, was a small purple orb.

That's it. She can sense it nearby and assumes that I'm armed with it. Thank God for this message; I would never have known.

She read the last sentence again. *'I should be back from the Abbey shortly.' He never came back, or someone would have taken this down.*

Letty looked up at Aleta. "Did you eat someone from the Abbey? Maybe a few centuries ago," Letty asked, dreading the answer.

Aleta was silent.

Letty looked back to the purple orb. *What to do with this piece of Counter-Argument? Maybe if I—* she reached out with a foot and tapped the orb.

A heavy and lingering jolt shot through her on contact with the orb. Despite the pain, her tap had knocked the orb a few feet further from Aleta.

Letty took deep a breath and let the pain wash over her until it finally subsided.

Is it far enough now? Letty glanced at the sphinx. *Probably not.*

She took a deep breath and kicked the orb toward the ravine. It rolled heavily towards the gap and silently plummeted in.

Letty felt like she had kicked an electrified block of steel. She stumbled back into a column, and slipped to the ground. Her leg was numb. "There! Are you happy now?"

Letty groaned, hopped back onto one foot, and carefully put pressure on her leg. Irritated, she limped towards the entrance. "And I bet there's nothing in here but a mountain of hairballs."

Aleta looked at her quizzically and spoke, "How can one enter so armed?"

"One can't! And one is not!" Letty yelled,

storming past Aleta's plinth.

She isn't going to pounce, is she?

Letty clenched her teeth as she passed.

Nothing happened.

Once inside, she stopped in her tracks.

Well, maybe that explains where the purple orb came from.

The wide entry way was lined with piles of bones and brutox husks. Ancient weapons and armor lay in haphazard piles. There were also two distinct nests made with what looked like cat fur and the softer linings salvaged off the collection of armor.

It's their bedroom.

Looking closer, Letty saw chew marks on countless bones. There were also a few skulls that didn't look human. They were elongated and malformed at the jaw.

Ryle.

Grateful that she wouldn't be joining the pile anytime soon, Letty continued, pausing to glance at a message written in pictographs on the wall above the door.

She was grateful for the burning sconces evenly spaced on the walls.

I wonder who keeps them lit? Or have they been burning forever?

She entered a wide and spacious chamber. The tables and tall rows of shelves had a look of ancient design, though not for any fault in their make, but for the simplicity of their shape. As her eyes adjusted to the space, Letty realized she was in a library.

I don't have the time to go through all this.

She approached a stone table covered with scrolls and wooden scroll containers. She stopped at one and saw more of the same pictographs.

Scrolls instead of books, and they're all full of hieroglyphics.

She approached another and saw several symbols from math classes that were a few grades ahead of her.

I think that's Greek.

She walked to another table and saw more of the same.

No! All of it's in other languages!

She paused as something caught her attention.

A book!

The odd book in a roomful of scrolls seemed important.

She rushed to the other table and carefully picked up the lone book, which, despite looking familiar in a room full of scrolls, also looked to be many centuries old. The cover featured a shining Infiniteye above a few words.

Vivere per hoc signum.

"Latin!" Letty yelled in frustration.

She nearly threw the book across the room.

"All this for nothing!"

She took a breath, kept herself from kicking the table, and then opened the book.

Latin on every page.

She paused at an illustration. It featured a character holding the Infiniteye up to her eye. The

297

next page featured a detailed drawing of what it was like to have the Argument inside one's mind.

It would have been nice to have this, in English, when I had to do it.

Letty read the title of that section. *Argentum Conspectu.*

She turned ahead in the book and saw illustrations of the orbs, and of characters wielding blades of light, along with other confusing diagrams.

This book is important. This is what I needed to find!

Letty took the book, which was heavier than she expected, and rushed to the exit.

She stopped in her tracks as Aleta blocked the way.

"Step aside, Aleta," Letty commanded.

Aleta shook her head and pointed at the symbols above the doorway. "Take learning, leave the words."

Letty nearly rushed past, but stopped herself and looked down at the pile of bones, husks, and abandoned weapons.

Chapter 11: Chimerax

Akri, the giant raven, perched atop a window cornice on the Weaver's Spire, listening to the tinkle of silverware floating on the air.

Damn this city and its spires.

Akri ruffled his feathers and cawed, before hopping down to a rail that rung the tower. His large black eyes blinked as he stared down onto the City in the Sea, a gleaming ryle capitol, nestled in a pocket between the scapes of Pansubprimus and Euboia.

Countless slender towers and turrets jutted from the murk, each supported by pole-thin buttresses, and all sheathed in glittering onyx sheets. These jagged peaks cast serrated shadows over those skulking in the washes and lanes below. The wicked height of the spires pressed down on the spirits of the creatures beneath, while those who had schemed and climbed found them quite the contrary. To those ryle, who, in the culmination of their decades, made residence in the high, thin air, these spires were their own intangible, undeniable greatness.

To Akri, the towers were unsightly hazards one moment, and a convenient selection of perches the next.

These ryle, Akri thought, *they speak to and fro, and sit to meals, but* friendship *is a foreign word. One trembles and thinks, "See me." And when one ryle truly looks at his brother, it is with a shark's eyes, and beneath thoughts of betrayal.*

Akri shuffled on his rail, towards the sounds of

dining, and took a swift peek around a corner to the nearby cafe. It was still too busy, and he pulled back. In minutes they would begin closing for the evening, and he would have a chance to alight between the still laden tables and take his pick of mussel soups and racks of split-shell pill-bugs the size of his skull. The ryle never split the shells far enough; they always left the choicest meat. Akri preferred to eat up here, and not scramble with the murk-dwellers for garbage.

His black eye rounded the bend once more and spied the cafe.

Only one couple left.

Two ryle, a male and a female, sat at a shaded table near the rail. Each took careful bites and sips, wary of making a mess on their tentacles. Their hands moved to place the flatware precisely so. Words passed. These concerned a world of peers and fiefdoms built by a merchant lord, now bloated and beyond. Though plans of violence and maneuvering swirled and formed and dispersed between the two, their eyes were ever concerned with each other. One saw weakness in the tilt of a spoon placed just shy of ninety degrees. The other spotted a speck of shellfish clinging to the underside of a tentacle. In these minor signs of weakness, the conversant ryle hedged for and against alliance, supposing imagined futures where this ally would be a foe. "Is this ryle a worthy ally?" begs the question, "Is this ryle a worthy foe?"

Their meal truncated by a feathered thrall, the ryle ended their analysis with a common phrase of parting, "To one day kill you," "And you." These words rang with a respect that moved the thrall to look up and away from the table.

In this moment, Akri, with practiced speed, rounded the corner with his long neck. He snatched a half-eaten pair of pill-bugs, and was back around the corner before the thrall returned to his table. While there was far more food lying around, further in the cafe, Akri was grateful for the easy scoop of two pill-bugs, and lucky he didn't have to fend off the thrall with his powerful wings. He recalled brutox doormen chasing him once. One had leaped onto his back, as he swooped away, and battered his skull halfway across the city.

I was never a ryle, no matter what they say.

He hadn't killed the brutox, but tossed him off over a canal, and endured a throbbing headache for days.

His feathers standing on end at the memory, Akri hopped further away on the rail before he felt alone. He split the shells and gorged on the fine meat before croaking out a thunderous caw and stretching his wings.

A burst of ultraviolet light pulsed through the city. Akri leaned over the edge and watched.

The Maelstrom is up to something.

He saw a massive, shooting tentacle whip around a spire.

They're out hunting again. Someone's been bad.

The tentacle craned upwards.

Hmm.

The tentacle barreled towards him at blinding

speed.

I see.

Akri hopped off the Weaver's Spire and tucked his wings tightly for a dive. The tentacle snapped at him, but missed, and slammed into the side of the spire.

Akri looked up and watched it arc around to continue the chase.

What did I do now?

Akri swooped low, beneath and between the dozens of bridges connecting the spires, hoping to force the tentacle into an untenable knot.

What do I do? What do I do?

Akri twisted and turned, occasionally colliding with pedestrians foolish enough to be on the bridges.

"Sorry!" he croaked, beating his wings at thunderous speed.

Maybe I'll fly out to Degoskirke and roost in the Guilt for a while. It was closed off the last time I was there—but those wheel-locks of theirs...

Akri cawed in fright as a second, then third tentacle appeared.

He dropped at the last moment, coaxing the new pursuers to slam into each other.

Akri flapped as hard as he could, refusing to look back, though he heard the tentacles crashing into buildings and ripping bridges apart not far behind.

Just keep flapping!

He spotted another pair of tentacles wrapped around a ryle female.

They're rounding up everybody today. She doesn't have wings though!

She was struggling to tear the tentacles to pieces with her Counter. He was certain that they would subdue her.

Those tentacles are maelstrom spawn, and the purple blade is loath to hurt its own.

Akri cawed and banked hard towards the ryle. He dived and corkscrewed between the tentacles she was fighting.

Come on! Tie yourselves up, you stupid things!

He heard a crash and a sickly smacking and breaking. Akri saw the tentacles had bound into a disgusting mess.

He flew up to the ryle, who was cleaving a final tentacle in half. Akri eyed her grip and stance. Her blade had a touch of rusty red and substance to it.

She's trained in the forms and has mastered the hone.

He eyed the cleaved tentacle.

Otherwise she wouldn't have been able to do that.

Akri tried to speak but found himself too flustered. His beady eyes darted around, searching for more pursuers. It was quiet, at least for the moment.

"Caw!" Akri sputtered, "I mean, why are they after us?"

She looked up from the severed stump. "Oh, not you! They're taking me in with you? I've kept the city's library for decades; what the hell do you do? Eat brutox for lunch?"

"Ocaw—asionally!" He spat. "We might make it across the sea to the—"

Akri paused. His black eyes rolled upward as a ragged white beak, connected to a massive tendril, loomed silently over them. It inspected them. At least a dozen other tentacles slithered up on all sides.

"They really are serious," she said, staring.

"To hell with this, climb on!"

"Don't be stupid!" she replied. "There is no escape."

Akri cawed and flapped, hoping to take off, but was held fast by a sudden rush of tentacles.

The ryle sighed and let herself be taken.

The tentacles pulled backwards to their source with speed, through the city.

"They're reeling us in to that shiny pond of theirs," she said.

Akri felt the whiplash of his many dives and twists between the bridges being reversed on him.

The Maelstrom, little more than a shimmering pool of undulating purple vapor, was hidden beneath a gargantuan structure of cavernous ribs, linked by green glass panes. The pool was surrounded by a dozen ranks of seats, and, opposite the entry way, sat the white beak, silently presiding over the pool.

The tentacles and beak receded to their places. The many tentacles, now only a hundred feet long, floated, like swaying trees, over the pool. One held Akri in place, while the ryle was allowed to stand.

The beak snapped, and a purple blob coalesced in the air above the Maelstrom. The Archealexolix, a frighteningly tall, green-skinned ryle woman, and her subservient Lixovore, appeared from recessed coves. They took their places around the pool and raised their arms towards the undulating blob, which bulged and grew.

"Caaaw—hell! What did I do to deserve this? I'm just a raven!"

The beak bent towards him for just a moment, and then it snapped. Thrown by the tentacle, Akri slammed into the blob and sunk beneath its surface.

Akri saw the woman fall in moments later, and then, something else crashed into the blob from above. Akri could barely see in the inky soup, but he did see the third figure as it came to a rest nearby. It looked like a red stone.

Akri felt a sudden pulling and then ceased to be.

The Archealexolix lowered her hands, and the Lixovore followed her lead.

The undulating surface of the blob sucked inward, and the bodies of the creatures given up were replaced by something altogether different.

A monster slipped through the now slack and empty blob to land on the steps surrounding the Maelstrom.

Its body was that of a hyena, taller in the forelegs and shorter in the rear, with a scorpion's tail, complete with serrated stinger. It bore massive black, feathered wings, and the heads of both jackal and raven, but between them was a third, clad in purple and black scales.

The central head opened its long jaw and exposed its midnight blue teeth. Smokey letters and symbols crisped through the air. They flowed, like exhaust, from its snout.

The Archealexolix snapped her claws and flaming letters appeared in the air before them.

"Here, anointed before the sight of the Lix, stands the God-creation, Chimerax!"

The Lixovore bowed deeply.

"You, living fusion of loyalty, perspective, and the refined power of ascendance, are born for this purpose: to discern the fate of the city of Hyadoth. False ryle are striving to avoid ascendance and are connected to a cataclysm. If any responsibility is exposed, it constitutes high treason. Determine the facts, find the perpetrators, and know that you are allowed any means in pursuance, and any end as punishment. The false-Argument is detected in quantity, and signs of Caspian manifestation have appeared. If Caspian is come, capture his body, alive, and return it here. Untangle these signs and discover the truth. With these tasks are you charged! The hand of God upon you!"

"His Voice within," the Lixovore intoned, before rising.

Chimerax bowed deeply to the great beak, turned, and loped into the city.

Chapter 12: Among the Elazene

Letty brushed her tears away when she finally heard a voice calling her name. It sounded like Quill.

She walked softly through the trees and peeked from behind a bough. She saw Quill calling out, while Staza inspected leaves.

"I can't! The trail goes in circles! She has to be around here somewhere," Staza said, sounding defeated.

Letty wanted to run to them and break down in apology, but was afraid and ashamed, because she found nothing to justify that lost time.

She kept herself from crying and followed Quill and Staza for only minutes before Staza paused, turned, and spotted her.

"Letty! Is that you?" Staza cried, grabbing Quill and rushing towards her. "Where have you—were you going in circles? I couldn't find you!" Staza rambled, embracing her.

"I'm sorry," Letty burst out. "I didn't find anything—I followed the sphinx and got inside a library, and there was a great book—but everything was in the wrong language—you don't read Latin, do you?"

Overwhelmed, Quill shook his head.

"It's okay," Staza said, straightening Letty's hair, and brushing it from her eyes. "You're back now and it hasn't been that long. The mice will be happy to know you're safe, and Emma and Dean too."

"They're okay?"

"Yes, and a little afraid. To be honest, they

thought you were eaten," Staza said.

Letty recalled the piles of bones.

"I nearly was."

"Hold on and tell the story when we get back. Everyone will want to hear it," Quill said.

Letty followed and was surprised to find a camp set up in a clearing. Logs and rocks surrounded a healthy fire, while clean clothes were up on drying lines. The watch-mice spotted them before they entered camp and called out to the others. Emma and Dean greeted her with a flurry of questions and demands that she never leave them again.

Letty accepted a tin cup of coffee and a protein bar from Emma before sitting down at the fire.

"What happened out there? Did the sphinx try to eat you? How did you escape?" inquired Dean.

"Give her a minute," Quill said.

"It's fine," Letty spoke between bites, before relating her past few hours.

"This book, it would show us everything. Everything to do with the Argument. It had new ways to use it, and a hundred things Andy and I don't know."

Fidelio interrupted, "It was an ancient training manual. The ryle hunt and burn them whenever they can. You might have found one of the last." Several mice nodded at these words. "The old Praetor, he had some of that knowledge. He used it to train the few Seers they found."

"I'm sure I can find the temple again, but does anyone read Latin?" Letty asked, looking across the faces of her friends, and then to the mice, who bent their ears or fiddled with their tails, as if ashamed.

Quill shook his head. "I studied a few brutox dialects, but it hardly comes up, they almost never speak."

"They speak in Degoskirke," Staza said.

"Whatever, forget the brutox," Letty complained, "we can't use the manual. We're no better off than we were before—worse even, we've burned through more food!" Letty said waving an empty wrapper.

"Wait," Dean mumbled, producing his cell phone, "try pulling up a translator," he paused. "No reception... Well, next time we go up, we download a translation program and come back. We can try again."

"We don't have the time for that," Letty said, stretching and realizing how exhausted she was.

"What's that?" Emma asked, pulling at the piece of parchment Letty had in her pocket.

"Oh, this," Letty handed it to Emma. "It was a message from some priest at the Abbey. Remember the goblin town? Steustace they called it. It's actually St. Eustace, and the monks that used to live there worked in the same library the sphinxes guard. One left this message for the others. It helped me get past Aleta," Letty yawned.

"Wait, there are two of those monsters?" Dean asked.

"Yes. Aleta has a sister, Typha, who is out hunting right now."

"Hunting? Near here?" Dean asked.

"Possibly," Letty answered.

They all shared a look before breaking camp, shouldering their bags and following Staza away from the hills.

"Letty, here is your pack," Emma said, returning the backpack.

"Thanks, I thought I lost it."

"You did, they found it in the woods," Emma said.

Letty checked and found the pistol and cartridges were where she had left them.

They managed an hour's trek back through the woods and towards Steustace before complaints of tiredness became incessant.

"We're not far enough," Staza insisted. She was immaculate next to the surfacers, who were sweating, disheveled, and dragging their feet.

"I need to sleep," Dean said, taking the opportunity to lean against a tree.

"Fine," Quill said, "we'll put up a watch for the night."

Staza raised a brow in irritation, but noticed that even the mice were flagging.

Minutes later, the sleeping bags were out and shoes had been tossed aside. Dean and Quill had taken to gossiping about the differences between the surface and Caspia. Staza helped direct the mice to the best trees for watching, and Emma was lying in her bag looking at the parchment.

"Hey Letty," Emma said.

"Yeah?"

"Aren't we going to Degoskirke?"

"Yes, we are. They have portals there."

"So, we could use a map of the city, right?"

"Of course," Letty said, suspicious.

"Well, this might help," Emma said, turning the parchment over and waving it at her.

Letty sat up and snatched it.

"You've got to be kidding me."

Quill, Staza, and Dean all clamored in to get a peek.

The word, Degoskirke, stood out above a faded map. In the center was a mark and the words: refuge, cache, mouseport.

"Well done, Em," Letty said, surprised that she hadn't noticed the map earlier.

I was worried about being eaten.

"Cache," Dean read, curiously. "Like a collection of stuff?"

"How about mouseport?" Staza asked, looking at Fidelio, who shrugged.

Emma held up the parchment and showed the damage. "But the tear. We can't read all of it." Emma held the damaged parts together and a fair sliver of map was gone altogether.

Quill leaned in. "Despite the damage, we should hold onto it. We might end up in the sewers."

"Why do you say sewers?" Letty asked.

Quill held the map for them to see and said, "Roads don't usually go through the buildings and places of note. Look here," he pointed out a few examples. "This has to be the sewers."

"I still think we should check it out," Staza said.

The surfacers, and Letty included, weren't keen on slogging through the sewers.

"Even if there is a cache, it's probably looted by now, and who knows what might be living down there?" Dean said.

"Should we add it to our plan, like the cat-chase?" Staza asked.

They were silent for a moment.

"What is the plan, exactly?" Emma asked.

Letty spoke, "Our plan, as it stands, is to make it to Degoskirke, travel by portal to ryle controlled parts of the Netherscape, and hunt down the locations of Ziesqe's palaces. That's only part one. Then we have to raid them, maybe capture and interrogate one of his servants, to hopefully find and free Andy."

Staza shook her head. "That's ridiculous. Even if we do discover the exact locations of the palaces, and if we learn which one houses Andy, the place will obviously be guarded. If we can find more Argument in this cache, we need to search it. Even with a thousand mice, we are too weakly armed as it stands."

Staza's point was convincing. Letty looked from face to mouse face, and saw the mice were determined, as were Staza and Emma, but Quill looked concerned, while Dean was no more anxious than usual.

Fidelio approached the sleeping bags and spoke, "We have agreed to take on the complete burden of the watch. But we beg allowance for the sentries to sleep in backpacks, or possibly on someone's shoulders, come the morning."

"Of course, Fidelio, I'll carry them," Letty said,

stifling another yawn and taking off her socks.

She rolled over in her sleeping bag and was asleep in an instant.

She slept soundly, until a slight rattle, as of small metal instruments clanging, stirred her.

Letty yawned and cracked an eye. She saw a group of nearby mice. Frozen in fear, they were staring her way. They had built a few small fires and were cooking acorns, berries, and carved pieces of root. A pot-full of acorn stew had fallen off its stand and clattered.

"Terribly sorry, Mistress," A mouse bowed pathetically, and the others followed.

"Don't call me that," Letty said, almost too loudly. She rolled back over and tried to get comfortable again.

"Letty?" Emma whispered.

"Ugh—yes, Em?"

"What's that noise?"

"Someone dropped a pot."

"No, the other noise," Emma said, sitting up and looking around.

"What noise?" Letty also sat up. "You're crazy."

"Will you two please shut your mouths? It's Dean and Quill, they got up early," Staza said, before throwing a pillow at Emma.

Letty tried to get back to sleep, but she heard the noise Emma mentioned. There was a tapping. It was frequent, but also random.

After five restless minutes, Letty stood and stomped towards the sound, nearly kicking up a dozen mouse campfires in the process.

She found Quill and Dean striking at each other with sticks.

They're training.

Letty felt a querulous smile appear on her face. She wanted to laugh as Dean stumbled, but then she felt something else, something painful. She was behind.

That's actually a good idea. If I'm supposed to fight, I'll need practice. I can't just depend on the Argument for everything. I'll meet a ryle with a purple orb at some point.

Letty stomped back to camp, and the mice cleared a path as she came, carefully balancing their breakfasts as they did so.

"Get up," Letty said, smacking Emma with Staza's pillow.

"Why?" Emma complained.

Letty nudged Staza, who glowered at her and cast a hand out for her dagger.

"We need to practice too; we can't let the boys get ahead," Letty said firmly.

Emma sat up in her bag. "I can't fight, Letty. I barely weigh a hundred pounds."

"Oh, shut up," Letty said, and then to Staza, "You're lethal, I've seen it. Please teach us."

Staza sat up. "Fine, every morning, before breakfast, and we start before the boys."

Letty smiled, and went to find a new set of clothes. "Get dressed, Em, nothing frilly."

"I didn't pack any clothes!"

"Fine, wear something of mine," Letty replied, getting ready.

They went a safe distance from the many camps

of mice and practiced blocking and striking with sticks.

The mice watched, giggling when one of the surfacers stumbled.

"They're laughing, Letty," Emma complained.

"Get used to the pressure," Staza replied.

Practice continued until they were sweating and aching with hunger.

"We need to get a bow for Emma; she has a good eye," Staza said, as they entered camp.

The boys were sitting together, snacking away. Dean had a heavy club tied to his belt.

"Practicing?" Quill asked.

"Dancing?" Staza replied, and the girls laughed.

Quill shared a knowing look with Dean and the two continued taking bites out of their respective bars.

A few minutes later, Fidelio reported the mice were fed and ready to go. Camp was broken, the many small fires doused thoroughly, and they were on the move.

The sentinels from the night before had strapped themselves to various packs, while Emma cradled one in her arms.

"What?" She responded to Letty's curious look, "He kept falling off my shoulder."

The mouse twitched in his sleep, limbs kicking this way and that.

"And besides, they're kind of cute."

Letty laughed, and the mice in earshot grumbled with concern.

"We are not cute," one insisted.

"Maybe a bit—in the right light," another responded.

"Anything's cute when it's asleep," a third said loudly, hoping to catch Emma's ear.

Emma, however, didn't notice.

Quill hummed a few tunes, and Staza occasionally stepped in to sing, though she was bashful about it. The mice joined in with a well-timed tapping of their weapons on the ground.

The tedium of marching melted away, and they found themselves back on the road and approaching Steustace.

"There it is," Letty said, pointing at the ramshackle wall surrounding the abbey and town. "It wasn't that far after all."

"We covered a lot of ground before we slept, yesterday," Staza replied.

"No one wanted to be eaten," a mouse muttered, reminding Letty of Aleta's sister, who she hoped was feasting on birds at the waterfall, far from the goblins.

As they approached, Letty noticed a few carts and a curious group idling around the gate.

Dean stopped in his tracks and pointed at a cart. "What the hell is that?"

There were several lumbering creatures harnessed to the carts. They looked like a cross between insect and gorilla.

"That's a bruton," Quill answered, "beast of burden and distant cousin to the others, which are the brutox we told you about." Quill squinted as he looked at them. "Though they are no strain of brutox

I've ever seen."

Letty didn't recognize them either. Though her experience was nothing like the Caspian's. These brutox moved too gracefully, and their plates from limb to limb were discolored or oddly patterned. One beetle had red arms and a green chest, though both were offset by a white head.

"Whatever strain they might be, they're also traders," Quill said, "and therefore, peaceful," he concluded uncertainly.

"Brutox traders?" Letty mumbled, "I thought they all served ryle."

"What do you think they have in that weird cart?" Emma asked, pointing to the largest.

It had a patched tarpaulin tied down over something tall and bulky.

"Let's find out," Staza said.

Letty agreed and led the way. The others were slow to follow.

"So, these are brutox. Aren't they our enemies?" Dean asked from further back.

Letty palmed the Argument, while Staza and Quill had their hands on the hilts of their blades. Emma caught up and had drawn her club.

Staza smacked Emma's hand. "Put that back in your belt!" She hissed, and Emma obeyed.

"We need to look prepared, but not openly hostile," Quill added. "There's more going on here than we understand."

They approached, close enough to hear the goblins on the wall arguing with a tall brutox of indeterminate type.

"He must be the leader," Letty whispered.

The lead brutox had the head of a fire ant, and the body plates in the coloration of a wasp, though he lacked a stinger.

"Have you ever heard of an ant-wasp?" Staza asked.

Quill and Letty shook their heads.

As they approached, they could hear the discussion was heated.

"We have fulfilled our end of this bargain, you damned points! Get out here and pay us!" The lead brutox waved a fist in frustration. "We've carted this thing halfway across the scape! You can't do this to us!"

Letty stared at the Caspians, surprised. "Are brutox known to yell?" she asked.

Quill shook his head. "It's known that they can talk, though they almost never do."

A goblin, wearing a large gray wig, poked its head over the wall.

"Open the gate!" the lead brutox yelled again.

"It's not safe t' be consorting with strangers when there's a gobeater afoot!"

"There's nothing out here but us!"

"Look," the wigged goblin rejoined, "we undershtand and sympet'ize with the trialy tribulations o' onesuch as yourself such, but the's been a vote. The vox populi o' Steustace says to maintain a self 'mposed blockade o' the town, from the inside, until furhder notifications."

Letty nearly broke out laughing at the ridiculous language.

The lead brutox turned from the wall and stomped towards his cart. He cut the ropes that held the tarpaulin over the bulky cargo. He whipped the tarp away and revealed a statue, hewn from marble, that depicted a heroic-sized figure with oddly goblinoid features. She saw pointy ears, a sharp cleft chin, and minimal body fat, though the rest was idealized human. He carried a book with the word, Goblinomicon, emblazoned across the front, and with his other hand, he gestured widely with an olive branch.

The word "Steustace," rose from hundreds of voices. Letty looked up and saw countless goblin heads peeking over the wall.

The lead brutox clambered up his cart, readied a hatchet, and prepared to cut away at the statue's prominent nose.

A horrified chorus of exclamation echoed from the wall. Letty could see the goblins pulling at their ears and hiding their eyes from the sight.

Eager to help, Letty rushed up to the brutox and yelled over the noise, "Hold on, let me try something!"

The lead brutox nearly stumbled in surprise at her sudden presence. "Guards!" He yelled, dropping the hatchet and drawing a polished mantis claw, fixed with a handle.

The other brutox, as mismatched as their leader, drew weapons and faced off against Letty and her friends. Staza and Quill had their blades free in an instant, and even Emma was ready with her club, though Dean looked like he was keen to bargain.

A moment later, a guard approached and tried to grab Letty by the arm.

Letty summoned the blade and pointed it inches from his face. He stumbled backward in fright, smacking into the cart. The impact sent his ant-like head flying off. But, much to her surprise, a human face remained, staring at her with a shaken expression.

The other guards backed away at the sight of the blade.

"The blood—" One muttered loudly, lowering his spear and stepping away.

"Don't be afraid; I'm trying to help you." Letty said, and then to their leader, "Call your guards off my friends, please."

The caravan leader motioned to his guards, and they lowered their weapons.

Satisfied that both sides had calmed, Letty released her blade. The caravan guards drew close together and struck up a mumbling fit in harsh accents that Letty couldn't decipher. The leader stepped down from his cart and looked at the newcomers, unsure of what to say.

Letty addressed the town wall. "Goblins! We have returned! The sphinx is—"

Dean had approached and gave her a quick nudge.

"What?" She hissed angrily.

"Leave this one to me," Dean said, oddly self-assured.

"What are you—"

"I've got a plan."

Dean approached the caravan leader and spoke, "Sir, we see that you have run into some trouble with these goblins. I am certain we can clear up this impasse."

"Ada!" A voice cried out, and a slight form darted from one of the covered carts and rushed towards the caravan leader. "Ada! Who are they, and why are they naked?"

The voice belonged to a young girl, though she was dressed as a ladybug. Her long, curled ocher locks spilled out in places from beneath her helm and face mask. She hugged onto the leader's leg and gawked at the newcomers.

Naked? Letty thought, and noticed that her friends were inspecting themselves as well.

"Yes, yes, dearest," he said to the girl, "get back to the cart now, hurry." He gave her a nudge, and she ran off laughing in a way that sounded as frightened as it did joyful.

"Please, excuse her, friends, but it is strange to see humans go unclothed, especially this close to the Nomark," the man paused, as if awaiting an explanation.

"I'm sorry if our appearance offends you," Dean said protractedly, not sure how to deal with the issue. "We are new to the area, and ignorant of the customs. I hope that won't keep you from making a deal with us."

The man took off his ant helmet. He had olive skin, short cropped hair, which was ocher, like the girl's, and his face was crisscrossed with scars.

"I am Ahmet, Elazene trader, and onetime

provisioner of rare luxuries," he finished with some venom for his cargo.

Dean raised a hand, he went for the handshake, but Ahmet grasped him by the forearm instead. "Uh," Dean murmured, "I am Dean Loggia, student."

Ahmet gave them a wide smile. "Ah, pupils of the Python then. I see what they say is true. She lets her wards wander naked, unashamedly bearing the name Caspian, but so far afield from her den." He made a 'tut-tut' sound and eyed Staza and Quill, who had donned their Caspian armor in the morning. "I have always had an eye for the Python's craftwork, but this new form..." he paused, looking over Dean's khaki pants and knit blue sweater with a raised brow.

Quill and Staza didn't like the man's dismissive and almost insulting tone. Letty saw them share a look and each returned a hand to their weapons.

Letty took Staza by the shoulder and whispered, "Let's give Dean a chance."

"Yes—" Dean tried to speak, but Ahmet rolled right over him.

"Very good, now that we know who we are, how is it that you can help me? I see you interrupted your leader. I suspect she had a way of getting these gates open."

Dean stammered. "I—yes, we can get these gates open, but I think an equitable deal could be made between our two parties."

"Indeed? And why should I pay for that which would occur freely? Let her open the gates, and then we can speak of deals. I am fully laden at the moment anyhow," Ahmet raised an annoyed brow at Dean, who seemed lost.

Letty approached. "Dean, you're blowing this," she whispered.

"No, hold on," he said, thinking.

Ahmet inclined his head, and grinned slightly, as if prompting his young opponent to surrender.

Dean looked up, bright eyed, "Certainly, we will be on our way. I had only hoped that we could enter together, but it seems that you would prefer to make your own arrangements."

Ahmet scowled. "Once the gate is open, it is open."

Dean laughed and looked up at the goblins on the wall. "We have news of the sphinx! Let us in please, so we can tell you."

There was a rumble of deliberation among the goblins.

"Just you!" The wigged leader called out.

"And my friends!" Dean yelled back.

Another huddle.

"Fine, your friends too. But the carts must stay!"

"Why?"

"Because t' embargo!"

"Right, your self-imposed embargo," Dean murmured, and then loudly, "What if we told you that the sphinx has been taken home?"

There was a sudden ruckus on the other side.

"Well, that's very nice and all, but t' embargo stands!" The wigged goblin grunted as if he was being beaten.

Letty watched several goblins try to pull their

leader off the wall. With a stone-headed club, he swatted them away.

"Didn't you vote for the embargo?" Dean asked.

"Yes! And the will of the people—oof—it still stands!"

"Have another vote!"

The wigged goblin nearly fainted at those words. A cry of, "Another vote!" resounded from the populace. Letty, her friends, and the traders stood about, regarding each other cautiously as the goblins engaged in democracy on the far side of the wall. Though shrieks and fleshy thuds punctuated the occasion, it was a relatively calm proceeding.

Letty shared suspicious looks with the traders while they waited.

The final count was overwhelmingly for abandoning the embargo.

"You idiots! I's goin to do that in a minute! Now we've to pay full price for the statuary!" The wigged goblin's cries reached over the ramshackle palisade.

"Ha! Did you hear that?" A guard guffawed.

Ahmet's eyes widened in surprise. "I didn't think they had it in them," he laughed. "They were working me over for a discount, and I thought they were simply stupid. That's what I get for underestimating the points." He clapped Dean on the back. "You are a sloppy negotiator, young man, but you ended up ahead, despite that. Now I owe you a favor."

The gates creaked open and the caravan entered along with Letty and her party. The goblins swarmed the statue, which turned out to be a likeness of

Steustace himself, creator and name giver of the goblins.

"A' least that's 'ow I heard it," one goblin remarked after telling the story to a curious crowd of humans.

The goblins assembled an array of pulleys, ropes, and booms to transfer the statue from the cart to a slightly lopsided pedestal they had waiting outside the abbey.

The wigged goblin, who wasn't keen on paying for the statue, complained, "Damn thing was never my idea. Dead mayor has all the credit, and I gets a bill!"

The goblin, ex-judge, now accidental mayor, chewed on his nails, and didn't notice his wig was askew, as the bags of loot promised to Ahmet were produced, tarried over, and loaded into one of the covered carts.

"What could the goblins have to pay you with?" Dean asked.

"They find treasures in this old abbey. Other things, I don't know where they find them, traders I suppose. Either way, I'm not asking questions," Ahmet said, inspecting a bag of silver candlesticks. Ahmet gazed their way for a moment before continuing, "I have never seen anything so remarkable as you," he said to Letty and her friends, loading the last bag. "The old blood walking fearlessly at the head of an army of mice. It's almost like a scene from the stories. How is it you rid the goblins of their sphinx? Was it truly her, or were they confused and merely suffering a mountain lion in a wig?"

Letty laughed. "It was her, though she has a twin sister too."

Ahmet's face became serious for a moment. He calmed his expression and continued, "They tell these stories in the Python's den, of course. It is nothing strange that you should know this. But how then—" he looked closely at Letty. "The blood is strong," he said under his breath, several mice repeated the saying, "but the mind is soft, you go doubly naked!"

Ahmet walked up to the Caspians and to Dean and Emma. He looked each one squarely in the eyes. "Three doubly naked Seers in a group of five. What damnation and war would break out on the fields at the sight of you," he rushed to a cart and returned with a bag. "Here! Eat, you must eat! What do they teach in that snake pit?"

The bag contained small, deeply purple carrots.

"Why?" Letty asked.

"Are you stupid?" Ahmet rejoined, waving the bag drastically, as if the reason were self-evident.

"They hide their violet eyes. Something in the carrots changes your eye color, but not forever; they have to be eaten every day," Quill said.

"But we have these," Staza took out a pair of sunglasses and put them on.

"Insane!" Ahmet replied. "This will only draw more attention. And you go shamelessly forward as human too." He paused for a moment, and looked as if suddenly enlightened, "I see now, she teaches you none of this, so you cannot hope to escape and survive!"

Letty saw Staza and Quill tense in anger.

I need to step in.

Before Letty could speak, a new chorus of shrieks and whining rang through the town. Goblins went running between their tumbledown shacks screaming, "Another's coming! A second sphinx!"

Who told them about Aleta's sister?

Ahmet, Letty, and her friends approached the source of the commotion and found a confused mouse, the mayor, and the caravan guards. The mayor and one guard were shaking hands.

"What's going on here?" Ahmet demanded.

The guards ignored him.

Letty approached the mouse. "What happened?" she asked.

"I might have let slip that the second sphinx travels the countryside in search of food," the goblins groaned at the sound of this. "But it's okay!" The mouse insisted. "The mayor has already made it better. The caravan guards are going to stay on as town guards until it's safe."

Letty cringed.

Ahmet flung his helmet into the air and started a vitriolic, one sided, argument with his chief guardsman, who ignored him and headed for the cart that bore the guards' possessions and payment.

"You can't abandon me! We're so far from home!"

"They pay ten times what you do," the guard answered without stopping. "And it's safer here, no ryle for leagues, no brutox patrols, no cult abductions."

Letty and her friends slinked away from the roiling argument, cloistering themselves around the far side of the abbey.

"Hey, Caspians, do you know if Degoskirke is likely to be close to the caravaneer's home?" Dean asked.

Quill considered for a while. "Well, he can't be going into mouse country. There's only one road, and it goes further sur and pacward. Either direction takes us closer to Degoskirke, though every important road in Pansubprimus terminates in the central city Yyonvere, and we do not want to go there."

"Why not? It has a pretty name," Emma said.

Staza shook her head. "It's the ryle capitol of Pansubprimus."

A moment later, Ahmet came stomping around the corner, his eyes aflame, and his hand gesticulating wildly.

"You did this!" He insisted, taking in Letty and all of her friends.

Dean stepped up, with his hands wide in supplication. "We did."

"There's no point in denying it," Ahmet barreled forward before processing what Dean said. He looked baffled for a moment and was then immediately suspicious.

Dean continued, "And to make up for it, we offer you our service as escorts. We only ask that you show us the way to Degoskirke after we get you home."

Ahmet stopped, mid-tirade, and stared for a moment, before bursting out in wheezing laughter. "You! Escort me! Hahaha! And you want to go to Degoskirke? Where they kill Seers! And you go naked? Hahahaha!"

The surfacers and Caspians stared at each other, embarrassed by the barrage of laughter.

Finally, Ahmet wiped his eyes and the laughter slowed to a simmer. "Maybe you will help mellow my daughter. Seeing how stupid you are should keep her on a cautious path. The deal is struck!" He held out a hand, first to Dean, but then to Letty, who reached out, and was surprised when he grasped her forearm.

"You will guard my caravan. I will supply you with purple carrots, food, and carts to sleep in. We will split the cost of chitin armor to clothe you, at the first possible chance. Until then, you stay in the covered carts. You fight with plain blades, and not artifacts, if it comes to combat. Though the purpose of an escort is to dissuade attack far more than it is to fight—never forget that. Do not start a fight, no matter what happens!" Ahmet looked from face to face, as if sniffing out trouble. He rounded on Letty and Staza. "You two especially. Chaos follows in your footsteps—I can see it. You must swear to obey my rules, or our agreement is forfeit."

He's serious about this. It must be dangerous out there.

Ahmet went around the group and listened as everyone swore to obey his rules. He also insisted that those with violet eyes eat a carrot.

Letty eyed the putrid looking thing with

contempt, then braced herself, and swallowed it in one gulp. She felt slightly sick but noticed that Quill and Staza were only annoyed.

"Not too bad then, and you won't stand out so much. It's a small price to pay," Ahmet concluded.

Finally satisfied with his new escort, Ahmet walked them to the caravan, shared another long string of obscenities with his former guards, before haggling with two for their suits of chitin armor. Neither cared to part from their equipment.

Ahmet grumbled as he filled the feed bags of the hulking, ape-like brutons that pulled the carts. "Petri, dearest, please array them, Oktuz followed by Elmaza, and I'll do the rest."

Petri, Ahmet's daughter, leaped at the order, and even laughed as she pulled on the bridles of the beasts to rearrange them, facing away from town. "Ada, they need to graze; we'll waste feed this way," she complained.

"Yes, yes, dearest, but I desire to be away from this place, and these traitors. We will graze them in a few hours."

"Is there anything we can do?" Letty asked.

"Yes. Please do your best to stay out of the way," Ahmet answered without looking up from the bridle of his beast, Oktuz.

Letty hoped he would be in a better mood tomorrow.

Caspians and surfacers stood back from the caravan as father and daughter prepared. There were five carts and seven brutons. Four of the carts were simple covered wagons, though the fifth was much larger and resembled a ship's hull on wheels. Two brutons were harnessed to this cart.

"What do you suppose they use that one for?" Dean asked, pointing to the ship-cart.

"It looks like it floats," Letty said, "maybe they use it to ferry goods across water."

Staza sighed. "I don't like this man, Letty."

Quill agreed. "He is insulting to the point of outrage, but we have learned a great deal."

"Right, like how we can't travel to Degoskirke dressed as we are, oh and how we need to eat carrots to hide our eye color, and how they kill Seers in Degoskirke." Letty sighed, thinking of all the troublesome details.

"Yes," Dean rejoined, "but imagine if he was polite, and didn't mention anything, out of fear of offending us."

They all shared a grave look.

"The goblins certainly didn't know any of that, and neither did our local experts, the Caspians," Dean addressed Quill and Staza, "no offense to either, but this is for the best. We can learn more from him, and we have only to look intimidating. So, let's ignore his rudeness and see if we can learn more handy ways to not die."

The Caspians agreed, if reluctantly.

"Come, come, children, let us drape you in bags and hide you in the chief cart until morning. I expect I can find you proper attire by tomorrow at noon," Ahmet said, motioning them towards the largest cart, which they had to climb to enter.

They were almost ten feet off the ground,

peeking over the sides of the cart.

"You don't think he'll try to sell us off somewhere, do you?" Emma asked.

They shared a tense silence before Dean shook his head. "He just lost his escorts, and we witnessed it. He genuinely needs us."

"If he plans to arm us, we can rest assured that he will honor the agreement. We'll need to be on guard, until then," Letty reasoned.

"My Lady?" A small voice queried.

Letty nearly leaped out of the cart. It was Fidelio. The mouse was abashed, tugging on a whisker.

"Yes—oh, God, what about the mice?" Letty asked.

"Yes, indeed. I already spoke to Ahmet," Fidelio said sadly, "and he considers us too great a security risk, as there are few mice further sur, and never a large force like ours."

"But we might need you in Degoskirke," Letty said.

"And what if we need to fight off raiders or something worse? The mice could be handy in a pinch," Quill added.

"More than handy, sir," Fidelio replied, "But as it happens, we have a plan."

"Oh?" Letty asked.

"Indeed. Since we will be a hindrance on the road, I have considered how we might be of use instead. After deliberation with my lieutenants, we have decided to found a new settlement in conjunction with the goblins here at Steustace.

We are close to our lands, and we know that others would abandon the Vychy if word got out that Seers walk the scape again. We also know that many of our older brothers, the mice from Sentinel's Watch, are nomads now. If we could get a message to them, they might join our new endeavor."

"Well considered, Fidelio, but what did the mayor say? Will he welcome mouse neighbors?" Quill asked.

Fidelio nodded. "I have a mouse working out a contract with him now. We would receive pay, like the mercenaries, for defending the town. They don't know that sphinxes and mice have a long history, and that keeping the town safe won't be an issue. We learned the goblins are lax watchmen; they simply failed to close the gate when she approached."

"What if the Vychy get word of what you're doing here? Won't they come and attack?" Staza asked.

"It is likely, but they won't know what to do with walls this size," Fidelio gestured at the wooden palisade around the city. "And any small, mouse sized, access ways through the walls will be sniffed out and filled or guarded on our first day. I can promise you that," Fidelio closed with a flourish.

"Combined arms," Quill responded. "It sounds like they have given it thought. They will be doing their people good if their plan succeeds."

"Indeed, we can only hope that our old brothers can forgive us. They may never allow a former Vychy into the Occidentus Obscura, but at least the order will have a place to put down roots again." Fidelio concluded, looking down, as if ashamed.

"I'm sure the others will accept you, especially if they see your commitment. We wish you the best of luck, and we'll be back to check in on you as soon as we can," Letty said, patting Fidelio on the head.

"Thank you, my Lady, for your kind words, and for helping to give us a new start. If it weren't for you, we'd still be on patrol in that traitor's land." Fidelio was about to leave before he stopped short, "There is one other detail. I didn't want to bother you with it, but we captured a prisoner a few hours ago. He is one of our kind, so I felt it unnecessary to raise the issue, but he is from Degoskirke by birth, and claims to have met your ally, the boy Andy."

"What!" Letty cried. "Where is he?"

"Andy, or the mouse?" Fidelio shrunk under the noise.

"Andy!"

"He doesn't know, but I'll bring him to you," Fidelio rushed off, his ears flattened.

"Off we go!" Ahmet called out, grateful to be leaving.

Letty popped her head out of the cart and said, "Just a minute please, we still have business."

"Absolutely not," Ahmet answered with a smile, as his daughter raced up to one of the moving carts and hopped on.

Fidelio reappeared on the grass near the cart, he was running alongside a blue mouse, who appeared angry at first glance.

"Come on!" Letty called out to them.

The mice leaped aboard, and Fidelio helped the

other, who was less mobile, due to his chains.

"Here he is, my Lady," Fidelio said, leading the other mouse by his chains.

"Hands off, traitor!" The blue mouse spat, pulling away.

"He is a handful, as you can see. Should I leave him with you or have him executed for spying?"

"For God's sake, leave him with us—but take those chains off, please," Letty implored.

"As you wish." Fidelio freed the blue mouse. "Fate will argue in your favor, young surfacers and Caspians, I see it in the sky." Fidelio bowed deeply.

"Fate and argument, very cute," the blue mouse sneered.

Fidelio ignored the jab, came out of his low bow, and leaped over the side of the cart. Letty looked over and saw him rejoin his mice.

"Fool's venture, founding a new town without me. I have more experience with goblins than any mouse alive. And that Fidelio, unfortunate choice for a leader too, all pomp and no circumspection," the blue mouse said harshly.

I'm seeing why Fidelio dumped him on us, but I better be polite.

"Hi, I'm Letty, and this is Emma, Dean, Staza, and Quill. We're all friends of Andy's. We've heard that you have met him. Is that true?" Letty asked.

"Met him! I taught him everything he knows— well, Clang and Martin helped, a bit. The boy was a fool when he fell in with the teeth, but he's a damned killing machine now. He butchered a ryle lord in his own fortress, with some good calls from myself, of course."

The humans shared a sidelong glance.

"Name's Blue, former executive officer of the Broken Teeth: mercenaries and fixers extraordinary. We were recently contracted by your Mistress," he gestured to the Caspians before continuing, "It's been a while since I've seen the Teeth; could be anything has happened by now."

"So, when did you see Andy?" Letty asked.

"We were together for the assault on the Nicomedian Ossuary," he paused at the blank looks on everyone's face. "It's an important Juncture between the surface and the Netherscape. I had been working on cracking a back-way into the fortress for weeks, before the lad came along. With a bit of the silversight, he figured the last, and tiniest, piece of the puzzle. We stormed the place, took out the occupiers, and then watched Andy leave with Pythia, deeper into the fortress."

I wonder what happened to him there.

"Andy returned alone. We managed to get him past the other goblins, who weren't with the Teeth. They had standing orders to hold Andy if they saw him. That's Pythia for you. We got past her loyalists and had Andy through a portal to Caspia. He was off to meet—" Blue paused and pointed questioningly at Letty. "Are you the one?"

Letty nodded, her face stern, yet slightly red.

"Hmm," Blue grumbled, staring her way. "Well, not long after, Pythia returned from the Juncture, quite furious. One of the unaffiliated goblins found out what had happened and let loose that we helped

Andy get away. Of course, we lost our contract. Though I expect she was even angrier to find a few of her pets missing," he looked over at Quill and Staza.

"You're lucky she didn't cast you all into the sea," Staza said snidely.

Blue only nodded before continuing, "We signed on with a schooner that works the lanes between Degoskirke and the Yyonvere tributary. Martin and Clang, de-facto leaders of the Teeth, deiced to send me on a mission to mouse territory—which I've never seen before in my life by the way—I'm born and raised in the free city. They wanted me to find Andy." He scoffed before continuing, "I managed to find a human trail outside the ruin of Sentinel's watch, and following it led me to your unsavory rear-guard. It's for the best that we're leaving them behind; those Vychy types have traitorousness in their blood."

"Wait, back up for a moment—how can we trust that you worked for our Mistress?" Quill asked.

"There's enough you don't know about your Mistress to fill a library, lad. She has deals going on every side imaginable, cross-scape, even on the surface, and has for centuries uncounted."

"Let's just stick to the facts, please," Staza said, annoyed.

Blue considered her with a cruel look. "You're just her little lapdog, aren't you? She must really mold her students with care to make them so obedient—"

"Watch your tongue, mouse," Quill interrupted,

"or I'll throw you so high, you'll wake up embedded in the ceiling."

Blue was about to rise to the insult, but Letty stepped in first, "Peace, please! We can't start fighting, there is too much at stake. Let's just agree to be courteous. Can we do that?" She looked to the two offended parties.

Quill narrowed his eyes, and so did Blue.

"Well," Blue spoke, taking another tack, "we delivered you the lad and you lost him. Anyone care to explain that?"

There was a long pause. Letty looked around, but no one met her eye.

"Yeah, Letty, what exactly did happen?" Dean asked.

Letty shook her head. "We almost got away, but Ziesqe was ready for us, and had an ambush waiting at the circle of portals."

"Andy fought them off with the Argument before he was captured. He bought time for us to escape. If he hadn't, none of us would be here now," Staza finished.

"Sacrificing one to save many," Blue muttered.

"We need to go over our plan," Letty insisted. "New information has come up and we need to discuss it."

"One second," Dean interrupted. He looked pale, and then stuck his head over the side and threw up.

"Really?" Staza asked in a demeaning way.

Quill and Blue abandoned their posturing to snicker at Dean.

"We've only been moving for a few minutes; we

have days to go yet," Quill said to Dean's back.

Dean raised an index finger, calling for them to wait, and heaved again.

Even Ahmet was laughing.

"That's it, just shut up all of you!" Emma yelled, her face contorted in rage.

The bullying ceased, and they remained quiet until Dean returned. Staza passed him a canteen full of water and he took a few sips.

"Sorry about that. Let's get back to the plan: escort duty with the trader and then Degoskirke to hunt down Andy," Dean croaked, trying to reset the conversation.

"You know that he's in Degoskirke?" Blue asked.

"We know he's with Ziesqe, and we know Ziesqe is probably keeping him in one of his palaces. We learned where those are, to a degree, and the plan is to use Degoskirke as a base to search out those palaces, and question anyone who might work for Ziesqe," Letty replied.

"Well, that is a plan," Blue said, tugging the whiskers on one side of his face.

Is he being sarcastic?

"It has good and bad points." Blue continued, "The good: You are with an Elazene chief, whether you know it or not, and they have ways across the Nomarky. Also good: You have me, and I know Degoskirke. The bad: Your eyes are still colored, that means enslavement out here, and likely death in the city. You also don't know where your target is, but Degoskirke is the proper place to start; there are portals and means of travel to almost everywhere in

the reachable scapes, but they are quite expensive.
I hope you have something worth trading in these
bags."

"What exactly is the Nomarky? And who is the
Elazene chief? Do you mean Ahmet?" Letty asked.

Blue laughed. "All that surface ignorance. What
good are your automats and victrolas now, when you
know so little?"

Automats? Victrolas?

Blue had expected a laugh from the Caspians as
fellow Netherscapers. There was only silence.

Blue huffed before moving on, "The Nomarky
covers the bulk of the land in the central portion of
Pansubprimus. Pansubprimus, also known as the
part of the Netherscape we're in right now—we're
clear on that much, right?"

There was another protracted silence.

*He knows too much. I can't just kick him out. We'll
have to get used to his bad attitude.*

"Well, the Nomarky consists of over one
thousand domains, each commanded by a fortress
or fortified settlement. The ryle have been warring
against each other for this land since the shattering.
Ancient human clans still live on and work the land,
yet they do so beneath an ever-shifting series of
ryle warlords. These clans are the Elazene. They are
technically outlawed, but, since they add more to
the value of the land than any other tenant, the ryle
warlords have come to accept them. The concession
being—can anyone guess?"

"The Elazene have to wear brutox plate armor,"
Dean said, unsure.

"Well guessed, sick boy. Yes, the chitin armor is now the human uniform in the Nomarky. I expect the caravaneer remarked at your being unclothed, or some nonsense, when first he saw you."

They nodded.

"The only problem with this charade lies in the capitol of ryle-controlled Pansubprimus, the city of Yyonvere. It is ruled by an abort-ascend ryle who has set up her own cult in recent decades. The failed ryle who couldn't secure a fiefdom or domain in any part of the scape or the surface have always had little to do but live as mercenaries. The ruler of Yyonvere," he bowed and flourished with his hands sarcastically, "her highness Supthoi, offered them a chance for riches and glory. They have only to hunt the Nomarky for the local Elazene. This makes it difficult for us," Blue concluded.

Hearing this unnerved them. Letty felt that the comfortable hull of the large cart wasn't as safe as it had felt moments ago. She peeked over the top and looked out onto the wooded hills. There was no sign of civilization, save the rutted path. The brutons lazily scraped up a mouthful of grass or a shaving of bark from nearby trees as they went.

"Well, I'm glad we know what to look out for," Staza said, also looking over the edge. "Local warlords will likely let us pass, but cultists from the capitol are a problem."

"He is very astute for something so small." Everyone nearly jumped at Ahmet's deep voice.

"You won't call me small after I claw out your eye, Elazene!" Blue growled, shaking a fist at the man, who had suddenly appeared, crouching, at the head of the cart.

"Fiery, this one," Ahmet replied. "But he is quite correct. We will fly local colors and present local papers to the Nomarks. May the Voice protect us from Supthoi's cultists. Keep a sharp eye on the horizon for banners bearing a golden face with eyes of crescent moons and bursting suns. They are—" he stopped short, his eyes pinched in apparent pain. A moment later he stood and was gone.

"He must have had a run in with them," Emma said.

Quill nodded. "That's probably why he was so insistent on an escort."

"Speaking of Ahmet, do we know on what side of the Argument they rest? They are persecuted by the ryle, but does that mean we are allies? Ahmet knows what we are, but he hasn't said much about it, unlike the mice," Letty said.

"Overly religious mice," Blue rolled his eyes and sneered. "We do it best in Degoskirke, where faith is personal and we avoid the endless, cringe-inducing statements about the blood. I could never tolerate the O.O. and their sermonizing."

Staza raised a brow. "She asked about the Elazene, and they are a controversial topic. Pythia dislikes them. Our stance is to only do business with them, and no more."

"Why?" Letty asked, "What could Pythia have against them?"

"They failed to join Caspian in his revolts against the ryle, even though it is suspected that they possess great wealth," Quill answered.

"They sound like merchants, more than crusaders," Dean commented.

Quill nodded. "Though they have risen in occasional revolt, they are known for being cowards," he muttered quietly.

Blue made a disgusted face. "There's a good pet, vomit up your master's drivel."

Letty leaned in and glowered at him.

Blue took a moment before going on, "Can you even imagine living out here? Hordes of rampaging ryle coming from every direction, some want to clothe you in the dead skin of insects and tax you for the privilege, while the others want to execute you for no other reason than your species being on the wrong side of a war lost centuries ago. I'd bet my tail that you couldn't make a living out here like the Elazene do."

Quill's fist tightened, but he listened.

"Blue," Letty said, hoping to calm the mouse, "would you take a look at this map? I found it at the sphinx's library."

"Sphinx?" Blue muttered as Letty laid the map down on top of a chest for him to examine. "Hmm, it's a very basic map of the sewers in central Degoskirke. No, wait. It isn't the sewers at all." Blue leaned in. "These tunnels are too few to be sewers for the whole city. Perhaps they are something else altogether. Cache? That's interesting. I wonder if it's still there. And there's something here about a mouseport."

"Do you know what that is?" Letty asked.

Blue shook his head before answering, "A way for mice to get in possibly, or maybe a security measure. If we ever make it that far I'll try to sort it out." Blue flipped the map over and read the old message on the other side. "You say that you took this from the library?"

"Not exactly, it was stuck into a column outside."

Blue nodded, his eyes narrow. "Old mice tell stories. I heard once that the sphinxes guard written histories, artifacts, and other, more ethereal treasures. They supposedly devour interlopers."

"That last part is true; Aleta kept me from leaving with a manual on how to work with the Argument."

That satisfied Blue's suspicion. "The mystery of this map aside, our plan is set. Are any of you decent fighters?"

Quill and Staza were both confident as they raised their hands. Letty produced the Argument.

"Two Caspians. Whatever they say about Caspia, it is known to produce skilled fighters and quality equipment. The surfacers are useless, save the one who wields the Argument."

"We're not useless!" Emma complained.

"We're pretty useless," Dean replied.

"We've been training," Emma countered as she produced the wooden club. "Well, we trained once, but we plan on training every morning."

Blue stared at the club with a small grin. "Hopefully the Elazene can talk us out of any trouble we might run into."

I hope so too.

Letty folded up the map and saw Emma pull a handful of protein bars from a backpack. "I don't know what time it is, but I'm starting to get hungry," she said, passing the bars around.

As the hours passed, the countryside smoothed into plains, the hills disappearing into the distance. The trees gave way to tall, patchy shrubbery, which then thinned into grazelands dotted by the occasional farmstead. The ceiling, far above, had lost its chaotic flux of color and settled into an array of purples and reds, interlaced with bands of gold. The faintest trace of Amber raced off lanticward.

Searching through one of her bags, Letty felt like she was being watched. She looked up and spotted an insect face peering over the side of the cart. Letty nearly shrieked as she reached for her Argument, Staza and Quill also noticed, but in their rush to arm themselves and stand, they all collided.

"Hahahah!" The voice was small and female.

"Petri! Leave them be!" Ahmet called from a cart further ahead.

The girl pulled up her face mask and smiled at the group.

"That's not nice, little girl," Emma said, rubbing a sore spot on the side of her head.

She laughed again. "Put some clothes on, or you'll wake the dead," she said before leaping off the side of the cart and rushing to her father's side.

A short while later, they stopped to rest. Ahmet accepted help from Letty and Emma in unharnessing the brutons and grazing them, while the Caspians started a fire and took watch. Ahmet considered the sky carefully and then raised a banner over the lead cart. It featured a mauve field, crisscrossed by crimson and orange hearts.

"For the locals," he said, as Letty and her friends stared at the banner.

Ahmet and Petri worked together to cook a few strips of meat and boil something akin to orange cabbage.

The surfacers shared a look of concern as they were served that orange cabbage with chunks of unknown meat and vegetable. The Caspians only took moments to finish their dinners.

Never squeamish, those two.

"Usually, it falls to my guards to stay up and watch, but tonight I will share the duty, since we are so few," Ahmet said, before deciding the order of watch. "I will lend the watcher my helm. Even if it is big, you must wear it, in case we are spotted. My armor will be too large, but the watcher will shroud themselves in a blanket. This should be enough for any patrols we might find here."

Letty cautiously accepted the first watch. She put the helmet on and draped the patchwork blanket over her shoulders before looking on from the head of the largest cart. She watched her friends unroll their bags and settle down in the hull, while the brutons nudged each other in a nearby rut. Ahmet and Petri enjoyed the privacy the covered carts afforded. Petri was pleased to have a cart all to herself.

They had pulled off a fair distance from the road, but Letty could still see the main path, some ways through the brush. She looked at the bowl of water that Ahmet had placed at the head of the cart. Inside it was a smaller bowl with a tiny hole poked in the center. The hole allowed water in at a set rate. She was told that an hour would pass before the bowl clunked to the bottom. She was to sit out two clunks before her watch was over.

Everything is so calm now.

After her first hour was up, Letty stood to stretch and reset the bowl. She heard a rhythmic thumping in the distance. She spied something like a snake on legs, traveling down the main road. As it got closer, she realized it was an insect.

A giant centipede?

Letty felt her skin crawl as she palmed the Argument.

Should I sound the alarm?

The huge creature made little sound as it approached. She spotted riders wielding lances, topped with the same banner Ahmet had raised on his carts.

The centipede halted, and a few riders considered their caravan.

Letty was eager to call up the comfort of her blade, but she remembered Ahmet telling them to remain calm if approached.

After a moment, the centipede lowered itself onto its knees and a pair of brutox leaped over the side. They walked through the brush and came upon the caravan. The brutons woke at the footsteps, but they didn't bother getting up.

They looked over the carts, casting a long glance

her way. She felt suddenly hot inside the helmet and under the blanket, but she didn't move.

One brutox nudged the other and they moved off. A minute later they were back aboard the centipede and on their way.

No one said anything about giant centipedes.

Chapter 13: Degoskirke

Andy opened his eyes. The sky was crimson and motley. The motley colors melded and twisted among themselves, distinct from the crimson. Andy watched the sky dance and noticed a thin arc of mauve jut through the other colors with the force of lightning, before shattering into tiny pockets.

He rubbed his eyes, wondering if he was still asleep, and dreaming about a lava lamp.

Sitting up, Andy realized he was on a mattress, which sat atop a square roof, lined with cracked tiles. He saw chains, bolted to the ground, but the shackles were lying at his sides. Red welts stood out on his wrists.

Right, I'm a prisoner. But shouldn't these shackles be on?

Andy thought back to the last clear moment he could recall.

I remember Thrag, and the ravager, and Ziesqe's allies. They each arrived with a team of bodyguards. We made it to that city, Hyadoth, and then something happened.

Andy looked at his robes for a clue, but, save their disorder, they were only familiar. He felt the obsidian jewelry still in place on his wrists, ankles, and neck, but there were no clues.

I remember a helmet; that was important. But why?

His head spun with unbelievable images, each poorly stitched together, like a preview for an action film. One upsetting recollection featured a stranger's voice coming from his mouth. The voice, through his body, had been talking amiably to a towering, malformed ryle. Andy doubted the recollections, reasoning they were more likely to be dreams.

Eager to be rid of them, Andy stood and stretched. His head throbbed, and his muscles were weak. Scared, he walked to the edge of the roof and leaned against the crumbling plaster wall.

In every direction he saw crumbling city. Sprawling and half-ruined, the field of buildings looked like a rugged forest. Fires lit the occasional window, but most were dark or broken. The silence that accompanied the desolation made Andy's skin crawl.

What's that?

Deeper into the city he saw a misshapen wall, lined with equally ramshackle towers. Every span of the poorly made wall was unique from the rest. A mile of it looked to be of one design, with crenellations and blue square towers, where the next consisted of wooden stakes and a few round towers, plopped onto already present structures. The overall effect was shoddiness, and that effect grew as he viewed more of the city.

Looking past the walls, Andy saw three spires that jutted so high, they reached the ceiling. He rubbed his eyes and traced the lines of the spires.

They don't end in a point; they reach the top.

A sudden movement caught Andy's attention. He spotted a brutox on a nearby building. It moved across its roof and leaned against a wall.

Is it one of Ziesqe's?

It scanned the city, as if on guard. Andy

crouched and, after careful minutes of watching, spied several brutox he hadn't seen a moment ago.

There's one in almost every building.

He leaned over the wall and looked down onto streets littered with debris and wreckage.

There!

He saw a brutox crouched behind an overturned cart.

Andy crept to the other side of the roof and looked down.

A huge crater split through the middle of the street and a nearby mansion. The fissure pierced into the sewer below. And in the sewer, something large blocked the way. It was covered in tarpaulins.

Andy stared and stared, until the tarpaulins swayed ever so slightly. There was movement beneath. A long, pointed leg shifted from underneath and was visible for a moment.

It's a ravager, kneeling, and covered up. They're hiding it in the sewer.

Surrounded, and unsure of where he was, Andy felt paralyzed.

They're everywhere, but I'm unshackled. This doesn't make sense. Should I try to escape? Or is this a trick? It almost has to be.

Andy crawled towards the rooftop doorway. He expected it to be locked, yet the handle turned. He opened it gently and then saw a slip of paper drift to the floor. It was a note.

Andy felt suddenly exposed. He crouched against the wall and read the note.

'*I've freed you. Meet me in the nearby palace with the*

fountain. Go now, while the Masters are distracted!'

Andy glanced at the empty shackles.

You don't have to tell me twice.

He slipped through the door and onto the stairs, moving slowly, as the stairs threatened to creak under his weight.

He descended three floors, and listened as the walls and floors nearby groaned, likely under the movement of armed brutox.

A moment later he heard someone getting up too quickly from a chair.

"She should be here!"

I know that voice! It's Ziesqe.

"She'll be here. Viqx has many faults, but traitorousness is not one of them." Andy recognized Kal's voice too.

She is close to Ziesqe, and they're talking about Viqx. She was red, with wings.

"Of course, Viqx is too belligerent to be a traitor. It's Veloiz! She might have given Viqx the slip."

"She's a coward, Ziesqe," Kal countered.

"Yes, but she's seen too much. If she goes to the Maelstrom, they might stop us before we enter the city." Ziesqe sounded calm, though there was an edge to his voice.

Using their conversation as cover, Andy slipped down a few more stairs. He peeked around the corner and saw Ziesqe and Kal, as well as Zava, and Inxa, the ychorons. The ryle wore shabby robes, while the ychorons dressed like paupers in rags.

That's nothing like them. What's going on here?

They had mismatched chairs and couches

set up around a few rickety tables that had been pushed together. The tables held maps and pieces of kitchenware, which Andy suspected represented their forces.

"There is good news: Another pair of ravagers arrived from one of your fiefdoms in the Nomarky. Though the creatures are the smaller savanna breed, they will be welcome. Another battalion of foragers and light infantry have come with them," Kal said.

A smaller breed. That might explain how they fit in the sewers.

"And what strain are the foragers?" Ziesqe asked.

"Locust, I believe. Their commander expressed interest in beginning immediate raids into the inner wreck. They believe that illicit commerce moves through those parts and into the old Niechenheim."

Ziesqe glowered at the maps. "These brutox are too eager. They do not understand the danger here."

"If they stay away from the queen's district, the Locusts will be effective. We need the forage. As it stands, our force is too large to feed conventionally. We're raising too many questions," Kal replied.

Inxa, orange and blue beneath her peasant's clothes, stepped forward and moved pieces on the map. "In a related subject: We have just captured three outer bridges and cleared a few abandoned back-roads. This widens our supply line to the outer city, and will take some pressure off our foragers. We have the hands to occupy what the scouts are now calling, the mussel-shell route. Occupying it will ensure that supplies arriving from fiefs enter the city without drawing attention on the regular routes through the wreck." Inxa spoke the last sentence quietly, looking away from Kal.

"You think this new route will ensure us better supply than engaging the Locusts in their usual purpose?" Ziesqe asked.

"Certainly, my lord. Foragers *could* supply us stolen provisions, though, not to contradict the Mistress, they will suffer attrition from contact with the local queens, who travel the whole city, not just their own district. There is risk of total catastrophe for our forces, if just one queen questions a captured forager."

Kal raised a brow before responding, "It is a fair point. I will concede that I know little of the city and the queens in particular. I never expected to be here."

Ziesqe nodded. "The city breeds a traitorousness that would hamstring any explicit invasion." He looked over to his ychorons. "Even you, girls, the image of fidelity, would find your hearts torn if you wandered too deep."

Zava and Inxa shared horrified looks, "I would never," "We will die for you, Master," they spoke over each other.

Andy's eyes met Zava's for a moment. He nearly gasped.

She saw me!

Zava remained silent while Inxa put a hand on the table and continued, "It is unnatural for the so-called, free ychorites, to live as they do. Despite that, I will obey. We will stay on this side of the wall, until the time comes."

Ziesqe fixed them with a blank expression for so long, the room became uncomfortable.

He finally turned to Kal and spoke, "Detailed planning, at this stage, is pointless. We need to wait for Viqx and Veloiz, as much as it galls me."

Kal walked to his side of the table and laid down a pile of charts. "Let us then go over the standing orders, perhaps we can improve our position here in the wreck."

Ziesqe was frayed and unlike himself. Andy wondered if their plans were falling apart, and cracked a smile before continuing down the stairs, which ended one floor further down.

I can try to sneak out since they're distracted. Maybe Zava didn't see me.

Andy looked around a corner and saw a pair of guards by the large entryway.

This must have been a mansion at one point.

He went the other way, peeking around corners as he went, until he found an empty room that was once a greenhouse. The planters were overflowing with vines and silver-fleshed palms, which had ripped through the glass ceiling.

Maybe I can climb out.

Andy hopped into a planter and felt his robe tug on the vines. He grasped the palm and pulled himself up. When he reached the height of the ceiling, he spotted a door at the other end of the greenhouse, behind some tall reeds. The door looked like it led to the back garden.

Really?

Andy considered sliding back down.

It's probably locked anyway, he decided, and continued up the palm. He reached for the iron support that framed the glass panes and pulled himself up and onto it.

The roof creaked. He held still, but a moment later it groaned ever so softly.

This wasn't the best idea.

Andy shuffled closer to the house and grabbed onto a drainpipe, putting as much weight on it as he dared. He followed the pipe to the edge of the greenhouse and then down. As he inched down the pipe, he had a sudden thought.

Does it rain down here in the Netherscape? It must, if they bother with drainpipes.

A moment later, the pipe creaked. Andy froze.

He cringed, expecting the fixture to tear free from the wall and send him plummeting to the ground.

When nothing happened, Andy dared to look down, and saw the ground barely a foot away.

Embarrassed, he released the pipe.

I'm in a backyard, a regular old backyard.

The sense of familiarity was uncanny. He kept low, moving through the overgrown plants and was about to climb a wall when he heard footsteps. He shrunk down and listened.

Brutox in the streets.

A minute later, they had come and gone, and no alarm had gone up from the mansion.

They don't check up on me that often. Andy hoped that whoever reported his absence to Ziesqe wouldn't end up executed. Putting that aside, he thought, *I must find the palace with the fountain.*

Andy hopped over the wall. The flagstone street was littered with the crumbling remains of buildings, broken down carts, scorched roadblocks, improvised weapons, and swirling pieces of paper.

I'll check the buildings nearby. Hopefully I can keep out of sight.

Andy crossed the street, pausing at the sight of a long dagger embedded in a charred barrier. Feeling exposed, he rushed to it and pulled on it as hard as he could. The barrier crumbled into pieces, releasing the dagger. Without thinking, Andy took the dagger's blade between his teeth and clambered over the wall into the next yard. He landed softly on turf and looked around. He was in a splendid rose garden that featured a large fountain at its center and a gazebo off to the side.

What luck!

Crouching behind a shrub, and with a dagger between his teeth, Andy felt like a pirate.

This is ridiculous, he thought, taking the dagger in one hand.

Andy crept to the fountain, put the dagger on the stones, and ran his hands through the cool water.

He cupped his palms and took a sniff. It seemed fresh.

He sipped, and then gulped down more. He drank his fill and washed his face, using his robes as a towel. Refreshed, he wondered if he should wait, or hunt for a yard with some fruit trees and return here later.

Andy took the dagger, walked over to the wall that separated this yard from the next, and was about to climb over when he heard a door creak.

He bent low and turned to look.

Zava?

The verdant ychoron stepped out of the mansion and into the garden.

"Lysander?" She called softly. "I know you're back here."

She was silent for a moment.

She did see me. That or these bracelets give me away, he thought, looking at the obsidian bracelet on his wrist.

"I know a better way," she said, still speaking softly. "They don't know you've awakened yet."

She said nothing, because she released me.

Andy readied the dagger and came out from hiding.

"There you are," Zava said, her face downcast.

"What did you say? They don't know I've awakened. How do you know then? Did you release me?" Andy asked.

"Yes—Ziesqe made you my ward, my responsibility—but listen, there isn't much time before they realize. I need to get those off you, and you need to get into the city."

She came towards him, but Andy raised his dagger. "I just heard you announce loyalty to Ziesqe. How—"

"Do you think I'm stupid? Or is it possible that we become skilled actors?" she spat, slapping the dagger from his hand.

Andy bent for the weapon. "Don't you want those off?" Zava asked, she pulled a black glove onto one hand. "And besides, there are far more potent weapons in the city."

Andy let the dagger lay and watched as Zava removed the bracelets and anklets as if they were simple jewelry.

That's the trick; you need the glove to get these off.

"And the last one," she said, pulling the necklace over Andy's brow.

She dropped the necklace onto a pile with the others. Andy looked at his arms and touched his throat. He felt no different.

"Come on, let's get inside," Zava said, kicking the obsidian jewelry into a planter.

"Okay," Andy said woodenly, still uncertain of her change.

She led him up the stairs, into a battered bedroom, and to a window facing Degoskirke proper.

Why is she doing this? It can't be what Ziesqe ordered, but—

"Do you see those giant pillars?" she asked.

"Yes," Andy replied, keeping the suspicion from his voice.

Zava pointed to the pillars as she spoke, "The central one, it shines brighter than the others, is Carthago Sundra. The one that's further lantic was Insyreth, though I believe it has another name now; it is off limits. The last one, Panobscura Talionis, was once closed, but we've just learned that it reopened some years ago." That last detail sounded important to her.

Why does it matter if the last one was opened again? Hell, why does any of this matter?

"The city is virulently secular. Their church denies that the Axiomatic wars ever occurred. Seer and ryle are outlawed, though we now suspect that both still live here, in secret."

"Why are you telling me this?" Andy asked.

"Right, excuse my excitement," Zava thought for a moment. "Ziesqe plans to conquer this place, to excuse his past failures and to secure his future against ascendancy. We loyal ychorons have a peculiar sentiment about the free city. Our—less than loyal kin—have made a home here. They even changed their name. We revile the so-called, ychorites, but it is critical that they remain free."

Andy scowled. "If you were really disloyal to Ziesqe you would leave him and live with the ychorites."

Zava's color twitched a few shades darker for a moment. "It is a difficult problem to explain. I must serve my master, but I do this for my heart. You might understand this old argument: A human can endure any agony, as long as he may freely end his life, and therefore end his agony."

What? Andy stared incredulously.

"For us, the situation is reversed, but the analogy remains. Degoskirke is the possibility of being born. We live and die in service to tradition, knowing it exists. If it were not so, I might find service impossible."

Andy shook his head.

"I'm sorry. We've always struggled to express this sentiment."

"Okay, you freed me to stop Ziesqe from taking Degoskirke. How do you expect me to do this? He has an army hiding all around us, and I'm alone."

Zava walked over to a cabinet and unlocked it with a key she had hidden up her sleeve. Inside the cabinet was a round bundle. She took it out and unwrapped it.

"I have brought you something," Zava said, a quaver in her voice as she produced the Casque.

Not that.

Andy's eyes flashed with a rush of memory. He backed away from Zava and the Casque as a sudden impulse to grab it almost overcame him.

"Focus, Andy," Zava said firmly. "Look back out to the pillars."

Shaking, Andy did so.

"Which one is Panobscura Talionis?"

Andy pointed.

"Yes. In Panobscura Talionis there are dozens of fountains and burning pillars, all containing a piece of the Argument. Above all of these is the Cogito, the largest piece of Argument known to us. You must find and claim it. Take the Casque and travel into the city, touch the Cogito," Zava pleaded, holding the helm out to Andy.

"No!" He stumbled backward. "I—I destroyed..." Andy mumbled as the memories of violence returned to him.

"It was a blessing. That hell-hole was torture for

millions of unwanted beings!"

"If I put that helmet on, it will happen again!"

"No, Caspian, you won't destroy this city, I swear!"

Andy felt his arms reaching out for the Casque. His legs pulled him closer and he felt his eyes roll into the back of his head.

"No!" He cried, breaking away. "That's not my name!"

He came to his senses and rushed from the room, barreling down the stairs and bursting out into the street. His heart was nearly beating out of his chest. His body quivered with the memory of his arms and legs obeying another master. He ran down the street, pushing tears out of his eyes, and trying to dodge the tall piles of debris littering the streets.

I can't, I can't! Get out of my head!

Andy slammed into a brutox, which stumbled, turned, and gave him a wide-eyed look. Surprise was so alien on the insect's face, that Andy could only stare.

They gawked at each other for a long moment before the brutox backed away and entered a nearby building.

"What?" Andy burst out, his face torn between confusion and outrage. "Don't you want to take me in?" he cried.

Andy looked around at the other buildings and saw the shapes of brutox on the roofs and in the windows. As his eyes passed their way, the brutox would back off the edge, or pull away from their watches at the windows.

Indeed!

Andy paused, and looked down the long street towards the pillars.

"This is his plan. This is Ziesqe's plan," Andy said to himself.

"There's a lad," a voice responded.

Andy took a deep breath and turned.

Ziesqe emerged from a doorway.

"I won't put it on," Andy insisted.

Ziesqe walked up beside him and looked out onto the pillars.

"I don't blame you," he finally said.

"I believed her," Andy whispered, thinking back to Zava, and looking at his naked wrists.

"I expect she did as well," Ziesqe said absentmindedly. He continued, with more focus, "Why did you refuse the Casque?"

Andy pondered, considering which reason he would spout first.

"Wait, let's walk for a moment before you answer. I want you to think it out," Ziesqe said, leading Andy back down the street and towards a tall bridge.

Andy spied brutox in the buildings and on the roofs. He even heard their heavy footsteps close behind.

They're paying attention now.

"Don't let them distract you," Ziesqe said. "Consider my question."

What does he want me to say? I won't put the Casque on because I remember what I did—what happened—back in Hyadoth. I don't want to be like that again.

They approached the bridge. It was only a few blocks from the mansion he just escaped. Ziesqe motioned to a nearby tower where a pair of ychorons stood.

"We have a brunch waiting for us in the spire," he said, as they mounted the stairs, the ychorons right behind.

Now I'm having brunch with him. He must want something, but why not use force?

At the top of the spire they found a table set for two and a many-eyed spider brutox staring out onto the streets. The brutox bore a heavy crossbow. He didn't break his watch, even when Ziesqe appeared.

An ychoron rushed to pull out his chair, but Ziesqe waved him off. "We eat simply today," he said.

Andy took his seat. The lunch featured cuts of meat and fish, served with mossy greenish-golden cheeses and hard slices of bread. There was also a ryle tea served from a tall, brass, table-side samovar. Andy ate nervously, as Ziesqe kept a watchful eye on him and his movements throughout the meal.

"I expect you've come up with an answer to my question," Ziesqe said, carefully tapping at his tentacles with a napkin.

The image was so inherently absurd that Andy felt a nerve split in his mind. It was possibly the funniest thing he had ever seen.

I might as well jump off the tower if I crack a smile at him.

Andy bit down on his cheek, until he tasted blood, to keep himself from laughing. He took a deep breath and looked down at the table.

"I will hear your response."

"Right, excuse me," Andy took a deep breath and looked up, "I refused the Casque because I remember what it did to me, and what I did with it on."

Ziesqe nodded. "Dissolution of agency, and moral reprehension at the scale of life lost. Typically human and, in this case, positive."

Positive, how?

"My plans have changed, Lysander, and it is best that you refused the Casque, but I must tempt you once more." Ziesqe stood and directed that Andy follow, before pointing out to the city. "There is Degoskirke. A resourceful young man like yourself might find a way to the surface through that city. To that end, I empower you."

Ziesqe tossed Andy a small leather pouch. Andy opened it and found an assortment of silver and gold coins.

"Be careful with that, and I expect you could be home in less than a day."

"Why are you doing this?" Andy snapped, surprised at himself and infuriated at the sight of the gold, which he left on the table.

Ziesqe cocked his head. "You feel manipulated. Quite the contrary. I do indeed hope that you stay, but you must make that choice."

Andy opened his mouth, but Ziesqe held up a hand.

"Yes, yes, I know where to find you and all that. Listen. I have lost my mandate on the surface; you have probably heard as much from my gossipy attendants. I can follow you at great personal risk—I of course remember where you live—but I am in a pathetic situation. My freedom is almost lost. I must capture this grand absurdity they call Degoskirke, before I can ever step foot in any ryle city, or even my own palace, ever again. You could leave now, go home, and have your family moved in two days, and I would never find you."

Is that true? I knew he was in trouble, down here and on the surface. Could I find a way back home? The only way I know is through the mouse fortress, but it was conquered. Even if it is true, there has to be a catch; he admitted that he wants me to stay.

"You are wondering how I can give you this knowledge, coin, and freedom, yet hope that you stay."

Andy was silent.

"We expect Viqx to return any moment. She is at the head of a large and brutal host of modified strains. Though I haven't spoken with her about our plans, I already know her conclusion, and that is for invasion. Kal also believes that fighting is unavoidable. I do not." Ziesqe took a sip from his teacup. "I also hope that you do not," he said, watching Andy.

"If you wanted me to stay, why have Zava offer me the Casque?" Andy asked.

"I wanted to confirm my suspicion, that you are not hopelessly idiotic. I have also discerned that your table manners are passable, though you suffer from emotional outbursts."

Andy felt himself clench. He paused and took a

breath, realizing that Ziesqe wasn't wrong.

"Fine, but why is any of that important?"

"I am assessing a plan, a plan which I could employ on my own, to some effect, but with your aid..."

"What's the plan?"

"Saving the millions of lives in this city."

"Of course. Pretend like you aren't the one attacking in the first place," Andy blustered at Ziesqe's false morality.

"It's past that now, I'm afraid. I cannot overrule Kal and Viqx. They will push for war. Only I arguing in favor of a peaceful assumption of control."

Andy nearly stormed out of the tower.

"Wait!" Ziesqe called out, there was a tremor of desperation, even fear in his voice.

Andy paused.

"Think—think back to the surface. For your whole life, you never knew the truth. You and your kind live in peace; you have your prosperity. You must admit that life under the ryle is more than fair, especially when compared with your own, human prisons."

Andy wanted to scream.

It's true. I never even suspected, but I can't go back to that.

"Our paths are thinning, Lysander. Kal is pure utility: She will do whatever is necessary to achieve her goals. Viqx is bloodthirsty: She will destroy this city out of pure joy. They will do this with my own warriors; my hand is forced by our combine. A venture into the city, in disguise, is our only chance to prevent invasion."

"You say that ryle rule has brought peace, but you break your own people's rules, and you chose Viqx and Kal to be your allies!" Andy retorted.

"Yes! I failed," Ziesqe snapped.

The brutox twitched.

"I—events did not unfold as I expected, but we must move forward. The final truth is that, if you leave, I will have a slim chance at keeping Degoskirke from the torch. If you join with me, we will save millions."

"I can't—"

"There is one more unfortunate detail," Ziesqe interrupted. "Your old friends, Titus and Taptalles, have escaped to this city."

Andy felt himself buckle. His stomach sank and he grasped the chair to keep upright. He opened his mouth, but the words wouldn't come. The pain felt like choking, and tears stung his eyes. He stood in agony before looking down at his finished meal.

Dine with the devil.

He felt a hand on his shoulder.

"Think on it," Ziesqe said.

Andy pulled away and slammed into the wall. "Don't touch me!" He spat, and wiped the hair out of his eyes. "Fine! Fine! I'll do it! I'll help you conquer these people—because it is better than them dying!"

Ziesqe watched him with an indecipherable expression. "Remember, I could have forced that helmet back on your head and released you into the city."

Andy shivered at the thought.

"It was Kal's notion," Ziesqe said decisively. "Come now, I have something for you, but it must wait until your eyes settle from the weeping."

Andy nearly attacked, but Ziesqe eyed him harshly, as if aware.

I can't believe it's come to this.

Ziesqe led Andy back down the tower. They met laden ychorons at the base.

"This should pass for a moderate display of wealth," one said, holding out a blue robe embroidered with gold braid.

Ziesqe regarded the aged and foppish clothes with contempt.

A moment later, a cart laden with boxes and barrels arrived. The driver stepped off and stood guard at the bridge.

Ziesqe went inside. Andy followed and was dressed in a plain, white robe, crosshatched with large red rhombuses. It was appalling.

"You are to be his apprentice and assistant," the attending ychoron said. "I don't know much about the free city, save that it is chaotic. What manner of courtesy rules here is beyond me, but I would just keep quiet if I were you. Always err on the side of caution, and be more polite, rather than less, if you are confused."

Andy nodded, trying to take it all in.

"There is one more thing," the ychoron said, leading Andy outside. Another approached from the cart, bearing a small box, which he handed to Andy.

Andy gave it a cursory glance before peeking inside. He saw two blue irises floating in glass containers.

"For your eyes," an ychoron said in a hurried tone, looking back at Ziesqe.

Andy stared at them awkwardly, feeling his skin crawl at the thought of putting them in.

"Here," the ychoron said, snatching the box. "We need to be quick; he's not pleased."

The ychorons had Andy kneel and lean his head back.

"They need to rest in this solution if you are not wearing them, which should only be when sleeping. Do not let the locals see them, and let it be on your head if you walk the streets without wearing these. The Master is skillful in the use of the lenses, but I wouldn't bother him about it, unless he's in a better mood," the ychoron stammered as he put the contacts in.

They finished and pulled Andy to his feet before pushing him towards the cart.

Wha—

Andy gawked at the figure sitting in the cart. It was human, and familiar.

"What are you staring at, damn it! Get up here and take the reins!"

It's Ropt! The lenses keep me from seeing what he actually looks like.

Andy needed another push from the ychorons before he hopped up and took the reins. The Bruton they had lashed to the cart's yoke looked back at them and regarded Andy.

"How do I get him to go?" Andy asked.

"Just a slight tug on both reins to go forward,"

One of the ychorons said, eying Ziesqe nervously.

Andy pulled back on the reins slightly and the Bruton groaned before lumbering into motion.

Chapter 14: Gifts

Letty felt the curved hull of the cart beneath her sleeping bag. Footsteps were approaching.

"So, my wayward sentinels, which one of you slept through your watch?" Ahmet asked, a brooding edge to his voice.

"I didn't," Staza said, aggravated by the insinuation.

"Neither did I," Letty replied.

"Well, someone did, because there are fresh ravager tracks!" Ahmet gesticulated at the road. "Did someone just happen to not see the giant insect?"

"I saw it," Letty said, sitting up. "They stopped, and a pair of brutox came to look at the caravan. They didn't do anything."

Ahmet sighed in relief. "Well, in the future, please mention it to the next watcher, so I do not suffer such a fright come the morning."

"Fine," Letty said, getting to her feet. "Will we have time to train before we get moving?"

"This morning, and likely this morning only. I have a stop to make in a few hours; you will have some time then. Though, you should rearrange the space in the tub here and practice on the move," Ahmet looked down at Dean, who rolled over and covered his ears. "Up boy, there's no time to lie about. We must meet the sun and the wind," Ahmet said, giving Dean a slight kick.

"Uhhh, fine," Dean mumbled, sitting up.

Ahmet hopped over the side.

"What did he mean by, 'meet the sun?'" Letty asked. "There is no sun down here."

"That's Elazene mysticism, they think they can sense the sun and moon," Staza said, yawning.

"It has to do with the wind," Blue interjected, showing himself. He had bedded down in a basket full of silks. "They can feel the moon and sun in the wind. I haven't gotten the hang of it myself, but it's serious enough for them. If they fail to greet the sun properly, they won't travel."

"I haven't seen them greet anything," Dean said.

"They're secretive about it," Blue responded.

They poked their heads out of the cart and saw Petri in the brush, facing away from them. She had her hands raised to sides of her face; her fingers spread open as she raised her palms to the sky.

Maybe it's their ritual. Or she might just be stretching.

"Let's not waste any time," Emma said, about to devour a packaged pastry, but Ahmet re-appeared, bearing food.

"Eat, and have some tea, it might wake up the *melekh* here," he said grinning at Dean.

They had their tin cups at the ready, before enjoying a musty tea with a thick vegetable stew.

The groggy morning conversation died down as they ate.

"Good breakfast," Emma mumbled between sips. "Beats the food at school by a mile."

Dean and Letty agreed.

Petri appeared a minute later and cleared their bowls.

"That was delicious, thanks," Letty said.

Petri looked her way and nodded. Letty could see that her eyes were smiling beneath the helm.

Emma readjusted Petri's ladybug helmet, which was askew and caught up in her curly hair.

"Thank you," Petri said, giggling and rushing off with the bowls. There was a clatter, and Letty looked over to see the tin bowls rolling on the floor and Petri bent to gather them.

Ahmet whistled a few minutes later, and the caravan was on the move. The side trail they had camped on was bumpy, but Ahmet led them back to the main road and a smoother ride.

"Let's make some space," Letty said, pushing cargo around.

"There's a hatch there," Blue said, pointing at a covered door on the floor.

Inside was more space. They put some of the cargo away, after asking Ahmet's permission.

"Fine, but keep your heads down, you're still not dressed properly," he replied.

With the space cleared, Staza led them in stretches. They did as well they could, considering the limited space, and the jostling of the cart. Dean and Emma weren't steady on their feet. They tipped over mid-stretch.

Quill and Staza faced off with the wooden clubs, and Quill made a better showing than Letty expected, but Staza still had the edge.

When it came time for Emma and Dean to spar, Emma tripped over a basket, and Dean stumbled to the side of the cart to throw up again. Letty scowled.

Emma was patting Dean on the back and

looking embarrassed as the Caspians scoffed. Ahmet yelled at them about a wasted breakfast from his position on the lead cart.

"Practicing in a moving cart might work for you guys, but we're not ready," Letty said, standing by Emma and Dean.

"I have an inkling," Blue said, watching the events from atop a pile of cargo. "Why not wake up early, like the Elazene, and spar before breakfast. You can make up the lost sleep by napping in the cart."

They considered Blue's proposal.

"I like it," Emma said, still patting Dean on the back.

"Ugh, me too," Dean mumbled, his face still over the side.

They agreed on the new plan and put the cargo back in order.

"Get down back there! A patrol is coming up," Ahmet called out to them.

"Quick, get under the blankets!" Letty said, pulling her friends away from the sides. "The monsters they ride are huge. They'll spot us if we don't get down."

They clambered under sleeping bags and blankets. Dean groaned from under a pile of backpacks.

Ahmet stayed silent as the percussive beat of locomotion came closer.

Letty watched Emma under their blanket. Emma had a single eye peeking out. The creature was just in sight, and Emma's face contorted, first with disbelief, then with horror.

She might scream.

Letty grabbed her arm, which only made Emma moan in fear.

"Shh!" Letty whispered, pulling Emma towards her and putting a hand over her mouth.

The insects rumbled by without ceremony, and their riders barely cast a glance down at the carts.

A minute later, they heard Dean cackle. "This is completely ridiculous. We're throwing up—I'm throwing up, because I get motion sickness. We're practicing with wooden clubs, and there are things out there like that." He let out a painful cackle before continuing, "What the hell are we doing?" His head fell back woefully and smacked into the hull.

Emma started to cry.

They aren't wrong. Why didn't I freak out when I saw the ravager last night?

Letty hugged Emma reassuringly, while the Caspians wore silent sneers.

After a minute of despondency, Staza blurted out, "I didn't cry when we saw the metal snakes in the tunnels."

"The subway," Letty said.

"Right, the subway—or the herds of iron carts," Staza spoke mostly to Dean.

"They aren't the same!" Dean snapped. "Giant bugs ridden by human shaped insects! And they want to capture or kill us. The subway just—well—it just moves people around, it isn't dangerous!"

"No. You could fall onto the rails," Emma said, wiping her face.

"Right! But that would be your own fault, it isn't our fault the bugs want to kill us," Dean retorted.

"Call them brutox, not bugs, and yes, it is your fault. You knew the risks; I saw Letty berate you. She gave you a chance to go home," Quill argued.

"If someone had mentioned building sized centipedes..." Dean mumbled to himself.

They sat in uncomfortable silence for so long that no one wanted to break it.

The Caspians are disgusted with us and we need them, but my friends are useless, and I'm not much better.

"I suppose," Blue poked his face out from under a blanket and spoke, surprising everyone, "we should be grateful there aren't any ravagers in the free city. Now that you've seen one, the shock won't be so great when the next patrol comes along," Blue finished with uncharacteristic sympathy for the surfacers.

Everyone stared.

Blue looked uncomfortable. "But you put on a disgraceful performance during training, so, sick or no, you had better keep practicing," he finished snidely and poked his head back under the blanket.

Staza smirked. She stood and approached Dean. "Come on now, there's no going back," she said, smacking him in the shoulder. "And you need to realize that Letty could cut a ravager down to size."

Dean looked up with red eyes, "But then it would just fall on you."

Quill and Staza both laughed. Letty couldn't help herself and joined in. Eventually Emma, and even Dean, had to giggle.

A moment later, Ahmet was there, looking down on them. "Stop enjoying yourselves. We must halt for a while, and now you may practice. If you see anything, get back in the cart and hide. Keep an ear out for Petri's call, she has better eyes than even me."

Grateful for the interruption, Dean clambered out of the cart, and nearly stumbled on the last step. The others followed, with more grace. Despite its size, the cart was crowded with so many bodies inside.

Staza and Quill broke out into a spontaneous torrent of stretching. They goaded Emma and Dean to join in. Letty looked out towards the brushland, reaching off into the distance. She spotted Ahmet carrying a heavy bag.

He's armed.

Letty saw his makeshift mantis limb in one hand. She wondered if they should help him. Ahmet disappeared behind a stand of thorny shrubs.

Petri approached and regarded them speculatively.

"Petri, is your father safe out there? Should we go to help?" Letty asked.

The others stopped stretching to listen.

"Certainly not! You would wake the dead. Be ready, if anything should come up the road," she said, climbing up the cart to take watch. "And don't forget these!" She yelled throwing the bag of carrots down to Letty.

Oh right, these disgusting little carrots.

Letty took one before tossing a pair to the

Caspians. She regarded it scornfully, before gulping it down.

"Well, at least we don't have to eat those things," Dean muttered to Emma.

Letty tossed the bag back to Petri, before joining the others in the calisthenics. They ended the stretches with a painful set of toe touches before pairing off to spar. Dean with Emma, and Letty with Quill, while Staza walked between them, directing.

"You're gripping the club like it's a hammer! Don't learn the wrong lesson. Imagine what will happen when you have an actual weapon," Staza said to Letty. "Hold it like a pen, that way you have more control."

Letty watched Staza demonstrate with her dagger.

She's right. I'm much clumsier with a club than the Argument.

Letty faced off with Quill, who had been holding back. She swung, and Quill responded by deflecting her club with force, knocking it from her hand. Everyone saw.

"Damn it," Letty muttered, lifting her club from the floor.

"You also need to respond to what's happening, Letty. His whole body showed you he was going to put force in that swing. You need to change your grip as the situation demands."

Letty readied her club, but hesitated, not sure of her grip. Quill batted the club from her hand again.

"I know!" Letty snapped before Staza could lecture her.

She readied her club for a third try. This time she let Quill go for the first swing. She stepped back to dodge and then lunged forward, thrusting with the club as if it were a bladed weapon.

Quill caught her with an upswing. His club cracked into her fingers, knocking her weapon loose once more.

"Damn!" Letty snapped, cradling her hurt fingers. "It won't be like this – I'll have the Argument!"

Quill and Staza shared a look, and Dean and Emma stopped sparring.

"What if something happens? Maybe you lose the Argument; maybe you come up against the Counter. You need to know how to fight. Don't take it personally," Staza said, surprised at Letty's attitude.

Letty scowled, but then relented.

She's right, I don't know why I'm so furious—I just thought I had him.

Training continued, for better and worse, until Letty heard a rustling nearby.

"There, there, young warriors!" Ahmet's voice called out to them.

He had lost the big bag he set out with but returned with two others.

"Proper outfits!" he said, laying the bags down carefully. "Be gentle, we must take care about the leather, I'll grease the straps, but you'll have to polish the plates."

He pulled pieces of brutox plate armor out of the large bags.

"Petri! My grease pot, please," he called, laying

out the breast plates.

A moment later, Petri appeared with a small pot and brush. Ahmet took the brush and carefully applied a coating of grease to the various leather straps. He inspected the buckles and found that several fittings needed replacing. He was about to open his mouth when Petri handed him a toolbox.

"Aha, thank you, my dear. Now would you please take watch on the cutter? I would hate for us to be surprised," he said, opening the box.

"Yes, Ada," Petri whispered, before running off laughing, her arms waving as she went.

"She is a sweet girl, and she loves to laugh," Ahmet said, replacing a broken strap and buckle with pieces from his supply. "Like I said, I will get these in good order, but you have to polish them. I'll show you how. Some of these suits are quite handsome, this one for instance," Ahmet said, holding up a helm that featured piercing mandibles and at least six multifaceted eyes, "what is he?"

"A spider," Emma blurted.

Ahmet laughed and motioned with the helm as if it were alive. "A wolf spider, blue gray like a sky. He leaps on his enemies, but he also sees far," Ahmet said, almost lovingly, before throwing Emma the helm.

Emma nearly shrieked, but then laughed instead, as she caught the helm and inspected it.

"I have new helmet liners too, go on and pull the old one out."

It's weird, the way he talked about 'a sky,' like a singular sky, and not the sky, the way we refer to it. How does he even know what it looks like? They must have stories about the surface.

Emma pulled the old helmet liner out. It was stained dark brown in a few places. She held the liner out for Ahmet to see.

"Ah, the last keeper saw some action. Imagine if they hadn't worn the helm at all," Ahmet said as he snatched the liner from her and tossed it into a nearby refuse basket.

"Is there anything for me?" Petri asked ingratiatingly from her post.

"No, my dearest, only for these larger friends of ours. Your suit is new, anyway."

"But why do they get new clothes? *I* am your daughter, not them."

"Tut-tut, dearest, of course you are my daughter, but these suits are far from new. A few I suspect haven't seen use in centuries."

Letty saw that some of the straps had wasted away, though the plates were still glossy and solid.

"Many of these breeds have not walked the earth since before my grandfather's time. Look here, the green wasp. What a collector wouldn't give for this set," Ahmet mumbled as he brushed a fine coating of dust off the wasp helm.

"A green wasp?" Staza asked.

"Yes!" Ahmet said, tossing her the helm. "It suits you. You are the fastest, and the sharpest. I will teach you how to polish, and then you will teach the others," Ahmet said, as he laid out the rest of the wasp.

"Ahmet, sir, don't we owe you something for

these suits, and the work, of course?" Dean asked.

Ahmet surprised everyone by sitting up and jabbing an angry finger in Dean's face. "There must be absolutely no talk of business now!" He sat back down and shook his head.

Dean was shocked.

"Please excuse me, surfacer; I should have said something before," Ahmet apologized. He ran his hand over a deep-purple breast plate. "The dead have offered up their skins for us—" he tossed Dean a purple ant helm. "Twilight forma: Their queen holds court in the free city. They were one of the only breeds to show an aptitude for business."

Dean held the helmet at arm's length.

"Snow moth, with scorpion chest," Ahmet pronounced before tossing the helm to Quill. "You will wear them both. As you fly towards the light you must also keep a fury in your chest."

Quill looked thoughtful as he listened and admired the helm.

His suit is from two insects. Ahmet's old caravan guards had mismatched suits too.

"And for you, girl, I found something extraordinary," Ahmet said, holding the final helm and tossing it towards Letty.

I don't recognize the type.

The helm was a bright, creamy white, lined with metallic black at the segments and powdered red at the cheeks. The body was similarly colored.

What is it?

Ahmet sensed her confusion and pulled a heavy bundle out of a bag. He rolled the bundle out, and then it made sense.

A butterfly.

It was a cape molded in the shape of wings.

Everyone else gets to wear an aggressive suit, and I'm stuck looking like a princess.

Ahmet could tell that Letty wasn't pleased. "You would have preferred something more intimidating? Let me just say that you should be careful when you put on the cape."

That gave Letty some pause.

Ahmet cast a serious glance around at his novice guards. He stood and spoke, "Would everyone please put their helmets on the ground, facing me?"

It seemed a strange request, but his seriousness allowed for no argument, and they did as they were told.

"Heads bowed, and no talking," he said, carefully adjusting the direction of the helms to his satisfaction.

Everyone bowed their heads. Ahmet was silent. All they heard was breathing and the tinkling of wind through the bridles of the nearby brutons.

Finally, Ahmet spoke, but his voice came softly, and Letty strained to hear, "If we bear you as mantle, will you bear us as progeny?" He stopped and kept an eye on the helms, as if something might happen. When nothing did, his voice became louder as he continued, "When we bear you as mantle, please share your essence. Enemies once, kin hereafter, enchained alike in life and flesh, hear our promise to you, whose coil and duties shed centuries hence:

384

Our tears, through your eyes, fall to one end alone."

He's praying to the helmets? No, he's praying to the dead brutox. It's like a pledge. 'If we bear you as mantle, will you bear us as progeny?'

Petri burst into the silence. "It's good!" she yelled, picking up the spider and handing it to Emma. Ahmet seemed pleased by this and stood by as his daughter passed out the other helms.

"Don't hurt this one, Letty; it's going to be mine after you," Petri said, as she reluctantly handed over the butterfly helmet.

"You say that now, but you might not want to look like a princess when you get bigger," Letty replied.

Emma laughed, but Petri blurted, "Don't be stupid!" Before going to help her father with Dean's new breastplate.

Ahmet tried to be hands-off, but the sight of so many inept hands was too much. He bent to helping everyone work the kinks out of their gauntlets and pauldrons, which were the most articulated pieces. He handed out new helmet liners and showed everyone how to attach them. Blue and Petri looked on, one with fascination, and the other with a hint of frustrated jealousy.

"I've never seen this done before," Blue said to himself. "Far more care than I expected."

After Letty had donned the suit, she regarded the cape. The neck was tall, and the collar ran down from the throat to the base of the cape in a red arc. The wings were white, fringed with black, like the body. She put the cape on cautiously.

What could be dangerous about this?

She searched the cape and found handles where interior pockets would be. She held onto them and pulled. The wings went rigid. She pulled up on them and the wings bent and stretched as she moved.

"Hey! Watch it!" Quill yelled.

Letty turned as her friends shrieked and leaped away from her.

"What! What happened?" She asked.

Just then, Letty saw the edges of her outstretched wings glinted, betraying their razor-sharp edge.

The fringes of the cape are lined with blades.

Quill had his hand over his cheek. A small trail of blood wound its way down his face.

"Oh God! I'm sorry, I didn't realize," Letty stepped forward, but they continued evading.

The wings!

She let go of the handles and the wings slackened back into a cape.

"Now who isn't dangerous?" Ahmet asked, laughing.

"You could have said something!" Letty yelled.

"Yes, I could have, but now you have respect for the skin of a long dead queen."

Queen? The butterfly was a queen?

"Now, all of you, practice moving around. Feel if any joints stick and we'll get them working. Walk around, damn it!" Ahmet said to the confused faces.

They all stretched and moved.

"They look like people now," Petri said.

"They look like a bunch of mismatched, antique

brutox," Blue rejoined, staring from atop the cart.

"This is people in my land, mouse. You must know this," Ahmet responded with a smile.

They continued adjusting their suits as Ahmet showed Staza how to polish the plates with a heavy cloth coated in oil. When everyone was finally satisfied, Ahmet left for one of the covered carts, returning with a long, bulky bundle, which he laid on the ground and unrolled.

A collection of cobbled weapons appeared as the roll unwound. Letty saw another pair of mantis scythes, as well as swords and shields made from curved Bruton plates. There were crude flanged maces and axes and even a bow made of horn. Before anything else, the dozens of daggers made their way into belts and bootstraps at Staza's insistence.

"Arm yourselves as you please, but do not be careless with these weapons! Do not drop them on the floor, and do not swing wildly at each other as I have seen you do. Real weapons require finesse," Ahmet lectured as each found weaponry they preferred.

Staza and Quill had packed their old Caspian suits away, and Letty could see that they were the most uncomfortable.

They must unlearn some of what they knew to get used to these clothes and weapons, where Emma and Dean are like blank slates.

Emma took a bow and short sword, Dean found a mace and shield, Quill hefted a spear and brace of javelins, and, after much deliberation, Staza took a saber and parrying dagger.

Every time Letty reached for a weapon, she saw Ahmet shake his head.

Well, what about the axe?

She looked up and saw him disapprove.

At this point, everyone else was armed and staring.

"What? He isn't happy with any of it," Letty said, responding to their looks.

"You are already armed, your Highness," Ahmet said cautiously. "Bearing a regular weapon would lower your station."

Letty rolled her eyes.

"Please," Ahmet held up a hand, "sting me not with that face. There are weapons that belong to that suit. Sadly, they are rare."

"I can't use these wings. I'm likely to cut up my friends," Letty said, staring at the tip of the cape.

"You are deadly enough for now, and you should practice alone for a time. Eventually you will find the wings move like they are your own."

Letty wanted to argue, or even cast the cape aside for the absurdity it was, but she relented, realizing how rude she was being, not only to Ahmet, but to the long dead queen.

I'm wearing the daggers though, even if he doesn't like it.

Once everyone could run and jump in their new suits, Ahmet clapped. "Finally, you are useful. Now we can talk about reciprocity."

"What?" Emma asked.

"He means payment," Dean said.

388

They spent some time going through their packs and rooting around for things Ahmet would like. In the shuffle, Letty found Andy's notepad, which she had stuffed at the bottom of her pack.

I should have a look at this tonight, on watch.

She slipped the notepad into an inner pocket sewn in the cape.

"How about this?" Dean asked, gesturing to an array of two flashlights, two pairs of sunglasses, a compass, and a math textbook that came with them unintentionally, hiding at the bottom of a pack. Ahmet was intrigued by everything, save the text, which Dean added to the pile on a whim.

"As we are enriched, so to, I hope, are you," Ahmet said, as he took everyone by the wrist in succession. "The deal is struck."

"Can we go now? We don't have time for tea!" Petri yelled.

"Yes, dearest!" Ahmet said, putting his new glasses on over his helmet. "No time for tea—it's a disgrace," he mumbled, "but we should get going. As much as I love a day trading and arming, we are behind."

Dean interjected offhandedly, "You said the sun glasses were foolish before. I don't understand why you'd want them now."

"Never let them know what you want! The price goes up," Ahmet responded.

They packed up the equipment, and Ahmet showed everyone where they were expected to sit or stand in the caravan. "No more lying down on the job," he said, going from cart to cart, inspecting the brutons.

They were finally back on the road.

Letty found herself tired and sore after only an hour of walking, though the others were complaining far sooner.

"They are like children!" Petri whined, as both Emma and Dean made up excuses to sit on a cart.

"Why aren't we allowed to sit? The carts have seats," Dean muttered.

"More work for the brutons, and besides, you need the exercise," was Ahmet's response.

The rest of the day was one long, slow trudge, until finally, Ahmet and Petri led the caravan off the road and down past a culvert. There was a daub farmhouse hidden behind tall brush. Another couple of Elazene came out and waved at them.

"It must be getting time to stop," Letty said.

"This armor is killing me," Emma complained. "It wasn't that heavy at first, but now I'm dying."

"This is how we get stronger, Em," Letty replied, taking her helmet off for a breath of fresh air.

"I don't know how they do it," Dean said, as he slid down the side of a cart to the floor.

"A hard life makes hard people," Quill added.

They watched Ahmet and Petri go out to meet the new pair of Elazene near the house. Facing a certain direction, they raised their hands and made precise gestures. Soft chanting could be heard on the wind.

"Can you make out what they're saying?" Letty asked.

The others shook their heads.

"Can't you see it's brighter? The way they're facing is a little brighter than any other direction," Emma said.

Letty looked up at the colors and, after a long moment, realized that it was indeed brighter.

"Is it like the sunset?" She asked.

"That's what they call it," Blue answered.

The Elazene changed directions, and Petri pointed to the sky and said something indiscernible. Then they were quiet for a time. Finally, Ahmet and the others exchanged parcels.

"What was Petri pointing at?" Emma asked.

"They might be looking for the moon," Letty guessed, scanning that quadrant of the sky.

Blue snorted a laugh and plunged back down into the cart.

Ahmet and Petri returned with fresh food from the farmhouse. Ahmet was missing his glasses.

"I was right—Elmahad wanted the glasses. If you return to the surface, please bring more; I suspect they would be quite popular down here," he said.

"But why?" Dean asked, exasperated, "there's no sun!"

"Perhaps not, for a twilight ant," Ahmet said, smiling towards his daughter, who laughed.

They sat down to a fresh dinner of seared meats and loaves of sourdough.

"This is like something we would eat on the surface," Emma said, breaking a loaf apart and smelling the fresh bread.

"Well then, you must have good taste," Petri

said, trying to hold back her laughter. She looked to her father, who also enjoyed a joke the rest of them didn't follow.

The watch that night was uneventful. Letty had started the shift with her eyes glued to the sky, in search of signs and shapes she felt might really be there, but all she saw were the pulsing colors.

Maybe they can see something we can't.

She sighed and reached into her cape pocket for Andy's notebook.

She flipped past the pages she had seen already and settled on his sketch of a woman in robes. The woman was holding a set of unbalanced scales and, with her other hand, held an arrow to her right eye. There was Latin script on a building behind, and French on fallen newspaper clippings. She read the papers, *'La révolution n'a jamais pris fin. Le Lyceum se bat sur.'*

Letty thought back to French class.

The Revolution never ends? The Lyceum is fighting?

She wasn't certain of her translation.

The Revolution? Maybe the French Revolution? But what's the Lyceum? I've never heard that word before.

She turned the page and read a long account of adventures endured by an English Seer.

He's had some of the same problems we've had and, going by his account, we should be careful in Degoskirke.

The next sketch featured a sailboat, though it was far from finished.

Letty turned the page and was disturbed by what she saw.

It looks like people turning into mice.

She read the words, "They were once us."

So, the mice were human at one point? Did something curse them?

"That's not how it happened," Blue commented, and Letty nearly jumped out of her skin. "Sorry to bother you," he said snickering, "not much to do, so I figured I'd read along."

Letty calmed her heavy breathing. "Fine, but what do you mean, 'This isn't how it happened?' Were the mice people once?"

Blue tugged nervously at an ear. "Well, yes, that part is true. But the spontaneous turning into mice, that's not right."

"So, what did happen?" Letty asked.

Blue nearly pulled a whisker from his face. "I've already said too much. That's one vow that won't go broken."

"Why can't you tell me? You've made a vow?"

"Open your ears!" Blue snapped, and then drooped his whiskers before continuing, "That's right, all sentient mice, once called masons, occasionally called builders, keep this vow. Even if we go to war with one another, or abandon our duty to the Seers, this is one thing that is kept till death," Blue said, quietly.

"You didn't tell me anything about it, so don't worry. I won't even mention it to the others," Letty said, trying to comfort him.

Blue shook his head and gave her a sad look before scurrying into his basket of silks.

Letty sat in thought for a while, the notepad flapping lazily in the wind.

"Were you talking up here?" Staza asked, coming to relieve Letty.

"What? Oh—yeah, I was just thinking out loud—looking at Andy's notepad," Letty responded.

"How do you like the new clothes?" Staza asked, a slight edge in her voice.

"Oh, I don't know yet. I'm glad we don't have to hide anymore, and I guess it's good armor," Letty answered.

"That's true," Staza said holding her wasp's helm at arm's length while inspecting it. "Just don't expect them to keep us safe from a purple blade."

Letty nodded before asking, "Do you think I look absurd in this?"

Staza lowered her helm and looked on as Letty stood up. "I think it suits you," she said.

Letty scowled all the way to her bedroll. She continued scowling as she took off the suit.

I look like a princess in this thing. It could be worse though; I could look like a giant green wasp.

Letty grinned and tried to sleep, but her thoughts returned to Blue and his curse. She did finally fall asleep, but her night wasn't restful.

Letty awoke to Petri's ladybug helm. The girl was prodding her with an outstretched finger.

"Yes," Letty muttered, listening for a sign of the others. It was largely silent in the caravan.

"You wanted to rise early for practice," Petri said, before leaping over the side of the cart.

Letty sat up and looked at her suit of armor, which sat a few feet away.

I guess we should.

She yawned and stretched before getting to her feet and giving Emma a soft kick to the ribs.

"Letty," Emma whispered.

"Yeah?" Letty bent and leaned in to listen.

"I need to go to the bathroom."

"So?"

"There aren't any bathrooms."

"Are you telling me that you've been holding it this whole time?"

Emma was silent.

"There are shrubs everywhere, go find one."

Letty stood back up and looked out at the countryside. She spotted Ahmet, off the road and gesturing at the sky.

"Come on guys, let's get up."

Minutes later, they were all roused, dressed, and after waiting in line for the most private shrub, they had time for stretches and some sparring. No one would train with Letty while she wore the cape, so she had to do without it. There were several comments about the armor being lighter than expected, though, despite that, a half-hour's sparring had exhausted the surfacers. Letty used the lightest blade available, as it felt the most familiar. Staza showed her how to grasp the handle for the most control. Petri wandered by and scowled.

A short while later, Ahmet halted their practice.

Once they were on the road, Letty listened to the conversations between her friends. Quill and Dean were keen on the details and workings of their two worlds; today it was government that fascinated. Afterwards, they talked about trains and ravagers, airplanes and cyclostones. Staza mainly talked at Emma, who was intimidated by the aggressive girl. Blue and Ahmet occasionally argued about local history or exactly how useless the surfacers would be in case of attack.

Gratefully, the day came and went with a fine lunch and a single encounter: A ravager patrol passed within a hundred feet, but seeing the banner flying over the carts they ignored the caravan.

"It's about time we found some luck," Ahmet muttered loud enough for Letty to hear.

By the end of the day, most of the conversation had devolved into complaints about walking. Even Staza and Quill were wearing thin.

"We don't march for days at a time in Caspia; Our territory isn't that large," Quill said to Letty as he rubbed his raw feet.

They had taken to sitting in the cart and putting their feet against the hull to cool them.

"Letty, I don't think I'll be able to practice tomorrow. I'm starting to get blisters," Emma said.

Staza scowled, until she pulled her boots off and saw her own feet. "Just give it a few days. We'll grow used to the walking," she said.

"A few days?" Emma whined.

"Blue? I need to ask you something?" Letty called out for the quarrelsome mouse.

"What?" Blue asked, appearing at the cart's rim.

"About how long until we reach Degoskirke?" Letty asked.

The faces of her friends turned to the mouse in anticipation.

"Less than a week, I should expect. Though, the Elazene hasn't shared his itinerary with me. He might have other stops planned along the way," Blue said.

"A week?" Dean moaned.

"Less than," Blue answered, "perhaps five more days of direct travel. Though, I do not trust the Elazene. They are far too superstitious and all that solemn talk about your new insect suits..." Blue trailed off.

"What reason have you to doubt him?" Quill asked cautiously. "Ahmet has been clear since we first agreed to be his guards."

"No hard reason, only experience, and perhaps one minor detail. Have any of you heard the Elazene say we are headed to Degoskirke?"

There was an uncomfortable pause.

"Of course," Letty snapped, casting annoyed glances at her friends. "That was our agreement from the beginning. Anyway, there's nothing stopping us from finding out. We'll ask him again tomorrow, just to make sure."

Quill and Staza nodded, but Letty heard Emma and Dean whispering to each other. She approached their side of the cart.

They went silent.

"We're just a little homesick, Letty. Nothing to worry about," Emma said.

"That's what you're whispering about? Good. I was worried you two were taking a liking to each other," Letty said, with one raised eyebrow.

Emma rolled her eyes and Dean crossed his

arms.

I swear he's blushing, and she wants to deny it, but she's actually afraid of hurting his feelings now. God, look at her squirm.

Letty forced them to stew in awkward silence for a little longer before continuing, "I have no idea how long we'll be down here. I warned you at the beginning—"

"All right, we get it, you were right, and we were wrong! Could you leave us alone, please?" Dean snapped.

Letty's face reddened. Her eyes narrowed and her jaw set. She felt an impulse to attack and humiliate Dean with either an insult, or an open palm across the face.

Emma refused to meet her glance.

Staza, Quill, and Blue, were all watching.

Letty sighed.

He's right; I've been cruel from the beginning. Now they're stuck here, and they know it.

Letty almost apologized, but turned and sat with the Caspians instead.

"What's their problem? Running low on diapers?" Staza asked.

"They—" she started sharply, before pausing, "they're just having a hard time being away from home."

Quill sensed Letty's concern and spoke softly, "I'm enjoying a bit of adventure, though I also miss my own bed."

Staza scoffed. "I'm not the religious type, but I wouldn't mind killing a few ryle on the way to Andy.

I'd like a little payback for our species. My bed at home can burn for all I care. I've tasted freedom and I won't go back."

Quill and Letty stared with open mouths at Staza's sudden vitriol.

Staza crossed her arms and locked eyes with Quill, who was too shocked to speak.

"What about you Letty? Do you miss your bed?" Staza asked sarcastically.

"I—I don't know if I'll go home ever again. I also don't think we should be talking about this now. Our plans for the future should wait."

Quill ignored Letty and looked straight at Staza. "Where will you go then? The surface, with those weaklings?"

Staza looked away and let her head rest against the hull. "I think I might capture my own part of the city on the surface."

This will be a problem if I can't calm them down.

Quill was about to retort, but Letty reached out and grabbed his arm. She shook her head. Quill opened his mouth angrily, and then closed it, before turning away from the girls and going to his sleeping bag.

Staza stood up and went to take the first watch.

Letty crawled into her own sleeping bag, careful not to glance at Emma and Dean. She pulled the bag around her face, realizing the temperature dropped as the so-called night set in.

She couldn't sleep, and soon heard sobbing coming from Emma, and then soft consolations from Dean and even Blue.

Now I'm the bad guy.

Letty rolled over and tried to keep from crying.

I haven't even thought about my own parents, or the failures and bad grades waiting for me when I get back… if I get back.

Letty was surprised when a red-eyed Staza came to wake her for second watch.

Letty put on her helm and carried a blanket up to the watching post at the head of their cart.

At least it's beautiful out.

The rolling shrub-land waved under the gentle brushing of a soft, ever present wind. She watched the sky and, after a long moment, fancied that she might see the moon, hidden up there in the swirling mess of color. Almost every shade of red and purple were run through with thick cords of gold. She watched as off in the distance a long line of soldier brutox marched, their attendant carts and ravagers trailing along behind. Limp banners jostled as they sunk out of sight.

Letty swayed with the wind and thought of her friends, and her home, school, and a car she wanted to drive. She thought about Andy making a scene in Caspia and snapping her out of that nightmare haze Pythia had put her in.

Moments later, she spied people emerging from their homes, which were nestled away so expertly in the thick shrubbery, that she only noticed them after their doors opened. The Elazene, in their borrowed skins, greeted a phantom dawn and went to work on their farmsteads. Letty turned and saw Ahmet exchanging gifts and greetings with one of the local farmers.

"What are you doing?" Petri asked, her voice startling Letty.

The young girl was bearing a tray with cups and a steaming pot of tea.

"I'm on watch," Letty replied, yawning and stretching what she now realized were incredibly stiff muscles.

"Did you sit up all night? Aren't you second watch?" Petri asked, carefully handing Letty the tray before climbing up.

Did I? Was I up all night?

Letty grimaced and remembered the hurt feelings of her friends from the day before.

"Oh, Petri, one thing. Are we going directly to Degoskirke?"

The girl tilted her head, Letty saw mistrust in her eyes through the helm.

"Answer my question first, please." Petri said.

"Oh, right—yes. I guess I stayed up; I wasn't tired."

Petri stared for a moment before speaking, "We're going home first. It's on the way. But you shouldn't stay up all night, you won't be able to walk today. You need to look after yourself, don't be so foolish," Petri scolded her, while pouring a cup of tea.

"So, we aren't going to Degoskirke, after all," Dean muttered.

Letty saw that her friends were up and had been listening.

"It's on the way," Petri repeated herself, hopping

down into the cart. "Up, up, and drink your tea, then we have some fine bread—fresh baked."

Letty refused to look at her friends that morning, and, as Petri predicted, could only tolerate a few hours of walking, before nearly passing out from exhaustion.

She awoke in the shade, staring at the inside of a covered wagon.

I'm in the lead cart.

Petri laid a hand on her cheek. "She's awake."

"Give her water, but sit her up first," Ahmet said, slight urgency in his voice.

Letty accepted Petri's help in sitting up.

We aren't moving.

Letty took a water-skin from the girl and drank deeply. She rubbed her eyes and looked out from the wagon. Ahead of the caravan, she saw her friends practicing their footwork and parrying. Staza led them in the exercise. Somehow, the sight of it was enough to make Letty laugh.

Why does it seem so natural for Quill and Staza? Even when Emma and Dean are doing it right, they just look absurd.

"I see you are healthy after all," Ahmet said, handing Petri a bundle.

Petri opened the bundle and presented Letty with her uneaten breakfast.

"Healthy enough to laugh, healthy enough to eat," Petri insisted.

Ahmet chuckled. "Very good, dear, now go show them a thing or two—but don't get too rough."

Petri emitted a pleased warble as she flew from

402

the cart. She slid to a pause and turned back to grab her child-sized baton before rushing off again to join the others.

"I was right. A few days of you and your friends has done my daughter more good than a hundred lectures. Your helplessness has taught her to rise to this new height."

"Maybe I should rent out my friends to other Elazene parents with misbehaved children."

Ahmet raised a brow and his cheeks puffed out slightly before he let out an uncharacteristic cackle. He struggled to stop laughing. "Yes, it could be quite the profitable enterprise, though at some point, you surfacers would no longer be helpless, but a decade's worth of profit isn't to be scoffed at."

Letty grinned and chewed on a slice of bread with crimson butter.

"But look at her; fierce and wild, isn't she?" Ahmet said, watching his daughter strike at Dean's knees.

"She is," Letty answered.

"She mentioned that you know."

Letty paused. "Know what?"

"You know that we aren't going straight to Degoskirke."

"Yes, she told me. We are going to your home, first."

Ahmet nodded. "I hope this won't be a problem. It is on the way, and we will only stay a night, God willing."

Letty was quiet for a while. They watched the sparring, and both wore a smile as Petri stood in as

Dean's partner for Staza's blocking lesson.

"Okay, so long as you don't forget our agreement," Letty said firmly.

Ahmet scowled. "Yes, our agreement. You make excellent guards," he spoke sarcastically.

Letty felt her face redden.

"Think, girl. Petri could have done the job better. What I do for you is charity; let's be straight on this subject." Ahmet paused for a long moment. He took a sip from his cup of tea before continuing, "I do not begrudge what we give, if that's what you think. Life has been hard to my people, but we aren't lost until we turn away our own kin."

Ahmet reached for a bag and produced a carrot before passing the bag to Letty.

He's a Seer too.

They both ate their carrots before Ahmet rounded a heavy brow her way. "I hear that you are suffering in your role as leader. Your two groups of allies are rather different, but you favor one over the other."

Petri. She's been spying on us and telling her father.

Letty looked away, not sure how angry she should be about the breach of their privacy.

"Do not take offense, girl. I am here to aid. These words struggle to smooth the path before you. Please do not grow rigid; now is the time to learn, more than any other. You are going to a dangerous place. In some ways the city is worse than these dusty plains. You must be as one, not fractured." He paused. "But your plan: You go to rob a purple lord of his possessions?"

Letty nodded. "It's a stupid plan, isn't it?"

"Only if born prematurely, in haste. Your party is blessed with six perspectives."

Six? He must be including Blue.

"Take the time—this is essential—to let each set of eyes divine the truth of your challenge. There will be disagreement, but it is your duty to make sure there are no hurt feelings when one path is taken and another left."

"I never wanted to be leader; it just happened. At some point they were asking me what we were going to do, and I just opened my mouth and answered, but I have no idea if it's for the best. I don't think we have the right plan."

Ahmet smiled. "What is best, in this case, is faith, my girl. There is no perfect plan, especially when you go to worlds unknown, but even a turbulent course will be traveled happily if the pilgrims do so in good faith."

Letty sighed.

"It comes naturally to you. Do not second guess yourself, not for your own sake, but for theirs. If you meet the day with defiance and confidence, they will see. The animating spirit will flow from you to them. If you mope, they will shatter. Right now, your bearing is far more important than whining over a perfect plan, particularly if so much is unknown."

"I see your point, but what if I don't have faith in them?" Letty whispered.

Ahmet nodded and thought on it for a while. "This is much like your futile hunt for the perfect plan. You hunt for the perfect players."

"But you said yourself that Dean is useless, and Emma..." Letty sighed.

"We jibe others in the hope that they will rise. Dean suffers our critiques with good grace, and he will rise to the occasion in the way right to him. Emma will too. If there was no hope, I would have left them by the side of the road. I assume you made the same decision earlier in your trek?"

Letty was silent.

"They chose to go with you and the snake children?"

Letty nodded.

"They could choose to turn back down the road we travel, at any point?"

Letty looked away.

It's true. They could leave at any point, if they really wanted to.

"You cannot bear the responsibility of their lives. They made the choice, foolish or otherwise, and if you bear the responsibility of that choice, you deprive them of what is essential in life: the ability to learn from it."

Letty felt a tear form in her eye.

He's right. It was their choice. It's wrong of me to behave this way. They are stuck with us now. Making them suffer for it won't help.

"Do you feel like waving a stick about?" Ahmet asked.

Letty nodded.

"Join them."

She did so.

"Are you feeling better? Is it true, you didn't get

any sleep?" Emma stammered as Letty approached.

"Yes, but I'm fine," she said, raising her hands to keep the questions at bay.

Staza tossed her a club, and Letty joined in the exercise.

Ahmet looked on for a time, occasionally cheering for his daughter.

The caravan lumbered on after a quick lunch. That evening, Letty apologized to her friends. They had unrolled their sleeping-bags and kicked their shoes off for the night.

"Hey, Emma, Dean?" Letty started.

They looked at her, uncertain.

"I'm sorry for being mean about—well, I haven't been fair to you, and it'll stop."

Emma gave her a thankful smile, but Dean looked away.

"I'm not responsible for your decision to come down here, so I'll stop acting like it. I need to realize that we're a team, especially if we're going to stand a chance against whatever is waiting for us in Degoskirke."

Dean looked up. "It isn't easy for Emma or me—being away from home and all. We'll stop complaining so much, to make it fair."

Emma nodded, and Letty smiled.

"Cute," Blue sniped at them from across the cart.

Staza scowled at the mouse and hurled a pair of balled up socks his way.

Blue hadn't expected the socks and was bowled over backwards into his favorite basket. The struggling mouse feet kicked up a wave of laughter and light applause.

"That'll show him," Quill said, as Blue leered at them, before diving away into the silks.

Chapter 15: At the Scene

Chimerax landed on a piece of crumbled wall near the outskirts of Hyadoth.

Akri cawed and spoke, "We're here."

"It's about time," Ithyl, the jackal head, replied in her grating tone.

They both cast a glance at the silent and nameless dragon's head. Its glassy eyes scanned the ruins idly.

"Something terrible has happened," Ithyl said, sniffing the air. "The false Argument, can you taste it?"

Akri nodded. "The Nightmare is a fey creation, and the lightning as well. You smell the taint in the air."

"No. There is something more," Ithyl said.

Akri gasped.

"Look down into the city." He said, clapping his beak nervously.

The dragon took in a rattling breath.

"There's a sea of mutation stirring in the streets, likely bled from the missing Hyacap," Ithyl reasoned.

"We are too cumbersome for this," Akri grumbled. "That soup can rend or enmesh us further. We need to change. Agreed?"

"What will happen to us, if we change?" Ithyl asked.

"I expect we will become of one mind," Akri said.

"But who will be dominant?"

Again, they both looked at nameless, who simply stared down at the city.

Akri sighed, and then closed his eyes. "I hope they never open again."

Their body morphed. Limbs shrank and heads merged.

Chimerax blinked and laid a hand across his face. Two thick rents ran straight down from his crown, through each eye, and then down to meet over the heart. His hands felt scales between the two lines, fur on the right side, and feathers on the left.

Chimerax shivered and grumbled all at once. He tried to flex his wings, but found they weren't there. He held his left hand out and, palm open, a purple orb, the size of a boulder flashed into existence. He grasped his fist and an ultraviolet glow replaced the orb and shone across the rubble. He tightened his grasp and a blade shot into existence. It was perfect and indistinct from a material weapon, save the color. He released the blade, and a dark haze shimmered around his body. The power of the Counter refused to be contained and seeped out through his skin.

Remember the forms.

Chimerax focused on his disjointed memories and found the essential ones rushing to the fore.

Ahh.

He loosened almost every muscle in his body and let himself fall. A moment before striking the ground, he felt as if he were stuck to the sky.

So simple.

Chimerax floated to an upright position and

flew slowly over the roiling remains of the city, dodging the occasional tentacle or clawed limb that lifted to inspect him from the soup below.

What a waste. Xyth was a fool. Look at this butcher's attempt at a breeding program.

Chimerax spotted a cluster of slithers clinging to the underside of a half-fallen tower.

Let's see what they know.

Chimerax rotated till he was nearly upside-down, and felt his feet tap against the stone. He held a hand out for one of the slithers, which cowered in a nook.

"Come here," he said.

A slither, somehow tempted, crawled out of its hole and climbed onto the open palm.

"Here you go," he said, pointing a clawed finger at the creature. A thin stream of purple and orange light flew into the slither. "Very good, sit still."

The other slithers rushed from their holes to snap at his feet.

"Now, now, only the brave," he said before flicking a finger.

The other slithers went limp and fell from the tower.

He set the lucky slither down and continued feeding the stream into it.

The creature grew.

Moments later, it had the body of an adult ychoron. It clung to Chimerax, who walked up the underside of the tower, before setting it down.

"You can't always climb ceilings," Chimerax said, with a slight grin. "You're an adult now."

"Master," the ychoron said, bowing. "How may I serve?"

"In your primal form, you might have seen what happened to this, ill-fated metropolis."

The ychoron nodded. "Yes, yes I did. Ravagers rampaged through the town. They bore stripes and banners I didn't recognize. I expect that they were privately owned, not part of the city's fleet."

"Were they part of an invasion? Was the city attacked?"

"Not that I could make out; I was quite small, but it looked like they were trying to get across the city in a hurry."

"What happened to Xyth's tower?" Chimerax asked, pointing to a stump that was once the Hyadoth.

"I cannot say. I remember a flash of light, the false light, my Master. Then the tower crumbled, and the city was like this ever since. All that happened after was more flashing and the fleet of ravagers retreating. One of them, a cobalt, went down nearby, though it is all soup by now," the ychoron concluded, and pointed to what was once an intersection. A few ravager limbs, all different sizes, still twitched in the air.

"Not what I expected, but not useless either," Chimerax said, floating off the tower. "If you can use your newfound mind to navigate across this—waste, you deserve to live."

The ychoron beamed. "Thank you, Master! I'll never forget!"

Chimerax flew to the bank of waving ravager

limbs.

In life it was cobalt-toned.

Chimerax slowly descended into the filth.

He placed a hand on the thick and quivering floor of living liquid. Half formed mantis, lobster, spider, and ryle limbs rose from the muck and descended on Chimerax.

The heavy legs of the ravager also twitched and moved his way.

Chimerax inhaled and yelled, "Down!"

Every limb smashed into the ground, many with sickening cracks. The ravager legs bent at odd angles in their rush to meet the floor.

Not so dangerous after all.

Chimerax cast his mind through the muck, which was akin to listening to a few thousand outraged conversations while trying to find one voice.

Cobalt, ravager. Cobalt, ravager.

Chimerax called for a long time, before finally finding a primitive voice.

"Master... Master, fallen."

Are you the cobalt ravager?

"I, Juvan, cobalt..."

What happened?

"Pulled down... Master!"

Chimerax peered into the creature's disassociated mind and saw an image of a stout, muscular ryle. This ryle was with several others; they had a boy prisoner, and another.

Thrag.

Images of the wild man flashed through his

mind. He pushed them aside and focused on the ryle.

Where is this ryle, your Master?

A million voices sounded out at once, "There."

Chimerax's head nearly burst at the noise.

An image of something like the ryle in question appeared. Through the thousand perspectives he watched the ryle use Counter to shield his body. He clambered over wreckage, and escaped the city. Though not unscathed, he slipped into the jungle beyond.

Chimerax opened his eyes in sudden shock. He was enveloped by the soup.

He gestured widely with his hands. "Break!"

The mountain of flesh trying to incorporate him exploded outward, leaving him standing in a crater. He wiped the still undulating filth off his fur and floated up and away, a part of his body shivering, as if horrified.

So, a ryle rich enough to own a ravager escaped the city in that direction. Yet, this was a while ago, there is no need to rush. There might be more to learn.

He flew towards the severed stump of the Hyadoth.

I feel the Dead God here.

A gurgle alerted Chimerax to sudden danger, and he surged upwards.

A tremendous, muscled red arm exploded from the pool in the crater of the Hyacap.

Xyth!

The abort-ascend ryle pulled its colossal bulk out of the soup. Its red face hung with tentacles that were as tall as some of the local towers. The beast's insane eyes flashed with maddened hate.

He's far too large. Ten times what he should be. All that precursor—

The creature was bombarding his mind. Pain shot through his limbs, and he fell from the sky.

Change!

His body morphed back into the three-headed beast.

The wings flapped, but too late.

Xyth's clawed fist tightened around Chimerax's body.

Chimerax pointed and articulated his right claw. He focused through the crushing pain and found Xyth's shattered mind.

Down!

Xyth lost control of his body and shot to the ground, ripping apart more of Hyadoth as he went. Chimerax flapped his wings and climbed higher, hoping to get out of reach.

He felt Xyth's uncontrolled, etherium-addled mind, struggling to get out from under his control.

No!

Xyth's body cracked against the ground. It groaned at such a bass level that many of the half-collapsed buildings in the city crumbled the rest of the way to the ground.

"Did Caspian do this to you? I sense the false-Argument."

There was a sudden silence.

Chimerax tensed.

Xyth pulled its body up and leveled its gaze on

him.

"Did Caspian destroy your city?"

Xyth yelled, expelling a cloud of raw etherium. The force of it nearly buffeted Chimerax from the sky. The ground churned; even the trees in the jungle splintered and collapsed.

Chimerax felt his armored flesh being rent by the uncontrolled etherium, roiling into the air. He tucked his wings and dived towards Xyth. *If this fails, I will be consumed!* He extended a claw, and screamed, "Die!"

As if every muscle buckled at once, Xyth twitched and crumbled.

The pure Counter flowed through Chimerax's body. He let it fill his wounds and regrow the damaged flesh. He sighed, staring down at his foe's carcass.

It won't stay dead.

Chapter 16: The Last Leg

"Ahmet called the place a karwansaray," Letty said.

She, the surfacers, and the Caspians were standing guard over the caravan as hundreds of Elazene traders and locals milled about the impromptu bazaar. A false wall, made of tall, uprooted hedge rows had been set up to camouflage and surround the large meeting point.

"It's a secret place on the plains, rife with bustle and commerce for a week or so, and then it will dissolve back into nothing," Staza said.

"That's mostly right; the only thing that's permanent is a large house or inn. The meeting will only gather around a place that can play host for large trades. The Elazene need to drink tea and smoke together before they can close a serious deal," Quill replied.

"Well, I read that they can substitute a large tent for the inn, if need be," Staza said.

"It took four days, Letty. How long until Degoskirke?" Dean asked.

Letty ignored him, as Ahmet was approaching.

"Ah, there's my brave escort. We've arrived safely," Ahmet said, as he produced a small bag, jingling with the sound of coins. "Go to the fold house and have some tea. They might also have ices in the cold larder." Ahmet handed the bag to Letty, but before he let go, he added, "be polite, and do not embarrass me."

Letty nodded. "Of course."

He released the bag.

"Ice cream? Did he mean they have ice cream here?" Emma asked, suddenly excited.

"Maybe," Letty replied, leading the way into the mess of carts and traders.

Before a dozen paces, a flurry of hawkers descended on them. Rugs, pottery, bolts of cloth and silk, tall brass decanters and samovars, weapons, robes, brutox armor, juvenile ravager spawn, and even hewn mushrooms, that must have stood ten feet tall, were all in evidence.

"Mushroom trees." Dean muttered, eying the stockpile.

Emma shrieked as a pack of dog-sized lizards scampered over the pile, avidly sniffing at the logs.

Two traders stood by and watched until the lizards stopped their search and stood on one log. The lizards looked up, as if signaling.

"I suppose they are interested in that log," Dean whispered sarcastically.

"Yes, bloody hart-root from the border," the dealer said. "It will help them grow. Though rare, I have more in stock."

The man with the lizards frowned.

"Come now! It isn't even your money; you raise mounts for lord Zllyj. Having fine monitors like these, so far from the border, is going to be expensive. Tell that to your lord!"

Letty led her friends away as the haggling began.

"So, how many types of monsters can we expect to run into while we're down here?" Dean asked, in his least sarcastic voice.

Staza laughed. "You thought that was a monster? They were spawnlings, and even fully grown, the monitors are nothing compared to what crawls out of the sea."

"Now that's true," Quill chimed in.

"Is that the fold house?" Letty asked, pointing at a pair of stone doors cut into a large boulder.

One door swiveled silently open and a trader exited with his children. The children were greedily eating from small brass cups filled with amber ice cream.

"Yes, that's it," Emma said leading the way.

They entered through the large, though surprisingly light, stone doors and saw a stairwell leading down. They descended, finding themselves in a wide room full of low tables and cushioned seats. Despite being underground, the place was cool and breezy. People sat together, eating, drinking, and smoking. Letty watched the columns of smoke bend and flow towards slats in the wall.

"Vents," Dean muttered.

The mix of conversations washed over them as a round-faced young woman approached, smiled, and motioned towards a table for five.

"Friends, I greatly admire your armor. I haven't seen a green wasp since I was a child, and that one hid in a cache. What do you desire today?"

"What do you serve here?" Dean asked, right as Emma said, "Ice cream please."

The woman smiled. "Sweets after proper food, young spider. As for the meal, I will arrange the dishes. You just recline, and I'll have the boy come by with tea."

Though she had spoken, the woman stood there, expectantly.

"Oh!" Letty stammered, getting the coin bag out. "How much?" she asked, fishing through the various coins, they all looked heavily worn.

"Dear girl, you are quite foreign. Please, forgive my thoughtlessness," she said, looking through the coins and selecting a few of the smaller ones. "These shall do. Also, your eyes are showing."

Letty gasped, realizing they hadn't had their carrots today.

"It's fine, girl. You are among friends, just be more careful, and remember, not everyone is so loving of visitors. You should employ a guide."

"We're with Ahmet," Dean said, speculatively.

"Ah, that rascal," she said. "We mourn his son. Don't let him know I said so; he is very proud."

Everyone shared an inquisitive glance.

His son? What happened to his son?

"I see I've said too much. Please, keep my secret and I'll find you something especially rare and sweet." The hostess left them in silence.

"That might explain Ahmet's odd behavior. Remember when he told us about the ryle cult that hunts down the Elazene?" Quill asked.

Letty and Staza nodded.

"It sounds like they might have killed his son," Dean said.

"That's awful, and here we are, about to stuff ourselves with ice cream," Letty whispered.

A young boy in ant's armor served them hot tea

420

with a bowl of freshly cut fruit.

"Should we buy Ahmet something from the traders?" Emma asked.

"No. I don't think we should mention it. If he wanted to talk, he would have," Letty said cautiously, picking up her teacup.

"I agree. It's too sensitive, but I'm surprised Petri didn't say anything," Quill added.

"I see the logic. He wanted us around as a lesson for his daughter. He said that she might be more cautious after seeing us," Staza recounted.

Letty nodded. "He repeated as much to me when I was in the wagon."

They drank their tea in silence, ignoring the stares from other groups. At one point, a trader approached them and bowed ingratiatingly.

"Hello friends," he said in a syrupy voice, "please excuse my forwardness, but I wonder if you might have any trinkets or wares from the surface? They would be most welcome, and I would—"

The hostess approached and slapped the man on his outstretched hand. "Not in here, Yehemal! Leave them be! Start business outdoors, end it in here."

Yehemal flushed slightly, but he retained his composure. He bowed and stepped back. "Of course, please forgive me."

The woman stared sternly, unmoved by his handsome face.

He raised a brow and clapped twice. "Please, clear a place for us to dance; my girls would like to help me apologize."

The hostess let a small smile slip before ordering her children to clear away several carpets.

"What's this?" Emma asked.

"I don't know," Letty replied, looking around as the mood in the room changed. Everyone shuffled around the floor, getting their pillows into place to watch.

Three smiling women stood from Yehemal's group. Their faces were heavy with makeup, and their hands and bare feet were painted with intricate designs.

"Is that henna?" Emma asked.

Staza nodded that it was.

A few younger boys quickly built a stage from thick wooden mats, lying rolled in a corner. The dancers all drew daggers and strutted to the stage. The first leaped head over heels and stabbed the stage with her dagger, balancing her whole weight on the thick handle, while holding her second dagger out. Her baggy pants draped down and she pointed her feet deftly. She remained still as her partners tumbled in unison to join her.

"Amazing!" Emma said.

Dean's mouth was slack, and even the Caspians were impressed.

The dancing girls pushed off the ground and stabbed their other blades into the mat, while making wide circles with their legs and twisting their bodies around the handles of their daggers.

They leaped to their feet and suddenly struck at one another with lightning speed. Their daggers flashed as they attacked and deflected in time with their dance. Their feet made gentle wide steps, in contrast to the vicious speed of their attacks, while their faces met the glances of several audience members. Dean even blushed when one blew him a kiss.

"W—we are a little too close to the stage," Dean yammered when Letty looked over.

A sudden gasp rang out when a blade met its target, followed by a burst of red. Those gasps gave way to laughter when that red was only a silk scarf, pulled from a slit in one's tunic. They smiled as the scarves were flung violently into the audience, only to waft gently to the floor.

The performance ended with the lead girl being blind-folded before balancing on a dagger and fighting off her fellows, upside down, with only one hand.

"I wouldn't want to slip," Staza said, as the dancers bowed for their audience.

"You only slip once," Quill said, clapping loudly.

Yehemal stepped forward and took the lead dancer's hand before gracefully walking them off the stage.

"Do you see, Quill? This is what I was saying the other day. We don't do anything like this in Caspia," Staza said, smiling.

"Because it's pointlessly dangerous," Quill retorted.

"Let's get back to Ahmet and Petri," Letty said, before the Caspians could start arguing.

As they got up to leave, Staza approached the performers and thanked them. Yehemal rounded on her and said, "You are quite lovely, and I can see that you are fit for performing. Perhaps you would like to join our—"

"Staza!" Letty snapped, interrupting.

Staza rolled her eyes and made a quick apology before joining her friends.

"Can't you tell that he's a creep?" Emma asked.

"Someday I'd want to join a group like theirs," Staza said, ignoring the others.

They left the inn and weaved through the disorganized rows of dealers and merchants. Through the crowd, Letty saw something strange. It looked like Ahmet was clasping arms with a ryle. Letty and the Caspians gasped at the sight.

"What's going on?" Dean whispered.

They stood in silence as the ryle ordered his brutox to take charge of Ahmet's wagons.

"What are you guys upset about? So what if he sells his carts?" Emma asked.

Letty realized that Emma and Dean couldn't see the ryle for what he was.

"That person who was just clasping arms with Ahmet," Quill started, "he is a ryle."

Emma and Dean balked.

"He's just a man," Emma whispered.

Letty shook her head. "We forgot our carrots in the excitement today, and we can see it."

"Do we attack?" Dean asked. "Has it tricked Ahmet into giving away his caravan?"

Letty saw that the other traders thought little of their deal. A few gave the creature disgusted looks, but only when he wasn't looking.

"I don't know," Letty said, still shocked.

Once the ryle was gone, Ahmet turned to his escort. His face was somber and didn't match the enthusiasm in his voice, "Very good, we've lost all that dead weight, but you'll need to carry your packs now. We've only got the cutter left."

Petri was rubbing her eyes, as if to keep from crying.

"What the hell was that?" Letty snapped at him.

Several other merchants stopped what they were doing and watched.

"Careful, girl. A man may trade his possessions."

"That's not what I mean. Why were you dealing with one of them?"

"A man may deal with who he chooses."

"I knew we shouldn't have trusted him," Dean whispered in her ear. "He might be selling us out."

"No. There's something else. The ryle didn't give him any money," Quill pointed out.

He's right, we saw no money change hands.

Ahmet came closer and spoke softly, "Please, you are causing a scene."

Letty and her friends refused to budge, and finally Petri broke down. "He didn't want to sell our caravan; he had no choice—"

"Petri!" Ahmet yelled, cutting her off. He took his daughter by her hand and walked her to their one remaining cart.

"Maybe we're wrong about this," Emma said, watching Petri go.

Letty was silent.

They stayed away from Ahmet for an awkward

425

while, before he finally invited them to help prepare the cart.

"Are we leaving now?" Dean asked Ahmet. "What's our destination?"

"Yes, and we make one last stop before I send you on your way."

Everyone looked to Letty.

"Based on what we learned at the inn, I think it would be wrong to cause trouble, especially after how Petri reacted," Letty whispered to her friends. "Everyone keep an eye out, and we'll talk more tonight."

They agreed and joined Ahmet and Petri, who were organizing all their possessions in the limited space of the bulky, boat-shaped cart.

They left the karwansaray behind. Letty and her friends shouldered their packs, which felt heavier since they joined with Ahmet.

They walked the rest of the day in a tense silence.

With a fair amount of the cargo traded away, they moved briskly. Ahmet spent time keeping an eye on the brutons, which tended towards mischief when not encumbered. They tussled and threatened to confuse or tear their lines.

Blue sat on Letty's shoulder and whispered, "I don't trust him." He paused and looked up at the cart, "We should leave in the night. I can get us to Degoskirke from here. Do you see the crimson and mottled veins running through the sky?" Blue motioned to the ceiling.

Letty looked up. "Yes. I haven't seen those

before."

"That's because we've only just come within range. The city can't be more than a day or two away."

"Selling most of the caravan to a ryle was suspicious, but he must have his reasons."

Blue huffed. "He makes his living as a trader. He's far too young to retire, and he has to consider his daughter. There is something else going on, and you'll have no one but yourself to blame when he leads us into a trap."

Letty shook her head. "It doesn't make sense. If he sold us out, he would have gained money or carts or whatever, instead, he's destitute. It doesn't add up, Blue."

Blue was silent.

That evening, Ahmet and Petri slept in the cart, while Letty and her friends spread their sleeping bags on the ground, not too far from the brutons.

Letty sat on a nearby boulder, sunk in thought, while her friends trained in the tall grass off the road.

"Join us, princess!" Staza called out, inviting her to the training.

Letty looked over at Blue, who has holding on to his tail as if afraid.

Letty gestured to Staza to come to her instead. Staza whispered to the others, and they stopped practicing.

They sat in a circle around the now-dead fire.

"We need to be careful," Letty said quietly, keeping an eye on the cart. "I don't believe he would have gone to all the trouble of arming and equipping us, just to sell us out at the first opportunity. Still, something isn't right. I say we double our watch tonight."

Nobody disagreed.

"Tomorrow we'll make it to their home," Emma said. "Petri told me that she's excited to see her mother."

"I don't think Petri could tell a lie, but the woman at the inn mentioned—"

"Children," Ahmet said, hopping over the side of the cart. "You've done an excellent job, and our destination is in sight. There is one last thing I hope you will consider before I send you off to the city, but the details will have to wait until tomorrow. As it stands, I don't know how—" he stuttered his next word and looked ready to cry.

Before anyone could speak, he walked to the brutons and inspected their restraints.

Emma opened her mouth, but Blue held up a paw and looked back at Ahmet.

They forced a casual conversation about school while Letty went around the circle and whispered in everyone's ear. "I'll take the first watch with Blue, then Emma and Quill, and finally Dean and Staza. If you hear anything in the night, wake everyone up."

Letty stayed up with Blue. Though the mouse dozed off a few times, he never slept for more than a minute, and Letty couldn't bring herself to chastise him.

She reluctantly nudged Emma and Quill awake. They looked at her questioningly.

"Nothing happened," she whispered and slipped into the sleeping bag with her armor on.

She woke up sore, and noticed a drowsy Petri was approaching their circle with the usual pot of tea.

"Is everything okay?" Letty asked.

Petri didn't answer; she simply filled cups.

"Petri, what's wrong?" Emma asked.

"It isn't right," the girl muttered, before stomping off.

"That doesn't sound good," Dean said.

"We should go, now," Blue pleaded.

Letty shook her head.

"Look, I can race off to hide in the bushes, and they'll never catch me. But you—" Blue shook his head and pulled on a whisker.

Letty reached into her bag and found the Argument.

It's been a while since I've looked at it.

She didn't realize how much she had missed the small orb until it was in her hand again.

"I'll hold onto it," Letty said, showing her friends, before pocketing the Argument.

They shared a quick and silent breakfast. Petri stomped around the campsite, while Ahmet refused to say more than two words.

"Let's go."

They shouldered their heavy packs. Letty saw that Emma and Dean were in pain.

They're sore from all the walking and having to sleep in their armor. Yesterday was worse. Ten hours march was too much for everyone. But, somehow, they aren't complaining.

Ignoring her own soreness, Letty marched on, palming the Argument for comfort. Blue sat on her shoulder, his head swiveling at the slightest noise.

Before lunch, they arrived at a farmhouse, expertly hidden amid a pile of boulders on the shrubby plain. One of the giant centipedes was lazily swaying in the wind as they approached. Its crew of a dozen brutox and one fox-faced creature stood waiting under a purple banner that featured three lightning bolts over a navy and honey-colored palm.

"They aren't enough to capture us," Staza said confidently, as the warriors came into view.

"But what about the monster?" Emma asked.

"The ravager might be a problem," Quill said.

"But they aren't ready for a fight. Look at them, they're bored," Dean observed.

"He's right. Unless they're good actors, they aren't expecting a fight," Staza said.

Ahmet halted the cart outside the farmhouse. A woman rushed out, tears in her eyes. She wasn't wearing armor, though the creatures hardly noticed or cared. She lifted Petri in her arms and embraced the girl in a long hug before setting her down and commanding her to go inside. She then spoke hurriedly to Ahmet.

"I can't hear," Staza said.

"Neither can I," Letty whispered.

"What is that other thing?" Dean asked, "It looks like a feathered fox-monkey."

Staza laughed. "Don't let it hear you say that."

"It's an ychoron. They are the cleverer servants

of the ryle. Call them ychorites, if they are free. They aren't great warriors, or strong laborers, but they are crafty. I've read that some can change the color of their feathers," Quill said authoritatively.

"No, they can all change their color, but it's connected to their mood," Staza countered.

"You're both wrong," Blue interjected. "But now isn't the time."

Ahmet rushed to the ychoron, waving his arms and begging with the creature, who looked abashed, but decided.

Finally, Ahmet started yelling, "Fine, you cowards! Tell lord Zllyj that our pact is broken! If he cannot protect his people, his people no longer owe him a drop of sweat!"

The ychoron walked away from Ahmet, who was now on his knees weeping. The ravager bent its many legs, and the brutox and their officer mounted and quickly went on their way.

"It has to do with his son," Dean said.

The others nodded.

They stood in somber silence until Ahmet, aided by his wife, composed himself. He approached them and tried to put a smile on.

"I'm sorry you had to see that. I hope that you will please lend me your ears for a moment."

Letty and her friends formed a circle.

"This is it. If something bad is going to happen, it's happening now," Dean whispered.

"We should hear him out. He helped us. We wouldn't have come this far without him and Petri," Emma said.

The Caspians looked at Letty.

"I agree with Emma, but Dean has a point. Everyone, keep your weapons ready."

"I hope you're right about this," Blue grumbled.

Ahmet waved for them to follow.

"Why can't we talk here, in the open?" Dean asked.

"Please," Ahmet said somberly, "indulge me a simple gesture."

They followed, and Blue renewed his promise to dash into the shrubs at the first sign of trouble.

Ahmet led them around the rear of his camouflaged house to a tall stand of dangerously thorned bushes. He reached deftly into a bush and firmly gripped one of the thicker branches. He pulled, and a wall-sized segment came away. Bending low, Ahmet entered a passage cut in the bush.

"Be careful, the thorns will draw blood. If you are snagged, do not panic; it is easy to become tangled," he said, looking back at them.

Letty followed along, and Ahmet stepped out into open space.

"There's a hidden grove back here," Letty whispered.

"Wow," Emma said, her mouth slack at the sight of blossoming trees.

"There's grass, even if it isn't exactly the right color," Dean said.

He's right, the grass isn't green—it's more like teal.

Ahmet was pleased by their reactions. He offered them freshly plucked tangerines and then

432

sliced a purple pomegranate on a small table by one of the trees. He bade them sit in low, cushioned chairs in the shade, while he served the fruit. Letty watched, and saw he ate as well.

He hasn't poisoned the food; he's cutting it right in front of us. Letty regretted her paranoia. *Blue must be getting to me.*

"I'm doing something dangerous, my friends, and I will speak plainly now. Please, at any point feel free to turn and leave. If these were normal days, you would never see this secret place, but they aren't, and I hope you see this invitation as the opening of my family's heart and most cherished prize to you. Please realize that this has never happened before; my wife refused to bear the shame of welcoming you here. Though, to me it is no shame! I do it for..." The man coughed back a sob.

"Is this about—" Emma tried to speak, but Ahmet held up a hand.

"I'm sorry," he coughed again and took a deep breath. "They have my son. Supthoi's cultists have him now, and they have kept him in my lord's hold. Our weakling ryle lord took my family's wealth as payment to secure his release, but here he only sends me an insult in the form of an apology! They refuse to challenge Supthoi. Though, this is my fault! I settled this land for my family, under a weak ryle lord. I thought it would be better for our trade, but here we are!" Ahmet spat. "My lord's envoy did offer one piece of news, and it may be what damns me. He told me when the cultists plan to leave the lord's holdfast, with my son as their prisoner."

There was a long pause.

"You're going, aren't you?" Staza asked.

"Do I go alone?" Ahmet replied.

Silence.

"We don't have to go, Letty," Emma said.

Ahmet nodded. "I expected as much. But listen, your—the holy weapon you carry would be enough to scatter them. There are less than twenty. They would fear you," Ahmet insisted.

"She's right, this isn't our fight. It wasn't part of the bargain," Dean said.

"He didn't know this would happen. His lord only betrayed him today. We were there," Letty blustered, ashamed of her friends. "Look, I don't care what you do, but I'm going to help."

"Letty! You have to stop!" Emma yelled. "You can't pretend that we're a team, and then run off to get yourself killed!"

Emma's sudden outburst was surprising.

"She's right, though," Dean said, "we need to make decisions together."

Letty sighed. *That's what Titus said before he left.*

"Okay, you're right; I accept that. So, what do we want to do? Are we going to abandon Ahmet after all he's done for us?" Letty asked.

"I'm willing to fight," Staza said.

Quill agreed.

Dean and Emma were silent for a moment.

"Wait," Dean said. "Blue, what do you think?"

Blue scowled. "I abstain."

"Well, that looks like a majority," Letty said.

Dean screwed up his face and sputtered,

"Whether we decided to fight wasn't the point. The issue was you running off and making life and death decisions on the fly, without saying anything to the rest of us."

"Okay then! And you can just stay here if you don't want to fight!" Letty snapped.

Ahmet stepped forward. "If we are going to do this, we must leave shortly. Give me a moment... You might want to prepare yourselves."

Letty and her friends gathered their weapons and tightened the straps on their armor.

"Drink some of the minoe," Staza said, allowing everyone a few drops. "It will refresh us and heal our strain before the fight."

Everyone drank.

Letty stretched in her armor after her few drops and found the soreness was gone, and the spring was back in her step.

Letty rooted through her bag while Dean walked nervously back and forth, muttering loudly to himself. "You think he might unhitch the brutons and ride them into battle; they look pretty useful, I mean, more useful than us, you would think, and what about those girls who danced with the daggers? They could probably fight like crazy. Hey Letty, what's that?"

Letty had pulled the revolver from her bag.

"Is that a gun?" Dean cried.

The others stopped what they were doing and stared.

"Why do you have a gun, Letty?" Emma yelled.

"I don't think you guys get it. We're going to

kill monsters. What don't you understand?" They only stared. "I might lose my weapon if there are ryle. I'll keep this ready, just in case." Letty loaded the cartridges, snapped the cylinder closed, and pocketed the weapon.

The sight of the revolver was too much for the surfacers.

Emma started to cry, and Dean was speechless.

"What's wrong with them?" Staza asked.

"We're not used to fighting. We don't train for it or anything—not regular people at least," Letty explained, disgusted at her fellow surfacers.

"But why aren't you behaving like them?" Quill asked.

"How could you forget what she did at the portal?" Staza replied.

Quill nodded. "You're right, there was a fury in her heart."

Blue crossed his arms.

"Look," Letty finally said to Dean and Emma, "stay back if you don't want to go... maybe hide in the bushes. Blue can get you back to the surface if we're killed or captured."

That wasn't what either of them wanted to hear, and they only sunk deeper into paralyzing dread.

"There you are!" Ahmet called out. He was with five other armed and armored Elazene, who clambered to see Letty. "We'll have some neighborly company for our little trip. So, what have you decided?"

Letty and the Caspians approached Ahmet and his neighbors.

"We're ready to fight; the others will stay behind," Letty said.

"It is for the best," Ahmet agreed.

The war party piled into Ahmet's cart and he took the reins.

"Wait!" Emma yelled.

Ahmet halted the cart. Emma and Dean climbed aboard.

"We might not be able to fight, but we can help pilot the cart if you're all hurt," Emma said, breathing heavily from running after them.

Dean had Blue on his shoulder and looked white as a sheet. He sat down and put a hand over his face.

"What's wrong?" Letty asked.

"I'm trying not to throw up again."

Letty put her arms around Emma and Dean and tried to stay calm. She glanced around at Ahmet's neighbors. Several fidgeted beneath their brutox armor, and most were looking at the floor. Only one met her glance with a nod and a slight raise of his axe. Letty nodded back, realizing momentarily that she still looked like a princess in her outfit, though no one cared.

The ride was over almost instantly. Ahmet halted the brutons and looked at the group. "I'll stand and block the road. I'll beg one last time, and when that fails, you must attack from the bushes. Stay hidden, and make no noise until I sound the horn."

Everyone leaped out of the cart. Letty nearly tripped on her cape in the process.

I'm not going to let this cape get me killed. I have the

Argument and the pistol and a handful of daggers.

Letty threw off the cape and tossed it back into the cart before rushing after her friends. They had hidden behind a growth of tall shrubs and were laying on the ground.

"The farmers are on the other side of the road. It's just us here," Quill said, flexing his grip on the haft of his spear.

Staza had drawn her rapier and parrying dagger. She gave Letty a coy smile as everyone's breathing settled. Dean held onto his mace and had kept himself from being sick in the shrubbery. Emma had her short bow ready, but a bunch of her hair had tangled in the bush. She struggled to rip it free and now looked frazzled and terrified.

Blue hopped off Letty's shoulder and climbed partway up the bush before stopping and looking back at them. "Do you suppose... no, it couldn't be."

"What?" Letty asked, angrily.

"Do you think that Ahmet's caravan guards abandoned him because they knew this was going to happen? They must have known that Ahmet had lost his son, and that he would confront the cultists. Do you suppose when he saw you wield the Argument outside the goblin town, that he put this whole plan together? He armed you, allowed you to train, and even fed us all, for nothing."

He did say we were useless as guards, that his daughter could have done a better job, but he also said, 'never let them know what you want.'

"Now isn't the time," Staza argued.

There was a noise on the other side of the

bush. They heard a percussive thumping, like dull jackhammers working away.

"That's them," Letty whispered.

Blue shot up the bush.

"Halt!" Ahmet called out.

The noise ceased.

"Clear the road, Elazene! Or your head will decorate our temple!"

"That's a ryle speaking," Quill said.

Blue appeared again at ground level. "There are two ravagers out there!" He whispered exasperatedly.

"How do we fight them?" Staza asked, sounding frightened for the first time.

"Go for the legs," Quill responded.

"Obviously! But the crews will shoot at us while we try to deal with their mounts," Staza replied.

They looked at Emma, whose eyes were still wide with fear. Staza snatched Emma's bow. "Give me that!" She also took a handful of arrows, before turning to Letty. "You'll have to go for the legs with the Argument while Quill and I try to suppress the crew."

Quill was about to speak when a shrill horn blew and the screams of charging Elazene rang out.

"Now!" Staza yelled.

They clambered to their feet and rushed out from behind their cover.

The ravagers were crimson plated with yellow chevrons running down their length. Each was crewed by a handful of brutox. Letty saw crossbows pointing their way.

439

Ahmet waved his curved blade at one of the ravagers, which bent low to snap at him with huge mandibles.

Staza bent the bow with lightning speed and loosed an arrow. It took a brutox at the throat. Quill threw a javelin, but Letty didn't see if it struck; she was rushing forward at such a clip that she forgot to summon the Argument. She headed straight for one ravager, while the Elazene converged on the second.

She tightened her grip, and the blade appeared.

The ravager reared, as if frightened of the light. One of its crew flew off and crashed onto the ground, only to be struck by an arrow moments later.

Letty swung at the creature's legs and cleaved a few apart before the pilot regained control and goaded the ravager into snapping at her.

Letty deflected the vicious mandible with her blade, slicing off a chunk. The creature raised a leg while she was distracted and struck her with such force that she went flying. Letty tumbled against the ground. Her head spun, and a blinding pain shot through her body.

She heard someone yelling her name but wasn't sure who it was.

I should be dead.

Letty rolled to her hands and knees and saw her breastplate fall away in pieces.

Even her shirt underneath the armor was ripped. Blood leaked out of the wound above her stomach.

Without the armor I'd be dead.

She struggled to regain her footing as an ominous shriek filled her ears.

A crossbow bolt jutted from Staza's chest. Letty watched as a second hit her in the shoulder.

Letty struggled to stand, as she summoned the blade and rushed towards the ravager, which was descending on Staza.

Letty lopped off another couple of legs before the creature pulled back, lowering its face, and raising the rest of its body, giving its crew a perfect view of Letty. She tried to close the distance to avoid another shot, but the ravager was still too quick.

Letty could only watch as a brutox trained its heavy crossbow on her. She felt the thud as the bolt pierced her plated thigh armor. The sudden sting of pain forced her down to a knee.

Seeing this, the ravager's pilot goaded the creature forward to snap at her. It moved so quickly that she could barely scream before it had her in its damaged mandibles.

"There, hold it steady!" A snake-like voice commanded.

Letty saw a ryle wearing golden armor. It wore a full silver helm that featured a crying face, but beneath it she could see the creature's red eyes. It wielded a blade at once golden and deep violet.

"It's a novice! It doesn't even know to hone its weapon. Watch this!" the ryle yelled as it struck at Letty's blade with its own. There was a loud crack and the Argument flew from Letty's hand.

"We wouldn't have to exterminate you if you behaved with dignity. Wielding the false Argument is the highest crime, child, and you will be flayed alive beneath Supthoi's throne for breaking our covenant."

Letty heard a snap and an arrow struck the pilot, who had the ravager's antennae wrapped around his wrists. The force of the impact knocked him back, and his weight tugged hard on the antennae, which elicited a shriek from the creature.

Letty slipped free from its grasp and fell heavily into a large bush by the road. The ravager tipped over and collapsed.

Letty saw Ahmet and his allies had somehow mounted the other ravager and had successfully defeated its crew, though they couldn't work out how to pilot it.

"Spiders, shoot those Elazene, I'll finish off the rest!" The ryle commanded, brushing the dust off his robes.

His remaining warriors trained their weapons on Ahmet and his Elazene, who ducked down.

The ryle, however, found himself facing Dean, who leveled his mace.

Letty struggled to free herself from the bush. In the effort, she saw that both Quill and Staza were down, with bolts sticking from their bodies.

"Dean! Don't try to fight him!" Letty yelled.

The ryle scoffed and sliced the mace in two before grabbing Dean by the hair and throwing him to the ground. "Don't make me kill you; I'd rather have a prisoner," the ryle said as it rounded on Emma, who was fumbling with her bow.

Finally, Letty tore herself free from the thorny

bush and raced towards her Argument. The small marble had rolled to a halt on the road.

Ignoring Emma, the ryle intercepted Letty with a swift kick, forcing her to the ground.

"No wish to see the golden city? You want to die here on the road?" The ryle mused.

An arrow bounced off the ryle's armor, and he raised a hand to slap a charging Dean off his feet. Dean drew a dagger and moved to strike, but the ryle laughed and slapped him across the face with such force that Dean stumbled backwards, dropping his dagger.

"Aren't you embarrassed?" The ryle yelled through his sputtering laughter. "All the rebellion in this blood! It only reinforces our conviction to see you exterminated. Don't you understand?" The ryle asked as he pulled Letty's helmet off. His eyes brightened at what he saw. "You aren't Elazene."

"No," Letty said, reaching for the revolver. "We're from the surface."

The ryle made a curious face as Letty fired a bullet into his throat.

Dean cheered, but nearly choked on the blood streaming from his nose.

"Shut up and get him off me!" Letty commanded.

Emma and Dean pulled Letty from beneath the ryle's corpse. Letty paused long enough to see that Ahmet and his men had thrown dozens of javelins, killing the last of the brutox, but they still could not pilot their captured ravager.

"I don't know how to get us down!" Ahmet

yelled. "I have minoe in the cart! You must heal your friends before they lose too much blood!"

"I'm not an idiot!" Letty insisted as she stumbled to the cart and saw Blue looking at her. He held up the strap attached to the canteen full of the healing liquid. "Thank you," Letty said, taking the canteen and racing to her friends.

She struggled to remove Staza and Quill's plated armor, noticing several new nicks and dents as she went. *A couple bolts made it through, but imagine how bad it would have been without the armor.*

Once the wounds were healed, Ahmet asked that his minoe be thrown up, so he could treat his neighbors.

Dean obliged. Letty was too distracted by the Caspians, whose breathing had finally normalized.

"I'm fine," Staza said, still lying on the ground. "How's Quill, is it bad? He keeps getting shot, the idiot."

"I'm fine," Quill groaned. "I should really write a poem about being hit by a crossbow bolt. The experience is like nothing else."

"Your turn," Emma said.

"What?" Letty asked, and then saw her thigh. "Oh, that."

Their personal store of minoe still held enough for these last wounds. Letty endured the treatment and was grateful for the armor, remembering her first run-in with a crossbow.

"Wait, the Argument! Where is it?" She cried.

Letty stood and returned to the ryle's corpse. She saw the hefty purple orb lying not far from his claws.

A bullet works well enough.

She shivered, realizing that they had all nearly died.

Dean reached into his pocket and produced his inhaler. Staring at it, he muttered, "I haven't needed it since we got here."

"Probably something in the air," Emma said.

Ignoring her friends, Letty spotted the Argument and ran to pick it up.

I must learn the hone. His blade was multi-colored, not just purple, and it even looked solid, where my blade looks like flaming light. When the purple and silver blades meet, there is a loud crack and we always lose ours, while they keep theirs. Maybe the manual—

"Mmmmhh!" A curious sound caught Letty's attention.

She heard a muffed voice.

She approached the capsized ravager, which, though it wasn't moving, didn't look dead. A large bag had fallen off the ravager and was writhing on the floor.

Letty tore into the bag and found a young Elazene man staring up at her. He was bound and gagged.

"Ahmet! I've found your boy!" Letty yelled as she freed him.

"Glory be! Jeva! He's alive?"

"Yes!"

Once free, Jeva leaped to his feet and thanked Letty before rushing to the sound of his father.

Ahmet was so desperate to reach his son that he

was trying to climb down the ravager.

"No! No, Ada! You'll break your neck! Tug thrice on both antennae. I've seen them do it."

One of the other Elazene did as Jeva said, and the ravager bent its many knees right as Ahmet stumbled to the ground.

"Ada, you fool!" Jeva yelled as he pulled his father to his feet and embraced him.

"Your mother will kill you!"

"Are you crazy? She'll kill you first!"

A moment later, Letty found herself surrounded by her friends, though they all leaned on one another for support. Everyone was silent as the father and son yelled their stories back and forth. They blessed and cursed each other for their self-sacrifice.

"But father, stop your tears. This a joyous moment."

"You first," Ahmet said, relaxing.

"Please, introduce me to our friends."

"Ah," Ahmet said with a start, "of course, forgive me. These young warriors found me in an unseemly state, outside a goblin stronghold. Here are two children of the snake—ahh, Caspians, Staza and Quill."

Jeva took Staza and then Quill by the arm in introduction.

"These others are true surfacers."

Those words caused a commotion among the Elazene.

"Well, they are clearly not our people, but how can you be sure they are surfacers?" Jeva asked.

446

"You can see it in their eyes, they know the sun, they know the moon, more than we."

The Elazene stared for a long time at Letty, Dean, and Emma.

Jeva nodded. "Perhaps they are."

"This one is Dean. He attacked the ryle with a mace, and then with a dagger."

Jeva laughed. "Fearlessness is remembered, but it is better to live, I think. Be more careful when you next give yourself to battle."

Dean was astonished by the praise.

"This is Emma. She killed the pilot," Ahmet said.

An approving murmur ran through the Elazene.

"I was aiming for the ryle," Emma said, bashful at the attention.

The Elazene laughed uproariously.

"Really?" Letty asked, remembering how close she was to where that arrow struck.

Emma shrugged, not keen on ruining the joke.

"This—most unlike anything we would expect of a surfacer—is Letty," Ahmet said with a flourish.

Jeva slapped his father's hand away and shook his head disapprovingly. "No, father, she is a Voice of God, the Child of Sky."

Ahmet's eyes widened at his son's words. "The Child of Sky?" he repeated skeptically, before turning to Letty, "Girl," he said, "will you please fly for us?"

Letty blinked.

"Ada! She is just born, but look, a surface Seeress, with a scape pair and a surface pair at her side, two seers and two lewed. She bridges the span,

447

bearing Argument and firelock, and she killed a ryle champion using both. Her builder is even blue as the sky!"

Blue did not appreciate the attention. Ahmet made no retort, and the Elazene concurred with Jeva.

"What does he mean?" Letty asked.

"Ahh..." Ahmet seemed afraid to speak.

Blue clambered up to rest on Letty's shoulder.

The Elazene nodded respectfully to Blue, who returned the gesture before whispering into Letty's ear, "They think the Dead God of the Seers has personally taken time out of his busy day to move your arms and legs in the battle. More specifically, they consider you the next iteration of the Child of Sky, a warrior saint, one of many they venerate and hope to see again. Though they expected you to arrive flying, and with a great host of warriors and weapons from their kin on the surface, they are still convinced by these other 'signs.'"

Jeva pointed at Letty's waist, "Would you raise this weapon, so we may see?"

"The revolver?" Letty asked, pulling out the gun.

The sight of it caused a stir.

"What's going on?" Letty asked.

Blue shook his head and sighed, "They will call for a convention of the disparate Elazene chiefs to discuss your ascension into sainthood."

"What?" Letty yelled.

"The men you see before you will be considered witnesses and will likewise have their names and stories written next to yours, if they beatify you, that is," Blue said, tiredly. "We should really get going, before any of this starts."

Jeva stepped forward from the group of Elazene. "The discussion may take months, though I am certain. You are the Child of Sky, your last body died ignobly, subdued by the Usurper, but I sense victory stands at your side."

Usurper?

Ahmet and Blue scowled at the religious speech, while Jeva and the other Elazene were confident.

Letty didn't know what to say.

"How may I serve you?" Jeva asked.

Letty shook her head and laughed nervously.

"Please, don't reject my offer."

"Letty," Emma butted in, "we need to get to Degoskirke."

Jeva heard this and looked at his father.

"It is true, they go to the city," Ahmet said.

"Well," Jeva replied with a smile, "let's go in style." He gestured to the ravager.

Half an hour later, they had loaded their equipment, forcibly hauled Emma and Dean onto the monstrous creature, and Letty had batted off the scores of questions lobbed at her by the religious Elazene.

"Tell my wife I'll be back in a few days, and take the other beast to Gylan! He'll know how to heal it!" Ahmet yelled to his neighbors as his son piloted the healthy ravager.

The other Elazene waved and cheered as the ravager backed up, then made a wide turn. The dips of the land next to the road translated into a bumpy ride.

"Letty, don't let them get to you. It's just like when those people in suits knock on the door," Emma said.

Dean leaned in and whispered, careful of Jeva and Ahmet. "I'd ignore them too, but it's hard to, when they say that you're a saint, or something."

"Yeah," Letty agreed, "but there's something else. Staza, Quill," Letty called the Caspians to her. "What did he mean when he said the Usurper killed my last body?"

"I don't know," Staza answered. "Don't tell me you're taking this stuff seriously."

"If they had God-powered saints, they would have won the war centuries ago," Quill added.

Letty cringed, but felt like she needed to know more.

"Ahme—"

Blue raised an insistent paw and shook it at Letty. "You don't want to go down that road," he said, "they'll have you leading an army, and you'll be dead at the walls of Yyonvere in less than a month."

Blue's admonition had a tragic ring of honesty to it, and Letty decided to let her curiosity die.

Sometime later, Ahmet walked back from the helm to sit with them. "You will have to leave what remains of your skins with us."

"What?" Emma asked.

"He means the armor," Staza replied.

"We will have it mended and anointed, perhaps we can have it sent to you. You might be needing it again soon," Jeva said from the pilot's position. "You go to rescue another warrior?"

"Yes, he's another Seer," Letty spoke loudly, over the rumble of the ravager, "he also fights with the Argument."

"Ah!" Jeva yelled. "Hear that, Ada! There is another! Two zealots stand as we speak! Perhaps your friend is another ancient! You must bring him to speak to our people!"

"As soon as I can," Letty said sadly.

Ahmet watched as she spoke and knew that she was only humoring his son. She felt ashamed and looked over the side.

It's many times faster than the cart.

"How quickly will we get there?" she asked.

"Before prayers tonight!" Jeva said, an almost permanent smile stuck to his face as he looked over his shoulder at them.

During the ride they enjoyed a meal, though Ahmet couldn't cook on the ravager, and they had to resort to packaged food, which the Elazene found fascinating, if not tasty. They removed their armor and helmets only to have Ahmet tut at them.

"This will never do," he said.

Jeva looked back at them. "Oh no, that will never work."

"What won't, our clothes?" Staza asked, a little annoyed.

"Yes, but we have a secret place in the Wreck. There are clothes we Elazene share in case we ever need to travel into the city."

"The Wreck?" Dean inquired.

"Ah, Ada, how have you left them so ignorant?

You shame me."

"Please," Ahmet said, directing his son to pay attention to the road, "you pilot, I'll talk." And then to Letty and her friends, "The Wreck is a considerable expanse of abandoned city that surrounds Degoskirke proper, which starts with the curtain wall. Though the curtain wall can be here or there."

"Are you saying the city walls move?" Dean asked, incredulous.

"Quite often," Ahmet answered, before moving on, "We will equip you with local clothes, though they will be of old styles, and the locals will think you paupers as a result. This will work to your favor, however. Once inside, avoid anything resembling a debate; this activity can have serious consequences."

"What does that mean?" Quill asked. "Should we avoid speaking with people? The whole point is to find out where they're keeping Andy. We'll need to ask questions."

Ahmet looked unsure. "I've never been to the city, only to the fringes of the Wreck. These are old tales given to me by courageous traders."

Letty glanced at her friends. They seemed unsure.

Ahmet quickly recovered and tossed Letty a large bag of the awful purple carrots. "Don't forget to eat these. I have let you go without them today, and I apologize for forgetting—my mind was elsewhere. One thing I can say for certain is that Seers are outlawed in Degoskirke, just as they are here. The same is true for the Argument, so do not

452

rely on it, unless forced. The firelock—the small thing that makes the loud bang—might attract attention as well. Keep it hidden."

Letty turned to Blue, who had his small mouse claws dug into her shirt, as the bouncing was too much for him.

"What?" Blue snapped at the sudden stares.

"Is that true, what Ahmet told us? What else can we expect in the city?" Letty asked.

"Damned if I'm a tour guide! I stayed in mouse works, mostly. We don't even use the city gates. I haven't been home—in some time."

"Damn it! Tell us what you know, mouse!" Ahmet snapped.

Blue glared at the Elazene. "The city is insane. Its customs are unlike anything else in the Netherscape, and though I've never been, I can speak with certainty that they are unlike anything on the surface as well. Debate is life there. Everything and everyone takes part. Law changes at a turn of phrase and life being turned upside-down is a matter of course. Millionaires are made in an instant and then destitute in another. Trade is constant but treacherous. They will seem rational in one moment, and then behave with deep religious mania the next, though they often call it secular instead. You will find every intelligent species I know of living and ruling in that city, every one, except the ryle. Though you'd be a fool to think that none live there."

They were silent.

Finally, Ahmet nodded. "This is what I've

heard," he said.

"Of course it is, you daft merchant!" Blue snapped, shaking a fist and nearly falling off Letty's shoulder.

"Careful now," Ahmet chuckled.

Dean and Emma smiled, but the Caspians looked uneasy.

They sat in silence and watched the plains roll by. With time, the land became rockier and there, among the foliage, grew large speckled mushrooms.

"Look at those!" Emma said.

Everyone leaned over the side in time to see a large lizard sunbathing on the cap of a nearby mushroom.

"Hart-roots. These are the speckled variety," Ahmet said.

"Perhaps tell them the history of this plant, Ada," Jeva said.

Ahmet scowled. "All you need to know is that they are food for the monitors."

They continued watching the countryside. The patches of tall mushrooms thickened, as did sightings of the monitors. Eventually they came upon pockets of ruined buildings. They passed other traders on the roads who pulled over and gave way, only to raise a fuss when they saw it wasn't brutox on the ravager.

"Will there be trouble for you if word gets out that you have this ravager?" Letty asked.

Jeva laughed.

"Immense trouble," Ahmet said. "We will have to go into hiding, my garden..."

"Forget the garden, Ada, war is on the horizon!" Jeva yelled as he reigned the ravager to a halt. He then flicked the reigns thrice, motioning it to bend down. "Please be quick, we are safest on the move."

Letty and her friends picked up their packs and hopped overboard.

Ahmet led them to a walled yard behind a sunken, two-story house. Approaching a shed, he searched and found a key between two bricks before unlocking the door. Inside the shed were racks of clothes and concealable weapons. There were also suits of brutox armor sitting in piles.

"Those are for people coming back from the city," Ahmet said.

They hurried to don the colorful and geometrically patterned robes. Ahmet took them out to the street. "The side roads out in the Wreck are dangerous. Stick to this path until it meets another, larger road before a bridge. Turn towards the three massive pillars and stay on that road. There are more secret ways, but this is the surest and safest path."

"What pillars?" Dean asked.

Ahmet looked up at the tall hills that obstructed his view. "Before long you will see them, there is no mistaking what they are. Good luck, my friends. Please return to us so we can begin thanking you for the gift you have given us. I will do my best to rid my son of his foolish notions about war and saints before you return; have no fear in that regard. I beg that you send word if you cannot come yourselves, or my heart will worry for you."

Ahmet gave them each a hug, before returning to the ravager. He waved as his son piloted the monster away.

Letty and her friends watched the Elazene fade into the distance before turning towards the road to Degoskirke. Somewhere in that tangle of ruined buildings was the way to Andy. Letty felt her heart skip, and with the warm presence of the Argument in her grasp, nothing would stop her.

To the reader:

Letty and her friends are at the outskirts of Degoskirke. Ziesqe has his plan, and Andy is within reach, but Caspian—and a certain three-headed beast—are circling. Thank you again, dear reader, for joining my characters on their adventure; I hope you'll return for this trilogy's conclusion: The Immortal of Degoskirke. If you enjoyed Letty's tale, I hope you'll recommend this series to friends, or younger readers who might be ready for their own adventure.

I would again like to recognize my editors and most helpful friends: Noa Zilberman, Jon Addley, and Oliver Pinchot in particular. They loved the crow, Akri, and insisted on more humor in subsequent works. It is their good sense that will improve these stories. I must also thank my exceedingly talented illustrator, Alexey Rudikov. He has outdone himself with this cover.